Praise for *Self-Portrait with Boy*

Long-listed for the Center for Fiction's First Novel Prize

"The conflict is rich and thorny, raising questions about art and morality, love and betrayal, sacrifice and opportunism, and the chance moments that can define a life. The novel wrestles with the nature of art but moves with the speed of a page-turner."

—Agatha French, *Los Angeles Times*

"A confident first novel . . . The moral dilemma Lyon sets up is explored with intelligence and grace. . . . Best of all is Rile's voice, snappish and self-aware and scared, taking on the world while being devoured by it, reaching out to touch the ghosts that float above the East River."

—Jeff Baker, *The Seattle Times*

"Striking . . . Think of the tough tone of something like Rachel Kushner's *The Flamethrowers*, or Olivia Laing's atmospheric nonfiction book about New York, *The Lonely City*. . . . *Self-Portrait with Boy* is a smart novel about the narcissistic ambition that's needed to succeed, especially in the art world, especially in New York."

—Maureen Corrigan, NPR

"Lyrically written, emotionally complicated, and surprising in many ways, it is hard to put down. It explores what constitutes success and fame and art. A single chance occurrence creates something out of nothing, and someone out of no one—but at an enormous expense. Rachel Lyon has given us much to think about."

—Diana Wagman, *Los Angeles Review of Books*

"Told in crisp, clicking, photographic prose and has the narrative momentum of a thriller."

—Brent Katz, *The Paris Review*

"A searing novel about the fraught relationship between intimacy and ambition."

—*Book Riot*

"A subtly elegiac yet fierce look at the blurred boundaries between life and art, loyalty and morality."

—*Chicago Review of Books*

"A gorgeously written story about ambition and responsibility."

—Ryan Sartor, *Vol. 1 Brooklyn*

"Lu quickly comes to see that the single most valuable commodity in the art world is reputation. At its core, this novel dissects the risks and sacrifices involved in coming to terms with this notion."

—Ryan Spencer, *BOMB*

"An electric and idea-rich debut."

—Ben Lasman, *The Rumpus*

"The descriptions of 1990s Dumbo feel so tangible that you want to walk under the rain-slicked overpasses while listening to the Pixies' *Bossanova*. But between Lyon's brilliant flashes of realistic prose, snappy dialogue, and brisk plot is the space of dreaming: Lu Rile's (or is it Rachel Lyon's?) philosophical fixations and the slight absurdism with which she sees her places, and others' places, in the world. . . . Lyon is a young master."

—Matthew Daddona, *Guernica*

"Lyon's first novel takes a deep look at the difficult choices artists make around their most powerful works, while also exploring the complexities of a female friendship founded on loss."

—*Apartment Therapy*

"Fabulously written, this spellbinding novel is a real page-turner. A powerful, brilliantly imagined story not easily forgotten."

—*Library Journal* (starred review)

"More than a book about art, or morality, it is a book about time. . . . Fearless and sharp."

—*Kirkus Reviews*

"Written in raw, honest prose, this is an affecting and probing moral tale about an artist choosing to advance her work at the expense of her personal relationships."

—*Publishers Weekly*

"Beautifully imagined and flawlessly executed, *Self-Portrait with Boy* will suggest, to some readers, the obsessive interiority of the great Diane Arbus, conjoined with an original and disturbing examination of the ill-defined borders between life and art."

—Joyce Carol Oates

"Lyon navigates a spectrum of loyalty and betrayal like a tightrope walker, with all of the attendant suspense. A life-changing moral choice powers this atmospheric novel, which shows what can happen when you do what scares you most."

—Amy Hempel, author of *Sing to It*

"A formidable novel, equal parts ghost story, love story, and riveting bildungsroman. Full of big ideas about art and love and ambition, with prose so vivid it gives off sparks, this debut won me over completely. Chilling and beautiful, just like the work of the artist at the heart of the story."

—Julie Buntin, author of *Marlena*

"Captures the furious beauty of a vanished New York, an irresistible whirlwind of passion, violence, love, struggle, and above all else, art. Rachel Lyon paints an unforgettable portrait of a true art monster—a young woman hell-bent on pursuing greatness, no matter the cost."

—Robin Wasserman, author of *Girls on Fire*

"With this gorgeous debut, Lyon will unravel you and then stitch you together again as something entirely new."

—Manuel Gonzales, author of
The Miniature Wife and Other Stories

"A remarkable debut, fierce and passionate and perfectly crafted with surefire prose and ambition to spare. It will fill you with inspiration and longing."

—Ivy Pochoda, author of
Visitation Street

Self-Portrait with Boy

A Novel

Rachel Lyon

SCRIBNER

NEW YORK LONDON TORONTO SYDNEY NEW DELHI

Scribner
An Imprint of Simon & Schuster, Inc.
1230 Avenue of the Americas
New York, NY 10020

First Scribner trade paperback edition March 2019

SCRIBNER and design are registered trademarks of The Gale Group, Inc., used under license by Simon & Schuster, Inc., the publisher of this work.

For information about special discounts for bulk purchases, please contact Simon & Schuster Special Sales at 1-866-506-1949 or business@simonandschuster.com.

The Simon & Schuster Speakers Bureau can bring authors to your live event. For more information or to book an event, contact the Simon & Schuster Speakers Bureau at 1-866-248-3049 or visit our website at www.simonspeakers.com.

Interior design by Michelle Marchese

Manufactured in the United States of America

10 9 8 7 6 5 4 3 2 1

Library of Congress Control Number: 2017061606

ISBN 978-1-5011-6958-8
ISBN 978-1-5011-6959-5 (pbk)
ISBN 978-1-5011-6960-1 (ebook)

Something amazing, a boy falling out of the sky . . .

—**W. H. AUDEN**

A photograph is a secret about a secret.

—**DIANE ARBUS**

Self-Portrait with Boy

summer

'll tell you how it started. With a simple, tragic accident. The click of a shutter and a grown man's beast-like howl. The silent rush of neighbors down our dark dirty stairs. The lights of a police car illuminating the brick wall behind our building. And a photograph.

I never meant for any of it to happen.

Or no. Part of me meant for part of it to happen. I was nothing but a kid then. Twenty-six, naive, and ambitious as hell. A skinny friendless woman in thick glasses with a mop of coarse black hair. There were so many people I had not yet become.

An article that came out later, I have it somewhere, described me as *ruthless*. I didn't know until years later what the writer meant. To me it was always about the work. Franke laughs at me because although my studio is in the garage, my art and its equipment insist on spilling out into our living spaces. Our kitchen table is cluttered with photographs.

Prints hang to dry in the bathroom. By *ruthless* he meant single-minded. And sure, I'm single-minded. After all, I have only one mind. Still, I understand now that some artists look out into the world and some look in. I am interested in the limits of, the prison of, the self. I am more hedgehog than fox. I am more turtle than hedgehog.

In art school years ago I had a professor, a former opera singer. An enormous man, completely bald, with a rubber face and body. He could make himself into any shape at all. He taught performance. Part of performance was improvisation. I was not what you'd call a natural. I was stiff. I overthought. I did not have a lot of charm. When he told us, *every action is a reaction,* I puzzled over it for months. But when he said, *an accident is just a change of course,* I got it. He meant the grace in making art is being alive to chance. *When you make a mistake, make it again,* he'd say. *There are only happy accidents.* Isn't that funny. Not funny ha-ha; funny strange. My so-called happy accident happened to be a tragic one.

I am not being flippant. Understand: the whole thing changed me deeply. Academics these days have developed an affection for the word *trauma*. The trauma of everyday life—the *trauma of painting*. It sounds good maybe but it is like *vexed* or *problematic*: overuse has leeched the word of meaning. I will say that now, more than two decades later, there is only one person in this world who is more traumatized by what happened than I am, and I barely know him anymore.

I did see him once a couple years ago. It was at an opening

for my old friend Casper. I'd driven down to the city in my little green E30. I love that car. I've told Franke more than once I intend to be buried in it. She doesn't think that's funny. I think she wants it for herself. It was a rainy night, warm for December. The slick streets glowed. Almost immediately when I walked in I felt that old familiar chill, or something like it. Some memory of it maybe. I looked to my right and sure enough there he was. The same, but older. Same stocky build, same snarled ponytail—though it was more white now than blond. What was missing in him really was elasticity. Some tautness of the jaw, a certain power in his stance. He caught my eye and the expression that came over him was unbearable to me. In the crowded gallery the past came rushing back. The vile way he treated me. The pain I felt for years. Not because of him exactly, but around him. He was in that pain. And then, somewhere among all those larger, major memories, there was this minor but foul little one: the feeling of being in my twenties at a party and looking out at some horribly attractive crowd. The feeling of them glancing at me with barely registered pity: *Oh, that thing in the corner. Isn't that funny. It thinks it's people.*

I did not leave. I went to the restroom, looked at myself in the mirror, and breathed. The same but older, of course. What did I expect? We are both just a couple of overgrown, badly damaged kids. I had as much of a right to be there as any of Casper's friends—more, in fact, because years ago I recommended him to Fiona, which put him on the map. I looked good too, in my way. Like myself: Lu Rile, five feet even in thick glasses, wild graying hair. A black silk jacket over a black shirt. Jeans and steel-toed boots. My uniform, my armor. I went back out and circulated, avoiding him.

The very act of recall is like trying to photograph the sky. The infinite and ever-shifting colors of memory, its rippling light, cannot really be captured. Show someone who has never seen the sky a picture of the sky and you show them a picture of nothing.

Still I have to try.

The thing you have to understand, the thing you have to keep in mind, is that Kate was my friend. At the time she was my only friend. She was so dear to me.

II

It was 1991. I'd just graduated from art school and was completely broke. I took the first job anyone would give me, which ended up being at a health food store called Summerland in ritzy Brooklyn Heights. It was half a windy hour's uphill walk from the riverside warehouse where I lived, in the deserted neighborhood down under the Manhattan Bridge overpass: DUMBO. I made minimum wage, $3.80 an hour. Can you imagine? Carob chips, soy milk, tofu, wheat germ. So much of the food we ate in the nineties tasted like old shoes.

The manager was this awful guy from California, Chad Katz. He wore a sarong. He was all about circulation, both physical and metaphysical. The store had chakras or some such shit and it was Zen, he said, to *circulate*, to *touch each point of the wheel*. So we all did everything in turn. The mindless labor I didn't mind—unloading the delivery trucks, taking stock, wiping down the juice counter—but I loathed checkout. When it was my turn to be at the registers I always tried to switch. Often enough I could find someone who preferred chatting with customers to, say, cleaning the walk-in. But if Chad caught us switching positions he'd be so *disappointed*. I couldn't get him to see that however healthy it might have been for us to *circulate,* it was not healthy to be face-to-face with our own poverty.

Being on the registers in the slow hours was not so bad. Midmorning the nannies would start filing in, women from Haiti or El Salvador or the Philippines pushing blond preverbal millionaires in four-hundred-dollar strollers, buying rice cakes or natural peanut butter or organic dish soap. I was curious about those women's lives: where they'd come from and why. Whether they had children of their own and who took care of their kids during the day. But around five their employers, those children's wealthy mothers, would surge through the Summerland doors en masse. That I could not handle.

I grew up poor among poor people in a poor town, but I never knew how poor I'd been until I moved to New York. These women with their fresh produce and diamonds and manicures. Even their skin was expensive. What got to me about them wasn't just the way they made me suddenly self-conscious about the ink under my fingernails or the haircut I gave myself in my own bathroom. It wasn't just that they'd spend more in one evening on chocolate, escarole, and jam than I did on the rice and beans and film and photo paper I needed for a week. What enraged me is that they didn't, *couldn't,* see me. I was less than a machine to them, less than a body. I did not even appear in their line of sight. I was nothing more than a couple chanted phrases: Cash or charge? Paper or plastic? Thank you, have a nice night.

I started bringing my camera to the register with me and taking covert pictures of these women. I quite like the way some of them turned out. The turn of a head, the glow of a pearl. The extended fingers of a manicured hand. Of course Chad tried to put the kibosh on that project as soon as he got wind of it. For all his bullshit about the human spirit he was really just a capitalist drone in a tie-dyed skirt.

Working at Summerland kept me more or less afloat. But a person needs more than remunerative work. Art school had been good for me. I'd learned to define myself as an artist. I'd thrived on the feedback, expectations, deadlines. Without those things my self-definition was flagging. I was not just broke; I was depressed.

What I needed was an *assignment*.

When I began shooting a self-portrait a day it wasn't about the idea of *self* at all. The idea followed the work. It doesn't usually happen the other way around, as so many people assume. In other words I assigned myself self-portraiture not because I was particularly interested in myself but because my own body was a subject I could count on. Wherever I was, there was it. It always showed up on time. The project was an exercise, really. Studies in technique. Experiments in the inkiness of shadow. The depth of field of a reflection. The gradations of light on skin. All while staying alive to chance.

I'd been using the same camera since I was seventeen. I bought it with the money I had saved working nights driving a snowplow, clearing the parking lot at Stop & Shop. It was a Sisyphean task. Sissy-puss, as my dad would say. I'd start at the north end of the lot and drive the plow from east to west until I'd reached the south end. By the time I'd gotten there the north end would be buried again, so I'd drive back and do it all over again. I spent all winter as the on-call night snow-plow driver, plowing through dawn and sleeping through my morning high school classes. In the spring I rewarded myself with a 1980 Pentax LX.

The Pentax was a tough little camera, rugged and weather-ized and sealed against dust, but compact and relatively light. I loved it but midway through my self-portrait project nearly ten years later I realized it wasn't capturing enough detail. In the photographs it produced, the hair on my arms had disap-peared, the wrinkles at the corners of my eyes blurred to invis-ibility. Those minute details were essential to me. So I spent a paycheck and a half from Summerland on my second cam-era: a vintage Rolleiflex. The Rollei can make larger and more detailed images, and it makes them square. Instead of looking into it at eye height you hold it at your chest and look down into the viewfinder. It reverses what you see but shows you what you're looking at in striking detail. My Rollei is black and was made in 1965, the same year I was. Its lens is made of lantha-num glass, which improves resolution and color correction.

I worked mostly at home in my loft—and what a loft! I had nothing, I'd always had nothing, but god, I had that loft. It was on the fourth floor of a building that had once been a fac-tory. A century of manufacturing had left a permanent layer of grime on the concrete floor, and in the winter it was so, so cold, but it was glorious. The light rose up off the corrugated river in the mornings and fell yellow and dusty through my windows in the afternoons. Those windows were enormous.

They tilted on an axis on the middle and you hooked them in place with a metal chain. Outside the ones that faced west were the Con Ed plant and rows of other warehouse roofs that stretched to the East River. The FDR Drive, where shining toy cars drove up and down the edge of Manhattan Island and the glinting jagged skyline above it, rows of towers that scraped the sky. My south-facing windows looked out on the Manhattan Bridge, where day and night the subway trains would flicker by. In the summer with the panes hooked open I could hear their rattle-rumble like a stampede of metal animals. Even in the winter with the windows closed I could feel them vibrate in the hollow of my chest. That view, that space, that noise, that light. When the sun shone in, illuminating the slides and negatives that I hung from clotheslines across the windows, I wouldn't have been anywhere else.

In a corner of the space there was an old wash-up sink, a relic from the building's factory days. Around that sink I'd rigged up a makeshift darkroom. Bought four heavy blackout curtains on the cheap from an experimental theater on the Lower East Side and hung them from the pipes that crisscrossed the ceiling. I had a boom box my dad found at a yard sale in Barnstable and I'd listen to WBAI or WFMU or WBGO or WNYC—or, if I was feeling really masochistic, Z100—while I developed film and made print after print after print. For every self-portrait I developed I'd make a tally mark on the flimsy drywall that set apart the bathroom from the living space. I was so naive I imagined that someday some collector would come in, rip out that drywall, and have it framed. They'd call it *Tally Marks, 1989–199*-whatever. They'd talk about it in artspeak: a register, a record of signs and signifiers. I *signed* that wall. Right in the bottom right corner. *Lu Rile*. That's how hungry I was.

That summer afternoon in June I'd been making a self-portrait a day for 399 days. We'd had a long run of the kind of heat that makes the whole city smell like garbage. Garbage wasn't a priority back then. Crime was a priority; arson and riots were priorities. On Dinkins's list of concerns garbage didn't even factor. It piled up on sidewalks and sat in the sun for weeks leeching greenish liquid that pooled at the curbs and shimmered. The stench of it saturated the still air. For weeks at a time the whole city smelled like shit.

But that afternoon the weather had changed. In the wake of a recent thunderstorm the humidity had lifted. The air was purer. A salty wind blew in from the Atlantic and the sky was a brilliant cloudless blue. I opened my windows and for the first time in a month my loft was almost cool. The seagulls seemed to feel it too. They flew over the river as if stirred by a spoon, round and round, yelping.

As a kid growing up on Cape Cod I was fascinated by seagulls. I used to walk to the beach in the late afternoon before my dad got home—even in the winter, bundled up— and watch them. Their flight looks elegant from far away but if you observe them closely on the wind you'll see that flying is a constant negotiation. Flight requires muscle. With their wings they fold the wind. What seems like rest when they are gliding is actually millions of minute adaptations. They lean a little this way, a little that way, on a current that resists them, pushing up while they slide downward. What seems like flying is actually falling.

Watching the gulls again I got it in my head I wanted that day's self-portrait to be about flight. I wanted to celebrate the wind and temperature. And because of that bright blue June sky I wanted to do it in color.

I mounted my Rollei on a tripod and set up the shot, framing the window perfectly, with just a fraction of wall space around the sill and casing. I took off my glasses and practiced leaping in front of the windowpane with a stopwatch, timing it, recording it to the fraction of the second. After half an hour or so I calculated the average time it would take for me to get to the apex of an arc in the air. Then I set the timer on the remote shutter release.

The sun was sinking. The skyscrapers across the river were aglow. Two stories up, on the roof, my neighbors were having a party. Voices and laughter wafted in through the open window. I stripped off my clothes. It seemed bizarre to fly in jeans and a T-shirt. I tried one exposure and heard the shutter release just as I landed. I set the timer a fraction of a second earlier. It was essential that I get it right with as few exposures as possible. Color film's expensive.

I tried ten or twelve takes before I got it. Before, I mean, it happened. At the exact apex of my leap into the air I heard the shutter release. By the time my feet hit the floor I'd heard a thump outside the window. Something had landed on the roof below. I went to the window and couldn't see anything much. Just the gulls and far away a tiny airplane glinting. Below a squat tugboat pushed a massive barge.

And then I heard him howl. Steve, upstairs, who'd realized. It was like no sound I've ever heard before or since. An animal sound, a complete release. Sometimes in memory I hear it still. I put my clothes back on and slipped into my ratty Keds and grabbed my keys and Pentax. If something was going on up there I wanted to document it—but I didn't want to waste my medium-format Kodachrome. That stuff was gold.

The hallway smelled of rat poison and turpentine, a century of dust, and roasting lamb. The lights were out in the stairwell. My neighbors were all rushing down the stairs, barely illuminated by the grimy skylight. I stood in the doorway and they passed me without a word. The painter Steve Schubert, who lived directly upstairs from me. Steve's wife, Kate Fine, looking thin and harrowed. Another painter, Philip Philips, who lived on the second floor. He was holding his hand to his mouth as if he were about to be sick. A few other people I didn't know—their guests, I guessed. I said, What's going on? Nobody answered.

When they passed I went upstairs and pushed open the door to the roof. The breeze rolled over me. With the great easy pleasure of that wind came the sounds of helicopters, a faraway siren, the smells of brine and smog and pepper from the spice factory. The decadent sunset illuminated a roof in shambles. Sunlight caught in upturned red-stained glasses. An abandoned joint smoldered in a tray of pigs in a blanket. Someone had dropped or smashed a wine bottle and shards of it lay reflecting in a black pool on the tar roof. I took a couple of pictures. The light was so good. I took a picture. The siren was getting louder.

I heard a low voice at my shoulder and turned to find Bob Maynard beside me. A sculptor who had lived for many years in one of the apartments in the third-floor passageway, Bob was more or less our default handyman. He had replaced the lock on our front door I don't know how many times. He'd installed the mailboxes. He'd helped us rig up the absurd tangle of doorbells by the front door. He was a heavy man, and drank. I remember he stank that night of wine and sweat. His lips were stained and his graying hair stuck damp to the back of his neck.

I couldn't go down with the rest of them, he said. His eyes were dark. All this shuffle and scuffle and. He dragged his palm over the back of his neck.

The siren was below us now. It cut itself off with a shrill hiccup. There were voices and commotion in the street below, on the other side of the low building behind ours. I could see the reflection of the blue-and-red police lights on the brick wall.

I couldn't look, Bob Maynard said again. I don't know how you can stand there and look like that.

Like what, I started to ask—but Maynard just stepped back, away from the edge.

I saw him last week, he said. Hanging out outside the building. He was singing. Sitting on the steps, swinging his legs. Waiting for Kate, I guess, or Steve. Waiting for Mom and Dad. The door was open. They were probably on their way. But they left him waiting alone. Swinging his legs, singing to himself. I couldn't tell the song. Maybe he was making it up. Didn't even look up when I walked by. This high little voice.

Maynard's eyes drifted to the skyline. That's the kind of focus I used to have.

I wanted to say, What do you mean? But all of Maynard's energy was being directed inward to force himself into composure. He let out a long breath and with his thumb and forefinger squeezed the bridge of his nose, pushed at his closed eyes. A noise emanated from his throat: half cough, half choke. Abruptly he turned and walked away from me toward the door to the stairs and disappeared.

Alone I turned back to the low roof. It was in shadow now, just a trace of bloody sun illuminating the tar surfaces and smokestacks, the piles of discarded scrap and, below, the edges of a large aluminum steam vent. What those smokestacks and vents were for I didn't know. They contributed to the alienness of the landscape: the rooftop steppes, skylight mesas, and brick-lined gorges. I raised the Pentax to my right eye and began to fiddle with the focus and depth of field, but was interrupted by a chorus of voices rising from the roof below.

The door of a stairwell exit, a sort of sloping little brick-and-tar hut on the rooftop, was kicked open and a group of people rushed out. It was the same group I'd seen running down the stairs a minute before. As I watched they dispersed, talking in distressed tones; among them were two cops. By the aluminum vent one of the people I didn't recognize let out a yell. Soon he was joined by the others. Then they were all yelling. Max! They were shouting. Max! Can you hear us? And then they were saying to one another, He isn't responding. He isn't responding. Max! And some of them were crying, Oh god oh god. A cop held up his handset and called in backup. I heard him say, Bring rope.

Another siren arrived in slow crescendo. Minutes later two more policemen burst out onto the roof. In the twilight I watched them throw their ropes down the vent again and again, pulling them back up empty. The cops conferred and the people held one another, making way, making space for two individuals: a man who paced the length of the rooftop smoking and a tall woman who sank to her knees. I recognized those two even in the dark. By his yellow tangled ponytail I knew the pacing man was Steve Schubert. The bent willow of a woman by the vent was his wife, Kate Fine. Stupidly, long after it should have come together in my mind, I began to make sense of what Bob Maynard had been telling me. This couple had a son, a manic boy of startling beauty. Max Schubert-Fine. I'd passed him in the hallway many times. He'd stare at me with the bald awareness of a boy who knew he was too old to stare and often I'd stare back—not for any reason other than he was wonderful to look at. A full curly head of his father's yellow hair; his mother's deep brown eyes and full lips. He was a devil though, a nine-year-old with the energy of an unleashed missile. I could see him now, breaking eye contact and racing up the stairs, leaving behind him a trail of mocking laughter.

I watched as below me Kate convulsed silently in the last of the light. I watched as she looked up into the twilit sky. Her gaze rose to the edge of the higher roof, where I was standing. The streetlights clicked on, flooding the scene and the brick wall beyond it in a pool of dirty light. Across four stories we locked eyes.

Suddenly aware of my own voyeurism I turned away, resisting the impulse to bring the camera to my eye. But something stopped me from heading back downstairs. It was that image in my mind. The contrast between the light reflected in the edge of the aluminum and the black tar of the roof. The flat disk tops of the policemen's hats as they bent their heads over their notebooks. The group of people seen from above, each of them doing something different—huddled in couples at the edges or pacing alone, cast by the streetlight in jaundice hues—and one woman at the edge of the crowd, crouching, looking up, a modern Madonna. It would have been a terrific photograph. I turned back toward the scene and put a hand to the Pentax that hung from my neck. Kate was still kneeling there looking up at me, a tiny figure in a crowded Brueghel, her excruciating expression a caricature of pain.

To take that picture would have been an awful thing to do. So again, without even looking through the viewfinder, I turned away.

It has often occurred to me in the intervening years that if I'd had a digital camera back then, the kind with a screen where you can look at the picture you've just taken—if in the very moment of taking that four hundredth self-portrait I had seen immediately how the picture had turned out—I might have just deleted it. These days, working in digital, I often delete pictures reflexively. But a strip of plastic, gelatin, and silver halide crystals doesn't just disappear. You have to burn it.

|||

Two twenty-two River Street was actually two buildings, both constructed in the late 1800s, just a year after Brooklyn was incorporated into New York City. They were factories originally. The one on the south side, where I lived, manufactured powdered soap. The one on the north side made things out of cork.

The layout of the compound was something like an H. The regular entrance to both buildings was on the first floor of the former cork factory, and the two were connected on the third floor by a long broad space: the middle bar of the H. The only direct access to our building from the street was a loading dock and freight elevator, which the sculptors used to transport their work. So to get to my loft from the front door I'd go in at the foot of one vertical, traverse the middle bar, and ascend the vertical on the other side.

That third-floor space would have been the depth of the building itself, but some of the building's first tenants who'd moved in back in the seventies had built lofts like rabbit warrens around the windows that faced the river. Because those windows were blocked by their apartments, the passage was a shady space. Masking tape arrows on the floor directed us from one side to the other.

Our landlord, Gary Wrench, bought 222 River for a song in the early sixties. It had already been abandoned for decades. Wrench was a Republican from Staten Island with abominable posture and a persistent case of eczema. Make a double exposure of the Cowardly Lion and Walter Matthau in your mind and you'll have an idea of what he looked like. Back then Wrench had a manufacturing business of his own: the River Street Box Company. I guess the cardboard box business was never particularly profitable. To make an extra buck he started letting artists squat for cheap in the empty floors upstairs. As the number of tenants grew, it became clear to Wrench that landlording was the better way to earn a living. He shut down his box business in the mid-eighties. By the time I moved into 222 River Street all that was left of the box company was some mysterious machinery on the ground floor and a collection of torn and dented moldering cardboard in the third-floor passageway. Meanwhile the majority of the building was occupied by artists.

It was really not until Max Schubert-Fine fell from the roof that I began to know my neighbors. I never had much to say to them before. Artists are weird people. Prickly and reserved. But because I lived directly downstairs from Kate and Steve, after Max's death I'd run into neighbors all the time, bringing up their various offerings. Casseroles or bottles of wine or flowers. People I barely knew would smile at me on the stairs. One morning I passed Gary Wrench clutching a limp bouquet of dyed blue daisies.

For some reason I always seemed to make Gary Wrench uncomfortable. I rather enjoyed that. Hey, I said to him, what are the chances you'll get around to replacing the light in the stairwell sometime soon? I almost broke my neck the other night.

He got a pained look on his face and scratched at the eczema on his temple. There's a ladder in the basement. You can change it any time.

How do I get to the basement?

Freight elevator. Bob Maynard and Cora Pickenpew both have keys.

So I should just do it then?

Somehow he managed to simultaneously nod and shake his head. Just takes a regular 60-watt bulb, he said.

Do you have one?

He slid past me on the stairs. You buy one, I'll reimburse you.

Cora Pickenpew lived on the top floor in a light-flooded loft everyone called the Penthouse. The former factory office, it had actual wood floors and paneling on the walls. Cora had a good relationship with Gary Wrench. Apparently when she was going through her divorce the two of them developed a friendship. He let her borrow his car. He took her to the movies.

Next time I ran into her, downstairs by the mailboxes, she was carrying a paper bag of bagels. Her salt-and-pepper hair was pinned up in a careless bouffant. Her voice was throaty and melodious, her tone always halfway to teasing: Hi, Lu.

Heading up to Kate and Steve's? I said.

Shifting the bagels into one arm, she pushed back her hair as if it might get in the way of her whisper. God, isn't it awful? Just awful. So sad.

I agreed.

Are you going to the memorial? Seeing my face she added, It's not by invitation. Everyone's allowed, I mean encouraged. Everyone's going.

When is it?

A week from Sunday. God, I just don't know if I can take it.

I have to work, I said.

A sage nod. Good for you.

Cora came from money. She was a woman for whom the word *work* meant *make art,* nothing else. What I meant by *work* was *work.* I meant I'd be ringing up out-of-season avocados for people like her.

Hey, I said, I know you're on your way up there but whenever's a good time could I come by and get the key to the freight elevator? I want to change the lightbulb in the stairs.

Oh, you shouldn't have to do that. Get Gary to take care of it.

I asked him. He won't.

Or Bob.

I can do it, I said.

Nonsense, said Cora. I'll talk to Bob.

I want to do it, I said.

She raised her eyebrows. Suit yourself.

So I ended up knocking on Bob Maynard's door later that day. He answered in jean shorts coated with plaster dust and a stained white T-shirt that emphasized the bulges of his midsection. He seemed surprised to see me. He wiped the sweat from his forehead with a torn, stained handkerchief.

I said, You've got a key to the freight elevator, right?

Sure.

Could I borrow it? I want to change the bulb in the stairwell. Gary Wrench said there's a ladder down there.

Maynard sighed. I imagine he was relieved that I wasn't there to talk about our moment together on the roof. Sure, sure. Come in.

His space was enormous, two giant rooms with windows that ran across the entire back wall. A wood-burning oven was rigged up such that smoke could be released via a vent that led out of a window. His lofted bedroom was accessible by a spiral staircase. Through two glass-paneled doors I could see his studio, a mess of dust and empty wine bottles and his heavy bulbous sculptures. A master glassblower, Maynard made enormous bloated objects that would wilt as they cooled; he twisted handles from their surfaces while they were still hot and somewhat liquid, and later threaded those handles with rope. I'd been to an opening of his work once; globular objects the size of small children hung from the gallery ceiling and rotated slowly, creaking. Trapping light in their translucent bellies, they seemed to glow. Here in his studio though, they were almost opaque with dust. Still and unlit like that, suspended behind the glass wall in the dark, they were like manatees in captivity.

He gave me the keys to the freight elevator and I rode it down to the basement and hooked back the collapsible metal fence with its dirty chain. The uneven basement floor was flooded with puddles of stagnant water that teemed with mosquitos. The ladder was metal and enormous and had been left leaning against a wall. When I picked it up I felt something soft by my foot. I looked down and saw a dead rat. A mosquito bit my neck and I cursed out loud. If I lived in a real apartment building, I couldn't help but think, the landlord would never allow me to witness that kind of filth.

I rode back up to the fifth floor, where Kate and Steve lived, and pushed open their fire door with the ladder. I was thinking, ruefully, of the basement, of decay, and of the thoughtlessness of men. I was thinking, How could a little boy grow up to be Gary Wrench or Bob Maynard? The bulk of their necks, the breadth of their thighs, the wheeze of their voices. I unscrewed the yellow cage that protected the dead bulb. It was covered in dust and I had to stop more than once to wipe my glasses. Even their accents seemed ready-made for adults: that Northeast warp to Maynard's vowels—Maine? maybe Rhode Island—and Gary Wrench's Staten Island umlauts. Did any actual children talk like that? If they ever had, it seemed to me, they didn't anymore. Not since television, anyway. Not since the democratization of mainstream entertainment had flattened out the differences between us all. On the other hand if you really listened to the Brady Bunch, those kids had some odd overcooked accents themselves. The fictionalized American voice of the television teen. . . .

These thoughts were interrupted by the awareness that someone was watching me. Awkwardly I turned around on the ladder to see Kate Fine standing in the open doorway. She was carrying a full black trash bag. Her hair was greasy and her face was wan, but her beauty was arresting.

What do you say to a woman whose son has died? I could not say, How are you? I could barely say hello. What ended up coming out of my mouth, idiotically, was: Taking out the trash?

She did not reply. After a moment I turned around again. She watched as I busied myself unscrewing the dead bulb and began to screw in the new one. When its metal end touched the metal in the socket it buzzed and lit up like an insect. I made a satisfied noise and turned back toward her. Having seen the process through to its conclusion she stepped through the doorway and started down the stairs. I watched her thin frame, the ruined posture of her elegant shoulders, the bend of her neck. At the landing she stopped a moment and looked back up at me. Her voice sounded muffled, as if she were speaking from behind a blanket.

Thanks for doing that, she said. Gary never would have gotten around to it.

No problem, I said.

She stayed there a minute.

Ever been down to the basement? I said.

She didn't answer. Just looked up at me with those miserable hollow eyes.

It's a nightmare down there, I said. It's like the set of a low-budget horror movie. Dead rats crawling with maggots.

Puddles swarming with mosquitoes. One bit me and now I'm coming down with the bubonic plague.

Ha, she said.

Yeah. Anyway.

Anyway, she replied. She gave me what on a person with facial paralysis might have passed for a smile. Then she heaved up her trash bag and continued down the stairs.

IIII

I guess I went to the memorial because of that moment. There was something about Kate's silence on the stairs, the way she seemed to want to stop and chat but couldn't. I remembered something my dad said once when I didn't want to go to the funeral of a coworker of his. It was a guy who was killed on the job. Someone else was holding a two-by-four and swung it straight into his head. Imagining the gruesomeness of a shattered skull, I told my dad I didn't want to go. I didn't even know him. In his simple no-bullshit way my dad replied: Funerals aren't for the dead.

So I got someone to cover my shift at Summerland and trudged uphill that Sunday afternoon to the First Unitarian Church in the Heights. It was overcast and humid. When I got there a group of my neighbors was standing around on the sidewalk. They seemed out of place somehow, removed from their natural habitat. Cora Pickenpew looked smaller than usual. Her smile was bright and false. Handsome

Philip Philips was sculptural with downcast eyes. Bob Maynard bowed his head over a cigarette by the No Parking sign. I didn't want to talk to them. I didn't want anyone to talk to me. I hoped a familiar hope, a hope I'd developed years before, in high school: that when they looked back on it no one would remember that I'd been there at all. I was wearing dark prescription sunglasses and I kept them on, even inside.

Kate was in the front row with Steve on one side and on the other a woman who I guessed was her mother. What I took to be Steve's parents sat beside him. Everyone had their arms around one another except for Kate and Steve. Steve was bent over like a rag doll, his head resting facedown in his hands, his elbows on his knees. Kate was sitting straight up and nodding as people came over to her and put their hands on her shoulders or kissed her cheeks or touched her hair. She was beautiful in the sort of way that made people think it was all right to touch her. Her body and face were unresponsive.

I took a seat in a pew near the back and picked up a hymnal so I wouldn't have to look at anyone. My neighbors filed in from the bright street and blinked as their eyes adjusted to the dim hot chapel. A few children about Max's age, dressed in black with clip-on ties, came in with their parents. The ceilings were high, the windows stained glass, the floors of the aisles covered with a thin fraying carpet. It smelled of mildew and stale coffee and old boots. Everyone was sweating. I watched one boy get down on the floor and start picking at the edges of the carpet. His parents ignored him. They held each other's hands tightly, bracing for what would follow.

Eventually the minister took the dais. She was dressed in long Indian cottons. Her white pillow face was set like a covered button in her frizzy woolen hair. She introduced herself with a compassionate hello. Greetings, she said. I'm Visiting Minister Sandra Weinstein. Then she read a poem. I don't know what it was. Her voice was slow and deep and resonant. It seemed to issue from some cavern in her belly. It filled the space. When the poem was done she let it sit and soak in the silence among the crowd.

When a child dies, she said at last, and looked around. When a child dies. We have a tendency to make him into an angel. Max Schubert-Fine was a brilliant boy. He was beautiful, he was loving. She smiled. He was *not* an angel.

The congregation sort of laughed and nodded and wiped their eyes.

God, I thought. The fuck am I doing here.

Kate in the front pew, haggard, her mother beside her, weeping. Steve on the other side of her, his face hidden in his hands.

The visiting minister continued: I heard Max referred to—several times in fact—as a hellion. His influence was irresistible. His energy was contagious. Max Schubert-Fine could get the most timid boy in school hocking loogies out a third-floor window. He could design elaborate practical jokes out of nothing but Vaseline, rubber bands, and string. He was a talented physical comedian. He'd perfected the Groucho Marx pratfall. His wise remarks and his inability to *keep his hands to himself* got him sent out of the classroom at least once a week. Kings County Academy isn't exactly known for its discipline, said Sandra Weinstein, smiling. The pair of parents clutching each other's hands nodded in sync, nodded desperately and kept on nodding, as if nodding their heads together like that would keep them from crying. And yet, she said, at Kings County Max became well acquainted with the principal. Max Schubert-Fine was irrepressible. He was a smart boy. He was so quick. He was more than clever. He had a habit of unnerving his elders with his perceptiveness. With small moments of poetry. His mother told me a story a couple of weeks ago that's stuck with me. They were making popcorn. Is that right, Kate?

Kate remained motionless.

These small cruelties, I thought. Don't make her talk about the popcorn.

Max had a friend over, a wealthy friend. A lot of wealthy children go to KCA. The kids were sitting on the countertop while she made popcorn on the stove. Max said to his friend, Do you live in Brooklyn or Manhattan? The child said, Manhattan. He said, I live at Windsor Court. Probably his mother had drilled the name of the building into him in case of emergency. And of course as any mother would, Kate felt sorry in that moment, sorry she could not give her son the kind of privileged life his friends were accustomed to. But Max? Max didn't skip a beat. With pride in his eyes he replied: I live in a building called Air.

Murmured laughter. Kate's head dropped.

A.I.R., as you might know, is painted on the front door of the building where Kate and Steve raised Max. It stands for *Artists in Residence* and it's there to let the fire department know that, in their sparsely populated neighborhood, there are people living in that building. But to Max, and to his mother after that—and to anyone who's heard that story—they live in *a building called Air*. Imagine after slogging home in the humid summer, or in the slush or snow or hail or relentless rain of winter, weighed down by groceries and book bags and purses, coming home to *a building called Air*? I'd like to thank Max for that moment of poetry.

Sandra Weinstein went on to talk about how love is life and Max was love. I had become livid for some reason. It wasn't any of my business but I was shaking with anger. How dare she try to make this into a beautiful thing. What happened was a kid died, period, and now his fucking parents were a mess. What happened was—

Well. Of course what happened was so much more than that.

What I mean is that when you die a boy you remain a boy forever. What I mean is, have you heard the seagulls call at the water's edge in a gray rain? Have you picked up among them the cries of a dead child? Have you felt the presence of an absence in the wailing of the wind? Because I have. I have.

Everyone was singing, many were standing, many weeping. I sat there clenching my fists and waiting for it all to end. And just as they came back to the inane chorus of whatever hymn for the thousandth time, I felt a chill, and gasped, and coughed. The woman next to me put a hand on my shoulder and goose bumps spread over my skin. Are you all right? she murmured under the noise of the song.

I was disoriented. The front of the room was its back; its left was right. Yes yes, I managed to say, yes. I touched my sunglasses to make sure they were still there. They were. I got up to go outside. I fumbled out the swinging doors and in the hazy sunshine by the iron fence I leaned back and closed my eyes. I rested my head against the fence and breathed slowly, trying to gather myself back together.

Eventually the door to the church opened again and the family stepped out, attended by a crowd of well-intentioned mourners. I felt a hand on my shoulder and turned to see the tearstained face of my neighbor Tammy Day. She had taken it upon herself to scratch down the address where the reception would be on the paper of a small lined notebook, and now she was tearing off little scraps and pressing them into people's hands. Seeing me, she did not waste a scrap. She only said, Everyone's going over to Kate and Steve's.

The mourners filed out of the church and we walked together back downhill to DUMBO. We made a slow procession through Cadman Plaza Park, which was deserted on a summer Sunday save for several men sleeping on the benches, their backs to the world. We passed below the entrance to the Brooklyn Bridge and marched quietly through the compound where the Jehovah's Witnesses worked and lived. Finally we turned to pass under the Manhattan Bridge.

It was beginning to drizzle and no one had an umbrella. The cobblestone streets were slick. Tiny beads of rain glimmered weightless in our hair.

I had ended up walking with Kate's brother and his pregnant wife. The wife was slow in her state and over the course of the walk everyone had passed us. I tried lamely to make polite conversation. How long will you stay?

Through the day after tomorrow, the brother said. We would stay longer, but.

He has to work, the sister-in-law said.

Where do you go back to?

Minneapolis, he said.

It did not take more than two exchanges for me to give up. For blocks neither of them said a word.

Amid the yellow poured-concrete monoliths of the Jehovah's Witnesses compound—READ GOD'S WORD THE HOLY BIBLE DAILY was emblazoned on one of them in clear block letters—we stopped at a Don't Walk sign and waited for the light to change, despite the fact that there was no traffic. It was just the three of us. The sister-in-law turned to me.

You're a neighbor?

Yes. Lu Rile. I live downstairs from Kate and Steve.

Polly Fine. And this is Tom.

I nodded again. They nodded back. The light changed. We stepped into the street.

Let me ask you something, Lu, Polly Fine said. Do you have kids?

No, I said.

Polly, said the brother.

If you did have kids, do you think you'd stay where you are—in your apartment, I mean? Or do you think you'd move?

Polly, the brother said again.

I'm making conversation, Polly replied. Turning to me, holding her round belly, she said: I mean seriously. Do you think you'd stay?

I don't know, I said. She seemed frustrated by my reticence.

I don't think this is an appropriate conversation to be having right now, the brother said, I really don't.

Why not? Polly said.

We walked a minute in silence, the rain wetting our faces.

I wiped my glasses. I can't imagine having kids, I said. I've never been able to imagine being a mother.

But you live in the building, she persisted. You have been there when the heat is off in the middle of the winter. When there was a gas leak—

There was a gas leak?

You weren't told? Tom Fine frowned.

What I'm asking is, said Polly, and you don't have to be a mother or a mother-to-be to have an opinion on this—do you think your building is an appropriate environment for children?

I—

Jesus fucking Christ, Tom erupted. Let up!

We were underneath the Manhattan Bridge now and a train was going by overhead so loud I could feel it in my skull, my feet: *ca-chunk ca-chunk* (beat, beat), *ca-chunk ca-chunk* (beat, beat), *ca-chunk ca-chunk*.

All I'm saying is—Polly was talking extremely fast, she was practically yelling, and her face was reddening, and we'd all stopped walking now (*ca-chunk ca-chunk*)—all I'm *saying* is it could have been helped. It could have been *helped,* Tom, I mean, *god*—a place like this—

He took her in his arms as she dissolved into the thunder.

I hesitated a moment. The train passed. Embarrassed, in the quiet of its wake I kept walking, leaving the couple behind.

The river was dull and gray that day. Back at our building I climbed the three flights up to the third-floor passage, traversed that long dark space, then climbed up two more flights, past my own loft on the fourth floor, to Kate and Steve's on the fifth. Privately I congratulated myself for having changed the bulb in the stairwell. The door to their loft was open and from the hallway I could see groups of people talking, hugging, eating, wandering, framed in the doorway. A crowded composition. I went downstairs to retrieve my Pentax and came back up once more and stood there in the hall to photograph it all. You might have seen the final print. It ended up on the cover of a novel that came out a few years ago. The book is crap, a cold, self-conscious story by a pretentious man, but I stand behind the image. So to speak. Clusters of mourners seen through a doorway lit from within. A woman passes with a tray of food while two overdressed children stand on their tiptoes and crane their heads up to see what she's holding. In the out-of-focus foreground two men hold each other. In the background a fat woman arranges flowers in a copper pot.

I did go in. I wanted Kate at least to see that I was there. I can't explain why. She was the sort of woman people wanted to please. I wanted to please her. I imagined finding her in some corner, left alone by all the well-intentioned people who thought she needed space. I wanted to go up to her and simply take her hand—no, that would be too much. To exchange a look, maybe, like the look we'd exchanged in the stairwell. A look that communicated on my end: You are bereft. I understand that you are bereft. You needn't be anything but bereft, bereft.

It was hot. Someone had put fans in front of all the windows and the noise of their heavy whir raised the decibel level of the whole space. A group of people standing together around the laden buffet, helping themselves to wine, were talking about what was going on in the Gulf. A couple of boys were wrestling under the table. Two men I didn't recognize were nodding and listening to Bob Maynard wax philosophical: Certain events, you know, you're one way before and you're another way after. The armpits of his T-shirt damp with sweat.

A young woman with a cherubic face was telling someone over and over: I just can't believe it. I can't believe it at all. I was his third-grade teacher. He was about to go into fourth grade. I can't believe it. As she shook her head Steve Schubert pushed past her. Her eyes fell and she blushed deeply.

An older woman I recognized from the ceremony as Kate's mother was saying, I haven't seen them since Christmas. They never come to visit. I live alone. They never come except for holidays. Not since Christmas had I seen him. Now I wish I'd made a bigger stink. As she spoke her voice rose up in pitch, became an awful whine.

Contrary to my fantasy, Kate was surrounded by people. She was standing by the window smoking cigarettes with several other long-limbed women. Each was beautiful in a different alien way. One had bright red lips and black hair cut to the chin like a fashion drawing. One was walleyed and wearing a kimono. One seemed to be afloat in a cloud of hair and looked as if she'd had her nose broken. I saw them smoking there and then I looked away. Of course Kate would be friends with model types. I had the distinct and immediate feeling that my idea of going up to her, of exchanging a look—or, worse, a squeeze of the hand—had been utterly insane. I could not go over to them. Of course I couldn't. My going over to them was just not a thing that could be done. Probably even if I tried they wouldn't be able to hear or see me. Probably their ears could not pick up sounds emitted below a certain altitude. Their eyes were not trained to perceive any differentiation between unbeautiful people such as me and the rest of their environment. I would be no more remarkable to them than a footstool or a trash can.

As I stood there by the wall, alone and staring, I felt a shush of fabric pass me and Cora Pickenpew steered herself into the harbor of models at the window. Katie, I heard her say, and her throaty voice was rich with compassion: If there's anything I can do, anything at all, you know I'm right upstairs.

I know, said Kate.

I am so sorry. So so sorry, sweetie.

Kate nodded.

I brought down a casserole. I put it in your fridge. You can eat it for days. You don't have to worry about a thing. All you have to do right now is rest, okay?

Okay, said Kate.

You just let me know if there's anything, *anything* I can do. Okay?

Kate sucked on her cigarette.

Okay. Cora stood a moment before turning around and surveying the room to locate her next port of call. Her glance moved right over me but I caught Kate's eye behind her and without really thinking shot Kate a sympathetic wink. Kate's face brightened a fraction of a joule as Cora, thinking the wink was for her, recoiled. The SS *Pickenpew* floated away. I almost laughed.

There were still a few hours of light left in the day. I went back downstairs to my loft. To drown out the noise above I turned on the radio. Finding nothing I liked I turned it off and pressed play on the cassette player. Cranked the volume on the Pixies and stripped off my sweaty black clothes. Nude, I filled a pot of water and put it on the stove.

In the studio I gathered my lighttight changing bag, film tank and reel, graduates, thermometer, and Kodak E-6 chemicals, which I stored in a gallon jug on a bookcase I'd nailed together from four wooden wine crates I'd found on the street. Ektachrome was so easy to process you could do it with the lights on. I put my roll of film, film tank, and reel into the changing bag, zippered the bag closed, and put my arms through the armholes. I wound the film onto the reel, put the reel in the tank, and covered it. Took the tank out of the bag. I mixed the E-6 kit chemicals with water, then went back to the kitchen.

The water was boiling. It was hot in the loft. With a dish towel I wiped my neck and armpits. I picked up the pot with two pot holders and lugged it back into the studio, careful not to spill any boiling water on my naked skin, then poured the water into the plugged studio sink and lowered the gallon jugs of chemicals into the steaming basin. The water level rose.

Hot water sloshed onto the floor. I hopped back from the scalding water, perspiring heavily. I took off my glasses. The chemicals had to be at just the right temperature to process.

Black Francis sang and sweat rolled into my eyes, stinging. I poured the various solutions in and out of the developing tank in time to the wailing guitars and smashing drums, turning the tank over every so often to dislodge bubbles and shake up the chemicals.

It was late in the day. Heat rippled off the tar rooftops, liquefying the view. A forgotten balloon floated in the empty sky. Havalina ended and the play button popped up. To drown out the voices upstairs, or at least mask them, I turned on the radio. It was the six o'clock news. Something about Boris Yeltsin. When the stopwatch went off I poured out the developing tank and filled it with stabilizer. Waited.

I lifted the film reel out of the tank, lightly shook it off, and twisted it until it came apart. Delicately I unspooled the film and washed it in the studio sink. Onto each end of the long strip of medium-format color positives I clamped a jumbo paper clip. Then I hung it from the clothesline I'd strung across my west-facing window. Light from the low sun poured in, illuminating the film. I tilted my head to look at the images without touching them.

The window in the background of *Self-Portrait #400* was a crisp square enclosing a swath of bright blue sky. My own body leaped from the right edge of the frame toward the left. The front of my form was blurred and ghostly, the back of my body a long veil. In the left-hand pane of the window there was something else, something I could not quite read. In just one of the exposures there seemed to be a reflection or a smudge, some imperfection. I heard myself make a little involuntary grunt of dissatisfaction. Stood up, pushed up my glasses, shoved the hair out of my face. Shut off the radio—it was distracting—and looked again but again I could not read it.

I'd let the film dry, I decided. I'd come back later.

I retrieved my one pot from the darkroom and brought it back to the kitchen to start dinner. Poured into it an inch of rice, water, and salt. Lit a fire under the pot, fetched a can of beans from the cabinet over the sink. While the rice and water came slowly to a boil I filled a short glass with ice and a shot of the cheap Polish vodka I kept in the freezer. The tenants had gotten together recently and chipped in to rent a generator, which made up in part for Gary Wrench's reluctance to pay Con Ed on time. The machine was finicky and our electricity was feeble. But as I took my first sip of the bitter alcohol and felt the hot cold run down my throat I was grateful for that generator.

The water boiled and I turned it down to a simmer. I threw on a dress—an ugly batik number I regretted buying on a whim for five dollars at a street fair—and climbed out my studio window to the fire escape. On the iron slats above me Steve Schubert was sitting with an artist I recognized but didn't know personally, a guy named Manny Cortazar. They were taking turns drinking from a tall bottle of whiskey. I nodded up at them and they nodded down at me. Manny lit a cigarette. We didn't speak.

Nursing my vodka I watched the sun set. With a moment of quiet to spare I felt overcome by sadness. On the low roof below us where the body of Steve's child had been extracted from the vent not two weeks before, the door to the stairwell had been left unlocked. It banged closed and creaked open again in the warm summer wind.

Above me I heard a door open and a voice say, You guys okay out here?

Yeah, said Manny.

Steve?

He's fine, Manny said.

People are heading out.

Okay, said Manny.

Thanks, said Steve. His voice was weak.

I finished my vodka and went back inside. It was dark. I turned on the dozen battery-powered camping lanterns I'd bought at the ninety-nine-cent store in Fulton Mall. I poured another small shot over a cube of ice. I heard the door upstairs open and close, open and close. The guests were leaving.

I plugged in my light box and retrieved my loupe and red pencil from the marinara jar where I kept them along with a collection of pens and other tools. The strip of color positives was dry by now. I unhooked it from its place in the window. I brought it over to the light box and peered at each image through the loupe. With the red pencil I made a small mark in the corners of those that seemed interesting. I started with the ones I was sure of—*Self-Portrait #388* had come out well. So had *Self-Portrait #394*. I stopped at *Self-Portrait #400*. What the hell was going on with that smudge beyond the window? There was the window in the background and there was the bright sky. There was my own body leaping from the right edge of the frame and there in the left-hand pane was that something else. It looked like a bundle of laundry falling from above. Actually whatever it was really balanced out the composition. Actually it was quite good. The square window fit perfectly in the square frame.

I cut the strip around *Self-Portrait #400,* brought it back into the studio, and mounted it in the enlarger behind the blackout curtain. I slid the square of film into the enlarger along with my color filters and focused the image, concentrating on getting the square window frame as sharp as possible. I closed the darkroom curtain so that it was entirely lighttight, then removed a sheet of Type-A Cibachrome paper from its package and laid it on the surface of the enlarger without bothering to crop or frame. I mixed the chemicals and began processing. That first print was just a trial run. It was just to figure out what was in the background.

It was hot and stuffy between the heavy curtains and after a minute and a half I was sweating again through the cheap batik. When the timer went off I picked up the paper with my thumbs and index fingers, removed the print from the drum, and washed it in running water. I flung open the blackout curtain and squinted at the print. The sky outside was sliced in half by one faint rosy gash of sunset. There was barely enough light to see. Leaning forward, peering in, I was almost able to make out the smudge. My whole body was prickling in the heat. But as I leaned I lost my grip. The print slipped to the floor and the stabilizer tipped. Clumsily I tried to catch it but only succeeded in upturning it. In a moment it was on the floor, the wet photograph wrinkled beside it, my dress drenched in formaldehyde-rich stabilizer.

I am rarely clumsy. I am usually careful and contained. I do not spill or trip or lose my bearings. I cursed, uncrumpled the photograph, washed it again, and pinned it to the clothesline.

In the bathroom I took off the dress and plugged the sink and ran a half capful of Tide under the tap. I scrubbed the toxic stabilizer from my skin with castile soap. When I turned off the shower the loft felt extra quiet. I stood in the middle of the bathroom a moment, toweling, listening. Nothing. The guests upstairs had all gone home.

I walked back to the studio wrapped in a towel. The sky beyond the windows was dull and dark. I would have to mop the floor but first I wanted to look at the wrinkled, wet test print.

I pulled at its corners to smooth it as well as I could. There was the frame around the window, perfectly in focus, perfectly crisp. There was the sky behind the windows, its smooth blue gradient. There was my own pale body floating ghostlike above the floor, midleap, translucent, caught in blur. There on the left, in the middle of the window, balancing the composition, was the vertical streak, a perfect counterpoint to the horizontal one that was my body.

It was not a bundle of laundry at all, of course. It was Max Schubert-Fine.

My throat closed. Despite the heat I felt a chill. I stood up straight and breathed and listened. The loft was eerily silent. I heard nothing but my own loud heart. I swallowed. I bent and looked again more closely. There was his tangle of yellow hair in the wind. A hint of silver zipper glinting brightly.

Five little fingers blurred upward like streaks of finger paint, just traces in the air. His little hand reaching up toward all he'd left.

Fuck, I said aloud.

A high-pitched muffled sob came from upstairs.

Fuck! I whispered sharply. Fuck, fuck, fuck, fuck. I paced the loft. The sun was down. Outside everything was dark and cooling. I paced and paced and stopped at the photo on the clothesline, then paced some more. I brought a camping lantern to the print and looked again in the dim yellow light. The composition was perfect. Serendipitous, just as I'd always wanted. At last my fucking project, my self-portrait a day, made sense. Falling boy on the left, leaping woman on the right. Flying and falling, because flying was falling. The problem was it was a terrific photograph. The problem was the photograph was fucking great.

It was unexpected. It was raw. It was startling. It was awful. It was beautiful. It was factual. Heartbreaking. Cruel. Fresh. Real. This photo could change everything, I thought, and I was thinking a mile a minute. It could transform me from the unknown photographer I was into the artist I wanted to be: serious, disciplined, honest, ruthless. I was dizzy with anticipation. I was hungry with ambition. *Self-Portrait #400* could change my life.

The smell of burned rice permeated the loft.

||||

They say a picture's worth a thousand words. I guess this one ended up being closer to a hundred thousand. Not to mention the toll it took on my sanity. I spent the next few days in a mania of indecision. Or was it weeks? The pain upstairs was palpable. It seeped through my ceiling in leaks and floods of tears and argument. I wanted badly to march upstairs and tell Kate and Steve all about *#400*. It was their child, their tragedy. On one hand it belonged to them.

On the other hand I wanted nothing to do with their misery. I'd never wanted anything to do with any of my neighbors, miserable or not. The fact that these two happened to be reeling in the throes of unimaginable heartbreak didn't make me any more eager to connect with them.

What was more, the test print of *#400* was so fucking good it seemed to speak to me. Passing the place near the cluttered dining table where it was pinned with tacks to the wall I'd stop to look at it, and every time it would respond—with fresh ideas,

Has the suicide on the wall?

new thoughts and theories, and boundless excitement. It felt *alive* the way the best art I'd ever seen had felt alive. I'd find myself comparing it not just to the work of other photographers I admired—Francesca Woodman, Robert Mapplethorpe—but to Cézanne or Goya. It bristled, breathed, *negotiated*. The photograph was so full of life it would literally pop off the wall. I'd lose the pins that held it in the cracks of the poured concrete floor. When I thought of what it might look like printed large, matted, and framed—my breath would become quick and shallow with excitement.

It gave me a proprietary feeling, familiar from childhood but long lost. When I was a kid growing up in our house on stilts in the seaside marsh I'd make little villages in the driveway, elaborate clusters and rows of sticks and shells arranged in the sandy soil. Somehow these little villages conjured the magic energy of the enchanted. I'd spend a day or two engrossed in building one but the process would inevitably end when it would be destroyed by wind or rain or the wheels of my dad's truck. I would be as crushed as it was. I'd mourn it and try to rebuild it, to recall its magic, but re-creation was impossible. Each village was different, each a little less magic than the last. Eventually I grew out of making them altogether.

I'd never realized until now how I'd missed this feeling, making art as an adult. *Self-Portrait #400* was like those villages of sticks. I felt an urgent need to protect it.

And yet. I'd hear Kate and Steve upstairs in their agony and know I had to say something. It was a matter of wrong and right. I tried to imagine every different way it could go, to prepare myself. I allowed myself one fantasy in which I'd walk upstairs, knock, and confess. I'd show them the image and, despite their grief, artists that they were, they'd recognize its power. They'd say, All right, thank you for showing us. This is a great fucking picture. You have our blessing.

I allowed that fantasy and then I squelched it. I knew I could not hope that they would give me the go-ahead. If I showed them the image I had to be prepared to relinquish it altogether.

It was around this time that my dad called and told me about his eyes.

Lulu, he said when I picked up.

Toby Rile, my only parent. That thin little voice with its thick Mass accent:

What's cookin'?

Hey, Dad.

How you managing down there?

Doing fine, Dad, doing fine. Making it work like always.

I know you do.

Still at Summerland.

Lu Rile, mayor of Tofu Town.

More like deputy sanitation commissioner . . . or something. What's up?

A deep sigh. Whenever I asked him about himself he'd deflect for about ten minutes. Been tinkering, he said. Found a piece of copper pipe down in the junkyard. Thinking of making it into a lamp.

I could see him in my mind's eye: deeply lined, tanned skin and wrinkled neck. Sharp nose, unfocused eyes. He always used speakerphone and would talk from his favorite chair with his hands in his lap, his face turned toward the sun.

That'll be pretty, I said.

Yep. Yeah. Jeff and Joey were over the other night. Helped me patch the roof in the garage.

Jeff and Joey.

From the VA.

That's good.

It was starting to rot. Stank to heaven. And after the hurricane in the spring I had to. Well. It's an uphill battle.

Dad, have you given any more thought to moving further inland?

An up. Hill. Battle. Old Sissy-puss.

It was a mispronunciation that I'd uttered once as a kid and that had somehow stuck. I let my nagging go. Sissy-puss, I rejoined.

Thing is I don't see so well no more.

I know, Dad. When's the last time you got new glasses?

It's not the glasses.

You've had those things for what, ten years?

It's not the glasses, Lu.

So stubborn.

Like kid, like dad.

I know. But you're out there all alone.

Martina comes three days a week.

I worry about you driving.

Well, yup. That's a worry. Another deep slow sigh. That's why I call, Louise.

What's wrong.

I been to the doctor. Says I ought to get surgery.

What surgery? Start at the beginning.

See, I knew you would—

Don't worry about me.

Long story short, it's cataracts.

Cataracts. Now I sighed. When do you have to go in?

It's not urgent. But in the next few months. I'll need you to stay with me a couple days, pal, maybe longer. It's a long recovery and even then it's not a sure thing.

Not a sure thing?

It's a fifty-fifty kind of situation.

What does that mean, worst case?

Why don't I give you the doctor's number and you can ask him yourself.

Dad, I really really need you to consider moving into a home.

Only home I'll ever have besides this one's a casket underground.

I'm worried about you all alone out there with all that junk around. What happens if you fall? What happens if you need help and can't get to the phone?

Isn't junk if I can fix it.

I took a breath. All right, I said. When do you need me.

Well. As I say, it isn't urgent. Might as well wait till Christmas. Then you only got to make one trip.

I don't mind coming up before then.

But you've got your life down there and no car, and. I don't want you taking too much time off work.

I'm not saving the world. I work in a grocery store.

Maybe by then you'll be doing something you like more.

All right, I said. Christmas.

Okay, he said. There was a pause. So I guess I'll go ahead and schedule the darn thing then.

Listen, why don't you ask Martina if she can start coming in five days?

Oh no. She's got things to do. She's got a kid.

She can bring him. That might be fun for you.

I don't want to put her out.

It's her job, Dad. I'll call her.

No. No.

You'll call her?

He cleared his throat.

You want me to send a little extra to cover it?

I know you're not exactly flush with cash down there.

I can manage.

The social security, you know, it covers things for now, but.

I'll cover it.

I had a habit of twisting and untwisting my index finger in the spiral phone cord. Sometimes it affected the connection.

Hello?

All right then, well, he said.

All right.

Keep fighting the good fight, Lu.

I always do.

All right.

Bye, Dad.

God, I thought. A week with Dad. I'm going to be bored out of my mind.

Then: Don't be a brat, Lu Rile. Do what you have to do. It will be good to spend some extra time with him. And what if it goes wrong? Someday it could be you who needs your kid to come take care of you.

Then: Who am I kidding. Kids? Me? Mama Lu, ha-ha. Not likely.

From upstairs I could hear an argument heat up and come to a boil. The Schubert-Fines were at it again. A door slammed. How they could slam those doors so loud I'd never understand.

It occurred to me: those two would never have a kid to take care of them.

I wandered over to *#400* and looked at it again for the umpteenth time. The boy's face was concealed by his sleeve, his upraised arm. Thank god. If it were visible the photograph would be absolutely ghoulish.

He must have been so frightened in those last moments. They didn't realize until afterward. He fell alone, unseen except by the Rolleiflex.

All right. Okay. I had to tell them. What was in the fridge? Leftover rice in a paper carton, half a container of wonton soup. A rubbery celery stalk, peanut butter, half a dried-up lemon. What was in the freezer? A mostly full bottle of third-rate vodka. I could bring that, I thought. It would be neighborly. It would also betray the fact that I had not bought anything special.

I dragged a step stool to the kitchen and climbed up on the counter to root around in the back of a cabinet. Behind a stack of cans from Summerland—black beans, tuna, artichoke hearts—I found an old bottle of wine. I'd slid it into my bag at a David Salle opening a year or so before, then felt too weird about my own thievery to open it. Now would be a good time. I brushed a film of dust off the glass and climbed back down. I put on my Keds, then changed my mind and put on my black steel-toed boots. Your battle shoes, Dad called them. I was going into battle. The disputed territory: their dead child's image. My diplomatic position: I'd like to use it, please.

I climbed the stairs to the fifth floor and stood at their door, wine bottle in hand. The detritus of their lives had overflowed into the dim hallway. Cardboard tubes and empty paint cans were piled by the door. Some rusted piping half-concealed a hamster cage. Here a blank canvas. Here a pogo stick. There two wooden horses, different breeds: a sawhorse for carpentry and a horse for play, bulbous head stuck on a rod body. Three bicycles hung on hooks from the ceiling: a man's, a woman's, and a child's. I knocked.

As I waited I heard their voices rise in volume. I could so often hear them from my loft downstairs but here beside the door they were clearer, more distinct. The subject of their argument had been forgotten amid a chaos of insults and generalizations.

You always fucking do this.

What do you want from me?

You *always* fucking do this.

I always—? That's a laugh. *You're* the one who—

That high-and-mighty tone, that fucking *poor me* routine—

Oh really. So that's how you're going to play it. Here I am feeling like garbage—

You can't even bring yourself to—

Some rustling, the slamming of a door.

You're acting like a real selfish—

A selfish what?

Don't bait me.

A selfish what?

Go fuck yourself.

Why don't you get the fuck out.

I will!

Leave me alone.

I am!

Then go!

The lock turned in front of me and I stepped back as the door was thrown open. Out came Steve in such a rush he didn't even notice me standing there with my back to the family of bicycles. But Kate did. We locked eyes as he barreled through the hallway and down the stairs, and I stepped forward into the light of their loft.

Her hair was unwashed. She was impossibly thin. In one arm she was holding a one-eyed teddy bear to her breast as if nursing it. The hem of her thin tank top brushed the elastic of a pair of cotton underwear. She stared down at me as if there were no explanation for what I was, or why I could possibly be there. As if I were a Martian. A space alien just dropping by with a decent Beaujolais.

I considered asking whether it was a bad time but that seemed gratuitous or cruel. For a long time every time would be a bad time. But I'd just screwed up my courage. If I left now I was liable never to come back. I held out the wine bottle, an offering. She let her head fall to one side, considering.

Yeah okay, she said at last. I could use a fucking drink.

I stepped inside. Should I take off my pants? I asked.

Again she looked at me as if I had antennae and gills. Then she looked down at herself and laughed suddenly, loudly, barking like a donkey. Her laugh was so startlingly ugly, I laughed too. She took the bottle.

When it was crowded with guests I hadn't really had the opportunity to take in their place. Now that it was empty I could feel how spacious it was. Though it was situated in the same corner of the building as mine, their loft was larger and, being one floor higher up, its view all the more stunning. Their kitchen was not laminate and unfinished pine as mine was, but stainless steel and cherry. Large antique carpets concealed the concrete floors. The walls were filled to capacity with art, mostly Steve's: tens of nudes crowded together, a convention of kinky wandering lines, deviant splotches, garish colors, lascivious protuberances of paint. But the place was a mess. Dirty dishes were piled in and around the sink. Stained glasses and empty bottles cluttered the table and counters and sat in bags near the door. And everywhere, on every surface, there were flowers, the souvenirs of grief. Not just in vases but in buckets, pots, and thermoses, in bowls and mugs and, in one case, a child's sippy cup.

Kate was in the kitchen working on the cork. The teddy bear lay facedown on the counter. I'm sorry you had to see that, she said. Hear that, I mean.

It's fine, I said. You're going through it.

She nodded, easing the cork out of the bottle neck. KCA—that's Max's school—is holding a memorial. Steve doesn't want to go, and I don't want to go without him. Actually, if I'm being frank, I don't want to go at all. Most of Max's friends' families are already out of town for summer vacation but that's almost worse, you know? The fewer people who come, the more I'll have to talk to. Still I feel an obligation and it really pisses me off that he doesn't. I should have expected it. I don't know why I didn't expect it. He doesn't give a fuck about social obligations and never has. Actually that's part of why I love him. But it makes me resent him now.

The bottle uncorked with a resonant pop. I stood just outside the kitchen, stiff and awed. Never could I have talked about myself with such ease, such honesty.

I hate the obligation of it all, she went on. All the *thank you thank you, yes I know, it's very sad*. It's such a tragedy, they say. As if I haven't noticed. I hate not being allowed to be alone.

She rinsed two glasses, used no soap. Problem is I also hate to drink alone. Which is inconvenient because I like to drink. You don't mind hanging out for a while, do you?

I said I'd be glad to. She filled the glasses both with wine. She handed me one, then turned away and set hers down on the counter while she rooted around in the refrigerator—which, I saw, was stuffed.

We've got so much to choose from, she said dryly. Prosciutto and melon? Pigs in blankets? Spanakopita? Cora Pickenpew's famous casserole? Chez Schubert-Fine is open for business.

I'm okay.

Well, I'm not. I'm starving. I keep forgetting to eat. She rinsed a plate and began piling on it a little smorgasbord of unmatched snacks. You work at Summerland, right? she said, her back to me.

Yeah.

Do you get an employee discount?

Of the five-finger variety, mostly.

She gave me a confused look over a Tupperware container of finger sandwiches, then seemed to get it. Oh. Like . . . stealing?

Everyone does it.

I heard the manager there's a real asshole. What's his name . . .

Chad Katz? He's horrible. Where did you hear that?

One of Max's friends has an au pair who dated him briefly. She paused over the sandwiches, just for a moment, then closed the Tupperware and put them back in the fridge.

He makes us do nags and brags, I told her.

Nags and brags? She leaned back against the stove to listen, chewing on a carrot.

At the end of every shift—when all anyone wants is to go home—we get together and stand around and we get one nag, where we can complain about something. Then to balance it out we have to tell everyone something good we've done recently, or that's happened to us.

Oh my god. I would die. What do people say?

She seemed to have stepped back into herself. It had taken a moment, following the argument with Steve, but now she was present, natural. She'd refilled her self with herself.

The thing is, I said, you'd think the nags would be more depressing than the brags, but the brags are really what get me. This is a minimum-wage job. It's not like anyone who works there has money. But people brag about all kinds of weird shit. Just the other day this asshole Sam bragged that he'd just leased a Jeep.

Jeeps *are* depressing. Bad taste bums me out.

It's beyond bad taste. Sam's just as poor as the rest of us. Obviously he's leasing it on credit. He's setting himself back thousands of dollars in debt.

Oh! Kate crinkled up a piece of prosciutto and deposited it in her mouth.

So that's depressing as hell.

What do *you* say?

Me? I don't know. I hate the whole thing so much I'm just a bitch about it.

I would be too.

My brag is always I'm about to go home.

Ha. What's your nag?

That we have to fucking *circulate*.

You have to what?

In the cluttered kitchen while she ate I told her about Chad Katz's bogus ideas about chakras and circulation. I more or less kept my eyes off her underwear. She laughed like a donkey and refilled our glasses. Let's go sit in the living room, she said. I want to smoke.

At the window she lit a cigarette and exhaled with relish. She glanced at me as if trying to decide whether to say something she wanted to say. She took another drag and seemed to decide to go ahead.

The first thing I did after Max. After it all happened. I mean after all the bullshit, after all the horrible shit. Oh my god, it was just last week, wasn't it? Was it two weeks ago?

She seemed to lose herself in memory a moment. She took a sip of wine. I waited.

The first thing I did for *myself* was buy a pack of cigarettes.

How long had you gone without smoking?

Nine years. I quit when I got pregnant.

Outside on the bridge a subway flickered by. Interrupted by its rumble-clatter we went quiet. She offered me the pack. I was not a smoker but I took one. She lit it for me and I inhaled poorly. My eyes watered as I tried not to cough.

I had my first cigarette when I was fourteen, she said when the train had passed. Behind the bleachers with Sally Mostel. In the suburbs of Rhode Island there was nothing to do but drive around and smoke and drink.

You were an athlete I bet.

She nodded. I ran track. I played basketball. Not because I was any good at it. Just because I was tall. Five eleven by the time I was fourteen. That year a modeling agent approached me in the mall, gave me his card. I never called but it put an idea into my head. An idea about New York, a certain kind of glamour.

I had that too, I said. In a different way. But an idea about New York that was there from very young.

You were an artist, though. You probably imagined your work in galleries—no, museums.

Exactly. In the Guggenheim or something. Totally unrealistic.

Not so unrealistic. You're good.

My belly seized up. Had she seen my work?

She didn't seem to notice my reaction. I can tell, she said. You're smart. You've got a mind of your own. You must be good.

Relief. I drank.

How did you and Steve meet? I asked.

God, I met Steve when I was seventeen. Can you believe that? Seventeen.

Where?

We met twice actually. The first time was at a show. A concert. Springsteen. I was there with a girl who was obsessed. Steve was a few rows away from us with another woman. He gave me a look over her shoulder. Really brazen. Really took it all in. I remember thinking, what a sleaze, you know? That's a real sleazy move.

I nodded as if I understood. People didn't do things like that to me.

The second time was a few months later. Immediately I recognized him from the show. I was taking classes at the community college while I finished high school. I just wanted to get the hell out of there as soon as possible. I figured in three years I could get my degree and move to New York. I didn't know what I wanted a degree *in*. I just thought of it as a passport.

Sure.

There was a girl in my art history class I'd become friendly with who told me about this gallery opening, this sexy local painter. She wanted me to go with her so I said sure. We show up and there he is. He didn't remember me at all. Not a flash of recognition. I was seventeen, I was a kid. I said to him, I know you. Thinking I'm so sophisticated, thinking I'm hot shit. He said, Absolutely not, you don't. I'd remember you. He egged me on. He made a bit of a fool out of me—which I loved, of course. Eventually I said to him, Paint me.

Wow.

I know. I'd never say anything so bold today. His work back then was not so different from what he does now. A little cruder, maybe. Thicker brushstrokes. It doesn't matter; they were nudes. I said, Paint me, and he just laughed. He said, I'd never paint you.

Why not?

Kate tilted her head at me. I got the sense she'd told this story a thousand times and no one had ever asked her why Steve had refused to paint her. Maybe other people took for granted the idea that a man might insult a woman to get her into bed.

He said my body was too boring, she replied. Which, I was totally offended—but I totally slept with him. Years later, though, you know, I get it.

I got up and wandered through the loft, looking again at Steve's nudes. The wandering lines, the curves and valleys of the form, the doubled and tripled lines suggesting movement, restlessness. I get it, I said.

Kate got up too and made her way to the fridge to refill

her plate. He likes a little substance to his models, she said. Heavy breasts and bellies, broad thighs.

It's more than that, though, I said. There's a stillness to you, the way you stand and move. He's interested in motion.

Huh, she said into the fridge. That's what he says too.

She retrieved her clashing snacks and brought them with her back to the living area, along with the teddy bear. We sat together on her couch. She threw an afghan over her legs. We talked about art.

What interests you? she said. As an artist. Her frank curiosity was disarming.

I answered slowly. Discipline, I said. The element of chance.

Art as meditation, she said.

Art as discipline, I said.

Very John Cage.

Not *very* John Cage, but sure. I like his ideas about practice. Leaving your work up to the environment.

I saw a show once of his prints, she said. He sort of scattered things on the surface of the paper, or lit fires and put them out by rolling paper through the printing press.

I felt myself fumbling, attempting to access the kind of frankness Kate inspired. I think that actually my feelings about discipline come from insecurity, I said. The knowledge that I'm really not all that good. I can't draw, for instance. I have poor depth perception. In art school I was weak in sculpture and draftsmanship. The kind of innate talent that Steve has? I don't have it. But I have an eye. I have my own mind, as you said. And I have discipline.

You're ambitious.

I took a deep breath. *Now,* I told myself. *Tell her now. There won't be a better opportunity.*

Well, I began.

She lit a cigarette. Holding the teddy bear to her belly she declared: I think discipline is all there is. Seriously. Without discipline raw talent is worthless. When I first met Steve he was almost thirty and he'd never lived anywhere but Providence and Teaneck. He was just fucking around. Drawing, painting, drinking, screwing a new woman every week. He had a little gallery and they were so enamored by him they let him produce when he wanted to produce, give them new work when he felt like giving them new work, and basically that was that. He was so spoiled. And he didn't have a future. He didn't have any future at all until he met me.

You wanted him to move to New York.

That's right, I did. I wanted this.

She looked around the loft and without warning, with a low, loud sort of sound that seemed to come straight from her belly, she began to cry.

I was taken aback. Suddenly hyperaware of my own presence in her space, I stood up. I'm sorry, I said, I'm so sorry. I'll go.

Holding her cigarette away from her body with one hand, her head bent over her chest, she reached her other hand out to me. No, don't go, she managed, feeling for me. *I'm* sorry, she said through her tears. Sometimes—

The moment lasted too long.

Don't be, I said. I sat back down. She found my arm and

clutched it tightly. I waited with her while over the course of a minute or two the sobs slowed, then quieted. The cigarette burned to her fingers, became a cylinder of ash, and fell to the carpet.

She said, There's a white Bordeaux in the fridge.

I went to the kitchen and brought it back to the couch. Through this bottle the tenor of our conversation changed. I admitted I'd never lost anyone close to me—at least not at an age when I could really comprehend it. Trying to explain the experience of her own grief, she seemed to brighten. It was as if, despite the insurmountable difficulty of it all, her curiosity had not been extinguished. She was fascinated by her own incredible pain.

Grief is so weird, it's so fucking weird, she said. Max was a part of me, you know, he was an actual part of me. He was inside of me for nine months before he ever breathed air. And now that he's gone it's like part of me is gone too and I can feel my brain stretching and warping to try to understand it, to compensate. I can feel myself trying to fill in the gap and then resisting filling in the gap because there would be nothing worse than filling in that gap. Nothing worse. Does that make sense? I just cannot understand how he can be gone and I can still be here. I cannot understand it.

Meanwhile all week I've been having these strange, intensely sensory flashes of memory. The day he was born, the feeling of his skin. The smell of blood, the wooziness of the drugs I was on. Steve next to me, breathing. Steve's coffee breath. That's one thing I've remembered. We'd been up for seventeen hours together and now there was this little being, and my body felt emptier than it had ever been, I was physically destroyed, and there was this creature, tiny nose, tiny hands, screaming so quietly, breathing gulps of air, hiccupping. And I kept thinking, this is a hospital, right? Does anyone have any mouthwash for my husband?

Or god, I remembered this this morning. It just occurred to me like—not like a memory but almost like an original idea. But it *is* a memory. I just hadn't thought of it in months, in years. When I first started noticing gray hairs I was pulling them out one by one, obsessively, in front of the mirror every morning. What vanity, right? Max was just four or something and he would sit there on the toilet and watch me. He'd get upset. *Mama, don't do that, don't do that.* I explained to him it didn't hurt, it was to keep Mama young and pretty, some shit like that, I don't know. One morning I woke up to him standing next to the bed yanking my hair, just yanking my hair as hard as he could. I didn't know what was happening, I'd just woken up, was totally disoriented. I yelled at him and he ran away crying. He hid under the couch for over an hour. That's what occurred to me this morning, just occurred to me out of nowhere. The memory of getting down on my hands and knees next to the couch. His back to me. And talking to him while he cried, his face to the wall. Saying, baby, it's okay. I know you were trying to help. I'm sorry. I know you were helping.

Or, Kate said—and she was getting drunk—it's like this. I have always been an emotional person. Steve and I have always had a tumultuous relationship. I mean, we fight like anyone. I get PMS like anyone. I cry. I have a shitty relationship with my mom, I guess. Maybe no more shitty than anyone else. But that's the thing. This whole thing—she gestured at the space around her with the teddy bear—has put everything else in perspective. Even when I've thought I was at my darkest, even when, I don't know, I was a teenager and thought I wanted to die, I had no idea. I had no goddamn idea how awful I could feel. It's like I'd been living in a world where the darkest I could get was a kind of light-to-medium gray. Now I know what black looks like. Real black. Not asphalt black or oil black or ink black or pupil black but true black. Empty-black. Nothing-black.

I'm sorry, I said again.

No no— She wiped her eyes, her nose. I don't want you to be sorry. I really don't want anyone to be sorry. I just want you to *understand*. It gets so bad. So. Fucking. Bad. I just want everyone to know. I want to be . . . I want to be a fucking ambassador for Sadland.

I laughed despite myself. She began to laugh too, through the snot and tears.

I just want everyone to know, she said: You're okay. You're all okay! Everyone is okay. Except for me.

More wine. More cigarettes. I was engrossed. I was committed. By the middle of the second bottle I was unsteady on my feet. I struggled up and announced I had to pee. Kate nodded gravely. On my way to the bathroom I knocked over a paint can of flowers. Water and snapdragons spilled all over the concrete floor.

Leave it, Kate called. I'll clean it up tomorrow.

In the mirror I looked at myself and was aggravated by my

ugliness. You don't belong here, I told myself. Stop drinking. Stop smoking. You don't even smoke! Go home. I washed my hands and splashed water on my face without thinking to take off my glasses. I wiped off the lenses on a beach towel printed with a cartoon Spider-Man. God, I said aloud. How had I thought I could just come up here and tell her about *#400*? Her grief was so much bigger than one meager photograph. That was just art. This was death and life. I felt foolish and thickheaded—and so, so ugly.

When I came back to the living room Kate was lying on her back on the floor, smoking quietly, the ashtray in the recess of her belly.

You know what, though, she said, as if I'd been there chatting with her the whole time. Despite everything. Or . . . among everything. All the other shit. The grief and the horrible pain and all that. And this is going to make me sound like a monster. But there's a small, a very small, a tiny part of me, that is relieved.

I couldn't leave.

I sat back down and poured another splash into my glass. I was afraid of what she might tell me. I was afraid of the darkness she described.

Motherhood is so hard. It is just. So. Hard. And Max was such. He was wonderful. He was so full of joy. He had so much life in him. He was so smart and sweet and curious. He was my best friend. I needed him so badly. It wasn't fair but it was true. He needed me too, of course he did, but I might have needed him even more. He was *such* a pain in the ass, though. He was worse than a pain in the ass. He brought out the worst in me and he knew it. He made me hate myself for how I treated him sometimes. There were times he'd be talking a mile a minute about something or other and bouncing around or running back and forth, god, or whatever he would do. He was always moving. And I'd just shut him down. I didn't want to *hear* it all the time. I didn't want to have to pay *attention,* to always fucking *pay attention.* He gave me no space of my own. No space to—to anything. To eat my own food or go my own places or say my own words or think my own thoughts. For nine years because of him I had no space to breathe.

She closed her eyes.

I'm not saying this is a silver lining. There is no silver lining here. Everything is horrible. But being able to smoke and drink and stay up late. To breathe.

She breathed.

It's a relief.

I stayed with her in the silence that followed her confession. Our glasses were empty. The bottle was empty. Kate seemed emptied too. Eventually I looked down and saw that she was sleeping there on the antique rug. I removed the ashtray from her belly and laid the afghan over her. Quietly, unsteadily, I made my way through her place and back to my own dark loft. It was colder downstairs. I felt shivery and nauseated. I got undressed and lay down on my hard futon. It was past two in the morning but I could not sleep.

I lay there with my eyes open, considering everything. Kate, the photograph, and grief. My dad and his declining sight. After what seemed like hours I must have finally dozed off, because I woke again with a start to an unfamiliar sound. At first I thought there was someone at the door. It sounded like a knocking or a tapping. It was an attempt to get in. I sat up and shook off the fog of sleep. Listening I realized it was not coming from the door at all.

It was coming from the window. But there was nothing there.

||||| |

On a day off from Summerland I left home early for the
Metropolitan Museum of Art. Outside the heat rose
up from the sidewalk and the day stretched out before me
long and promising. I took a hot slow uptown train scrawled
with graffiti to Lexington Avenue, where ladies carried dogs
in handbags instead of walking them. The glorious Met.
Every time I ascend those stairs and step into the grand and
fragrant air-conditioned hall I feel I'm at a peaceful intersec-
tion between worlds and time. Past encounters present, and
all these disparate worlds and subjects greet one another dip-
lomatically. Cruel and orderly ancient Egypt, silly frivolous
baroque France. Grayscale street urchins and sculpted lovers
intertwined. On a weekday there is little sound beyond the
echoed footsteps of a few dedicated visitors. It is as if we want
to emulate the stillness of the art.

A Brueghel happened to be visiting from Belgium: *Landscape with the Fall of Icarus*. I spent half an hour looking into

its painted world. The *with* in the painting's title tells you something about it. It is more landscape than Icarus. His white legs that kick as he drowns in the lower right quadrant of the painting are almost insignificant, and that's the point. In the foreground is a plowman with a horse. Delicate sailboats populate the bay. A fisherman with what looks very much like a cup of coffee throws his line into the water. A flock of sheep turn away from the drowning boy—except for one, which watches passively. A man with a knapsack frowns up at the sky, arms folded. He has noticed some disturbance up above, but the tragedy's behind him.

There are two mysteries in this painting. One has to do with time. Far off beyond the mountains, the sun is setting. Why? In the fable Icarus flies straight up toward the sun. That in the painting the sun's already sinking past the sea, rippling its light over the horizon, means Icarus's fall must have taken hours. I was staring into the painting, contemplating this idea and admiring the way the sun sets the leaves of the trees aglow, when I noticed the other mystery. Deep in a thicket on the left side of the composition, a head lies upright in the shadows. It is so small it is nearly imperceptible. But it is clearly a head. A person is lying in the shade. Who is he? A wanderer asleep. Or Daedalus looking upward through the branches above him, still waiting for his son.

Or maybe he is the artist, who sees what no one else can see.

I had two errands that day: to get a new sheaf of matte photo paper from B&H and to pick up a few negatives I'd dropped off to make slides. Emerging from the cool museum into the humid afternoon was like stepping into a warm puddle. So as not to spend the extra $1.25 on subway fare I walked downtown. The sidewalks glared up, mica sparkling. Square-shouldered businessmen talked loudly on phones the size of shoe boxes. Damp women in hideous power suits pushed past each other at crosswalks. Cyclists careened through traffic and sprayed up the oily water that pooled at the curbs. Taxi drivers shouted in Arabic and Urdu. Buses lumbered up and down the avenues, belching when they stopped. There is a William Carlos Williams poem about the very Brueghel I'd spent time with at the Met. Something about *the whole pageantry of the year* . . . *awake tingling* . . . *concerned with itself* . . . *sweating in the sun* . . . And then, *unsignificantly off the coast* . . . *a splash quite unnoticed.* These strangers knew nothing of Max, my art, or me. Tragedy is insignificant, banal. A falling boy goes largely unnoticed.

The farther south I got the emptier the streets became. Midafternoon on a weekday the photo district was quiet. I passed the Hasidic guy at the door hyperconscious of my summer clothes: Keds, jean shorts, tank top, no bra. I was not inside five minutes before the aggressive air-conditioning hardened my nipples into little rocks that pushed against the cotton of my tank top. Still I took twenty dreamy minutes to browse the Leicas and Canons, though I was down to my last two hundred dollars, though I had to keep my arms crossed over my chest, thumbs hooked in the straps of my backpack. At the checkout a grave and efficient seventeen-year-old— acne, *peyes*, yarmulke—did not look up from his register, did not even make eye contact as he bagged the matte paper along with two precious rolls of Ektachrome and took a non-negligible percentage of all the money I had.

To be interested in the work of my contemporaries was a luxury that like all luxuries I could not afford. Still it was imperative to keep pace with art-world trends. Though my feet were aching and I'd sweated through my shirt I wandered south toward SoHo and the galleries. The recession had softened the rental market and made it possible for a bunch of new spaces to open. At Spring Street I hooked a right and went into one I hadn't seen before. Its rough cement floors and patched walls gave it the feeling of a building in transition, but the air-conditioning made my skin prickle. On one wall hung a cluster of bronze and pewter heads, casts of baby faces, some of them a little warped—a cheek melting toward the floor, a forehead frowning, squished—their mouths open as if crying. Beside them hung a long mirror with an ornate plaster frame that on closer inspection was made up of a multiplicity of pornographic detail: vaginas flowering among conch shells, butts and breasts blooming between ivy vines.

I stepped back out onto the hot street and into another new gallery a few doors down. This one was dedicated to a solo show of large-scale oil paintings. The paint had been left thick on the canvases, pressed, molded, and shoved straight from the tube by what felt like a restless angry hand. They struck me first and foremost as expensive. A tube of paint is a costly thing. In the mounds and valleys of one canvas I found, like a gem set into the surface, an actual paint tube, wrapper and all, the lifeblood squeezed out of it. Red, of course. I went back out into the heat.

In those days Cherrystone Clay was on the corner of Grand and Greene. I'd wandered in a year or two before, when I was so broke that I was always hungry, to steal some cubes of cheese and a plastic cup of wine from the table by the window during a gallery talk. Cool-looking, moneyed downtown types stood beside middle-aged couples in raw silk and linen. A thin woman with a blunt black bob was interviewing a stocky, wild-looking man with a wide lewd mouth and long blond hair and paint on his black jeans. He was gesticulating lazily, as if doing the audience a favor, and talking about his work with disaffected eloquence. That was the first time I saw his paintings—nudes, of course: rounded, buxom, flat and square, all female, in vivid colors with wandering, tangled lines on raw unstretched canvas. Some sat with their legs open; some lay half hanging off invisible surfaces. All their limbs and faces had been painted and repainted a number of times in different positions. The effect was of motion, as if the artist had caught them in the middle of getting up, of walking away, and of collapsing, and had recorded every connected moment of the gesture. The lines that limned them were drawn, in a way, against the form, as if resisting depth, resisting reality.

Clearly he was an excellent draftsman. His painted bodies conveyed weight and depth convincingly with line. I stood at the table piling cubes of cheese into a napkin in my palm and listened. It's about movement, he was saying. There was a kind of drawl in his voice. I could not place his accent. A body is only a body as long as it is in motion, he said. When a body stops moving it becomes a corpse. And where is the human in the corpse? Not there. When we say *my body* we do not mean *me*. When a person dies, though they remain right there, we say *they're in a better place.* The body ceases to be the person herself when it ceases to move. That's why I have no patience for static portraits. They are not paintings of people. They are paintings of corpses. He raised a hand to show his audience what he meant on one canvas, an example. Women are alive, he said, women move. Women turn. I'm not interested in committing homicide by portrait.

It wasn't an accent at all, I realized after a while, but an affect. The stylized way of a man who wasn't particularly interested in consonants. With one ear on his monologue I wandered toward the front desk attempting an affect of my own: young downtown collector, just passing through. Not broke, not twenty-five, not eager. I picked up the printed list of work and checked the artist's name: Steve Schubert, of course. It seemed familiar, but I ate four cubes of white cheddar before it dawned on me why: it was scrawled in childish handwriting on one of the mailboxes in my own front hall at 222 River Street. I looked again at the prices of his canvases. They were as shameless as his disquisition. Why would an artist whose work sold for that much be living in Brooklyn? Either his work wasn't selling, I decided, or he was terrible with money.

It was not until a year or so later, at a party at Bob Maynard's, that I found myself actually speaking to Steve for the first time. It was an accident. We'd been talking in a group with Tammy Day and Philip Philips but Tammy and Phil had left to freshen their drinks. Steve did not try to hide the way he kept looking over my shoulder. I captured his attention though when I admitted to having spied on him at Cherrystone Clay. Flattered, he looked me in the eye.

You saw that, did you? One of my more bullshit performances.

Decent of you to admit it, I said. He gave me a cold look and I tried to smile. The moment was saved by Kate, who came up and weaved her thin arm through his. She was taller than he and looked down on us both with the benevolent resignation of the very beautiful. Cherrystone Clay? she asked.

Lu heard my gallery talk, said Steve.

Ah.

Chuck Cherrystone's great, he said to me. He's saved my life so many times. And Fiona's a smart cookie. If it were up to her they probably wouldn't have taken me on.

She took a risk and she's still paying for it, said Kate, and added: But you could say that about anyone who knows you.

Steve laughed without smiling. I was surprised at Kate's blasé cruelty. She turned to me. You're a—let me guess. Performance artist?

Photographer, I said, a little offended.

I love photography. Who do you show with?

I made a face that said, *You kidding?*

Well, you're young, said Kate breezily. You've got time. Hey, you should bring your portfolio over to Cherrystone Clay. Steve, shouldn't she bring her work to Chuck and Fiona? We can recommend you.

Steve made an inscrutable face.

What? Fiona said they were looking for photography.

Katie, that's not what she said. Or if she did she was being stupid. Chuck would definitely disagree.

Everyone's looking for photography these days. You say so yourself.

No. What I say is, you can't *sell* photography.

Then why would everybody be looking for it?

That's not what I *say*. What I say is, photography's *cheap*. It's a way to reach a wider audience.

I wandered away, leaving my neighbors to bicker behind me. But as I entered Cherrystone Clay now, the exchange rang in my mind.

I pushed open the door and stepped into the cool quiet space. Another group show. On the walls were paintings and drawings and prints and photographs arranged in clusters and vertical rows in the style of a traditional Paris salon. Sculptures made from metal and clay and poured plastic and glass populated the floor like guests at a poorly attended party. I took an information sheet from the front desk, where a girl with silver-blond hair and a black velvet choker eyed me skeptically. The list of artists was long and I browsed it for names I knew, but besides a few heavy hitters—including Manny Cortazar—Steve Schubert was the only familiar one. One of his nudes had been hung cleverly between a photograph of a nude and a wall sculpture made of knots and tangles of colored string, as if the Schubert between them were somehow a product of those two ideas—which, in a way, it was. As I looked at the painting, trying to decide whether or not I liked it, whether it had any real meaning beyond what was on the canvas, whether it was vaguely or overtly misogynist, I heard a soft but commanding voice behind me: Have the new frames been delivered yet?

Another voice replied in apathetic monotone. Not yet.

A clipped sigh. Can you call them? This is getting ridiculous.

The other: Sure.

I turned. The monotone belonged to the blonde at the front desk. She was maybe twenty-two, white and blank as an unpainted canvas. The other was the same thin woman with the blunt black bob who'd interviewed Steve at his gallery talk.

Kate's offhand encouragement: *We can recommend you.* It didn't matter that she had never seen my work or that I'd been only a sort of prop in their argument. I drew strength from it. You must be Fiona, I said, and walking toward her I smelled a whiff of perfume: amber, pepper, orange blossom.

There was a hint of impatience in her cordial smile. Can I help you?

Lu Rile, I said. I'm a friend of Kate and Steve's.

Kate and Steve, she repeated.

Kate Fine? Steve Schubert?

Oh, of course! Compassion made its way into her narrow features as she shook my hand. A vertical wrinkle appeared between her black eyebrows. Her painted lips pressed together. I noticed a dusting of delicate freckles that stretched from temple to temple over her cheeks and nose. What a horrible thing, she said, my god.

I know.

How are they holding up?

I shook my head. You know.

A silence fell between us. She seemed not to want to extract herself from the conversation, but also she seemed not really to want to talk to me.

I just wish there were something we could do, don't you? she said at last. It's just horrible knowing there isn't anything, *anything* you can do.

They're sort of inundated by visitors right now, I said. I think they're a little overwhelmed.

I can imagine. We sent flowers of course, but. Fiona rolled her eyes. That was Chuck's idea. When my mother died the *last* thing I wanted was flowers. You know what I wanted? Food. *Bad* food. Cookies and chocolates and cake and things. Things I would never normally eat. All the flowers I threw straight in the trash.

Her neck and wrists were delicate as a doll's. She shook her head and let her gaze drift toward Steve's painting.

Following that gaze, I remarked: I imagine this will affect his style.

Fiona frowned at me and we stepped together closer to the painting. How do you mean? she said.

I said: I just can't imagine him continuing to do this sort of work after something like this.

She nodded slowly, listening.

The bravado. The performance. Tragedy would change that, I think.

You're an artist too, she observed.

Yes.

A photographer.

I must have looked surprised; she nodded at my B&H bag.

Well, what do you think, then? she asked. How would you predict, if you could, the way Steve Schubert's work will change?

I looked at the painting and tried to put myself inside it. The way it had been made. All its arrogance and lust. I thought of Kate, her sudden sobbing on the couch, the quick window I'd been given into the depth of her pain. I think it will get quieter, I said. I think he'll become more interested in depth than in line.

She regarded me thoughtfully. Emboldened, I went on: The best art makes visual a metaphor we live by, right? One idea at work here is the urge or craving to fill a woman in. The idea that a woman is like an unfinished page in a coloring book: wandering lines and empty spaces. There is depth to the way she is perceived but it can never be resolved because she is always in motion. The lines never close the shapes they suggest. All the empty spaces are left open.

At the front desk a phone rang. Cherrystone Clay, said the blonde. Fiona glanced at her.

Who's this? I said, pointing to another work at random. I was trying to keep her attention but I immediately regretted changing the subject. Clearly she was less interested in the piece I was pointing to now than she was in Steve's.

Oh, that's Mel Vogel. One of Chuck's old white men. She lowered her voice to a wry murmur: Mel's been doing the same shtick since 1963.

I was glad for her conspiratorial tone. If it ain't broke, I quipped.

Too true.

Fiona? the blonde called. Wayne Salt is on the line?

Without turning from me she held up a finger at the girl, signing *one minute.* I've got to take this, she said.

Wait, I thought, *don't go.* Aloud, a little desperate, I managed: Nice meeting you—

It came out as a question.

Her thin freckled skin crinkled at the corners of her intelligent eyes. Pleasure's all mine, she said. You've given me some food for thought. She turned to go. I'll take it in my office, she told the blonde.

I blurted: I'd love to show you my work sometime—

Come find me at our fall show, she sang over her shoulder. Jessie will give you my card.

Her heels clacked on the gallery floor as she walked away into her office, closing the door behind her. Through the glass I watched her thin silhouette pick up the phone, lean over her desk, and write something down. Dutifully the girl held out to me a simple white business card.

Back outside I held my Pentax at chest height to take that day's self-portrait: my reflection in the gallery window. Plastic bag hanging from one hand, thick glasses, sweat-damp mop of hair. I looked childish, absurd, deeply uncool. I did not look like an artist anyone would want to represent—least of all chic, breezy Fiona Clay.

All through my ride home on the deserted rocking subway I ran my fingers over the thick edges of the card, obsessing. Over my stupid outfit. Over Fiona Clay. Her chumminess and her disinterest. Whether I'd said the wrong thing. Probably nothing would come of it. Probably Fiona would forget all about me. At High Street I got off the train and climbed the dirty stairs to the street. The homeless man who'd made a nest for himself in the entryway to our station was sitting there with his face to the sun. Hallelujah, he was called. His beard was woven with elastic and multicolored string.

Have a blessed day, he said to me.

Likewise, I said.

Hallelujah, said he.

I walked downhill to River and turned up the empty cobblestone street.

There was a small group gathered around our makeshift plywood stoop, beside the tangled network of doorbells that had been rigged up one by one over the years as new tenants moved in. Nancy Meister with her frizz of graying hair was leaning against the brick and her wire-haired gray dog was lying panting on the hot sidewalk. Tammy Day was sitting on the plywood steps and our landlord, Gary Wrench, seemed just to have wandered up. He was standing in the middle of the sidewalk, slack face drawn into a long frown, scratching his neck. They all watched me approach silently, bleakly. Rainbows shimmered in the oil at the curb.

Hi, I said.

They said nothing. They were still mourning.

I pushed my glasses up my nose and transferred my B&H bag to my other hand, standing awkwardly on the uneven walk, waiting. Then Nancy Meister moved closer to the brick to let me pass, and I went up the plywood stairs and pushed open the front door. Our lock was broken again.

Up the three flights of dirty stairs without touching the splintery wooden banister. Through the gaping passageway, past the moldering cardboard and other debris. Up the last flight on the other side with the old pipe banister and the lead paint cracking on the brick. Something wasn't sitting right with me about my neighbors' mourning, when the grief was so clearly Kate's and Steve's. Kate was in enough pain as it was. Hers was a depth of pain I could not understand, could only witness. It seemed presumptuous for them to mourn. Rude, even. Kate Fine, ambassador for Sadland, would have a message for them: *You're all okay. Everyone's okay except for me.* I fit the key into the heavy fourth-floor fire door, twisted the deadbolt, and rolled it open on its track. Max Schubert-Fine was no one's business but Kate and Steve's.

I slid the next key into the lock in my plywood door and pushed it open into my loft. There was some quiet indistinguishable talking coming from upstairs, but no sobbing, no yelling. I laid the B&H bag on the kitchen counter and stuck Fiona's business card with a magnet to the freezer door. There it would stay, I told myself, to remind me every day of the work I had to do.

||||| ||

I was at home halfheartedly eating a bowl of cardboard Healthy-Os and going through the mail when there was a knock at my door.

Instinctively I looked at the window.

It was definitely coming from the front door.

Kate was waiting in the hall outside. T-shirt and jeans, lipstick and bare eyes, clean hair pulled back.

You look great, I said.

I showered, she said. I put on pants.

What's up? You want to come in?

As soon as I'd spoken I remembered *#400* pinned to the wall by the dining table and regretted it.

Maybe. She shifted her weight. Are you going to the loft board meeting?

The what?

The loft board meeting. I've never seen you there but I thought that wouldn't necessarily mean you never went. I don't make it to every one myself. But today I don't know. I thought it would be good to have something to do. I was just hoping. Not that I need an escort. But I felt it might be easier to go with a friend.

Friend. I tried not to show that the word moved me. I—sure. I—when?

Twenty minutes.

I looked back inside, hoping it would seem as if I were checking the time, though my only clock was the AM/FM clock radio by the side of my bed.

Just give me a second, I said. I left the door half-open and ran back to the wall where *#400,* as if cooperating, had popped one of its pushpins onto the floor and was hanging diagonally, flapping. I pulled out the other pin and laid the photo facedown on the table with the mail I'd been going through. A catalog from B&H, a water bill, a reminder from my optometrist's office that it was time to get my eyes checked.

When I turned around I saw she'd already wandered in and was browsing the art books lined up on the raw two-by-four shelves I'd bolted into the walls, noting the pot in the sink that was encrusted with burned rice and full of cold soapy water. Your place is so bare, she said. Do you ever think about hanging anything on the wall?

I don't know. Maybe. I like a bare wall. The clarity of mind. I paused awkwardly before remembering to ask: Drink?

What do you have?

Vodka.

That's it?

I could make coffee. Wait, no. I'm out of beans. Water then. Water or vodka. I might have some tea.

She laughed her warm ugly laugh. I'll have a shot, what the hell.

I retrieved the bottle from the freezer and two short jars from the cabinet. So what is this loft—what did you call it? What's this meeting?

Essentially it's a bunch of neighbors sitting around arguing. Usually there's food. I'm surprised they haven't tried to recruit you. The day after Steve and I moved in Cora Pickenpew strong-armed us into joining. It's like a building association. Just a group of people trying to have a say in what goes on around here. You know, since it's not technically a legal living space, we're in a pretty vulnerable position.

It isn't legal? I watched Kate wander around, trailing her fingers over the dining table, picking up the loupe and peering down at the light box where a few negatives and slides were lined up in rows. Was *Self-Portrait #400* among them?

You didn't know that? We're all squatting. Technically.

What? Really?

She turned and raised her eyebrows at me. You didn't think it was odd that Gary didn't give you a lease?

I was just relieved I wouldn't have to give him first, last, and security.

Well, everyone does it. We've got friends in SoHo who've been squatting for decades. But their landlords are basically behaving themselves. Since the Loft Law passed in '82 the board has been trying to convince Gary to do some renovations around here. Just basic stuff: upgrading the sprinkler system, replacing rust-eaten fire escapes, installing working heat, et cetera.

The Loft Law?

Lu, shame on you! You're behind on your civics. Basically the Loft Law says that any artist who's been squatting for ten years or more has a right to live where he's been living, long as the landlord ensures that the space meets certain qualifications. Cora and Bob have been here since '78, which makes this building eligible for legal status. It's been nearly a decade since the law passed, though, and nothing's changed. I think Gary thinks if he holds out long enough he can just sell the building without having to invest in upgrades.

He thinks he can sell this dump? I laughed.

People are starting to notice DUMBO. Developers I mean.

It's such a shithole.

A shithole with a great view.

I poured our vodkas and handed one to her. I can't get a read on Cora Pickenpew, I said.

Cora's a piece of work, said Kate. She paints these total knockoff Rothkos? But funny story: Cora actually knew Rothko personally. She was thirty years younger than him but she knew him. She's a runaway. Her dad's the Milk King of the Northeast. Are you familiar with Pickenpew Dairies?

We sell their milk at Summerland. Hormone-free, pasture-raised, blah-blah.

They must have edged into the organic market. That's her family. Kirk Pickenpew: Milk King of the Northeast. I used to hear his radio ads all the time growing up. *I'm Kirk Pickenpew and these are my happy cows.*

So corny.

According to Cora she hated the milk business—

Who wouldn't?

—and had always loved art. As a teenager she'd take the train down to the city and go to the Met. She'd sit and stare for hours at the stained glass in the medieval chapel. One day who happens to come and sit down beside her but Mark Rothko himself. They get to talking—I guess she was a striking girl— and he invites her back to his studio on Sixty-Ninth Street. Shows her all the cables and pulleys and things that he uses to manipulate those enormous canvases under the skylight. Tells her about the chapel he's building in Texas. Cora stays all afternoon and then for dinner and then overnight, sleeping under a sheet on his couch, shivering and wide awake with excitement. One day becomes two, two becomes four. She never goes home. She falls in love with an assistant of his and moves in with the guy. Learns to smoke, hangs around the Village, starts painting. That assistant happens to be the unfortunate guy who found Rothko dead in front of his kitchen sink.

No kidding, I said.

That's the story. Kate raised her jar and I raised mine. We took our shots. She coughed. Fine vintage of rubbing alcohol you've got here.

We left the jars in the sink beside the pot full of burned rice and soap, and went upstairs together.

Cora's loft sat on the roof of 222 River Street like a little cottage dropped by a cyclone, skylit and wood-paneled and totally incongruous with the tar-topped skyscape of broken windows and water towers that surrounded it. There were windows on all four sides. A chandelier made out of a birdcage hung over a long heavy oak table where Cora set out cheese, crackers, and slices of pear. On the walls were her enormous color-block paintings, which made my vision vibrate. In the corner by the door to the bathroom there was what looked like an elaborate shrine, with tens of candles in puddles of wax, photographs, sheets of paper scribbled with writing, and other relics I couldn't identify. The proximity of the paper to the candles was vaguely alarming.

Philip Philips came up to greet Kate, his thin cheeks folded back in a wide smile. He was as tall as she was. While he held her in a long hug I waited awkwardly at their elbows. When they extracted themselves they were still holding hands. Philip, Lu; Lu, Philip, said Kate.

Though we'd spoken plenty of times Philip said, Nice to meet you.

Cora came over to greet us in bare feet and Eileen Fisher linens. She held herself like royalty. Hi, honey, she said to Kate, and took both Kate's hands. Her smile became a concerned frown. How are you holding up? Philip said you didn't want any company these days but I've been thinking of you every minute.

Kate seemed to have lost her voice. She just nodded. Philip squeezed her shoulder. Cora turned to me.

Hi, Lu, welcome. Is this your first loft board meeting? Her vowels were slow, her consonants deliberate, her smile fixed as stone under her bobbing black-and-white hair, held up in a bouffant by a wide silver clip at the back of her head. Can I get you two anything? A beer? Soda water?

Maybe a beer, said Kate.

Of course, honey. Cora floated away toward the kitchen area, where more old black birdcages hung like empty threats. Erika Kau, the Irish-Hawaiian sculptor who lived next door to Bob Maynard in the third-floor passageway, was sawing through a loaf of dark bread at the kitchen island.

Philip said: So, Lu, what brings you to our monthly loft board meeting? He spoke ironically, as if making a joke, though I couldn't tell what the joke was.

Kate brought me, I said.

I needed backup, said Kate.

What do you think of Cora's digs?

What I don't get, I said in a low voice, is why we've got a Milk Princess living right here in DUMBO? You'd think she'd be able to afford a place in the city.

Philip's laugh was high-pitched and melodic. This place is two hundred dollars a *month*, he said. She's saved so much on rent she bought a villa in Tuscany.

Really, said Kate.

Philip nodded. Tammy told me Cora invited a mutual friend of theirs last summer, who said it was literally a castle.

I couldn't tell what impression the three of us were giving off, standing together and whispering at the door. I could feel the rest of the neighbors stealing glances.

Cora came back with two beers, one for me and one for Kate. She was about to start speaking with us again when Tammy Day appeared behind her. Tammy's long brown hair was parted in the middle and her eyes were bright and wide behind a pair of overlarge glasses. Cora, she said—and proceeded to syphon Cora's attention.

Tell me about everyone, I said to Kate and Philip.

Well, Philip began, with guarded relish. That's Tammy Day.

We don't dislike her, said Kate.

Philip laughed.

How long have you lived here, Lu? Kate said.

Just over two years.

That long? said Philip. How have you gotten away with not meeting everyone?

I've met them, I said.

She keeps to herself, said Kate.

I decided they were not making fun of me.

How long have you been here? I asked.

Twelve years, said Philip. Kate said, Ten.

In the corner by the windows were Uri and Etta Rainer. They were standing over a skinny baby with a mess of plumy hair, who was banging a tin sieve on the floor. Uri was stubbled and gaunt. His mother was a seamstress, Philip told me, his father a subway conductor. He went out at night wandering, taking photos around the city that he called his clues. *Broken Sandal, Port Authority, 9:34 p.m., October 12. Red-Faced Man Slumped Against Wall, Surrounded by Cops, Port Authority, 9:41 p.m., October 12.* He'd pin these unrelated fragments up on a wall, plus a photocopied paragraph of an article in the *Enquirer,* let's say, and then connect them all with red yarn and pushpins as if he were a detective uncovering the details of a case, building a store of evidence of what or against whom it would never be clear.

The cases he comes up with seem so true, said Philip, I've caught myself gossiping about them at parties.

What about Etta? I asked. Uri's wife was dough-faced and guarded, with black watchful eyes.

She's a projectionist at Anthology Film Archives. An artist too, I think.

I've never seen her work, said Kate.

You've seen Erika Kau's, though, right? Philip's eyes moved over the room. Erika was tough as nails and built like a brick house. She was standing by the bread she had just sliced, arms folded, scowling. Her sculptures are amazing, he said.

Very vaginal, said Kate.

Huh, said Philip. Never occurred to me.

It wouldn't!

They're just bowls, said Philip, rolling his eyes.

Big fleshy oblong bowls with deep crevices, Kate teased.

They laughed and glanced at me. I blushed and drank my beer. Back at the kitchen island Nancy Meister had come up to chat with Erika. With her long neck and sharp nose Nancy looked a little like a bird of prey, but the effect was tempered by her soft gray frizzy hair.

Nancy's been here almost since the beginning, said Philip. She's a playwright. Comes from a long line of Bolsheviks and Marxists. She has an FBI file.

Kate said, Also she matches her dog.

I've noticed that, I said.

You'd never know it, Philip added, but she's a Christian. She converted.

She's pen pals with prisoners, said Kate.

Speaking of religion, said Philip, turning to Kate. Did you know Tammy used to be a Mormon?

No way.

She mentioned it to me the other day. She grew up in Salt Lake City. She married a pharmacist at the age of nineteen.

No no, said Kate. Her ex-husband worked in pharmaceuticals.

Philip said, I'm pretty sure he was a pharmacist.

Pharmaceuticals for sure.

All right then, pharmaceuticals. Anyway she got married, lost her virginity, and six months later left the church.

Tammy in her big silly glasses was still talking to Cora Pickenpew. She felt us watching her and turned to nod in our direction. She looked about fifteen years old. Philip waved back.

Why don't you like her? I asked quietly.

We don't *dislike* her, Kate said.

Philip said, She's a pain in the neck. She moved here like two years ago, same as you, but she thinks she gets it.

What's her work like?

Philip waved his hand and rolled his eyes. She makes these little paper cutouts: animals and dancers. I don't even know. Actually I guess they're kind of interesting. I just can't get past her personality. They're fine.

Max calls them paper dolls, said Kate. She gets all bent out of shape.

We drank from our beers and stood quietly together. Light fell in through the wide windows, making our beer bottles glow, transmuting the baby's hair into a halo. Cora extracted herself from her conversation with Tammy and stepped into the middle of the room. In her throaty melodious voice she said loudly: Should we get started?

As if on cue the door opened and Bob Maynard edged in. His shirt was stained, his hair unwashed. Sorry I'm late, he muttered.

Cora took it in stride. Should we get started? she repeated. Now that all the old farts are here? Bob rolled his eyes and Cora clapped her hands. All right! Tammy, what's on the agenda?

Tammy looked down at a lined notebook. Recycling, she said; replacing the boiler; and obviously renovations.

I don't know why I even bother coming to these things, growled Bob Maynard beside us. Nothing ever gets done.

Free beer? offered Philip, raising his bottle.

That's it, said Bob, and crossed the room to the kitchen, where he availed himself of the fridge.

Okay: recycling, said Cora. It has become clear to us, to some of us, that some people in the building have not been recycling. I just want to reiterate, as I did last month, that recycling goes out on the curb no earlier than Wednesday, six p.m., no later than Thursdays at eight in the morning. If you put out your recycling *before* Wednesdays at six it can result in a fine. Obviously we are trying to avoid getting fined. Since it isn't clear whose recycling is whose, it would be the whole loft board that would absorb that fine. In other words all of us would be paying for one. So let's avoid that.

And just to be clear, added Tammy Day, you do have to separate glass, metal, and paper. So paper goes in one bag, glass in another, metal in another.

Cora nodded and retrieved a pencil from the great accumulation of hair at the back of her head to check off the item on the notebook. It was unclear to me whether she was annoyed by Tammy or appreciated her.

Philip was squeezing Kate's hand. A tiny smile was creeping into the corner of Kate's mouth. Almost inaudibly Philip whispered: What else do you think Cora has hidden in her hair?

Kate snorted.

If recycling continues to be put out on the wrong days, Cora continued, I'd like to suggest we initiate a labeling system so that everyone is clear on whose recycling is being put out when, and so the loft board does not have to be responsible for absorbing this cost.

Jesus Christ, said Bob Maynard.

Cora's smile was fixed. Bob, would you like to weigh in on that?

No, said Bob, clearing his throat. No, I would not like to talk about it at all. I am here for one reason: to talk about the boiler. Scratch that—for two reasons: to talk about the boiler and to drink your beer, you petty tyrant. *Viva la revolución!* He raised his bottle and mugged at the room at large.

Great, said Cora. Moving on. Renovations! We are still waiting on—she looked at her notebook—sprinklers in Tammy's loft . . . for the third-floor passageway to be cleared of debris . . . replacements of all rusted-through sections of the fire escapes . . . a few other items. Funny, I feel like I've been saying the same thing every month for years!

No one laughed.

But it seems that we are making some progress on the

sprinklers. Gary told me he has made a call to the city and is in touch with a plumber, so we should see sprinklers installed by September or October.

That's terrific, said Nancy Meister.

I'll believe it when I see it, growled Erika Kau.

As for the other items, said Cora, I have been in touch with that lawyer friend of mine I mentioned last time. As we discussed, we will be meeting with the lawyer and with Gary Wrench in August. Anyone who'd like to attend that meeting please feel free. I'll post something about it downstairs by the mailboxes.

Just to be clear, said Uri Rainer rather timidly, the cost of the lawyer will be split among all of us?

For now he's doing this pro bono, Cora said. We'll see how things develop down the line.

I don't like this, said Bob Maynard. I don't like this at all.

Bob, said Cora: You wanted to talk about the boiler.

Bob stepped forward and went on at length about the state of the current boiler and the need for a new one, including the costs and relative functionalities of various models. Little whirlpools of side conversations stirred up around the room as he went on. Kate seemed to notice the tight grip with which I was holding my beer. She leaned over and whispered: This happens every month. The conversation falls apart and nothing gets accomplished.

Why do you come? I asked.

She shrugged. It's like going to the theater.

All right, Cora sang: Do we have consensus on the boiler issue?

No one replied.

Do we feel comfortable with Bob making the decision about the boiler himself?

There was general nodding.

All right. Then let's! move! on! to the next order of business. We also wanted to discuss the issue of the roof.

Beside me I felt Kate's body tense up.

In light of . . .

Cora paused, choosing her words.

. . . of recent events. Gary has let me know that he's going to be changing the lock on the door to the roof. The roof is going to be closed to all tenants.

A disconsolate murmur eddied around the room. Gary fucking Wrench, somebody said.

That's some paternalistic bullshit, said Erika Kau.

Bob Maynard said: It's not even July and my loft is already hot as fucking Hades. We've been going out onto the roof for years. We need to be able to get out of the heat.

It's just until he can get a railing or a fence put up, said Tammy.

Oh yeah, said Erika. Like that will ever happen.

People will still go up there, said Nancy Meister. They'll just break the lock.

I'll break it myself, Maynard rejoined.

I could feel Kate tensing up beside me. On the other side of her Philip called out: Can we table this discussion?

A fence would completely ruin the view, Nancy was saying.

What's the likelihood of it ever even getting installed? Etta Rainer asked.

I'd say the likelihood is zero, said Erika Kau. I've had a leak in my bathroom Wrench hasn't addressed for two god-damn years. The ceiling's caving in.

We've never discussed the black mold problem, said Nancy.

Every time the freight elevator goes up or down, more lead paint flakes off my wall, Tammy added.

Uri and Etta's baby began to cry. Etta picked her up. Arm's length from her father she hit Uri in the eye with the tin sieve. He dropped his wineglass. It did not break but red wine ran through the riverbeds of the old floorboards. Cora grabbed some paper towels and made for the spill. Philip went over to help her. Uri knelt too, apologizing. Cora waved him off. I glanced over at Kate and saw her eyes were squeezed shut.

About the fence, Nancy began again.

Enough about the fucking fence, snapped Maynard.

Nothing is getting accomplished here, said Erika Kau.

Excuse me, Bob, said Cora, rising.

We need to table this discussion, Philip said loudly from the spill on the floor.

It's not like it's going to happen *again*, said Tammy.

The room went silent.

Kate quietly handed her beer to me, turned, and left.

Bob Maynard put his beer bottle on the kitchen counter. Are we done here?

No, Bob, said Cora. No, we are not done here.

I put down the two bottles, Kate's and mine, and followed her.

The voices in Cora's loft faded behind me as the door closed. The stairwell was dark and cool. On the fifth floor the fire door had been left open an inch or two. I tugged it open and knocked on Kate's door.

The paint cans and forsaken hamster cage. The family of bicycles.

No one answered. I tried the handle. It was unlocked.

Kate was standing by the kitchen counter, pressing the palms of her hands against her eyes. She did not move when I stepped in.

There was no sound but her unsteady breathing. Tentatively I approached her.

When she spoke her voice was slow and trembling. They're talking about installing a railing *now*.

I nodded, though her eyes were concealed by both her hands and she could not see me. It's farcical, I said.

She took a shaky breath and let her hands drop. I don't think I'll ever be okay again, she said. Not ever.

I could not think of any way or reason to disagree.

She lowered herself clumsily to the floor and sat with her knees pulled up to her chest, her back against a kitchen cabinet. I sat down beside her. The rubber floor covering was shaped like honeycomb and though the rest of the kitchen was Ajax clean, in all its hexagonal reticula there were accumulations of dust and hair and crumbs and onionskins. Pressing her palms to her eyes again, Kate began to shake. When she spoke her words were warped by sobs. I want to die, she said. I want to die.

I felt almost physically ill. I felt unprepared and wrong for the occasion. I was a bicycle helmet at a football game. A book of knock-knock jokes shelved among Greek tragedies. Hesitantly I said: You need someone to take care of you.

Her body was shuddering. The sound she was making was as if her warm ugly laugh had been caught and warped in a fun-house mirror.

Where's Steve? I ventured.

Gone, she managed. At his parents' in Teaneck.

I put my arms around Kate's thin crumpled body. I rubbed her back.

I had not been this close to another human being for months—no, years. No, months. I had not been this close to another human being in I didn't know, don't know, how long. There had been a romance in my second year of art school with a dour scrawny philosopher whose ideas were like candy but whose body stirred nothing in me. Later, after I moved to New York, I had let unfold an angry sadomasochistic fling with a married art critic. Were there other lapses in what was essentially my celibacy? I'm sure there were but I'm also sure that they weren't much. In other words I don't remember how long it had been. I only know that being close to Kate in that moment in the kitchen seemed to open a window in me. I felt the wind flood in. I felt the drafts and canyons in her voice, experienced whole seasons in the chemical sweetness of her shampoo.

I felt that window open and through its opening I felt a threat.

For a long time I sat with her, scrunched and crying in the kitchen. For a long time I held her.

Then, almost silently, Kate's front door was pushed open again. Kate didn't seem to hear it. I looked up to see Philip's concerned face peering in, taking in the scene. I looked at him. He looked at me. Quietly he withdrew, pulling the door closed.

I pressed my cheek against her hair. I stayed past dark.

||||| |||

I came home that night wrung dry. How had I become this woman's friend? I leaned back against my closed door and all my breath seemed to escape me. There was a clenching in my chest. I almost wanted to cry too, but I didn't.

I flicked on the kitchen light and opened the refrigerator.

Nothing. Half a jar of peaches and a yellow rind of cheese. I closed it.

On the cluttered table in the dark, facedown, lay *Self-Portrait #400*.

Stuck with a magnet to the freezer door was Fiona's business card.

The magnet was a flat flexible thing I'd somehow ended up with from Trudy's Auto in Truro, Mass. It was a juxtaposition, a little on the nose: my past holding up my future, and all that. Trudy's Auto Truro; Cherrystone Clay.

I looked at that odd little assemblage a long time. The phone number on the magnet from Trudy's Auto Truro didn't even have an area code. At the top was a list of services—brake systems, cooling systems, engine repair, electrical, suspension—and between that list and the number and address at the bottom was a line drawing of a Cadillac. I remembered going to Trudy's with my dad when I was a kid. He preferred her place to the auto shop in Hyannis despite the fact that Hyannis was closer to where we were in Osterville. Hyannis would charge you an arm and a leg for an oil change, he said. Plus he liked Trudy, a broad middle-aged woman with greasy hands and a dirty mouth. When we went to see her in Dad's old beat-up truck she'd laugh at him for driving such a clunker—*clunkah*—and give me a lime lollipop.

I don't know whether I have imagined this or if it's true but looking back I thought I could remember a certain sadness between Trudy and my dad, some adult understanding. Either I knew or I imagined or I'd re-created it. We never talked about it, but something in me suspected that Trudy knew my mother.

Dad called me pal or kiddo. He called me good company. We'd always lived together, just the two of us in the house on stilts in the marsh where the salt flew in on the wet wind and bleached the wood and got encrusted on all the window frames. My mother had gone when I was so young that all I took of her into adulthood were a vague sense-memory—a shadow at the doorway, a shoulder half-concealed by hair—and my habit of standing at the window for hours and watching the road. Cars were infrequent but once in a while if headlights appeared in the dark on the other side of the marsh where the road split out of the woods I'd feel a thrill in the hollow of my belly, and hold my breath as the car drove slowly over the short wooden bridge and approached, and approached, and passed.

All this was contained in that one flimsy magnet. Memories of a lonely childhood. The longing of a young kid for a mother she could only imagine.

And behind it Fiona's business card, which didn't even state her title. Just a simple white three and a half by two with four pieces of information: Fiona Clay, CHERRYSTONE CLAY, the address, and the gallery phone number, area code 212. Blank and featureless as the future before me.

How could I be so many different people? I lay on the cool concrete and pinched myself: the skin of my belly, my arms and legs and small hard breasts. I took off my glasses. I closed my eyes. You are all one person, I told myself, but I wasn't convinced. I opened my eyes. I am all one person, I tried again aloud. I listened to my own voice echo in the room but still I did not believe it. I could not integrate that kid standing waiting at the window with the woman I was now, or the woman I might become. I could not even reconcile the woman I was now, lying on the cold concrete floor in a room alone, with the woman I'd been a moment ago upstairs, holding crying Kate. Certainly I could not square that kind woman upstairs with the one who'd taken *Self-Portrait #400,* and stuck that fucking business card to her freezer door as a challenge.

Sneaky Lu and loyal Lu, grown Lu and Lu the child. Had I always been so many Lus, or had I started as just one person and somehow proliferated over time? Ruthless Lu and awkward Lu and focused Lu and troubled Lu. Lying there and wondering, through the wondering I became aware that my train of thought had become a sort of rhythmic song. What was the metronome to which it played? What was that tapping on the window?

Whatever it was, it was getting louder. Less a tap now than a sort of slap.

And then there was a sound so loud that I actually startled. I put my glasses on and hurriedly got to my feet, my heart beating hard. Quickly I went to the window.

There was nothing and no one there. I stood at the glass and waited, trying not to breathe too loudly. Remembering something my dad had told me once when I was plagued by a nightmare, I began to count backward aloud from a thousand. Nine hundred ninety-nine, I said. Nine hundred ninety-eight. Nine hundred ninety-seven. Nine hundred ninety-six. Nine hundred ninety-five.

And then the slap was right in front of my head, so hard it visibly jolted the window in its casing. I jumped back with an inadvertent Fuck! I forced myself to breathe. I grasped the handle at the bottom of the frame and cranked the window open slowly. The rubber that I'd glued to its edges for winter insulation unsucked itself like an opening mouth, and the summer wind rushed in. I waited by the window, feeling that wind.

Maybe a wire had come loose, I thought, from the top of the building somewhere and was swinging in the breeze, slapping against the pane. Maybe someone upstairs was throwing things.

It was so unlikely but the wind was soothing, the wind was real. I looked across the river at the city, its glitter and its provocation. I listened to its sounds: the faraway traffic on the FDR Drive, the tiny *thub-thub-thub* of a helicopter circling the bridge. Beyond all that the low groan of a foghorn. What time was it? I wondered. It felt late but maybe I was just exhausted. I opened my mouth, feeling my ears open up, closing my eyes, but was interrupted midyawn by another slap against the glass, and this time it was accompanied by another muffled sound—like a sigh or a cry, like a child shouting into a pile of pillows—and when I opened my eyes I saw—unmistakably—a small, reaching hand.

It was more like an afterimage than an image. More like a handprint than a hand. Like the impression on the insides of your eyelids after you've looked at a bright thing. It wasn't moving. Wasn't falling or flying. Was simply there, static and lifeless but reaching, all of its curvature quite clear. Pale bluish wrist exposed, five fingers bright as some holographic snapshot, reaching—

Toward the sky?

Toward my window. Toward me.

I pushed up my glasses and leaned in to take a closer look and in an instant the hand snapped into motion. It all happened so quickly that I didn't know until it had vanished how the hand had flicked forward against the glass, a violent slap. Instantly my heart was loud and erratic in my ears and I felt a rush like vertigo, like the nauseating belly-up when an elevator descends too suddenly. My whole body went cold, my bare skin prickled damply as if with flu, and there was the sensation quick and weird of something passing through me—

I cannot explain it any differently. I've tried.

—and the little hand was gone.

Outside the city was alive and indifferent, restless and peaceful as it had always been. But peering through the open window, looking down and up as far as I could with that limited peripheral, I was a sweating shaking mess.

For all the different people that I've been, I've never been the sort who believed in angels, fairies, phantoms. I was not the kind of kid who got spooked by ghost stories. My nightmares always fade with daylight. I am reasonable. I am a realist. I have always been this way. But that night I was more than shaken: I was shaking. I was beside myself with fear. I tried to tell myself that it was nothing. But it wasn't nothing. It wasn't nothing, at all.

I closed the window and glanced behind me at the empty room. I paced. I sat down on the floor. I stood. I sat in a chair. I stood.

I poured myself a vodka.

I paced.

I stood.

At the cluttered dining table I looked down at *#400*. I'd left it facedown, I was sure, by a pile of mail near the corner.

But there it was lying in the middle of the table, faceup.

fall

ⅢⅢ ⅢⅢ

With Steve staying at his parents' in New Jersey the neighbors rallied around Kate. Her startling horsey laugh, her generosity, her beauty, and that we knew she was suffering—it all drew us to her like moths to a flame. The weather was getting cooler and it was getting darker earlier and we spent many nights together upstairs eating, drinking, talking. Kate brought out everyone's best. Because she was so shaky we showed up solid, determined to be good to her and to one another.

Those were great nights. Philip was in bartending school that fall and from his own loft on the second floor he'd bring up fixings for cocktails plus his faux rose-gold cocktail shaker and we'd have whatever he was learning to make that week. The so-called school was a scam but we were its happy beneficiaries: me and Kate and often Tammy Day, who was growing on us, but who couldn't have more than half an old-fashioned before her face turned pink, and sometimes Erika Kau, who'd have three or four, get raucous, and deliver scathing tirades to which we'd clap and yell: Hear! Hear!

I'd never had anything like a community before. Now because of my friendship with Kate I was no longer the weird little photographer downstairs. I was a part of things. I knew—everyone knew—that any night we could knock on Kate's door and be welcome. Once in a while we'd be joined by Uri and Etta and we'd pass around the baby and Uri would tell us in his quiet rapid way about his most recent fictional investigation. Sometimes Nancy Meister would make an appearance with her wiry dog and conversation would lean political, and while she talked about the prison industrial system and institutional racism and the dog snored heavily at her feet Kate would lean back, listening, patient, and Tammy would lean in, listening, flushed, and Philip would narrow his eyes before yawning performatively, standing, stretching, and leaving without a word.

Then sometimes Bob Maynard would stop by with a magnum of red blend and wax elegiac about the good old days when he used to hobnob with Judd, Serra, Smithson, and all the other greats at Max's Kansas City. The Manimalists, Philip called them. If Cora Pickenpew happened to be around too we knew we were in for a treat. She'd hung around with that crowd too but she remembered everything differently.

God, Bob, she'd snort, holding her wineglass with her wrist thrown back. Leo *never* said that. That was Penny.

Penny who?

Ar*cade!* See, girls? *This* is how women get erased from history.

Penny's doing fine, Maynard would mutter.

The only people who tell the goddamn stories are men who drink too much.

Don't kid yourself, Maynard shot back. History is written by the winners and the only winner in this game's the market. That may not be you, but honey, it sure ain't me.

The hours would pass so warmly at Kate's with her rugs and her candles and her endless wine. No one ever wanted to leave. Around two or three when my eyes began to cross with exhaustion I'd say my good-byes and heave open the fifth-floor fire door and stumble back downstairs in the dark, tipsily gripping the filthy handrail. After a night at Kate's my own place always seemed so dark and cold. I'd lie awake listening to the radiators clanging with futility and to the laughter upstairs, which always seemed to outlast me.

But sometimes I would be joined by a different kind of company.

I could hear it from the futon where I slept.

I didn't have a bedroom, just a shoji screen I'd found on a curb in the Village one night and brought home with me on the subway. It was ripped in one corner but I'd taped a sheet of tracing paper into that panel and most of the time it did the trick, separating where I slept from where I worked at least psychologically. What it didn't do was buffer any noise.

This may sound as if I'm trying to avoid responsibility. But if you've ever been deprived of sleep for an extended period of time I trust you'll know what I mean when I say I blame a lot of what ended up happening on that goddamn tap-tapping.

‖‖‖ ‖‖‖

I remember exactly what I wore to the opening of the fall show at Cherrystone Clay. As usual my steel-toed boots. As always my thick-framed black glasses. And a black raw silk Helmut Lang sheath I found at a Lower East Side consignment shop. I remember I debated whether or not to shave my legs. In the end I decided I would feel too exposed and didn't. At the last minute though I pulled on some opaque black stockings. I wore no jewelry. I mussed and crumpled my hair.

I asked Kate if she wanted to join me. She'd been saying she wanted to get out of the house. With Steve still in Teaneck she was lonely, always lonely. But in the end she said she was too raw to meet new people. Since she wasn't ready, I went alone.

It was a humid fall night and the space was crowded. The show was called *Love Letters to a Battlefield*. Enormous six-by-six-foot canvases painted in blood reds and sand and peach and shadow, they looked like bird's-eye views of ravaged desert landscapes but were in fact near-photographic studies of Kaposi's sarcoma, that cancerous augury of HIV.

I heard a woman in a cloche say: It's enough to make you lose your lunch.

Cherrystone Clay has gotten so *safe*, her companion said. I'm so tired of these compromises. Political art that looks like abstraction by an outsider who isn't outside.

But he's gay, though? the cloche objected.

He's gay. But he's a gay white man from the Upper East Side. He went to Yale.

She waved a hand dismissively. Everybody went to Yale.

I wandered from painting to painting and took them in, keeping my eye on Fiona Clay, who was circulating expertly.

Are they from photographs or from life? I heard a young woman ask tentatively.

Oh, from life, replied a woman in a blue scarf, casually. His boyfriend is dying.

No no, objected a third girl: I heard that wasn't true. I heard his boyfriend is completely healthy.

What's worse? the blue scarf mused. Being an opportunist about AIDS or being an opportunist about neo-Expressionism?

The largest painting in the show was a complex mess of brushstrokes: skin and pockmarks, lesions, blood. I stood by it awhile, letting the death of it sink in.

I heard a familiar voice and turned to see Philip Philips beside me in lipstick and rouge and a beautiful ragged pink dress. He was on the arm of an older, shorter, whiter man, dressed in a silk suit.

Philip! I said.

Lotte, he corrected me.

Lotte. You look wonderful, I said.

Thank you, he said with a little sashay. What brings you out tonight? Do you know Ken?

He was referring to the artist. No, I admitted. I'm just trying to make the rounds.

Smart, he said, and winked and turned to his friend and introduced us. His friend shook my hand, looking over my shoulder distractedly.

I smiled at Philip/Lotte. I didn't know, I said.

Oh, everyone's in drag here, he said breezily. Even you!

Self-consciously I looked down at my own dress.

Lu the lady, he teased. Lady Lu.

Philip's friend saw someone he knew and they moved away from me.

As he walked away I heard another man murmur, Gorgeous.

Making my way around the perimeter of the room I looked again for Fiona but she had been obscured by a group of people laughing.

I heard an older man say: Echoes of Lucio Fontana.

The woman he was with: Oh, but Fontana was so much more elegant.

I moved closer to the wine table to complete my circle around the room, fill a plastic cup, and see if I could find Fiona. Too late did I discover that Philip was not the only person I happened to know there. As I considered red or white I heard a familiar voice quite close to me. Steve Schubert was standing on the other side of the table, talking to another man.

They were the same height and build and would have been a comical pair, both short and thick, except that Steve's expression was desperately tragic. His chin was rough with stubble and he had dark soft circles under his eyes. I'd never seen him look so old.

Heartbroken, Steve was saying to his friend. He tugged at his snarled ponytail. It's a cheesy word, right? I thought so too. I didn't understand it's not a metaphor. Heartbreak is physical. It fucking hurts. I feel like my chest is caving in most days. I feel like I can't breathe. I feel like I'm going fucking crazy, to be honest with you. It's hard to explain. I've been sleeping in my childhood bedroom, right, living with my parents in the burbs? It's freaky out there, man. Age is shifty. Time's unstable. Their house is dark, curtains always drawn, I never know what time of day it is. My dad's like this sad old guy from Jersey, worked his whole life, retired now, watches golf all day. I look at him and I'm like, Who are *you*? Meanwhile, I keep looking around for Max, like, *Dad?* I want him back. You know? Of course I want him back. I'd kill myself tomorrow if it meant I could spend ten minutes with him today. I want him back but I want him grown. I want to be *his* child. I want him to take care of me.

Psychedelic, said the friend, shaking his head.

Steve noticed me listening and raised his eyebrows at me confrontationally. I nodded quickly and walked away. I didn't hear what he said as I made my way into the crowd.

Fiona was engaged in conversation with three people who all looked like money. I veered into another small group, which opened to make space for me, and listened for a minute as they discussed other openings they'd been to recently. I sipped my wine and tried not to look uncomfortable in my black dress. Philip's words—*Even you!*—were still ringing in my mind.

I was relieved when Fiona joined the same small group I had. She said hello to everyone and asked if we all knew one another; when we didn't she made the introductions. Lu, right? she said when she came to me.

I nodded, gratified. Lu Rile.

Right! Photographer. Lu lives downstairs from Steve Schubert, Fiona told the group.

They nodded. Everyone said how sad it was about the little boy. Everyone seemed to know. Eventually the rest of the group fractured off and left the two of us to talk. Do you know Ken? she asked.

Not personally, I said.

Oh, you should meet him. He's lovely. I'm so glad we were able to take him on.

We had been talking maybe a minute when Steve shoved through the crowd to join us. So you're the new best friend, he said to me. His voice was thick with wine.

Hi, Steve. Fiona squeezed his arm.

Hi, Fi, I see you've met my neighbor. His eyes were wild and his mouth was wet.

How are you holding up, sweetie? she replied.

Her question seemed to distract him from me. He turned to her heavily. Fuck, I don't know, he said. It's weird. It's so weird. I'm on another planet. I'm in another world.

I'm going to come visit this week, okay?

Steve shook his head.

No I am, said Fiona.

Let me know when you're coming, said Steve. I haven't been spending a lot of time at home. He wiped his mouth and looked at me. He seemed to waver on his feet. I had the distinct feeling he wanted to punch me.

You want Jessie to call you a cab? said Fiona.

Around us the crowd surged and ebbed, an uneasy sea.

No no. Steve downed the last of his wine. I'll catch the train, he said. He was still looking at me, pressing his lips together. Wobbling, he raised a finger and pointed at me. Out of the corner of his eye he seemed to notice Fiona again. He lowered his finger and said to me: Well, how is she?

What could I say? I fumbled: She's—sad—

There was a ragged edge to his laugh. What do you know? he said. Fuck, he said. Well, word to the wise, he said, leaning in, locking eyes with me: Don't be fooled. She puts on a good act. Affectionate. Hospitable. Guess what. She doesn't love you. She doesn't even like you.

I could not speak. I could not look away from him. Beside me I could feel Fiona grasping for something to say.

Steve dropped his empty cup on the ground and turned and pushed his way through the crowd.

The vertical wrinkle appeared again between Fiona's perfect brows as she exhaled. God, she said. There's nothing sadder.

I nodded. We stood together braced against the tide.

Finally she managed a polite smile. Excuse me, she said, I ought to—

Wait, I said, before she could turn away: While you're visiting Steve why don't you stop in at my place? I'd love to show you my work.

Her face lost its animation. Fuck, I thought. I scrambled for something else to say. At last I added: I would be so grateful for your feedback.

Oh, she said, I don't know if—

My heart was pounding. Five minutes, I insisted, smiling wildly. That's all I ask. I'm literally right downstairs.

Of course, she said at last, and smiled back. I'd love to.

Beckoned into another conversation Fiona turned away from me. I finished my wine and pushed my way to the door.

I did it, my heartbeat seemed to pound. Did it. Did it. Did it.

I didn't know whether Fiona Clay would follow through but in the event of a visit I had to be sure the place was spotless and professional. I set to work after my shift at Summerland the following day. Blasted Sonic Youth and scoured the oven and the stove. Disposed of the crowded roach motel under the sink and set out fresh poison. Washed the scuff marks off the walls by the door where I kicked off my shoes. Ajaxed the tub and sink and Cloroxed the toilet. Swept all my two thousand square feet. Wiped the windows, standing on a ladder to get the uppermost panes. Got down on my knees and cleaned deep in the dirty cracks in the poured concrete floor, scrubbing with soapy water, wiping the mud away, scrubbing harder.

Tap-tap-tap.

Turned up the music. Went through the clutter on the dining table, sorting mail—throwing out the old and the irrelevant, filing the unpaid bills—separating mediocre test prints from the few that really worked, among them *#400*. I stood and looked at it for the thousandth time. Falling child, rising woman. God, it was good.

I allowed myself to consider the inconceivable. I could show it to Fiona. Ask for her feedback. Act like I wasn't sure how good it was. Just ask her what she thought.

I played it out in my mind. She would say, I imagined—so politely—*Is it staged?*

Yes, I would say. I could just say it was staged!

But what if she asked, *How did you do it?* Or what if it came out later—surely it would—that I'd stretched the truth?

Okay. Okay. *It was pure chance.*

She'd know it was Max. Immediately she'd know.

But what if she couldn't see how good it was? What if she didn't understand?

I went into the studio and retrieved my ancient thousand-ton projector. I set it up on a tall stool by the dining table and plugged it in. It whirred to life and a faint white square appeared on the wall. I flicked off the lights. I slipped in the color slide of *#400*.

It was out of focus, a blurry rectangle of blue, black, and white, blotches of beige and red. I brought it into focus until the crisp edges of the window frame resolved around the vivid blue sky. There was the red sneaker, a streak beyond the windowpane. There was my rising form on the right, his falling form on the left. *Fuck* was it good. Anyone would be able to see how good it was. There was no chance Fiona Clay, of all people, wouldn't.

It's an incredible photograph, she said in my mind. And then: *Have you told them?*

I felt queasy. My own guile appalled me. But not showing *#400* was not an option. And when I thought of the way Steve had spoken to me at the opening, the nerve of him, how he'd made me feel at once naked and defensive, insecure and furious. With fresh viciousness I felt that he deserved not to be told. If he were told, he'd stand in the way of everything I'd worked for, everything I wanted, out of spite.

Clearly, though, if I didn't want to tell Steve, I couldn't tell Fiona.

I would keep *#400* quiet a little longer.

I set it on the table and pinned up a few other prints that were not brilliant, but were good enough.

I'd tell Kate, I thought. I would tell Kate first and get her blessing. Kate would understand. Kate was a friend. She knew how much I needed this. She knew how hard I worked. She'd as much as said so. *You're good. I can tell. You're smart. You've got a mind of your own.*

But then. Perhaps that was just her way. What if Steve was telling the truth? *She doesn't love you. She doesn't even like you.*

As if lifted by a sudden wind *#400* slipped off the surface of the table and landed faceup on the floor.

I jumped back from it as if from a live snake, yelling aloud: What the fuck? My voice mingled with the music raging from my old boom box and I felt dizzy, suddenly overwhelmed by doubt and need and noise. Stop it, I yelled. Stop! Leave me alone! And then on top of the music and my own yelling there was a third noise, the noise of knocking, heavy knocking. Leave me alone! I yelled again.

The knocking stopped and under the music I heard a little voice.

I could not understand it but it bound my guts in knots. I went to the boom box and stopped the tape and listened, nauseated. It came again:

Lu?

What? I yelled.

Hello, Lu? Is this a bad time?

I felt a relief so palpable it was like having the wind knocked out of me. I half collapsed, laughing at my own mistake. Be right there, I called. I pulled myself upright, readjusted my glasses, wiped the smile off my face.

I opened the door to Tammy Day, eyes wide behind her outsized glasses. Is everything okay?

Oh yeah, I said. Yeah. I was just. Working.

She nodded sympathetically. Sometimes you really have to wrestle with the work.

That's the truth, I said.

She said, Just yesterday I got myself so worked up about a grant application I threw a mug at the wall.

I waited for her to tell me why she was there. She was holding a clipboard. Clipboards have always made me uneasy.

After a moment she seemed to realize I wasn't going to invite her in. Okay, she said. Well, so I'm just going around and letting everybody know what they owe for legal fees. For you—she looked down at the spreadsheet that was clipped to the board—it's going to be three hundred nineteen dollars.

What?

Unless, she said, you don't want to be included in the suit. Which would be fine but I do have to say that if you are *not* included in the suit you really won't have any legal protection.

What? I repeated.

She blinked at me. Do you not know about the suit?

Suit?

I—oh! I'm sorry. She laughed. I can see how it would be weird for me to just knock on your door and ask for three hundred dollars if you didn't know. Well, okay. So I guess you haven't been to a loft board meeting in a while. Right. Well, I'm sorry, we should have asked you earlier. We just assumed that you were on board. But if you're not that's fine, I'll just have to do some recalculations.

Who's *we*?

Me and Cora and Erika Kau and Nancy Meister. And Philip and Bob Maynard. Oh, and Uri and Etta. And Kate and Steve. Is that nine? I think that's nine. Uri and Etta count as one since they share a space, as do Kate and Steve obviously.

Tammy, back up. What's this about?

Do you mind if I come in? she said.

With *#400* flying around like a thing possessed? Not likely! I'm sort of busy, I said.

Well, okay, she said, and pushed her glasses up her nose and took a breath. Gary Wrench has disappeared.

Disappeared?

He left a forwarding address in South Carolina but the mail keeps coming back. We all voted. I guess you weren't there that day. We're filing a formal suit. Apparently that's the best way to get these things done. Cora says there's a whole mess of buildings in New York doing the same thing, so eventually we will join forces and boom! Legal residency. Anyway Glenn Delaney has spent five hundred hours on us so far, which is way past his limit for pro bono stuff.

Glenn Delaney?

Cora's lawyer friend. He says this sort of work is pretty Sisyphean.

Sissy-puss, I thought reflexively.

He says he won't waste his time without payment. So we're all getting together and chipping in to keep this thing going. And from you we need—she checked the spreadsheet again— three hundred nineteen dollars. Not so bad.

I laughed. I said, I don't have three hundred nineteen dollars.

We're all strapped for cash—

You don't understand. I don't have three hundred dollars. I don't have nineteen dollars. I don't have nineteen cents. I'm not a Cora Pickenpew or a Bob Maynard. I'm not even a Kate. I don't get help from some kindhearted family offstage or from a spouse who's more successful. I'm not slumming here.

We all love the building—

I don't live here because I like it! I snapped. I work in a goddamn grocery store.

Health food store, she said, as if to make me feel better.

Tammy, I make minimum wage. I have no savings. I have no health insurance. My rent is two hundred twenty-five dollars a month—and that's supposed to be some kind of deal! But the only way I can afford to live here is I steal food from Summerland.

You pay two-twenty-five for this place?

I nodded.

She said, I pay five hundred.

What? I laughed. Do you get like heat and hot water that the rest of us don't have?

She raised her eyebrows.

My smile faded. That son of a bitch, I said.

Anyway, she said, sorry to bother you. She stepped backward into the hall. She pushed her glasses up again and took another look at her spreadsheet. I can recalculate, she murmured.

I took pity on the poor woman. Cora had forced her to do this, I imagined, to go around to everyone's apartment and ask for money. They were like the good cop and unwilling bad cop of the loft board. Meanwhile she was paying double to live downstairs from me in a loft that faced the street, where garbage trucks rattling over the cobblestones woke her every morning before daylight. No matter how I felt about her, that wasn't right. Gary Wrench was a scumbag and deserved to be sued for all he was worth.

I said, How likely is it do you think that the building will be sold?

She looked up at me. One hundred percent.

And what happens then? I asked.

She shook her head. We have no legal rights. Glenn says they can kick us out overnight.

I looked at her standing there so small in the dark hallway. Okay, I said. I'll come up with the money.

Her face brightened.

It might not be this month though.

The longer you wait, the more it will be, she warned. Glenn's working day and night on us.

He better be, I said.

All right, she said. Thanks, Lu. Thank you.

Don't sweat it, I said.

She's psycho but the author (book?) doesn't want her to be - she can't be so emotionally callous while also be

‖‖ ‖‖ |

That week at Summerland I asked Chad for a raise. I said I'd been there two years and it was time I at least got assistant manager. I pointed out there were people I'd started with who already had keys to the front door and loading dock. I worked hard and I showed up on time. What else could he want?

He told me my work ethic was admirable but my approach just wasn't there yet. I said, What does that mean *isn't there yet*? He suggested I cultivate an *attitude of gratitude*. He told me I should work on my smile. I suggested he grow the fuck up. I told him I wasn't getting paid minimum wage to act like a fucking beauty queen. He said: See? Like that. Like right there. You see what you did? I was trying to help you and you turned it around on me. You turned it right around. It almost feels to me, Lu, as if you don't *want* to be helped.

Go back to Berkeley, Chad, I said. This is a job, not a self-help seminar.

He said: I strive to cultivate an environment—a web, let's say—of interconnectedness and support. And it seems to me, Lu, that you're the weak link.

I told him he was mixing his metaphors. He told me I was lucky I still had a job.

That shut me up.

I came home from Summerland scowling. It was only six but the sun was already setting. It was going to be a long winter. I had to find another job.

Also: Fuck Chad. My attitude was perfectly appropriate. If he'd wanted someone who would smile on cue he shouldn't have hired me in the first place.

My meditations were interrupted by the sounds of women's voices above me. One was Kate's but the other I was not sure of.

I took my key in hand and went upstairs. The fifth-floor fire door was open. Quietly I went to Kate's door and put an ear to it.

I'm sorry you missed him, Kate was saying.

Glad I got to see you though, said the other voice.

Soft, firm, polite. Fiona Clay.

I stepped away from the door and ran back downstairs. In the bathroom I retrieved my mop and brought it out to the hallway. I heaved the fire door back open and propped it that way with the mop handle. Then I went back into my loft, leaving the front door open, and washed my face, brushed my teeth, and splashed some water in my hair. My plan was this:

when I heard her open and shut the door I would grab my jacket as if I were going out and accidentally bump into her in the stairwell.

I went to the dining table, where several prints were laid out, and turned *#400* right side up, then upside down. Which was best? I could not decide. I was distracted by the voices upstairs.

As it happened my plan did not work out. I heard the door open and close. Hurriedly I turned *#400* right side up again, then upside down. I threw on my jacket and went out into the hallway, then ran back in and turned *#400* right side up again. I rushed back out and stood in the doorway. Kate and Fiona must have been lingering with their good-byes. At last I heard footsteps descending. I retreated quickly so as to come back out just as Fiona was passing. But upon stepping back into the hallway I realized the door was still propped open. I hurried to remove the incriminating mop, but when Fiona turned toward me in the stairs I froze in the doorway.

Hi, I said quickly.

It was obvious I was up to something.

Hi, said Fiona. She looked at me oddly. She looked at her watch. She was wearing a white jacket and black leather pants. She looked terrific—and terrifically out of place in the dirty stairwell.

Five minutes, I said. Seriously.

You're persistent, she said, smiling stiffly. I'll give you that.

The fire door upstairs rolled open and I heard more rapid footsteps behind her and Kate's voice: Fiona, I'm glad I caught you! You forgot your—

And Kate appeared behind her, holding a hat. Oh hi, Lu.

Hi, I said again.

Coming out to mop the stairs?

I laughed uneasily.

I told Lu that I would take a look at her work while I was here, Fiona said, taking the hat.

Lovely! said Kate—and then she added: Lu, my god, I can't believe that in all the time we've known each other I've never seen your work. What a terrible friend I've been.

I fumbled: Of course you haven't. I've never, uh.

Can I join you?

Please do! said Fiona.

This was an unforeseen snafu.

I led Fiona and Kate into my loft still holding the mop, feeling a bit like the grand marshal of some sorry little parade. Just a minute, I told them, and ran over to the dining table. I propped the mop against the wall and flipped *#400* over so that it was facedown again. My thoughts were racing. So this was how it was fated to happen, I thought, then chided myself. Fate indeed. It was just an introductory studio visit. Probably nothing would come of it.

Unless she saw *#400*. Compared to *#400* the rest of my work was so inferior. It wasn't a question. *#400* was genius. In comparison nearly all my other photographs were practically amateur.

Relax, I told myself. Just do what you can.

Your place is so *clean,* marveled Kate from the kitchen.

Great view, said Fiona. She stood at the window, looking out at the river and Manhattan glittering on the other side.

She was faking it, I knew she was. She'd just seen the same view, but better, from Kate's.

Can I get either of you anything to drink? I said.

Kate came and stood with us.

Oh no, said Fiona, I can't stay. I have to be at a dinner uptown.

I showed them into the studio, where my darkroom setup piqued Fiona's interest. I showed them a few prints I had been working on, pinned to the fiberboard wall. *Self-Portrait #161,* which I'd been struggling with for what seemed like forever, cropping and recropping it, turning it upside down, sideways. *Self-Portrait #322.*

I watched as Fiona and Kate bent toward the wall to look at my images more closely. I had never had anyone in my studio before. I wasn't sure whether or not to speak. As I weighed my next words, as I worried in their silence, a whispered shrillness seemed to rise up among us. Neither Kate nor Fiona seemed to notice it. Slowly it became a fraction of a decibel louder. I froze, listening for the tap-tap-tap-tap that had been plaguing me. But this sound was coming from upstairs. I might have thought it was in my imagination or worse if Kate hadn't said suddenly: Oh! I put water on for tea! I'm sorry, I completely forgot. Lu, thank you for letting me crash the party. These are wonderful. I'd love to see more.

She gave Fiona a kiss on the cheek and Fiona grabbed her arm and gave her a meaningful look. Tears filled Kate's eyes; she extracted herself from Fiona's grasp and ran out, closing the door behind her. In a few moments the teapot shriek ceased and my studio was quiet again.

The emptiness that Kate left behind was an enormous relief.

I have more prints by the table, I said, and showed Fiona back into the living space.

Color prints, she said. You do these at home?

Yes, I said.

What do you use, Ektachrome?

That's right.

And what about for a larger print? Where do you go?

Duggal.

She shook her head. They're expensive.

They are. There are a few that I really want to get printed large, really large, in full color. But that's two weeks' pay. More, maybe.

You teach? she assumed.

No, I said, and I felt my face get hot. I . . . do this and that. Odd jobs.

Summerland was an odd job, to be fair.

One of my artists is a part-time customer service rep, a waiter, a dog walker, and I don't know what else.

I loved the way she said *my artists,* the way they seemed to belong to her. I ached to belong to her. You do what you can, I said.

She nodded, browsing the work I'd pinned to the wall. You do what you have to, she agreed.

While she was standing with her back to me I turned over the test print of *Self-Portrait #400* so that it was lying faceup.

She came to it slowly. She looked at all the others first. My hands were shaking. Of *#388* she said: I like the contrast here.

Your black is true black. And that gesture—the way the model is pinching her own skin—the skin, its folds and its creases—it becomes so sculptural. Is it you?

They're all self-portraits.

That's right, that's right. So you use a timer.

I use a timer, I said. I rig up the camera in all kinds of ways. For this one—I picked up *#292* to show her—I tied it up with rope and strung the rope around a pipe in the ceiling.

Aren't you afraid of damaging it?

I am very careful, I said.

She nodded. Her eyes grazed over the table. At last they settled on *#400*. She picked it up.

That's one of the ones I want to print large and in color, I said. I gripped the edge of the table to conceal the shaking of my hands.

She looked at it a long time. I watched her putting it together. She did not ask whether it was staged. She did not ask me about it at all.

The sun had set. I flicked off the overhead light and turned on the projector. Its little fan got to whirring, slowly, loudly. On the wall on the other side of the table *Self-Portrait #400* appeared in all its vivid color, crisp and perfect. Fiona stepped back and put her hand over her mouth.

We stood together staring at *#400* a long time. In my memory hours passed—are still passing. We are still standing like that together, looking. I am breathless. I am shaking. I cannot read her reaction at all. The image is magnificent. She steps forward into the projection and the colored light becomes a mantle around her. Over her white jacket my blurry body ripples, caught in flight. Over her silky hair Max Schubert-Fine's body falls: a blur of blue and red, a shock of hair, a hand. She turns to look at me, shielding her eyes from the bright bulb. Her thin hand casts a black shadow over the contours of her face.

If I were you, she says slowly, I would have this printed large. Yes. This is an image that must be large. As large as it can be.

The biggest color print that Duggal could do in those days was 72 by 120 inches. The reason for this had to do with the dimensions of the room where they kept their mural enlarger, a machine as big as a cannon. Traditionally an enlarger hangs from the ceiling and light shines down from above it through the slide or negative to expose the paper below. Duggal's mural enlarger was set on a track, and light projected through it horizontally.

A large color print at the time was one hundred fifty dollars.

Meanwhile since Tammy's visit days before, the amount I was expected to pay the lawyer Glenn Delaney had gone up. Already I had to steal all my food. Already I barely had $1.25 for the subway.

Because I was about to be tied up financially in the whole lawsuit thing I started going to loft board meetings again. It was October and the light in the Penthouse was golden and sweet. Kate wasn't at that month's meeting. It was Cora Pickenpew, Tammy Day, Erika Kau, Nancy Meister, and me. We sat around Cora's heavy oak table and drank hot cider and ate sharp cheese and discussed what was going on with the sale of the building, which at that point was still hearsay. I suggested that if it was just hearsay we give Glenn Delaney a break. I said the expenses were a drain on my finances. I must have looked desperate because Tammy Day put a sympathetic hand on my arm.

We really appreciate you joining the fight, she said.

Did I have a choice? I said.

She retracted her hand.

Where is Glenn anyway? said Erika. I thought he was going to be here today.

Last-minute thing, said Cora. He had to appear in court.

Around the table were a couple of exasperated sighs.

Folks, Cora said, I know it's a drag. But at this point it is critical that we stay in the game. There are cases like this all over the city right now, buildings full of artists fighting for their rights. If we back out now we lose the opportunity to become part of something much larger, something really big. We're looking at potentially a class-action suit against the city. We're looking at making this city a place where artists can live cost-effectively without threat.

Wouldn't that be something, murmured Nancy.

First we're suing Gary Wrench, said Erika loudly, then we're suing the city. I recognize that sometimes this is what it takes but this is not what I signed up for.

Has anyone heard from Gary? asked Tammy.

You're friendly with Gary, aren't you, Cora? Erika said. Have you talked to him?

Not that friendly, Cora said.

Nancy said, He left his ex-wife in charge.

Gary Wrench's ex-wife was Carmela Mola, a thick-bodied, fast-talking character who drove a red Chevy Silverado with a bumper sticker that said Bush Quayle '88. She wore thigh-high white pleather boots and had a fake tan the color of an old clementine. She did not give a shit about us, we knew.

This is bigger than us, said Cora firmly.

I said, That's all very inspiring, but what are we talking about here expense-wise? Years of legal fees? Decades?

Lu, said Nancy, do you need a job? She was sitting with her back to the window. Her cloud of gray hair was a halo in the sunshine. At her feet her dog let out a guttural sigh.

Nancy Meister, guardian angel. Yes! I said. Yes I do. Thank you. I mean please.

A friend of mine teaches photography at Kings County Academy in Brooklyn Heights.

That's a good school, said Cora.

Isn't that where Max went? said Erika.

Max who? said Tammy, then shut her mouth quickly.

Nancy said, My friend has had to miss a bunch of work because he's been in and out of the hospital. I visited him at Saint Luke's the other day and he said the substitute they brought in to cover his classes doesn't know what the hell she's doing. Apparently the last time he went in half his students were trying to expose their photographs on the wrong side of the paper.

Seems unlikely, I said.

She shrugged. I could ask him if they need someone else to substitute teach or if they're hiring.

Really? I said. That would be great. That would be so great, Nancy. So great.

I got a phone call a few days later from someone at Kings County Academy asking me to come in for an interview. You're a photographer, right? she said. Bring a portfolio of your work. Gideon will want to look at it. Gideon? I asked. Gideon Isaac, she said. The headmaster.

KCA's main offices were located in a thirteen-story, nineteenth-century stone building enclosed by two stories of blue scaffolding a couple of blocks from Summerland. On the ground floor, large display windows like a department store's showcased student art: a troupe of funny-looking puppets with lumpy papier-mâché heads. One of them had dozens of cardboard teeth and a black wig and was wearing a ripped Nirvana tee. Another was painted green and had antennae and gills and was holding a plastic martini glass.

I passed through a vaulted lobby where yelps and laughter echoed loudly, then up a flight of red-carpeted stairs draped with languid teens. At the office of the headmaster I knocked. A striking woman who might have been Chinese waved me in and told me Gideon Isaac would be with me shortly.

I sat in an orange plastic chair by a short flight of metal stairs in the cramped dark waiting area uncomfortably close to the woman, who neither asked me who I was nor made conversation but instead passed the time reading a library book. Through the small square window in the door I could see people passing by: slouching kids with backpacks slung over one shoulder; teachers in pairs gossiping.

Eventually a door at the top of the stairs opened and a man appeared who looked exactly—but *exactly*: gaunt cheeks, furrowed brow, white mustache, and all—like that portrait by Rembrandt *The Man with the Golden Helmet*.

Though the man in the golden helmet is not and was never meant to be Don Quixote, around the time that I first saw the painting projected onto the wall of a darkened lecture hall I happened also to be reading Cervantes. So in the laundry pile of my mind the portrait became folded up with the character. Upon my seeing Gideon Isaac, a third fabric was jumbled into that pile. I still cannot think of Gideon Isaac without thinking of windmills. Years later that Rembrandt-Quixote-Gideon pileup has become further wrinkled by two bits of history that I've learned: (1) Gideon Isaac was born Gurion Isaacson; (2) scholars now surmise that *The Man with the Golden Helmet* is probably not by Rembrandt at all but is instead a product of what they call his circle. Painted by some other artist or some group of artists now forgotten, like so much great art its authorship has split and disintegrated over time. It is the product not of some individual genius but of time.

So Gideon Isaac became for me a quixotic character, a product first of his own making and then of many related thoughts, memories, impressions, and stories.

Then again, who among us isn't?

Ah, Goethe, he said now, nodding at the Asian woman's book: We need not visit a madhouse to find disordered minds.

She laughed.

He looked down at me. And what waits here? he said.

I stood up and held out my hand to shake his. Mr. Isaac?

I'm Nobody! he replied. *Who are you? Are you—Nobody—too?*

I'm Lu Rile, I said, a little confused. I'm here for an interview?

He looked back at the striking woman with an expression that could as easily have been despair as inquisitiveness.

For a substitute in the art department, she told him.

Ah, he said. To comfort the disturbed and disturb the comfortable. Good good. For we want all our children to be comfortably disturbing.

I brought my portfolio, I said, showing him.

He turned back toward the door, considering as he went: *Oh, do not ask, 'What is it?' Let us go and make our visit.*

I followed him into a spacious office with thick blue carpet on the floor. At the far end was a massive oak desk and a wall-width bookshelf. On all the walls around us were paintings and drawings, many of them nudes.

Our little atelier has been terrifically productive, he said, noting me noting the pictures.

Students made these?

I think you'll find that at KCA the teachers are the students and the students are the teachers.

I felt like I'd stumbled into Wonderland. As if replying to my mind he said: Yes, we're all mad here. Are you mad enough for our little experiment? Tell me: What is your peculiar brand of lunacy, Ru Lile?

Lu Rile, I said.

Riled up, are you? Is that the folly you prefer?

I hesitated.

You do not strike me as the sort of artist who'd be inclined to cut off her ear. Do you have, as Hippocrates might have suggested, an excess of black bile? I have often thought that artists must have a little extra. They do certainly shit blacker than the rest of us. But perhaps that's just the wine.

He selected a book from the packed shelf behind his desk and started to read as if I wasn't there. I wondered whether his office was soundproofed; standing under the low ceiling in the dim light on the thick blue carpet I could hear my own heart beat.

I don't have any teaching experience, I said, attempting to bring our conversation back to Earth. But, I added firmly, I am a great photographer and I am fearless.

He perked up. Fearlessness, he said. That is a kind of madness, yes.

I set my portfolio on the round table and unzipped it. He meandered over with the languid interest of a tomcat, still holding his book—which, I saw now, was Vasari's *The Lives of the Artists*.

In our own time it has been seen, he read aloud, . . . *that simple children, roughly brought up in the wilderness, have begun to draw by themselves, impelled by their own natural genius, instructed solely by the example of these beautiful paintings and sculptures of Nature.* He turned to me and demanded: What do you think he means by *these beautiful paintings and sculptures of Nature?*

I left the portfolio open and stood back so he could flip through it. I think he means god, I said.

He closed his book on a finger to mark his page and squinted at me in the low light, standing back so he could take all of me in at once. Do you believe in god, Ru Lile?

I hesitated, unsure whether he was the sort of person who thought there was a right answer to such a question.

Put another way, are you more aligned with Plato—do you believe that art is a dangerous illusion, that art obscures truth?—or do you as Aristotle allow that by witnessing art the viewer experiences catharsis, which can be a moral good?

I don't believe there is any relationship between art and morality, I said.

I was struggling to remember something my onetime fling, the dour art school philosopher, once told me. We were lying in bed. I wasn't wearing my glasses. It was a relief not to be able to see his face. He was waxing romantic in his dull way. What did he tell me about myself? I remembered and declared it now rather triumphantly:

I am an existential nihilist.

Gideon Isaac nodded approvingly. He put the book down on the tabletop. Silently, without much of a reaction at all, he began to go through the pile of prints I'd brought. Halfway through he stopped and sighed.

To be honest, he announced, photography bores me. Go and show these to Antonio Morecki in the art department. Good-bye.

He sat back down behind the large oak desk, reading the Vasari where he'd left off. There was nothing to do but reassemble my portfolio and zip it up again. In the front pocket were a few copies of my résumé. I pulled one out and approached his desk. Tentatively I slid the paper onto his desk. With one hand—without looking up at all—he slid it off the polished oak surface and into the wastebasket.

I paused a moment before gathering up my things. At the door I turned around. Thank you for your time, I said.

As Fortune, he replied, *when she has brought men to the top of the wheel, either for amusement or because she repents, usually turns them to the bottom, it came to pass after these things that almost all the barbarian nations rose in diverse parts of the world against the Romans, the result being the speedy fall of that great empire, and the destruction of everything, notably of Rome herself.*

Behind me the door opened and the woman from the desk appeared. Gideon, she said, Pat Parker's parents are here.

Send in the barbarians, he replied wearily, and she ushered me out as two angry, well-dressed, middle-aged people went in.

How had a simple human person become a character like Gideon Isaac? He was a true eccentric and to me he was a marvel. I walked rather dizzily to the paint-splattered art department in a brownstone across the street from the main building. Antonio Morecki turned out to be a more accessible man. He was small, just a few inches taller than I, with a thin, dark comb-over and large black eyes and a rapid subdued speaking voice with the hint of an accent. Over paper cups of coffee he took in the contents of my portfolio with wisdom and intelligence, pointing out areas where I might consider dodging, burning, cropping. Our meeting was less interview than master class. I remember the texture of the decades' old paint that coated the table, the smells of tempera paint and clay. How midway through the interview a stampede of little children in overlarge backpacks tumbled past the open door, a few of them stopping to yell shrilly: Hi, Antonio! and laugh and run away when he replied.

Max Schubert-Fine was a student here, wasn't he? I ventured.

Antonio looked up and nodded. Those sad black eyes. You knew him?

I'm a neighbor.

Antonio shook his head. Tragic thing. Some of his classmates still don't know he's dead.

What? How?

He sighed. It was the choice of the school to let each parent deal with the incident as they felt would be most appropriate. There was a memorial but it was poorly organized. Attendance was optional. Max's parents didn't even show up. Parents who thought their kids wouldn't be able to handle it just didn't tell them.

Antonio sipped his coffee. A couple of students actually went to his memorial—but they're children. They disagree on specifics. I suppose their parents were too upset by the whole thing to tell them much. Of the kids who are certain he's dead, only a few actually know *how* he died. I recently overheard one girl say that Max was trampled by a carriage horse in Central Park. There are arguments, as you might imagine.

He shook his head in bafflement. Meanwhile all these kids

are clinging to this idea that he's still alive somewhere. The rumors you overhear as a teacher are really amazing. Some kids are saying he transferred to another school a couple blocks away. Others are saying his family moved to Michigan of all places. Those who don't know tend to be the more sheltered, quieter kids anyway. They're understandably confused, even threatened. When the other children say he's dead they feel they're being made fun of. I heard one boy get really bent out of shape, swearing up and down that he saw Max on *Think Fast*.

Think Fast?

A TV show apparently, I don't know. I don't have cable. But the rumor proliferated. Now there's this subrumor going around that Max Schubert-Fine left KCA to pursue an acting career. Max Schubert-Fine is going to be a movie star.

It seems wrong that the school wouldn't be more clear about it, I said. On an official level. If only to put an end to the conversation.

There was talk about that in faculty meetings, said Antonio. Some teachers thought the memorial was sufficient. Others thought it would be best not to upset the children. Others, like me, wanted to send a letter home with all the students explaining what had happened. But in the end it was a moot point: The family wouldn't approve a statement. No one could get ahold of the father, and the mother wouldn't make a decision without him.

And so my interview came to a close. What else was there to say? Max Schubert-Fine had left us quiet. By the time I walked back out into the street with my portfolio the light was already changing. The wind had picked up. There was a chill in the air. A beam of sunlight reflected off the windows of a tall building on the next block, illuminating a small group of kids who were playing on the scaffolding outside the main building. I pulled up my scarf and stood for a moment watching them dangle and balance and jump, whooping like monkeys. One boy swung from a horizontal steel pipe by his knees. Another climbed up and taunted him. A little girl did a gymnastic front walkover, ending in a handstand against a vertical pipe. I raised my Pentax to my eye and took a picture.

Max would be there with the best of them if he hadn't fallen, I thought. And perhaps for the first time I really understood the magnitude of his absence—beyond Kate, beyond Steve. I understood the space he'd left behind.

||||| ||||| ||

It would have been ideal to work at Kings County Academy full-time but despite the increasingly frequent absences of Nancy Meister's friend Ernest there was no room for me. The regular photo teacher, a severe woman I recognized by sight from openings, had been teaching there since the school was founded in the sixties and didn't plan on leaving any time soon. Substitute teaching proved to be rare work and notice was always short: a last-minute phone call at eight a.m., a sleepy-sounding voice—Hey, Lu? Are you around this morning/afternoon? Photo teacher is a no-show/Figure-drawing teacher's down with the flu/We need someone to supervise in the puppetry studio during lunch. Too often I had to turn them down.

The slapdash way they did things there was irritating but KCA also proved a valuable resource. When I didn't have to be at Summerland I forced myself to be flexible, to postpone whatever developing or printing or photo shoot I had planned for the day and walk up to the Heights—uphill from the ruins of DUMBO, under the Manhattan Bridge, and through Cadman Plaza Park, where the London plane trees made a yellow canopy—to teach forty-five minutes of drawing or painting or once in a blue moon a ninety-minute photo class. After the children left I'd take advantage of the quality enlargers, thick matte photo paper, and all the other expensive trappings of my craft, which the private school provided free for its thankless high schoolers.

The students came from stunning wealth. I overheard countless conversations about their expensive hobbies: tennis, violin lessons, squash, dressage. *Dressage!* I had to force myself to appear indifferent. Whole worlds separated me from them—worlds of experience, worlds of possibility—and galaxies of money. Yet when I did manage to conceive of them as the odd little individuals they were, I found I actually enjoyed their funny company. The children in the Lower School were tiny, self-contained creatures who spoke with remarkable eloquence about their crude scrambling art. The middle schoolers were boisterous and funny and strangely affectionate despite my own awkwardness around them. I think I have a crush on you, one tiny fifth-grade girl admitted to me once, blushing like mad, after a painting class, and what could I do but try to smile and reassure her that crushes were normal, crushes were okay.

It was the high schoolers I liked best though, the tough and miserable high schoolers. Though many of them lied to me, often and transparently, about due dates, canceled classes, deadlines—about everything they could—a couple of kids really took to me. A runty Goth, freckles and dog collars and corkscrew curls. A boy who wore women's pants and had a homemade tattoo on his shaved scalp. A girl with a red birthmark that spread over her cheek like the map of a continent. Outcasts like these hung out past sundown in the ground-floor art room and talked with me earnestly, angrily, about their fucked-up parents, their fucked-up friends, their anxious, incipient love lives. It was the first time I had ever felt anything like needed by anyone but my own fucked-up parent. I was glad to stay long after the janitor had come and gone to mine whatever unpolished wisdom I could from the bleak quarries of my own barely begun life.

One boy I will never forget: George Washington Morales. He was so unlike the rest. An import from the Gowanus Houses projects, he'd ended up at KCA through a program that relocated promising minority kids from shitty public schools to fancy prep schools around the city. I remember his dense, well-kept hair and worried brown eyes. He was a little heavy and the extra pounds gave his bald cheeks a sweet childish wobble. They also surely contributed to the way he tended to skulk around, pouting, attempting invisibility. He was a terrific draftsman, could draw anything and did—on tables, all over his notebooks, all over his baggy jeans, backpack, and sneakers. There was some graffiti-type stuff, bubble letters and jagged lightning bolts, but you got the sense that with the graffiti he was just experimenting with a trend. He had that rare truly graphomanic impulse; I'm sure if he had been older and it had been ten or twenty years later he'd have been covered in tattoos. Perhaps today he is.

One cold afternoon in early November I commented on something George had drawn in blue ballpoint pen on the leg of his jeans. It was a simple angel—just a face and tunic and two geometric wings—but he'd clearly taken care with it. Its eerie androgynous tranquility and the thickness and deliberateness of its lines recalled for me the strange placid seraphim I'd seen in slides of stained-glass windows in European cathedrals.

This? he demurred. I don't know, I just drew it.

But have you seen them? I asked. Have you been up to the Met? Or to the Cloisters?

He shifted uncomfortably. The what?

There was a full wall of art books in that ground-floor classroom. I found a book on art of the Middle Ages from among the battered paperbacks. It was large, about twenty years old. Half its pages had come unglued from its spine and their edges were soft as cotton. Most of the illustrations were in black and white but there was an insert in the middle featuring color reproductions. There we found the rigid, weirdly idiotic angels I was looking for. Some stained-glass character from a cathedral in Norfolk playing a stringed instrument we didn't recognize. A French *ange* with great curls of blond hair reading from a book. An organist from Oxborough whose body seemed to be covered in scales, her head lifted toward the sky in a way that looked really uncomfortable. The odd tilts of their heads became funny to us, the stiffness of their necks. Look at that one, George Washington said, pointing at a glowing figure playing a double flute whose eyes—either in pleasure or in boredom—were rolled back in its head and

I saw that a look of genuine pleasure had come into his own worried eyes. He began to laugh and so did I. Pushing up my glasses I admitted, I never noticed how sassy they all are! We made a plan to go to the Cloisters together once it got warmer.

At Kings County Academy I learned how to teach. No, I learned that I *could* teach. How to teach came later. More important, I learned that, though in my private life I was often strange and out of place, as a teacher I could inhabit a different persona, a Lu Rile who was stern but poised, and almost wise.

It was late in the day and the janitor was wheeling his garbage can through the emptied halls. I stepped out into the chill and walked home through the yellow-lit park, where a lone man in a black wool coat walked a black dog and a homeless man slept on a bench and a morose nanny pushed a stroller encased in thick plastic. As I left the Heights and entered DUMBO the sidewalks were more crumbled. Everything was emptier, eerier under the streetlights. The train rattled over the bridge (*ca-chunk ca-chunk*). There in the entrance to the subway slumped homeless Hallelujah, wrapped in a filthy comforter.

Have a blessed day, he called.

Likewise, I said.

And there was my own barren street.

I came home to a cold loft, an empty refrigerator, and a ringing telephone.

Hello?

Hey, Kiddo. What's cookin'?

My dad of course. Who else would it be?

How's the mayor of Tofu Town?

Actually, I said, I just came home from a new job.

Look who's talking now.

It's just part-time but it's pretty good. I'm teaching at this private school.

How much they paying you?

It'll come out to an extra couple thousand or so a year.

La-di-da.

Thanks, Dad. I think I'm still going to have to find more work, to be honest.

What, and take a third job?

I need to get this photo printed and that's not cheap. And with the lawyer fees adding up . . .

Lawyer. You in trouble?

No no. Nothing like that. I'll tell you all about it when I see you. Are we still on for Christmas?

He cleared his throat. That's why I called. We got to talk about the surgery.

All right, I said.

You know what, pal? he said. We're living in an amazing time. Amazing. I just came from the doctor. He explained it all to me. I trust the guy, I got to say. He's from Brockton. You remember the Fitzes? Brian and Willie?

No.

He's their uncle.

Did you drive there yourself?

Good guy, I think. Decent guy.

You shouldn't be driving with your eyes.

Anyway he says to me if I'd got these darn cataracts back in the old days, once they took the lens out, the lens of the eye, I mean, they'd of had to give me these big thick glasses the rest of my life.

You already wear big thick glasses.

Ha-ha. Like kid like dad.

Like kid like dad, right.

I took off my own glasses and pressed my thumb and forefinger against my eyelids while he talked.

Worse though. I'm talking scuba goggles. Anyway that was the old days. Nowadays what they do, they give you this little lens—they make it out of silicone—and just slip it right into the eye. He'll give a little drop, a little anesthesia, make the cut, and then—get this, Lu—he slides in a little probe. It lets out sound waves. *Sound waves.* Just amazing. The waves break up the lens so he can suck it out. Then he slides in the silicone, and thank you, ma'am. No stitches, nothing. Ten minutes, he said. A ten-minute surgery. How's that for modern medicine?

You sound relieved, I said.

Well. I'll tell you what. I'd be a lot more relieved if it weren't going to leave me eight hundred bucks in the red.

Eight hundred dollars?

Four hundred for each eye.

We were both quiet a moment, taking that in. I said: And Medicare?

That's after Medicare.

Okay, Dad. When's the appointment.

December twenty-third.

All right. Okay. I put my glasses back on, then removed them again.

Louise, listen. You don't have to—

How else are you going to pay for it?

A long sigh.

Listen, I said, can you *please* get Martina to at least drive you back and forth to the doctor and so on?

Sure, sure.

I'm serious, Toby. I'll call her myself if you don't.

All right, Lu.

All right. I love you.

Okay.

I hung up the phone and unwrapped the spiral cord from my index finger. I poured myself a vodka and put on a sweater. I was worried about my dad. I was worried about my work. I was worried about everything. I was so goddamn sick of being poor.

So I took on a third job: part-time night shift at a 24-Hour Photo in the back of a drugstore in Fulton Mall. The store was dingy and the street was dark and sometimes I heard gunshots. When my shift would end at six thirty a.m. I'd walk quickly with my hood up through the chilly gray dawn past a silent audience of crackheads. Hallelujah was a model citizen compared to the men who slumped against the steel gates that protected the closed stores at that hour.

I won't lie. I was afraid. The bloodshot eyes of the people who came in just to skulk around and browse without buying:

they scared me. The shots I heard once in a while: they scared me. I'd heard of burglaries and muggings near River Street but I'd never heard of anyone getting shot.

I took refuge in the knowledge that I was never alone in the store. There was always someone at the front register. The night cashier was a tough old dwarf with leather skin and a tattoo of a teardrop next to his right eye. He would be the first line of defense. I didn't have a register of my own so I wouldn't be a target. And if things really went south I could hide in the darkroom, where there was a lock on the inside of the door.

I tried to occupy my increasingly paranoid mind by calculating every hour how much money I'd made so far that day: $4.25 an hour for a six-and-a-half-hour shift minus taxes and mandatory unpaid breaks. Minus the twenty-five cents I paid nightly out of pocket—not out of any sense of duty but because of the security cameras—for the Big Red I chewed to stay awake. How much was that?

The only benefit was getting to develop other people's photographs. The pictures were intimate and strange. Babies in high chairs with food all over their faces. Families picnicking in Prospect Park. Nudie pics of heavy women taken in low light. A parrot in a cage. Busy parties shot in the dark, just a few faces caught in motion, illuminated and flattened by flashbulb glare. A shirtless man flexing in his bedroom mirror, holding the camera above his head, its flash a ball of light. A woman at a Chinese restaurant, mournful, distracted, looking out the window at a delivery guy blurring past on his bike.

Company policy was that if any pictures came out really poorly we should just discard them. Customers had a habit of shooting the messenger when it came to getting shitty pictures back. So we accumulated a vast collection of what were photographs but not quite pictures: blurry hands or fingers that had blocked the lens; bright, overexposed, unreadable forms; underexposures that came out black or almost black, dark and shifty as a still night lake where something's swimming below the surface.

I pocketed them. They weren't worth anything to anyone but me. At home I began to assemble a quilt of rejected photographs. Glossy snapshots of blurs and fogs, mists and streaks and darkness. I arranged them in a grid, alternating and contrasting their colors. I sewed them together with the kind of thread that's meant for stitching leather.

When I wasn't working at the 24-Hour Photo, teaching at KCA, or counting the minutes at tedious Summerland, I was working on my photo quilt or developing film or exposing prints or cropping, reprinting, and otherwise perfecting what I was increasingly thinking of as my body of work.

I was barely sleeping. I was losing all sense of time.

You might say I was losing my grip.

When I lay down to get a quick nap in before a morning shift at Summerland, just as I began to lose myself to sleep, I'd hear that fucking tap-tap-tap.

What! I'd yell.

Tap-tap-tap-tap.

Sometimes I'd just lie in bed and holler. I can hear you, little fucker! Quit it!

Sometimes I'd get up and run over to the window, try to catch him in the act. Soon as I got over there the tapping would quiet down. Sometimes I'd think I heard a little peal of laughter, a high-pitched ha-ha-ha! that faded as soon as it became audible. Sometimes I'd slap the window myself with the kind of desperate rage that can only come from sleepless-ness. I'd plead with him to stop it, stop, please stop. I'd try to reason with him. I had nothing to do with it, I'd say.

Or, as compassionately as I could manage, I'd whisper: Wrong floor, kid. She's upstairs. Go upstairs.

I'd stand by the window as long as I could, feeling the min-utes tick toward the time I had to leave again for work. I'd let my eyes lose their focus in the blue gray of a morning sky. Or I'd watch the cars pass on the bridge as the sun came up over the city, shimmering the river. Or I'd look out at the glow-ing city as a ferry went by after dark, its lit windows casting unsteady light on the water's surface. No matter the time of day all I ever wanted was to sleep—please *please* to sleep. Still, sleepless, I'd wait. When I had waited long enough, when I had almost convinced myself either that he'd taken pity on the poor exhausted woman that I was or that he had simply been flushed back to wherever world he came from, I'd pad as silently as I could manage back to bed.

But no sooner would I be huddled in the sheets than it would start again. Tap-tap-tap-tap.

|||| |||| |||

It was after one of these nights on a bitter day shortly before Thanksgiving that, nodding off at the juice machine at Summerland, I heard a couple of familiar voices. I looked up to see two high schoolers from Kings County Academy: a pale blonde named Eliza I'd taught in a life-drawing class and her best friend, Margo, the tall, frizzled, outspoken daughter of a well-known novelist. They noticed me and came over to the juice counter.

Hi, Lu, drawled Margo.

Hi there, I said. How are you two doing?

Good, said Eliza, and laughed inexplicably.

Good, said Margo. How are *you*?

Good good. I pushed up my glasses and readjusted my hairnet. What's new?

Margo just got cast in the play, said Eliza.

Margo brightened. I can't believe they gave it to me and not to Jennifer P.

Jennifer P. sucks, said Eliza.

What's the play? I asked.

Hamlet, said Margo. I'm Gertrude.

Congratulations.

Are you going to straighten your hair? said Eliza.

Margo put a hand to her hair reflexively: I don't know. Do you think I should?

Let's commemorate this moment, I said. I grabbed my Pentax from the produce bin under the counter and raised it to my eye. The girls mugged and held each other tightly. I pressed the shutter release. It wasn't quite right. I said to them: Now one without smiling. They let their expressions go slack and their hands fall to their sides. I pressed the shutter release again. Something about the picture suddenly seemed hilarious to me: two gawky girls standing together so seriously between the barley flour, sweet potato chips, rice cakes, and stone-ground mustard. I laughed. Now act natural, I said.

Chad Katz, who'd been doing billing at his desk near the front of the store, noticed the activity by the juice counter and came over to chat. Oh god, I thought. Here we go.

Hey hey, he said. He put his hands together and performed a little bow. How's it going over here?

Fine, sang the girls.

Eliza said: Lu, can I have a juice?

Me too, Margo said. I want a juice too.

Sure, I said. What do you want in them?

While they stood there watching me, fending off Chad's efforts to chat, I blended the spinach and carrots and beets and so on. The blender was loud and after making the first juice I had to rinse it out. Being exhausted I screwed up the second order, starting with an orange juice base instead of apple, and had to rinse it out again. When the absurd process was over and I handed them their plastic cups they smiled at me and in singsong unison called out: Thanks, Lu!

You're welcome, I said, wiping my hands on my apron.

Do they make you wear that hairnet all the time? Margo said. Eliza bent her head over her juice and let her hair fall in her face to block her expression.

I said, That's a good question for Chad here.

I don't make the rules, said Chad. His affect was a performance of regret but it was clear he was delighted to have something to talk about. Unfortunately that one's up to the health department. If they came and paid us a visit—and that's been known to happen—and the person manning the juice station, or wo-manning, in this case, wasn't wearing a hairnet? We could be in deep doo-doo.

Eliza snorted. Doo-doo, she echoed.

What kind of doo-doo? Margo asked, wide-eyed. Eliza laughed.

Oh, they'd probably fine us, said Chad. We'd be looking anywhere from fifty to a hundred and fifty dollars.

I'd pay, said Eliza. If I were her.

Would not, said Margo.

To not have to wear a hairnet? Would too.

All right, I said.

A hundred fifty dollars is probably more than she makes in an entire *week*.

Okay, I said more loudly. You can go ahead and leave now, girls.

Chad Katz shot me a look.

Margo opened her mouth wide. What? she said.

Go on, I said.

Sorry, Eliza muttered.

Falling against each other in their magnetic way they turned and giggled toward checkout. Chad started to reprimand me in his ingratiating way about my negativity, about how you can't turn customers away no matter how they make you feel. But I wasn't listening to him. I was listening to them, to their bubbling laughter. Trying to decipher their overloud whispers. I heard Eliza say to Margo at the cash register: I didn't know she was *poor.*

Thanksgiving Day, Summerland closed at noon but the 24-Hour Photo remained stubbornly open. The drugstore was understaffed due to the holiday so I took on some overtime and worked a double, afternoon through midnight. When the bleary-eyed art school dropout who worked the graveyard shift came to take over I walked home in the dark cold past the shuttered ninety-nine-cent stores and pawn shops and discount clothing stores and electronics shops.

The street was quiet. In the windows of Brooklyn Heights brownstones I could see warm lights left on, dining room tables laden with the remains of celebrations. Stacks of plates, trays of half-eaten cookies. An empty brandy glass on a windowsill. A pot of coffee left beside a lamp. As I came up toward the courthouse, flakes of weightless snow appeared around me. I was exhausted and frustrated and alone but I was saving money, I told myself firmly. It would not be much longer that a couple of nasty teenaged girls would be able to make me feel less than. I walked slowly through the park, past the empty benches, between the ever barer plane trees, and felt the miniature flakes melt on my face. Almost there, I told myself. Almost there.

At 222 River Street I climbed the stairs slowly. My legs were like jelly. All I'd eaten in the last twelve hours was a drugstore Snickers bar (minus seventy-five cents). In the third-floor passage after midnight the dusty windows let in only the faintest yellow light. I squinted to see where I was going, then stopped. On the other side of the long space the light framed a small figure. It seemed to be approaching without approaching. It seemed to be growing. It seemed to be missing an arm. In its one hand it was holding an enormous knife.

I was frozen in place. You are being ridiculous, I told myself. It is not what you think it is. I watched it, paralyzed, from the doorway. It is a trick of the mind.

But it *was* approaching, weaving unsteadily, growing in space. The silhouette of the knife dangled from its hand carelessly and I could do nothing but wait for it to reach me. If it wants to make a deal, I told myself wildly, don't let it. Do not under any circumstances negotiate.

It ambled into the pool of light cast immediately before me by the stairwell where I stood and I saw that it was Tammy Day, petite in jeans and a sweatshirt, long hair pulled back in a bun, holding a carving knife in one hand and a large bowl in the other. Hi, Lu, she said, wrinkling her nose to push up her glasses. You all right?

Hoping I did not seem too relieved I said: I'm fine. I'm fine. I was just thinking.

Oh. Well. Happy Thanksgiving! she said. Her face was a little flushed. She'd had a couple of drinks, I gathered. It was a pretty great spread. I ate so much I feel like I'm going to die!

Happy Thanksgiving, I managed.

You're wet, she observed.

It's snowing, I said.

You coming from family or . . . ?

No no, I said. Just from work.

She made a sympathetic face, a sort of smile-frown with raised eyebrows that made me prickle with resentment. There are still a couple people up at Kate's if you want to join, she offered.

Okay, thanks, I said.

All right, well, she said.

Good night, I said, and walked quickly away from her through the passageway. That short conversation with Tammy Day was the first I'd had with a friend in days. Weeks maybe. I should go upstairs, I told myself. I should hold out a little longer before sleep. Go and talk with Kate and whoever else was there. Have a conversation. Eat. Be a human being. I dropped off my things at my place and loaded up my Rolleiflex with my last roll of medium-format Ektachrome. I hadn't used the Rollei in a while. I figured Thanksgiving was a special occasion.

At Kate's door I heard a little muted conversation, and knocked. Getting no answer I tried the handle and found it unlocked. Kate's warm loft was fragrant with the smells of butter, roast turkey, and pie. The kitchen was clotted with dishes and pots and pans and glasses, the dining table with ten or twelve empty bottles and plates that held the remains of pie and empty ice cream cartons and scattered utensils and more glasses half-full of water or stained with wine. All along the center of the table were candles in varying states of melt, burning tall and straight or flickering or sputtering, their light dancing in the glass and silver and porcelain plates. At one end of the table in a copper roasting pan was the decimated carcass of an enormous bird. At the other, leaning back in their chairs, talking quietly, were Kate and Philip.

I knocked on the wall. They both looked up. Hi, I said.

Lu! said Kate. We haven't seen you in ages. She stood to give me a hug. My head came up to her chest and I could feel her laughter before she let go. You're so cold! Your hair is wet.

It's snowing, I said.

Is it? Philip got up too and we all went to the window and looked.

It was falling harder now, half obscuring the lights of the city across the river, collecting on the rooftops below us, making everything glow. Our three silhouettes were reflected in the glass. I looked down into the viewfinder of my Rolleiflex and took a picture.

It almost makes this ugly city beautiful, said Kate.

Where are you coming from? Philip asked me.

Work, I said. Work work work. Always work.

The health food store is open on Thanksgiving?

No, it closed at noon. I went straight from there to the 24-Hour Photo.

That's in addition to working at KCA? Kate asked.

I nodded, suddenly overwhelmed. In my drained state their friendly interest was too much for me. I felt my face get hot and my throat close and my eyes begin to sting.

Oh, honey, said Kate.

Wine! Philip decided. She needs wine.

Wine and pie, said Kate, and cut me a generous slice of pecan.

We sat down together at the table and the way Kate pulled out a chair for me while Philip filled my glass I could hardly bear it. These lawyer fees, I said loudly. Wow! They are really taking it out of me.

The way they looked at each other I could tell that to them the cost wasn't outrageous. But Philip said: And let's be serious. What is Glenn Delaney even doing for us? We haven't heard from him in a month. Cora assures us that he's hard at work defending the poor citizens of DUMBO but honestly—

We haven't even met the guy, Kate said.

Meanwhile Gary Wrench hasn't been heard from in months.

Flown the coop to Myrtle Beach, Kate said.

And now we've got Carmela Mola, I said through a mouthful of pecans.

She's a witch, said Philip. No, I mean an actual witch. She practices Wicca.

You lie! said Kate.

I mean, probably.

I saw her the other day, said Kate, leading around a couple of guys in suits. They were looking up at the facade of the building. It looked like they were assessing it for structural issues.

Developers, Philip said, shaking his head. I guarantee it.

Their hair was *full* of pomade, Kate said, disgusted. They were like Ken dolls.

I hope you told them to go fuck themselves, said Philip.

Oh, said Kate, I pulled down my pants and stuck out my ass and wiggled it at them. Mooned them right there in the street.

You did not! I said.

Kate laughed her donkey laugh. No, of *course* I didn't. What do you think I did? Do you even know me? I said hello politely and minded my own business and went inside like a pussy.

Philip said: When the history books are written about the great DUMBO real estate coup, Kate Fine will not appear in their pages. And why?

Because she's a pussy, said Kate.

Pussies don't get into history books, I said.

History is written by the winners, Kate agreed.

Also! said Philip. Have you noticed how cold it's been in the building?

I said, Is there something wrong with the radiators? I think there's something wrong with my radiators.

Oh no, said Philip. Your radiators are fine. It's freezing in here because Carmela turned off the heat.

It's so cold outside. It's snowing! Why would she do that?

Doesn't want to spend the money, said Kate.

Philip shook his head and held out his hand: It isn't just that, Katie. I'm telling you. It's a cold war.

Kate snorted: So to speak.

It's like what they used to do to foxholes. You know, in war?

Kate and I both began to laugh.

Come on, said Philip, amused by our laughter but dedicated to finding the words he was searching for: *Smoke 'em out.*

She's the one who needs to be smoked out! Kate managed amid laughter, her giddiness growing. Maybe it would relax her a little.

Speaking of! Triumphantly Philip produced a little plastic baggie of green from his breast pocket.

Oh, Philly.

Oh, Katie.

You're so good to us.

Lu? Philip said, gesturing with the little bag.

I'd better not, I said. It puts me to sleep and I haven't been sleeping.

Perfect! said Philip.

I mean I'll fall asleep right here, I warned.

Kate said, You are welcome to fall asleep at my dinner table any time of day or night.

Okay, I said. What the hell.

Philip rolled and lit a joint and we listened to its susurrus crackle as he inhaled. He and Kate were both so beautiful, had such an ease and grace to them. We passed the joint around and Philip talked about his paintings. He made these luscious portraits of members of the cross-dressing community, thick colorful paintings where the paint itself was often punctuated with feathers, fabric, rhinestones. Their expressions were the hardest part, he said. He wanted them to communicate something deep and real, and yet he also wanted to exaggerate their smears of lipstick, twilit eye shadow, their rouge and penciled brows. He was working on one now, he said, of his friend Priscilla, who had been a runaway and homeless and struggled with addiction. Priscilla was now sixty-six and Philip loved her perfect posture. During her first sitting he'd asked her about it and she'd said: I go through life upright. I don't bow to anyone. Isn't that great? Philip said. I have been thinking I want to try to incorporate those words into the painting, to actually paint in the words. *I go through life upright.* But it might be too much.

As the pot did its work, drying my eyes and filling my ears and neck with its warm foggy tickle, I became fascinated by the way Philip's hands moved as he talked, his long fingers and perfectly manicured nails. The graceful way he gesticulated took on a kind of dancing quality to the tune of the lilt of his voice.

Incorporate words, Kate echoed. Like Barbara Kruger.

No no no no, said Philip. Not Barbara Kruger. She's so direct. Too direct. Anything that direct, you can't trust it. It's like the words of politicians. *Read my lips: no new taxes.*

His Bush impression was spot-on. Kate dissolved into laughter. I watched the way she threw her head back and let that guffaw escape. Her laugh was an animal bounding through an open gate. The abandon of it, I thought—and I considered that word *abandon* and thought that actually there was no better word to describe how Kate laughed, none at all. Abandon! I said through my own weird laughter, and both of them turned to me and said: What?

Oh, I said, and slowly I stopped laughing. Oh nothing. Abandon. It's a great word.

Kate smiled at me indulgently.

Lu, said Philip, are you still doing a self-portrait a day?

Oh! I said. Oh. No. Not really. Not consistently.

I became distracted by the way my own voice sounded: scratchy and childish and gruff and unpleasant. It felt scratchy too. My mouth was awfully dry. I raised my glass and drank a little wine, felt the pleasant heat of it—but after I'd had a sip my mouth was even drier than before. My tongue was a velvet slug.

Why did you stop? said Philip.

Huh?

The self-portrait project. How did you know when it was finished?

I looked at Kate, who was pretty zoned out, staring more or less in my direction.

How did I know when it was finished?

You'd been doing it for a couple of years, right? Philip prompted.

Yes, that's right. A couple of years. How did I . . . I didn't stop, actually. It just sort of petered out. Or. The thing was, I made my best one. The best self-portrait, which wasn't even so much a self-portrait as . . .

I looked at Kate again. She didn't seem to be paying attention.

A happy accident, I said.

Kate had become absorbed pushing the crumbs on the surface of the table into a small square pile.

It was sort of a masterpiece, I said. The word sounded good to me. It sounded right.

Huh, said Philip.

Yeah. Yeah. I made . . . sort of a masterpiece. And then it turned out the whole project had been leading up to that one image the whole time. So that's how I knew the project was through. I knew when I saw this one image that I never had to do another self-portrait again. Because I had made the best one.

Philip was nodding rhythmically. Kate was pushing crumbs. I went on.

It was like . . . pinball or something. I played the game on the self-portrait level for a while. For a long time. And that was the first level. I played that level for years. I played it until finally I played the winning combination. And when I played the winning combination, I realized that, although I hadn't known it while I was playing, that winning combination was the *point* of it all. So: Bingo! or whatever. I guess Bingo is a different game. But you know what I mean. So now I'm on Level Two.

Wow, said Philip. So what are you doing now?

I don't know. . . . I don't know. I glanced at Kate. I tried to relax. I said, I'm making a quilt.

AIDS quilt, Kate murmured.

Photo quilt, I said. A quilt made of photos. And I guess I'm taking pictures of other things, and seeing what comes next.

Remembering I had my Rollei, I stood up from the table and stepped back and looked down into the viewfinder. Philip was leaning back with one arm draped over the back of his chair. The candlelight shone in his eyes. Kate was leaning forward, focused on the surface of the table, her face obscured by shadow. I took a picture, then adjusted the exposure and took another one. I rested the Rollei on top of an empty ice cream carton and adjusted its position to get the angle right. From down there closer to the tabletop the composition was interrupted by the long vertical candlesticks so that both Philip and Kate were in their own separate compartments: Kate on the right and Philip on the left. From the far left jutted one long turkey drumstick, bone and ragged meat. It was blurry in the depth of field but it fit perfectly into Philip's body. I couldn't tell whether or not it was a good picture. Certainly it was weird. I made sure the Rollei was steady on the carton, then pressed the shutter release to take a long exposure.

Neither of them looked my way. They knew not to. Brushing the crumbs on the tabletop, focusing madly on brushing those crumbs, Kate said: Where you are right now sort of sounds like where Steve is too. He's turned a corner. The work he's making. I visited him.

She looked up at Philip. Did I tell you that? He shook his head no.

She looked back down. Yeah, I visited them. I took a train down and they picked me up at the station. His parents are awful. Just awful. I mean his mother is nice and everything but she's a meddler. First thing she said to me when she picked me up was, You're not eating. I can't stand it when women make comments about each other's weight. It's like yeah, I'm not eating. I'm not fucking eating. My fucking son died and I'm not fucking eating. Leave me alone. She said, You're not taking care of yourself. God. The nerve of that woman.

Philip and I watched Kate and waited. I sat down again and took another picture, focusing closer on her face. Nothing could make her anything but lovely, but there were dark circles under her eyes and her lips were chapped. Her unbrushed hair was pushed on one side behind her ear; on the other side it fell against her face. I snapped photo after photo. As she talked her expression changed so radically, moment to moment, that I could hardly keep up.

Steve's been staying in his old bedroom down in the basement, she went on. He's nearly forty and he's sleeping in the same basement where he lost his virginity to Lisa Carleton in 1970. Oh yeah: I know all about the night he lost it with Lisa. I know everything about this man. We've been married twelve years. I know how and what time of day he jerks off. I know what he smells like in the morning and how much he has to drink to feel drunk. I know how lonely he was as a kid. I know about how when he was thirteen he experimented with an older boy under a bridge. I know what he really thinks of his father and how he feels about being an artist. His resentment of the art world and his weird sense of entitlement and this other darker feeling that happens simultaneously somehow. Worthlessness, I guess. The anxiety of the impostor. Oh god. I could write a book about Steve. Maybe I would, if he were more successful. If his career really took off. Ha-ha. *Steve Schubert: The Unauthorized Biography*. By his long-suffering wife.

It was happening. It often happened this way late at night. It was like Kate had a dimmer switch deep inside her and late at night after she'd been drinking someone went in through a secret door and slowly darkened her beautiful lights.

But see, that's why I can't spend time with him right now. I know all of this about him but I don't know what we're doing, I don't know where our marriage will go from here, I don't know whether we'll get a divorce or figure it out and stay together, but that doesn't even matter. After Max died everything else just started to seem so fucking meaningless. Who cares if we work it out or if we don't. I just know that right now I don't want to be—no, I can't be—around him all the time. I can't watch him grieve. The way he walks. The way he speaks. It's like looking in a mirror. I see my own grief reflected back at me and it is horrible. Every gesture, every sigh. I resent it. It's like, who are you? Who do you think you are to be this heartbroken? *I'm* the one who gets to be heartbroken here. His mother's right: I can barely take care of myself. I certainly can't take care of him. But he's *never* taken care of me.

Even when we were first married. I was twenty-one years old. I was practically a baby. I didn't know the most basic things. But it was me taking care of him from the very start. When he came home sick from drinking I'd hold his hair back over the toilet. When he went on a painting binge and stayed up for three days straight I'd make sure he ate. When Max was a toddler Steve broke his hand. He punched a goddamn wall and broke three fingers. Do you remember that, Phil?

Philip nodded.

And suddenly I was taking care of *two* babies.

I remember, said Philip. What were you saying though, he asked gently, about where Steve's at artistically? And how it's sort of like where Lu is right now?

Kate looked up at Philip and gave him a genuine smile. He smiled back. This was their friendship, I realized: he gave her the space to talk about it, all of it, and when she veered off into self-pity he'd nudge her back on track. Meanwhile she offered him good company and the freedom to be his most natural self. Her company must have been a relief to him, this man who was so often performing a different self or selves to the world. Their friendship must have been a relief to both of them.

And it was a friendship totally inaccessible to me, one I could not have with either of them and that maybe I could not have at all. I began to feel very much as if I did not belong, as if I were worse than a third wheel. As if I'd stumbled into a party to which I'd specifically not been invited. Which made me think: *Had* she invited me to Thanksgiving? I couldn't remember. Far as I could recall the first I'd heard about the gathering was from Tammy Day in the hallway an hour before. Surely, I thought, if Tammy were invited I would be welcome. Tammy, Cora's little henchwoman, who went around with a clipboard demanding money. People liked me more than they liked Tammy, surely. Didn't they? Or if they didn't like me they respected me at least. Didn't they? Was I a fool? *She doesn't love you. She doesn't even like you.* My head was spinning.

To quiet my mind I tried to focus on what Kate was saying. Something about Steve's new work. Something about how she'd gone down to this basement room where Steve had slept as a teenager and now slept again as a nearly forty-year-old man. He had been making art, she was saying—but this art was not like the nudes he was known for. It was not fun, it was not colorful. It did not bristle with energy or sex. He'd been drawing with charcoal on paper, had been drawing faces—no, just one face, the same face—over and over, obsessively. The portraits were poorly done in that they were not good representations. But as works of art they were interesting. Here and there, she said, were moments of resemblance. The fold of an eyelid; the curl of a bottom lip. Here and there she saw hints of the boy they both remembered. None of the faces was exactly right but the work was so much better than anything she'd ever seen him do before. What made it better was its utter lack of stylishness, of stylization. These ham-handed portraits from memory of the boy he'd always love. They were totally artless, she said, and that was what made them art.

She was going on in a sort of meditative voice so slow and methodical I barely noticed she was talking to me when she asked, What's your image?

Philip looked at me too.

Sorry? I said.

With what I feared was a hint of irritation, maybe even mockery in her voice, Kate said: Your last self-portrait. Your *masterpiece*.

I hesitated. This could be the moment. Nothing, I knew, would make one moment any better or worse than another.

If I was going to tell her, I was going to tell her, period. She may not like me anymore, may never have liked me, but I could hope that she'd respect me. On the other hand there was something about the way she'd been talking about Steve's work that I envied badly. Artlessness was what made his new charcoal portraits art, she'd said; I wanted her to tell me what made *#400* art. Because it was. It surely was. It might have been the only real work of art I'd ever made. I wanted her to come and see it some quiet afternoon and I wanted to give her the space, as Philip did, to unravel a little. I wanted to believe that would bring us closer. But maybe even more than that I wanted her intelligent perspective. Kate knew art. She understood it. I wanted her to see my best piece and to evaluate it. I wanted to be good enough for her.

As I weighed whether or not to go on I watched Kate push all the crumbs from a small radius toward one another, then pad the sides of the pile with her thumb and forefinger to make it a square. She was making sure to collect all those crumbs before increasing the radius, addressing a wider swath of table space. It was an inefficient way to play the little game; every time she increased the radius she was bringing more crumbs across the same space she had just cleaned before, which inevitably left even more smaller crumbs behind—which meant she had to clean it again.

Philip began to chuckle. I looked at him with alarm. It had happened, I thought wildly, it had finally happened: I had embarrassed myself completely. I felt my body tense up and my heart begin to pound. You weren't invited, I told myself. You're not welcome here.

Wow! Philip laughed. You two are *stoned*.

We looked at him, then at each other. It was true. We were completely stoned. Kate began to laugh too. Relieved, I stood up. I have to go to bed, I said.

Okay, they said—and the fact that they'd spoken in unison triggered their laughter anew.

Good night, I said.

But they were absorbed in each other's hilarity. Without waiting for anyone to respond I left the table and let myself out.

‖‖ ‖‖ ‖‖

By the end of November I had saved enough money to get *#400* printed large. I dropped off the slide at Duggal and came back for the print a week later. A young guy who worked there unveiled it for me on the counter and though it was enormous, its colors so vivid, its content so shocking, lines so sharp, blurs so beautiful, the guy's expression bore no recognition of its magnificence. As I pored over its every highlight and shadow, inspecting it for technical imperfections, I found details I hadn't even known existed. A wrinkle in the coat of paint on the window frame. The impossibly pale reflection of my own body in the right-hand pane. Far off in the sky, beyond the yellow blur of Max's hair, a shining pinprick of light: an airplane. Max's shoelace, untied, sticking straight up from his high-top.

Cash or credit? the guy asked dully.

Cash, I said, still staring into the image. Cash.

He handed me my change along with the slide, wrapped

in paper, which I slipped into the pocket of my coat. He wrapped up the print in acid-free paper and cardboard and masking tape and I brought it home carefully as a treasure. When I got out of the subway there was Hallelujah.

Hallelujah, he said to me.

For real, I replied.

He must have sensed the buzz in me, must have noticed the excitement in my eyes. Well, he said. The Lord's light truly shines from all His creatures.

I stopped at the top of the steps and looked at him, really looked at him—the colored thread woven into his coarse beard, the crust on the edges of his shining nostrils—and smelled his filthy comforter. It was a bright day but nearly freezing, and due to the cold, tears were streaming from his bloodshot eyes.

I set down *#400* in its cardboard, leaned it against my leg, and raised my Pentax. Hallelujah laughed and leaned his head back against the tile and called up to the ceiling, his voice a froggy echo: You seeing this?

I pressed the shutter release and pressed it again. He was a natural model. He mugged and laughed. Then his face was overcome with solemnity. Then he grimaced at me. That's enough now, he growled.

All right, I said, and took one more.

Enough! he snapped.

All right, all right. I put the camera down.

He said: Five dollars.

I shoved my hand in my pocket and felt around but all I had was a quarter. I held it out to him, poised to apologize, but quickly, all in a gesture, he leaned forward and spat in my hand. I jumped back and the quarter fell to the ground. The Pentax fell against my belly on its strap; I nearly fell, myself, down the subway stairs. With the spit-covered hand I grabbed at the pipe railing; with my clean hand I caught *#400*.

Hallelujah laughed at me and his voice was like an electric saw echoing in the stairwell. Dumb bitch, he snarled. For a quarter you can suck my dick.

I grabbed *#400* and half ran from the subway. Hallelujah's voice seemed to follow me down the hill toward the river and up River Street. Dumb bitch! he yelled, and his voice was so clear I was convinced he was running after me. Breathless I reached 222 and realized I'd been running alone the whole time. I hurried up the stairs to the fourth floor and fumbled with my key, furious with myself. How could I have let down my guard like that? I *knew* old Hallelujah was crazy, of course I knew he was crazy, but I'd let myself believe he was some kind of wizard or a saint, his blessing rising up to me from his pile of rags. I'd thought myself such a good woman for responding to him every time he said, *Have a blessed day.* He'd been nothing but an ego trip to me. I was a dumb bitch. He was right.

In my cold, sunlit living space I laid down a clean sheet on the floor and unwrapped *#400* again. Just looking at it calmed me, settled my angrily beating heart. It made me feel as if I was all right after all, as if I had a future, a fortune, to look forward to. Still in my winter coat I got down on my hands and knees on the cold concrete and looked at it closer, closer. It was so odd an experience to see it there under the window where it had been taken six months before. There outside the window on the enormous sheet of photo paper it was summer. Here in three-dimensional space outside the same window it was winter. There in the print I was naked, floating, flying, oblivious to everything that click of the shutter would set in motion. Kneeling here beside it, bundled up in my winter coat, I was its servant, its prisoner.

I was crouching before the print when I was startled by a loud slap on the windowpane. I did not look up at first. I had been shaken up by my interaction with Hallelujah. I did not want any new insanity. I kept my head down, kneeling there. I addressed the falling boy in the image. Go away, I told him loudly.

But the next sound was so loud I had to look up. It was less a slap than a booming *crack*. I raised my head and saw the glass in the left pane of the window had developed a long fissure, a crack that began in the middle and ran down all the way to the sill.

I heard my own voice say: What the fuck? I got to my feet and walked to the window slowly. I had the sense that I was on a rocking boat, that the ground below me was tipping, sloping. My center of gravity was a pendulum. My legs were weak. I stood with my arms held out for balance, my eyes on the glass.

Another *crack*. I gasped. A couple of feet from the window I stopped. This time I saw it. I saw it. It materialized in a moment, sudden and shocking as a triggered memory: flat palm and outstretched shadowy fingers. His hand, that little hand, the hand that had been tapping, then slapping, then cracking my windowpane. No sooner had it appeared than it was striking the glass. The fissure in the glass spread—this time up the window, toward the top of the pane, and out toward the edges on either side—and again that palm, those five fingers, retreated into the cold sunshine as if into shadow.

I was beside myself. Please stop! I yelled. Stop! Dizzy I fell to my knees on the hard concrete. Pain shot up my legs and through my hip sockets. Stop! I pleaded—

The view behind the window was rippling as if it were underwater. The sky, the buildings, the river beyond, the skyline, all of it was undulating. Something was behind the window, something as invisible but real as the heat waves that come up from the sidewalk in deep July.

I watched from my knees. The hand reappeared—outline first, just the contours. Then behind it was conjured like dust or shadow on an invisible thing the boy's body and face. There he was, pillow lips and windblown hair. I could see him. Unsteady and colorless, flickering like a bad connection. I could see him. Not as he was in my photograph, but as he'd been in life: standing four feet tall in untied sneakers and a sweatshirt pressed against his skinny body by the wind. He was both visible and invisible, both real and unreal. I wish I could explain it better, wish I could convey how unlike anything else in the world he was. He was ripples and he was dust. He was wind and memory and dream. More than anything else, he was *real*—not in the sense that he was tangible but in the sense that he was actually *there*. Maybe better to say he was *alive*—not in the sense that he wasn't dead, but in the sense that he actively *existed* there, breathing or seeming to breathe, looking or seeming to look. I could see him, but what was more frightening was that—I could tell!—he could see me. We locked eyes, and there was desperation in his expression. He could see me—no, he could see *through* me—no, he could see *beyond* me, into my space, my loft. He could see the photograph. He was looking at *#400.*

I staggered to my feet and stepped backward from the window and, keeping my eyes on him so that he wouldn't disappear, I pointed down to the floor, to the clean sheet where I'd laid down the photograph. Is this what you want? I asked him. My voice was loud in the empty loft but it somehow wasn't loud enough. Is this what you're looking for? I yelled. Screwing up his face, squeezing shut his eyes with a child's blind fury, as if he were just another kid throwing a tantrum, he smacked the windowpane with his whole hand so hard it actually shattered.

Glass rained in, reflecting sunlight. I shielded my eyes with one arm. The gust of wind was bitter cold and sudden. Shards of glass stuck in my winter coat. Splinters of it stuck in my hair, my scalp. Throwing down my arm I ran to the broken window and—gasping, wide-eyed—stuck my head and arms out through the broken space. I reached out and felt for him, but he had disappeared. It was as if the effort of finally breaking the glass had been too much. All that was left where he had been was freezing wind. I stood in the chill with my mouth wide open, gulping at the air like a fish.

At last I put on my gloves, carefully removed each fragment of glass from the matte surface of the photograph, and deposited them in a paper bag. Thankfully—unbelievably—none of the glass had scratched the image itself. There was one small abrasion on the far left side in the white unexposed area around the print, but that could be concealed by a frame. Carefully I wrapped the print back up in its tissue and cardboard and looked for somewhere to stow it. I decided I would keep it under my bed. I thought if I kept it concealed he might not sense it.

Still in my winter coat and gloves I removed the last fragments of glass from the window and dropped them too in the paper bag. Crunching over the broken glass in my shoes I went to the studio to retrieve my duct tape, then to the bathroom to take down my plastic shower curtain. I measured the window and used a straightedge to draw a corresponding rectangle on the plastic with pencil. I cut the rectangle with heavy scissors and held it up to the empty frame. The sun was going down and the wind had picked up. My nose was running in the cold. The draft that came in through the open window whipped the plastic out of my gloved fingers and pinned it to my face. I took off my gloves so I could hold it more firmly and my hands became numb as I wrestled with the duct tape, but at last I secured the plastic to the window frame. With violent inhales and exhales it was sucked in and blown out by the wind. I taped it again from the top left corner to the bottom right and the top right to the bottom left, making a giant X; then again from top to bottom, and then from side to side. By the time I was done the whole space where the windowpane had been was dark with duct tape.

I swept the last of the broken glass from the floor, taking care to dislodge the pieces that had gotten stuck in the cracks between the concrete. My fingers ached and my face was numb. I plugged in the space heater my dad had given me my first winter on River Street but the ceilings were so high that the old thing was totally ineffective. I went to the bathroom to take a hot bath. The water was frigid so I let it run. Waiting I looked in the mirror and saw my own pale face. A fragment of glass had struck me on the temple, leaving a shallow but bloody mark, and a dark river of blood had dried to a crust down the side of my head. I cleaned it with rubbing alcohol and watched myself wince. A tear formed in the corner of my eye. I did not wipe it away. I let it run down my face. I let the next tear form and fall.

The water ran ten minutes and never got any warmer. Carmela Mola had turned the boiler off, I guessed. I filled my one large pot and let the water heat up on the stove instead. When it came to a simmer I brought it into the bathroom and poured it into the tub. It was only half an inch deep but I undressed and took off my glasses and got in and sat down and cleaned myself carefully. I was shivering uncontrollably. My skin was gooseflesh and my teeth were chattering and I did not care to stop the tears that were coursing from my eyes. When I had removed every tiny shard of glass I drained the tub and stepped out and dried off, still weeping. I bundled myself back up in my winter coat and hat and, though it was not even nine o'clock, went to bed in all the warm clothes I had. Through the violent suck and blow of the duct-tape-covered plastic, through the tears that wet my pillow and froze in my lashes, through the wails of sirens outside and the calls of the gulls, I slept fitfully until morning.

‖‖ ‖‖ ‖‖

Two things became clear to me after that. First, I had to get *Self-Portrait #400* out of my home—and in front of Fiona Clay—as soon as possible.

Second, I would have to cover the window if I didn't want Max, or whatever he'd become, to visit me again. I tried hanging my blanket over the window during the day but at night, even bundled in my hat and socks and winter coat, I was so cold I could not sleep. I had spent nearly all I'd saved on the color print of *#400*. Even taking on extra shifts at the 24-Hour Photo and extra classes at KCA, I was spending almost all the rest on the invisible lawyer Glenn Delaney. I didn't know how I was going to help my dad with his surgery. I didn't know how I was going to eat. I could not afford another blanket.

I called Fiona Clay at the gallery so many times that the girl at the front desk, Jessie, now recognized my voice. Cherrystone Clay, she'd say when she picked up, and I'd say: Hi, may I please speak to Fiona? After I'd called four or five times she started replying in that affectless monotone: Hi, Lu.

Hi, Jessie, I said. Let me guess. Fiona's not available right now but you will let her know I called.

I may have imagined it but I felt I could hear the hint of a smile in her voice when she replied: You got it.

Listen, Jessie, I said. What's going on? Is Fiona having you screen my calls?

I'm sorry, Lu, she said, and coughed. Fiona's in a meeting right now and she'll be out of the office the rest of the day.

She's a busy woman, I said.

She said: I will let her know you called.

I said: Jessie, please. It's very important.

I will let her know you called.

Can you give her a message?

Of course.

Please tell her, I said, just tell her please that I had *Self-Portrait #400* printed large, that's the photograph she saw at my studio, the photograph she *told* me to get printed large, and, Jessie? It is glorious. It's better than glorious. Tell her it's a masterpiece. I'm not exaggerating, Jessie. I don't use that word lightly. It's a goddamn masterpiece.

Okay, Lu.

Can I describe it to you?

Um, sure.

First of all it's enormous. It's a huge photograph, the biggest they can do. And the colors are so unbelievably vivid, the textures so crisp you can see every detail. Imagine the bluest sky, the most pristine level of detail in the paint on the walls,

Rachel Lyon

the dust on the windowpane. In front of the right-hand pane of the window a nude, a thin female nude, is flying. She's airborne, leaping. An ecstatic blur. She's all motion and color. Behind the left-hand pane on the other side of the window, a form is falling.

I'm sorry, Lu, I've got to go. I've got a call on the other line.

Wait, wait! This is the most important part.

I'll let her know you called.

And then again for the hundredth time I'd hear the glottal click of the handset being set down on the receiver. I was a sucker. I was a loser. I was a loser and a sucker. I'd misinterpreted Fiona's politeness for encouragement. I'd let myself believe that when she told me to *print it large* she meant print it large, then show her. I was worse than a dumb bitch. I was an arrogant naive child.

There is nothing more pathetic than being the only person who believes in you.

It was December. I spent a long day substitute teaching at KCA: third graders in the morning, middle schoolers at lunch, and high schoolers until four thirty. When the last kid slumped out—huddled up in his North Face, JanSport backpack slung over one shoulder—I climbed the marble stairs to the theater on the fourth floor. A few kids were up there rehearsing the play. The drama teacher, Lief Zuckerberg, was sitting on the risers in the seating area, leaning forward with his chin on his fists and his elbows on his knees.

The set was unfinished. On the black rubbery floor were a few strips of glow-in-the-dark tape. Offstage where the wings would be a couple of kids were painting what looked like a plywood bridge. Onstage was the boy who'd been cast in the role of Hamlet hamming it up for a monologue that despite his remarkable enunciation and faux-British accent it was clear he did not completely understand. His voice was deep but ungrounded. In the way of teenaged boys' voices it seemed still to be hovering, reaching for its lowest register. I listened for a moment then turned to go—but turned back when Lief Zuckerberg read: *Look, my lord, it comes!* And in walked George Washington Morales, who'd apparently been cast as the ghost of Hamlet's father.

I was impressed by George Washington's posture. He was carrying himself with a degree of presence I'd never seen in him before. *Angels and ministers of grace defend us!* the boy playing Hamlet said with an overwrought gasp, and Lief stifled a laugh.

From the costume shop I could heard the low buzzing of sewing machines. I stepped back into the hallway and glanced toward it; the door was open.

It beckons you to go away with it, read Lief.

I turned back to the stage to watch the two boys act out their scene. Strangely, as I watched, the world around me— the buzzing sewing machines, the painters, Lief Zuckerberg, my own body—seemed to dissolve. *Mark me,* said George Washington. He delivered the line with a hint of pain in his voice. He spoke too quietly for the stage—Speak up! yelled Lief—but I was impressed by his nuance, by the urgency in his eyes. I was engrossed. *My hour is almost come, when I to sulphurous and tormenting flames must render up myself.*

The language was strange and musical in his treatment. It was hard to tear my eyes away. Not because of George Washington's performance or because of Hamlet—although that boy said, *O my prophetic soul! My uncle!* with such a wild roll of the eyes and head that he looked almost as if he were starting to seize—but because of the story itself. *Mark me,* the ghost said, and although it was George Washington Morales who had delivered its line the words gave me a chill. *The glow-worm shows the matin to be near, and 'gins to pale his uneffectual fire: Adieu, adieu! Remember me.*

Mark me. Remember me. I stood limply, half leaning against the wall, those two directives ringing in my ears. I was so distracted by them that I barely noticed Lief Zuckerberg noticing me. He waved at me while the boy playing Hamlet continued to chew the nonexistent scenery and raised his eyebrows as if to ask whether I was looking for anyone in particular. I stood up straight, pushed up my glasses, gave him half a smile, and shook my head—No! Not at all, no. Spooked I made my way out of the theater and back into the fourth-floor hallway, where the costume teacher was just leaving, throwing on her coat as she pushed open the door to the stairs.

Though it was late in the day there was still a student in the costume shop, busy at one of the sewing machines that sat in regular intervals on a low shelf around the perimeter of the little room. I went to the door and stood there for a moment before knocking. She was small for her age and wore large glasses and her red hair was pulled back in a lumpy bun. Her old T-shirt had been cut liberally around the collar to expose her bra straps and show off her sizable breasts. Was she trouble or was she meek? Probably both or somewhere in between. She looked up at me briefly before going back to her work.

Do you know where I could find some fabric? I asked her.

Up there, she said, jerking her head toward the ceiling. I looked. Probably a hundred rolls of fabric had been stuffed into three or four deep shelves built into the walls high above the sewing machines.

I'm looking for the kind they use for blackout curtains, I said.

She was training a hem steadily through the machine. I don't know about that, she said.

There was a stepladder leaning against the open door that led to the backstage area. I opened it and climbed it and reached up to run my hand over a few fabrics that looked promising. Here was a deep red velvet. Here was a black silk. What would be warmest? What would be darkest? I didn't want to take anything too expensive. I climbed down and moved the stepladder a few feet and climbed back up. Here were the thick wools and felts. I found an ample roll of dark blue felt and yanked it out from the stuffed shelf.

I don't think you're supposed to take those, said the red-head casually.

It's for an art thing, I said vaguely.

She shrugged, still focused on her work. Whatever.

The roll of blue felt was new and probably twenty pounds. I carried it down the back stairs to the first floor. Although it was not even half past five it was already dark, and it was snowing again. I turned to the security guard, a good-looking Jamaican guy. I asked, Do you have a trash bag or something I can put this in so it doesn't get wet?

He said, Let me see what I can do. He left me waiting there by the front desk. I positioned the roll of felt behind me just in case. I stood there with it for several minutes. A small group of boys in shorts and sneakers passed me, carrying gym bags and laughing loudly, faces flushed, hair damp. The basketball team, maybe. They opened the door and cursed at the cold that filled the lobby but did not stop to put on their jackets. I watched them tumble outside, their bare skin exposed, and let the door shut slowly behind them.

The security guard reappeared with a couple of black garbage bags and helped me fit the roll of felt into them. When it was covered he opened the door for me and I walked out into the snow protected.

I spent that evening securing the felt to all my windows. I started with the window that Max, or his specter, had broken. I cut a swath of fabric and nailed it to the walls around the window frame. It was not quite wide enough; I cut another swath and nailed that too, letting it overlap the first. Then I duct-taped it securely around the perimeter. It looked almost ominous. But I believed it would dissuade him from coming back—and I noticed it cut the draft considerably. I poured myself a vodka, turned on the stereo, plugged in the space heater, and got to work nailing and taping up the rest of the fabric over all the other windows.

When I was done my home looked like an insane asylum. But for the first time in weeks it was not freezing cold. For the first time in weeks I could take off my coat. I could breathe again. I felt almost safe.

Since I'd lived at River Street I'd never had to set an alarm. I'd always been woken by the light in the sky, the light dancing on the river, the calls of the gulls above me, the screeching of garbage truck brakes down below—or, lately, by the tapping on the window. But with the thick blue felt over all the glass my loft was almost as quiet as it was dark. I could sleep again. When I woke again the next morning it was past ten, and I was late for my shift at Summerland.

||||| ||||| ||||| |

After calling Cherrystone Clay enough times I began to get a sense of their schedule. The gallery opened at ten. Jessie took a lunch break around one thirty. If I called between one forty-five and two fifteen the chance of Fiona answering the phone was a little higher.

I started being more strategic about my approach. If I was working at Summerland I would take my own fifteen-minute break when I guessed Jessie would be out getting her salad, and run over to the subway entrance at Borough Hall, where there was a pay phone. If I was at the 24-Hour Photo I'd try the pay phone by the bus stop on Fulton Street. If I was at KCA the journey was shorter: there were two pay phones on the wall by the art room across from the elevator.

Sometimes they were occupied and I'd have to go back to work without talking to anyone. More often I'd get through, but not to Fiona Clay. I had hung up on Jessie, an art handler, an intern, a junior staffer I didn't know, and Chuck Cherrystone himself before at last I recognized that quiet, commanding voice. I was in Fulton Mall. A preacher was yelling. He was an African guy, a Jew for Jesus, tall and thin in a gray-and-white pinstriped suit and a down jacket left open to the chill. He was standing on a milk crate around which he'd arranged a display of pamphlets. A small crowd had gathered on the sidewalk: a couple of bored shopkeepers, skeptical women with baby carriages, and an outspoken grandmother who seemed to have taken it upon herself to argue with his premises.

I had called and hung up so many times, and was so distracted by the preacher, that I almost hung up on Fiona Clay when she said hello.

Fiona! I blurted. I've been trying to reach you.

Who is this?

Lu! Sorry, it's Lu. Lu Rile.

Lu Rile.

You came to my studio for a visit back in September.

I remember.

You saw my *Self-Portrait #400* and told me I should print it large.

Yes, well—

I've been trying to get ahold of you. I wanted to let you know that I printed it large and it's magnificent.

Jessie delivered the message—

It's better than magnificent, Fiona. I don't know if Jessie told you this. I told her to tell you but I don't know if she—

Listen, I don't overuse this word: It's a masterpiece. It's my only masterpiece, but it's a masterpiece.

Across the street the Jew for Jesus was getting heated up. One! Sovereign! God! he yelled, thumping a copy of the Old Testament. Existing in three persons! Father! Son! and Holy Spirit! Perfect in holiness! Infinite in wisdom! Unbounded in power! Measureless in love!

Are you . . . in a church?

I'm on the street. I'm in Fulton Mall. I am—on my lunch break. There's a guy out here. It doesn't matter.

Lu, I'm sorry, I'm sort of in the middle of something.

No no, *I'm* sorry—but I'm so glad I caught you. Please listen to me.

Lu, I—

You don't understand—

I do—

No, you don't. You think you do because you know so many artists, but you don't. You're a gatekeeper. And I understand how hard that must be for you—making potentially life-changing decisions for so many people, answering calls from crazy frantic women in the middle of the day—

She laughed uneasily.

But gatekeepers have one job and the people on the outside of the gates have another. I didn't just make this thing because you suggested it, but you did suggest it—and you were right. The print is amazing. The print is—I worked three jobs for it and I'm not sorry. For months I haven't slept. I've made sacrifices, real sacrifices—and all I want is for you to take a look. I'm not crazy; I don't believe you'll see it and necessarily think it's god's gift. If you don't like it, fine—you don't have to like it. If you don't like it, I'll leave you alone. But if you do—

We believe in everlasting blessedness! the preacher was shouting. In the bodily resurrection of the just! and the unjust! The saved will find everlasting blessedness! The lost everlasting punishment!

You fulla shit! the grandmother barked back.

I just want you to take a look, I said.

Lu, came Fiona's voice in the crackling handset: I'm sorry, but I'm finding this extremely disrespectful. You have called here a hundred times. You have spoken to my assistant a hundred times—and actually I'm quite impressed with her equanimity given your—tenacity. If you haven't gotten the message yet, I don't know what else to tell you. We're just not interested.

You can't not be interested in something you've never seen.

Actually I can. The fact is we do things a certain way here. You don't have a track record. Your CV is just *so* paltry. You've been in zero group shows. You have gotten zero grants, zero residencies. The number of times Cherrystone Clay has taken on an unknown like you—I'm not going to say it's never happened, but it's negligible. *Negligible.* What makes you think you should be a special case?

The work! I exclaimed. The work. It's as good anything you'll see at the Guggenheim right now. At the Whitney.

She let out a sharp frustrated sigh.

I'm serious. I wouldn't come to you like this unless I truly believed I had something incredible, Fiona, something that would shake foundations, that would get people talking—talking not just about me but about Cherrystone Clay—about *you!* This could be as good for you as it is for me.

The Holy Spirit is eternal! He participate in the creation of all things! He convict the world of sin! He regenerate! He sanctify! He baptize! He illuminate! He bestow His gifts upon all believers!

Fiona, I said, I just. I have to get this photograph out of my apartment. I have to get it out of my house. You don't understand.

Excuse me, interrupted a recorded voice on the pay phone. *Please deposit five cents for the next two minutes or your call will be terminated. Thank you for using NYNEX. This is a recording.*

I've really got to go, said Fiona.

I was digging in my coat pocket for a nickel. All I needed was a nickel. Wait, I said. Wait! Just a minute really. I know I have a nickel—

Lu, this is crazy. It's not that you don't have talent; it's that you're still just so green—

And Jesus the Messiah will return! In body! His body will come back to earth! And He will fulfill the prophesies of His kingdom!

Excuse me. Please deposit five cents for the next two minutes or your call will be terminate—

I found two nickels deep in the inside pocket of my coat and dropped one of them into the coin slot. Taking a deep breath I said: All I want in the world is for you to see it. I would give—I would give—

I fumbled wildly.

I have nothing to give. I would cut off a foot, both feet, my left hand—

Oh please—

If you see it and you don't like it I'll never bother you again.

It isn't that I don't want you to bother me, Fiona said. It's that I want you to bother me once you already have some *traction*. Once you have an established *career*. Do you see? There are steps to this process. You can't just skip these steps.

I said: This *photograph* is my traction. This *photograph* is my career. But in order for it to do what it is going to do it needs to reach an audience. Showing it in some gallery in Williamsburg or wherever isn't going to get it the audience it needs. I *have* to show it in SoHo. That is the only way it's going to make any kind of splash. Do you remember the image?

Liar! the angry grandmother spat at the preacher. You ain't a Christian! You a liar! And you'll burn in Hell with the rest of them! Jesus sees you! she yelled. *Jesus sees you!*

Even if I wanted to make another trip out to Brooklyn, Fiona was saying, I simply don't have the time. I'm busy all week preparing for an art fair and I leave town on Friday until mid-January.

Do you remember the image? I repeated.

She was quiet.

Do you?

I do, I do.

So you know what I mean when I say it needs to reach a certain audience.

An older man who'd been watching the preacher from the doorway of a discount shoe store stepped forward to try to reason with the grandmother. She hit him with her beige pocketbook. Liars like him, they must be stopped! she told him. What do *you* do for Jesus?

I can get it to you today, I said. If you can arrange for someone to be there after hours I can deliver it myself.

I can't—I can't be there. I have a dinner tonight. And I can't ask Jessie to stay late again.

Tomorrow then. I have to work at nine but I could bring it early, seven or eight—

No, Lu. No. This is crazy. God, this is crazy. You know, just for the record, I don't like this at all.

I know, Fiona. You won't be sorry.

This is *not* how we do things.

I know. I know! When's best for you? I'll quit one of my jobs, I don't care. I'll quit today.

Good grief! *Please* don't—

It's fine, I have three of them! I have jobs to spare.

I'll send a courier. I'll just send a courier to pick it up.

You'll do that?

There was a pause so long I thought perhaps she'd hung up. The godforsaken recording came on again—*Excuse me. Please*—and I slipped the other nickel into the machine. I watched the shopkeeper try to reason with the grandmother, who had gotten so worked up that even the preacher had stopped to listen to her rattle on.

Hello?

I'm here, Fiona sighed, and I could hear a certain degree of exhaustion in her voice. She had been beaten. I was just fetching a pen, she said. When should I have him come by?

Tonight, I said. Tonight! Any time.

It will have to be tomorrow. When tomorrow?

Before nine?

Your address?

Two twenty-two River Street 4D.

All right. He'll be there tomorrow morning.

Fiona, thank you! Thank you, thank you.

All right. Lu—

Yes?

No promises.

No promises. I understand.

The line went dead.

The courier knocked on my door at eight forty-five. Again I had overslept. My windows were covered with felt and I had no overhead lights. I yelled, Just a minute! and flicked on the battery-powered camping lanterns and set them out on the table and floor. Their weak light barely reached the ceiling. It was weird in there.

I opened the door to a young skinny kid, maybe not even twenty, with long black hair. You Lu Rile?

I am.

He blinked as he stepped in, accustoming his eyes to the dark. Whoa, he said.

The photograph is under the bed, I said. I hadn't had a chance to put on real clothes. I was still wearing the ratty sweatshirt, sweatpants, and thick socks I'd slept in. He followed me toward the futon where I slept, behind the busted shoji screen.

As I dragged out the photograph he wandered over to the window that faced the river and ran a hand over the dark blue felt. You probably got a million-dollar view behind this fabric.

Yep, I said.

Why do you keep it covered like this?

Hiding from a ghost.

He squinted at me.

It's my darkroom, I said.

Crucial, he said in a tone of respect.

Hey, so this isn't secured by anything, I said, holding the wrapped print. I mean I don't have anything to keep it in besides this cardboard. Can you be absolutely sure not to bend it?

For sure.

I was in front of the paper screen and he was standing by the window. There was a muffled thud on the fabric covering the vacant windowpane behind him.

Listen, I said loudly, hoping he hadn't noticed. Just promise me that you won't bend it at all. I paid a lot of money to have this thing printed. A lot of money I don't have.

I got you.

Give me your word?

I wouldn't be working for Fiona if I weren't one hundred percent legit, man. Fiona is a very particular woman.

I looked at him intently.

He laughed at me. Chill, lady! he said. I guarantee I won't bend your shit.

Okay. Okay. Thanks. I cleared my throat. This just means a lot to me.

I handed him the package.

He stayed where he was.

Well, I said, I ought to be getting ready for work.

Right on, he said. He stayed where he was.

Do you want a glass of water or something?

No, I'm cool.

There was another muffled thud.

Birds, I said.

Huh?

Like kamikaze. I jerked my head toward the fabric- and tape-sealed window.

Oh sure. He shook his head sympathetically. It's like a territorial thing? Like breeding season? They attack the other guy because they're trying to be the only alpha in the area. They don't get that it's their own reflection.

Wow, I said.

They're smarter than you think, he said. My ma's a bird-watcher. She goes out to Central Park with all her buddies. Thermoses of coffee, binoculars. I been along a couple of times. It's mad proper.

He wasn't moving. Thickly I realized he was expecting a tip.

Oh, I said. Hang on. I went to my bag and rummaged in it for my wallet. All I had was a twenty and a one. Twenty bucks was a lot back then and it was really a lot for me. Twenty bucks would last me a couple of weeks. But a dollar would be a laughable tip. With him standing there watching me in the poor light, hesitating over my wallet, I did a quick calculation. How much had it cost him to come all the way to Brooklyn? How much would it cost me for him to take care of *#400*?

Reluctantly I handed him the twenty. Take care of it, I said firmly.

He smiled. Thanks, man.

There was another muffled thud and this time I could see the fabric move. I felt suddenly frantic. I felt as if I were being pursued—no, as if I had been pursued and now here I was, trapped, and the courier with the long black hair was the dead end I'd run into. This kid was why I never invited anyone over.

Sometimes it helps if you tape an X on the glass, he was saying—

But I wasn't listening; I was standing there stiffly, remembering that strange wind-dust face, the expression in those barely visible eyes that looked at me, looked through me.

A thought occurred to me. It was not I who was being pursued.

You know what? I said. Actually let me give you a couple of other things too.

As he waited I went to the dining table and dug through my piles of photographs and gallery announcements and empty envelopes and unopened mail until I found the initial test print. I gave it to him. Stick it in that same cardboard, would you? I said. Obediently he laid it down and opened it there on the floor. I ran to the studio and rummaged through my slides.

#400 was missing.

The window was making a serious racket. Thumping had given way to hard slapping against an unbroken pane. Where the fuck was that slide? I stopped in the studio doorway trying desperately to think despite the noise. Oh. Obviously. I'd left it in my coat pocket after picking up the print from Duggal. I ran to the closet and retrieved the little paper package. Here, I said, walking back to him with purpose.

He could feel what it was. They don't usually need a slide, he said.

Just take it, I snapped.

He slipped it into his jacket pocket. There was something a little sulky about his tone when he asked: Anything else?

No, I said. That's all.

He made his way to the door and I followed him. When we reached it I saw that he had started laughing. What was he laughing at? Was he laughing at me? The batty little artist in sweatpants riddled with holes?

I pushed up my glasses and tried to stand up straight. Thank you, I said in what I hoped was a professional tone.

All right, man, he said, laughing, shaking his head. Hiding from a ghost. Ha. That's funny. He pointed at me: You're funny.

Thank you, I repeated stiffly.

He winked at me before stepping through the doorway. Hang tight, Lu Rile. Don't let the ghost getcha.

I felt a difference as soon as he had left. The air in the loft felt as if it had been diluted. The walls felt farther away. For the first time in months I appreciated my sixteen-foot ceilings.

Ripping down the dark blue felt from the windows was much easier and quicker than putting it up. A benefit of

working with entropy rather than against it. The whole process took less than fifteen minutes. I stood in the middle of
the living space and blinked at the vivid palpable white winter light and the jagged beautiful view. It was cold but the
cold was worth it for the light. I lived in a nest at the top of
the world.

I told myself I would not call Fiona again. I had work to
do. *#400* had limited my ability to move forward with my life,
my career. Now that it was out of my hands I would finish my
quilt of photos that were not pictures. It would be fifty-three
photographs high—as many as I could fit from floor to ceiling
in the loft—and forty photographs wide.

Meanwhile at Kings County Academy there were stirrings
of Christmas. The kids were abuzz with plans for skiing in
Aspen, theater in London, scuba in the Bahamas. These were
the children of people like me—like me, that is, but wealthy:
people who'd come to New York because they didn't trust any
other city to make them the best. And if these kids were not all
heirs and heiresses—though many of them were—if they had
not all inherited their parents' single-minded ambition, they
had all inherited the fruits of it. They had a certain awareness
of the wideness of the world.

I went to a performance of the high school play not so
much to support the students as to see how it had transformed
since I witnessed that scene in rehearsal. It wasn't very good.
The boy who played Hamlet overenunciated such that he spat
into the first row. Margo as Gertrude seemed to be channel-
ing Baby Jane. George Washington, old Hamlet's ghost, swallowed the ends of his lines and mumbled so that the audience

could barely hear him. It made me wonder how crazy I had been when I had been mesmerized by him weeks before.

Finally the time came for me to go up to the Cape for my dad's surgery and Christmas. I splurged on ten rolls of film—four color, six black and white—to shoot while I was there. I borrowed Uri and Etta's beat-up little Pontiac to make the drive. I went up to Kate's apartment to ask if she could check the messages on my answering machine.

She answered the door with the handset of her phone stuck between her ear and shoulder, holding up an index finger apologetically. The airline, she whispered. Standing back so I could come in she said more loudly: But don't you have Super Saver tickets for those same days? Uh-huh. Uh-huh. She signaled with one hand for me to sit at the table while she went and rustled around in the kitchen, still talking.

I booked the same ticket last year. We had two adults and one child. This year I will be flying alone. She came back out with a hunk of cheese and half a baguette and said: No, you listen to me, *Jennifer*. I don't care what kind of deal it was. I don't understand how your prices can fluctuate so wildly from year to year. How is it that you want to charge me double what I paid for the same damn flight a year ago?

She wandered back into the kitchen and I heard the tap run. Well, I didn't *know* I was going to be traveling solo, all right? Do you want to hear my sob story? It's a really good one.

She set two glasses of water on the table. I'm sorry, she said, that's just not good enough. I'm aware that your entire industry is going to pieces. I read the news, okay. But two hundred dollars to godforsaken *Minneapolis*? Have you ever *been* to Minneapolis, Jennifer? . . . May I speak to your manager, please?

She went back into the kitchen and I got up to wander while she haggled. Outside her windows the sky was empty white. I looked over the spines of the books on the bookshelves that lined the living space. There were some empty spaces where books had been removed and packed neatly into a couple of cardboard bankers' boxes on the floor. Here was another cardboard box with painting supplies in it: a bottle of turpentine, a palette, brushes, and tubes of oil paint. Were she and Steve separating for good? It felt like snooping to keep looking. I returned to the table as she was hanging up the phone.

Sorry about that.

I shrugged off her apology. Going home for the holidays?

Home. What's home? She sighed and cut herself a slice of cheese. I'm going to my brother's house. We haven't seen each other since the memorial.

That's a long time, I said.

I know. My mother kept offering. *I'll just come down there and take care of things for you. You need someone to take out the trash.* She was obsessed with coming all the way to New York to take out my trash. As if she'd just pop down and stay a couple of days doing *chores* for me. But one of the weird things that happens when your kid dies is: Suddenly you're facing a real lack of chores. I wish I had *more* chores. I don't have *enough* chores. You'd think she'd realize her argument was flawed. The same thing happened to her after my brother and I left home. Suddenly she had all this time on her hands—and it only made her miserable. She'd call twice a day just to tell me how the daffodils were doing.

Yikes.

I mean, I know she doesn't *actually* want to come and take out the trash. What she wants is to come over for a pity party. What she wants is for the two of us to just sit here and cry together and tell each other over and over how awful it all is. Thanks but no thanks.

Nightmare.

Kate nodded. Exactly.

But you're going.

It's the lesser of two evils. It's just for a couple of days. I've been avoiding seeing the baby. I have to see the baby.

The baby?

My brother's daughter. Did I tell you what they named her?

What?

Brittany.

No.

Swear to god.

That's an idiot's name.

Kate laughed. Oh, it had been too long since I'd heard that horsey bray. Polly would probably prefer her daughter were an idiot, she said. She's a see-no-evil hear-no-evil type. Are you going away?

I am, I said. I'm going up to the Cape to see my dad.

Oh, that'll be nice.

It'll be dull, I said. But he needs someone to be around. He's getting cataract surgery.

How long is the recovery from something like that?

I'm not sure, I said. I'm just going to stay as long as I have to.

That's good of you, she said.

I shrugged. He's all I got.

She smiled.

Actually that's why I came up. I didn't know whether you would be around but I was wondering if you'd be willing to check my messages while I'm gone. If you'll only be away a couple of days, would you mind popping in before you leave and when you come back, and just giving me a call at his place if there's anything important on the machine?

Of course.

I'll leave his number by the phone.

No problem at all.

Good.

I took a breath.

I'm expecting a call, I said. I mean, I'm hoping for a call. From Fiona Clay.

Oh?

Yeah. I. I'd been meaning to tell you. She took one of my photographs. I mean, she has one of my photographs. Right now.

What? Lu! That's great!

I cleared my throat. Yeah, it's exciting. Fingers crossed. She told me she's not interested in taking me on but—

But for her to ask to see your work is huge. Fiona's a star, Lu. She's no small potatoes.

I know. She didn't actually ask though. I think I sort of twisted her arm.

How do you mean?

It doesn't matter. What I really want is. I mean. I'd really like for you to see the piece. I'd like to know your thoughts.

I don't know that my opinion is all that important, said Kate. I don't know that much about photography but I'm happy to come see your work any time. The little I've seen is—

This piece is special, I said.

She raised her eyebrows and nodded.

I wasn't sure what else to say.

Is this your masterpiece? she asked.

It was an accident, I blurted.

What was an accident?

I . . . the photograph. It's an accidental masterpiece.

She waited.

That's great, she said uncertainly.

But that was all I could say. My heart had started to beat too hard and my mouth was dry. I wanted to tell her so badly but I couldn't bring myself to say anything more. I was defending myself not against the real flesh-and-blood Kate, who was sitting with me at her dining table, but against some other Kate, a Kate in my imagination.

She smiled at the cheese. Well, she said, I'd be happy to check your messages when I get home.

Thank you, I said, and I gave her my spare set of keys.

I started out in the early morning. It was an unseasonably warm day for December and the roads were slick after a light rain. I navigated out of the city and made it to the highway, where at times I was nearly blinded by the reflection of the sun on the blacktop. Yet as I made my way farther from the city the asphalt seemed increasingly blacker than New York asphalt, just as, when the sun went down, the night would be increasingly blacker than a New York night. There was more frequency to the shadows. A flickering followed my movement through the landscape, as if the drive itself were an old movie dug out of some long-forgotten box, only to be watched alone for sentimental reasons. The AM/FM radio/cassette player in Uri and Etta's car was broken. I had only my own thoughts to keep me company.

As I got closer I became increasingly attuned to the landscape of my childhood home. Strange and moving landmarks called to me, and I let the car idle by the side of the road as I got out to document them each in turn. Here a massive maple stripped bare by the season grew in a split in the road. Here a red mailbox jutted out from spindly shrubbery. Here a front-end loader had paused on its way out of a clearing with a mouthful of sod. A decrepit school bus, all its tires flat, sat in a grassy lot. The deflated pelt of a dead dog bristled in the light of the setting sun. It was slow going. Everything was bright and dripped with melting snow.

The house was a quarter mile down an unmarked path through a stretch of wetlands that flooded at high tide. Uri and Etta's Pontiac wasn't liking its change of scenery. Its axles whined and water sloshed in the tires as I eased it through the wide and shallow lake of salt water between the reeds. The sky was pink and lit the marshes bright. I tortured the car a little longer for the sake of another shot with the Rollei: in the rearview mirror the marsh reached out toward a horizon black and jagged with trees, the water afire with sunset sky. The whole framed scene was blurry as a Monet, streaked with reeds like brushstrokes, but outside the frame of the mirror similar reeds were perfectly in focus. The crisp silhouettes of four gulls swung aloft in the neon sky.

I reached my dad's house on stilts after the sun had gone down. Half the sky was drenched in vivid Yves Klein blue. I parked in the gravel driveway and killed the engine and sat a moment listening to the gravel still dancing in the tires, cyclical and rapid as my thoughts. There were the notches on the doorjamb my dad had made as I'd grown. There was the dent I'd made in the garage door with the first car I ever owned, a 1977 Chevy Chevette. And there above me at the living room window was the flutter of a curtain and, behind the muslin, the hint of my father's face.

winter

꜠꜠꜠꜠ ꜠꜠꜠꜠ ꜠꜠꜠꜠ ꜠꜠

He turned from the window when I walked in. The smell of my childhood home hit me like a poem. Low tide, cedar, buttermilk, laundry, dust. The faint stink of dog, though Baloo had been dead nearly a decade. The lights were off and my dad was wearing the thickest, silliest glasses I'd ever seen. I laughed despite myself and came over to him to turn on a light and say hello.

His turtle eyes squinted behind the thick glass in his round black frames, and his sharp old nose wrinkled in frustration as he tried to look at me. His pupils were hidden by two cloudy disks. It was as if resting on each iris was a tiny opal.

How you doing? I said.

He waved me toward the fridge. She left some deli meat and a couple of kaiser rolls in the bread box.

She—Martina?

He nodded. Thought you might be hungry from the drive.

I opened the refrigerator. Sliced turkey, mayonnaise. The foods of my adolescence. When I bit into the sandwich I thought of the Ramones: *I wanted everything. I wanted everything.* With his hidden eyes my dad rattled on about the weather and repairs he'd have to do to the house when it got warmer. I watched him as I ate, shoving the sandwich in my mouth without regard for table manners. As he groped his way to a stool at the kitchen counter it became clear to me that he could not see me, not really.

We caught up briefly. I was tired from the drive. Despite my exhaustion, though, I found it hard to sleep. In my old bedroom off the kitchen, its walls still papered with posters, I lay awake most of the night listening. To the clang of the buoys in the bay. To the fierce wind.

The next day I got up early and took a walk on the beach alone. It was frigid and I was wearing not only my own jacket but Toby's winter coat and a hunting cap that smelled like dust and a wool scarf wrapped three times around my neck and face. Winter on the Cape is all wind. The sand whipped up in eddies, mingling with flurries of light snow, and stung my cheeks. Out on the ocean the waves bared whitecap teeth. The only animals were the hardy gulls who spun around and around above me and called out in restless exclamations as the great gray clouds rushed by above, teasing them with sun. The sky was in a hurry. With my Rollei I took a picture of the sea and sky where gray met gray.

Somewhere in the dunes there was a rustling and I caught

a glimpse of a long black tail. A moment later a mangy dog appeared, half his coat worn off and the carcass of some other creature held between his jaws. He looked at me confrontationally and then ran off. In the afternoon I'd bring my dad to the surgeon, where they would use a high-frequency ultrasound to break up the lens of his eye and what I imagined would be a tiny vacuum to suck it out. Two hours was all it would take, he'd said, but that was hard to believe. I've always hated doctors' waiting rooms. Hate the corny music and the vapid magazines. Maybe I'd just drop him off and wait in the parking lot. I breathed on my frozen fingers, then shoved my hands deep in my coat pockets.

Lying on the sand was the exoskeleton of a giant horseshoe crab. I knelt down to admire the glossy surface of its hinged mahogany carapace, its frayed spines and lancelike tail, its punctured eyes. It was almost the size of a soccer ball. A cloud passed and clean white sun flooded the sand, refracted off the water. Far off the coast lobster boats were silhouettes on the blinding ocean. I took a picture, then thought maybe I would carry the giant crab back to Toby's house and photograph it there on black felt or velvet. An homage to or corruption of Edward Weston's *Nautilus*. I reached one hand out of my pocket to pick it up but dropped it when I found that the underside was hopping with sand fleas. I stood up quickly and backed away. The wind picked up and sand flew into my eyes. Momentarily I was blinded. In the harsh wind I took off my glasses and pressed against my eyelids until I saw red waves and yellow galaxies. When I opened my eyes a new cloud had moved over the sun. A gull cried out. The beach was dark again. Snow fell on the crab, then lifted in the wind.

In the afternoon we bundled into the car and I drove Toby to Yarmouth. He sat beside me in his enormous black sunglasses, silent. I wanted to make conversation but I didn't know what to say.

The ophthalmologist's office was in a massive building, dark square windows and corrugated brick. It was flurrying and the meager snowflakes got trapped in the waist-high juniper hedges that lined the parking lot. I helped Toby out of the car and we walked slowly on the curving sidewalk toward the automatic door. Inside a heavy woman in her forties with bleached blond hair sat at the front desk. Plastic holly hung from the low ceiling over her head and multicolored lights blinked on and off. I did the talking, checking in my father with his ID and his Medicare card. He seemed to expect me to.

The radio was tuned, predictably, to lite FM. A saxophone rendition of God Rest Ye, Merry Gentlemen burbled over speakers. A physician's assistant came to fetch Toby, who was still wearing his dark glasses, and led him away with a fat arm. In the waiting room I was alone except for an older woman wearing an eye patch on one eye, and over the other what looked like a clear plastic jockstrap, dotted with holes for aeration and held in place with surgical tape. She strained to look at me out of that contraption and nodded. It would have been a polite gesture if it hadn't felt so desperate. I considered going back out to the car but thought better of the cold and sat down in one of the ugly chairs. The old woman followed me with her whole head. I nodded back at her.

Still snowing out there? she said. Her voice was deep and husky, a smoker's voice.

Just a little, I said.

My nephew's car broke down in Barnstable, she said.

I nodded.

He was gonna pick me up but now with the snow. We may have to have Christmas here *(heah)*. She laughed nervously, rubbing her hands together in her broad lap.

It's just flurries, I told her.

She nodded and then kept nodding as if the gesture soothed her, as if she didn't want to stop.

I picked up a *Cosmopolitan* from the stack of magazines beside me. On the front cover was a thin blonde in satin smiling widely, laughing without laughing. Who was she posing for? Surely not for the women who bought such trash. She was posing for some concealed photographer, a man beyond the frame. It was that subterranean dynamic between model and photographer that women bought, not the model, not the pose itself. It was the lie that said, You too can be this accessible, this available. Beside the model's laughing head was an unbearable headline: Women Who Cannot Experience Intimacy. Are You One of the Lonely Ones?

Oh god, please no, I replied under my breath.

Come again? said the woman, jerking her head up.

I was a little startled. Nothing, I said. Just this despicable headline.

She seemed hungry for conversation. What does it say?

I turned it toward her but immediately realized she could not read it so was forced, embarrassingly, to read it to her myself.

She went back to nodding. My sister-in-law was like that, she said. No matter what my brother did she was never satisfied. He took her to Hawaii for their twenty-fifth and she cried the whole time.

Maybe she was depressed, I said.

That's the problem with your generation. You've got a reason for everything, no offense.

None taken, I said.

In my day a woman knew how to behave herself. You're expected to laugh? You laugh.

I felt a sudden surge of fury at this presumptuous woman. More or less without thinking I said: That sort of approach is probably why my mother killed herself.

Oh! The older woman shifted in her seat and began again to wring her hands. How horrible, she said.

I said, Maybe she should have laughed when she was expected to laugh.

Horrible, she said again—and then she shut up.

Inside the magazine was rife with lies and brainwashing. There were articles meant to make the reader insecure about her relationships and ads meant to make her paranoid about her odors. Deodorants, douches, hairsprays, perfumes. Turn inward, the magazine said. Do not look out. If you look outside of yourself you may begin to realize that you are trapped. If you look out you may begin to wake up. Stay asleep, the magazine said. Think only about yourself. The fragility of your ego. The size and smell of your body. Your health, your habits. Your deficiencies, your fears.

The truth was I didn't know if my mother was dead or alive. I barely ever thought about it. I couldn't remember what she looked like, what she smelled like. All I remembered was a shadow in the doorway, hair over a shoulder, a certain tone of voice. She was nineteen when she gave birth to me, nineteen and a half when she married my dad. By the time she was twenty-three she'd had enough and split. I didn't blame her. Most days, most years, I didn't think about her at all.

But now on the Cape, where vowels warped and snow met sand, in this purgatorial waiting room the question of my mother had woken up in me again. She would have been forty-five by now. She could have been anywhere or anyone. She could have been a bottle blonde at the front desk of an ophthalmologist's office. I didn't even know her maiden name.

The doctor led my dad out of the operating room himself. He was a beefy man with a broad face, flushed as if sunburned. A drunk probably. Poor Toby was wearing gauze patches over both eyes and holding out his hands for balance. I stood up quickly and grasped one outstretched hand and said, How do you feel, Dad?

He'll be a little woozy for a couple of hours, the doctor said. Don't ask him too many questions, okay?

I squeezed my father's hand and he squeezed it back.

Toby tells me you're an artist (*ah-tist*), the doctor said.

Photographer, I said.

Isn't that fine!

I felt for the Pentax around my neck and raised it.

Say cheese, Tobe, said the doctor, and put his arm around my dad and mugged for the camera. My dad stood up a little straighter but did not smile. I took the picture: a narrow older man with gauze taped over his eyes and a thick broad-faced man with a false wide-open smile, posing in a grim hallway below paper decorations and a string of sad little lights. On the far left side of the frame the quarter profile of the middle-aged blonde, a little blurred as she turns away.

They gave us two prescriptions and a couple of those clear aerated plastic eye protectors and warned us that Toby would need lots of rest. I led him carefully toward the door, one hand grasping his and the other on his back. The blonde got up and made her way from behind the front desk to open the door for us, watching us sympathetically, her lips pressed together.

She squeezed my dad's shoulder. We okay?

We're okay, he said faintly.

All right, she said. She shook her head at me with a sad look. I'm so sorry about your wife, Mr. Rile, she said. Merry Christmas, all right?

He raised a hand in recognition and we stepped out into the cold. I shot a look back into the waiting room behind us. The old woman was still sitting there wringing her hands.

What did you tell them, Louise? he asked quietly.

Nothing, I said, nothing. They must have misunderstood.

I drove home slowly, carefully, in the dark of five o'clock. It was snowing harder now and the headlights of the car illuminated the white flakes like a dense mist. I could sense that Toby was nervous but he let his hands lie limp in his lap. They would give nothing away. Had he always kept himself so secret? I think he had.

A couple of miles from home amid the glowing snow I saw two bright reflective spots in the road and stopped short. Toby raised his hand quickly to the dashboard to brace himself as we lurched forward in our seat belts. In the twin beams of the headlights I could see it was an animal—too large to be a raccoon, too small to be a deer. What is it, Lu? he said. What's going on?

It's a dog, I said, peering out the windshield—and in fact it was the same dog I'd seen on the beach. Black and mangy, half its coat worn off. Staring up into the light as if stunned or crazy.

Paul Boyle's dog comes out this way sometimes, Dad said. They shouldn't let her out so late at night.

It's only a little after five, I said.

That so? He sat back in his seat. Well.

The dog dropped its head and trotted off the road into the dark of the woods. There was a long gash along the side of its body that looked too bloody not to be a recent wound. I don't think that's Paul Boyle's dog, I said.

He nodded slightly and turned his face away toward the window despite the gauze over his eyes, as if to watch it go.

||||| ||||| ||||| |||

The days that followed were slow and painful. Toby set a timer to remind himself to change his bandages every four hours and did so privately, in the bathroom with the door closed. At mealtimes he made his way slowly through the dark cold house, trailing one hand on the wall. I tried to make myself useful. I brewed coffee, made oatmeal, turkey sandwiches. Warmed cans of soup. I did a load of laundry in the old washing machine, which rocked violently back and forth as if terrified, and hung the wet laundry up to dry on the living room furniture in the lame winter sun.

When puttering around the house got to be too much I bundled up in two coats and Toby's hunting cap and went out to the garage. I said I was going to try to organize some things but it was my mother that was really on my mind. I'd got it in my head I wanted to find some proof of her existence. It was weirding me out that I had thought of her so rarely. I thought maybe in the garage I would find something that would prove she had been real, at least. A snapshot, a necklace, or a pair of gloves. I went through a crate of unusable tools—half a pair of pliers, a wrench that was missing its lower jaw, mismatched nuts and bolts, a rusty hammer. I sorted through a collection of single buttons. I found an old guitar missing all its pegs and strings, and a wooden bird feeder that stank of mildew. A bicycle frame minus the seat and wheels. A small collection of ripped, bent beach chairs. A busted dehumidifier. A corroded pan and several pots of cobwebs. A medicine cabinet whose mirrored door had broken off. Three hurricane lamps, a mop bucket, and an old stiff-bristled broom. An antique shaving kit, its rock-hard soap about a hundred years old. A green glass pitcher coated with dust and dirt but actually in pretty good condition. No snapshot, no necklace, no pair of gloves.

In the late morning on Christmas Eve I helped my dad replace his bandages with the two plastic eye protectors that looked like sieves fashioned from jockstraps. I removed the damp gauze carefully to find that the skin below his eyes was raw and red. It was the first he'd let me see.

Does it hurt? I asked.

He shrugged.

Open your eyes, I suggested.

If his irises had been two round ponds it looked as if whatever dams had kept them that way had been removed. They bled unevenly into the whites of his eyes—which themselves were bloody red. I felt an involuntary wave of revulsion. Jesus, I said.

He raised his eyebrows, concerned.

Can you see? I said.

Ah, he said. Maybe a little.

How much is a little? I said.

What's the matter, it don't look right?

I squeezed his shoulder. We'll call the doctor, I said.

Give it a couple days, he said. He'll be with his family.

I don't know, Dad.

Fluid escaped from his eyes, clotting his lashes, wetting his skin. What's the matter? he said again.

I didn't want to worry him. I don't know, I said, maybe nothing. Probably they're just healing.

I can see a little, he offered unconvincingly. He gestured at the window. I can see the light.

I wiped the fluid from his face with toilet paper. We'll call after Christmas, I said. I attached the plastic eye protectors with surgical tape to his forehead and his cheeks.

The drugstore would close early that day so I got in the car before lunchtime to drive to Mashpee to pick up his prescription, antibiotic eyedrops. Uri and Etta's car was nearly out of gas so I stopped at the filling station on my way. There was a woman in the car at the pump beside me, a brunette in her late forties or early fifties. A little heavy, smoking a cigarette in the car while her husband went in to pay. I watched her, trying to see if I recognized anything. She sensed me staring and shot me a sharp look as if to say, *What?* I turned away.

The roads were empty and the trees were bare and the sky was cloudy white. I drove slowly on the quiet highway. The suspension in the Pontiac was busted. I could feel each pothole in my spine.

In the drugstore another woman caught my attention. This one was petite like me. She had dyed black hair and a fringe of bangs and was wearing a heavy shearling coat that looked expensive but worn and old. I overheard her at the counter refilling a prescription for Percocet. Her voice was soft and apologetic, which surprised me somehow. It seemed to clash with her hair. As the pharmacist went to work on her prescription she browsed the aisles, picking up and putting down vitamins and douches, plastic Santas and paper crèches, with fidgety disinterest. I noted the gauntness of her cheeks, her wide mouth and tired eyes. Was she like me?

There was a book we used to have when I was growing up. Probably you know it. A baby bird falls out of its nest while its mother is out. Anxiously it asks everyone that it encounters: Are you my mother? Each foreign animal replies with equal apathy. *I am not your mother, I am a dog.* Then, *How could I be your mother? I am a cow.* I don't know why my dad kept that horrible book around. When I'd read it as a child alone in the early morning while he slept, each time I reached the climax, when the idiot bird encounters a front-end loader and exclaims *You are my mother!*, I'd feel a shiver of dread.

Toby's eyedrops were ready before the stranger's Percocet. I waited in the car outside the drugstore for her to come out. My breath fogged up the inside of the windshield. When she got in her boxy gray Subaru I started my engine. She pulled out of the parking lot and I followed her out onto the road.

It was only a fifteen-minute drive or so to what I assumed

was her house, an unobtrusive split-level just outside Mash-pee. Fat multicolored outdoor lights had been wound around a stubby spruce on the brown lawn. I idled behind a grove of pine trees and watched her pull into the driveway behind another, nicer car. She got out and stopped at the side of her Subaru and glanced up at the window. The lights were on inside the house. I could see the silhouettes of figures moving past the half-drawn curtains. She leaned against the car and ripped open the paper bag and got out the bottle of pills. Popped open the childproof cap and put a pill on her tongue and swallowed it dry. Then she stowed the paper bag in her purse, made her way up the path to the front door, and opened it without unlocking.

I didn't know whether my mother lived in the area any-more. I didn't know anything about her. I had followed a stranger home from the drugstore in broad daylight. I recognized that my behavior was unhinged. But as I pulled out from behind the grove of pines and drove back toward my father's house the outrage and resentment, the fury and the grief, hit me like a cold front. I hadn't had a mother since I was three years old. Probably I never would. The chance that woman from the drugstore was my mother was ludicrously slim, but it was not impossible. *Someone* out there could be her. Hiding from the man and daughter that she'd left in the safety of another family, a private addiction, a shearling coat. When I was a kid I read enough stories about orphaned children whose long-lost parents somehow found them, who lived happily ever after in warm and well-appointed homes, that the infrequent headlights of every passing car would thrill me. Waiting at the window I'd have that same deep-in-the-belly feeling you get on a swing when the pendulum has reached its apogee. Just as you begin to fall back again your guts hover a moment, suspended inside you. Around ten or eleven I forced myself to quit the window game, forced my mother or the possibility of her out of my mind altogether. I have always been a determined person. In the fifteen years that had passed since then I'd rarely spent a thought on her. That she could be any one of the middle-aged women who lived nearby had never crossed my mind. I don't know why the thought happened to surface that winter I was twenty-six, but it did, and it was dizzying.

Back at home I gave Toby his eyedrops and hid out in the garage for the rest of the afternoon.

My dad was not a sentimental man. He did not keep photographs. I found a garbage bag of rags, a box of rotting kindling, an old shoehorn. I found a collection of postcards in a rusted tin box. They were mostly free; advertisements for Howard Johnson's and other restaurants. The handwriting on the backs was beautiful. They were from my dad's own mother, it turned out—my grandmother, who'd lived in Tennessee and died when I was very little. I went through each one carefully, searching for clues. Her messages gave almost nothing away. In one, postmarked November 1964, I uncovered a hint of resentment: *Toby—Feeling the chill these days. Timmy will come and clean out the drains this Sun. Giving thanks, 'tis the season I guess—xx, Mother.* In another, postmarked April 1966, when I was just a baby, some affection: *Toby—Nice morning here. The orioles are back. My love to little Louise—xx, Mother.* So these remembrances of his own mother he'd felt were worth saving.

I found too all the projects he'd been tinkering with—electrical in nature, mostly. There was a cheap set of speakers that he'd disassembled and apparently been trying to fix. An eccentric lamp he'd somehow rigged together out of a bit of copper pipe, a round flat stone, and a length of electrical cord. He'd even somehow lodged a foraged socket—appropriated from some other lamp, I guess—into the end of the pipe for the bulb. I found an outlet, plugged it in, and watched the 40 watts come to life. It was a pretty object: He'd polished the stone to make a reflective base, and the copper shone. All it was missing was a lampshade.

With numb hands I dug around in the boxes, shelves, and bins. In a wooden chest I found an old canvas sail folded in thirds and a coil of thick wire. I put on some heavy gardening gloves, retrieved a wire cutter from the toolbox, and formed two hoops—one small, one larger—from the wire. I cut the sail with pruning shears and folded it flat, just a quarter inch over the smaller hoop, and angled it out on a diagonal so that it would wrap a quarter inch over the larger hoop below. Then I superglued the seams. When I had finished, it made a simple lampshade, a little narrower on top than on the bottom. I rested it over the top of the metal hanger that surrounded the bulb. The light reflected against the sail and bounced back to the copper and refracted. It gleamed brightly.

Christmas morning I was up before Toby. The snow had cleared and the sky was bright and the gulls were a ruckus in the sun. I went out in bedroom slippers to retrieve the lamp from the garage along with the green glass pitcher. When I came back into the house I found him sitting at the kitchen table, like a cartoon cricket with his sharp nose and those bulbous eye protectors.

Merry merry, I called. I come bearing gifts!

He lifted his head. Lulu. Was wondering where you gone off to.

I found your project in the garage.

Only project I'm concerned about is coffee. You want to start a pot?

I set the lamp on the kitchen counter, unplugged the toaster, and plugged it in. It was a weird, almost eerie object—like a pile of trash that someone had cast a spell on. The copper and polished stone glowed. Pretty pretty, right? I said.

Ah! he replied.

I set the green glass pitcher in the sink to wash later on, maybe to fill with some pine branches if I could find them. I filled the electric coffeemaker from the tap. Over the noise of the coffee grinder I told him: I made the shade out of an old sail.

I glanced back at him to see if he had heard me. He wasn't looking at the lamp at all.

Pretty impressive electrical wiring, I said, pouring the grounds into the coffee filter. You're quite the tinkerer.

You find the lamp? he said. Was going to get myself over to the swap meet in a couple weeks, see if I couldn't get a shade for it.

I stopped and turned around. But I saved you the trouble, I said. See?

Oh sure, he said vaguely.

Dad.

These darn things, he said, tapping on the plastic over his eyes.

You won't be going to the swap meet, I said. You won't be doing any driving at all.

He murmured, Don't look like it, no.

I made us coffee and bowls of scrambled eggs and broiled toast with lots of butter. We had breakfast with the radio on, Crosby and Belafonte crooning Christmas songs. He ate messily, dropping forkfuls of eggs back into the bowl on their way to his mouth, biting the bare fork. He tried to conceal his agitation but midway through his meal he stopped and sat back in his chair and resigned himself to coffee. The winter sun was coming in creamy through the east-facing windows and his plastic eye protectors reflected the light. I got up from the table and retrieved my Rollei and took a picture of him like that, half-eaten bowl of food in front of him, glowing bulbous cricket eyes.

Don't, he said, hearing the soft *ca-chunk* of the shutter release.

I put the camera down.

He said, Guess I've got a little thing for you too. Nothing special.

You didn't have to, I said.

It's by the mail, he said.

The pile of unopened mail was on a table next to the door,

by the rotary phone. Underneath the stack of envelopes was a large coffee-table book.

They were having a sale at the library, he said. Thought you might like it. Didn't get to wrapping it.

It was a book of nature photography, its cover protected by a dirty plasticine cover, its spine still bearing a sticker with its Dewey decimal number.

I took a chance, he said.

I flipped through the pages. Glossy color photos of young green forests and beaches at sunset. Waterfalls that had been photographed on a long exposure so that their cascades looked soft and blurred as mist. I said, I hope this didn't cost you anything.

He shifted in his seat. You can leave it here if you don't like it. Martina's boy might get a kick out of it.

Outside the gulls were yelping, the buoys clanging.

I said, Dad, do you know anything about the kind of work that I've been doing?

You don't tell me much, he said.

I want to explain something to you about the sort of art I make.

He didn't reply.

It's not like *this*, I said. *This* isn't art, Dad. I mean, thank you for the gift. But look. This is a bullshit consumer product. You know what I mean? This sort of photography is created to numb the mind. The sort of work I do, and I want to tell you this so that you know, it's the opposite. It's meant to *unsettle* the mind.

He said, It was only a dollar. You don't like it, okay.

I said, It isn't that I don't like it. How can anyone not like a sunset or a fucking babbling brook? But these things aren't art; they aren't *art*. Maybe they're beautiful in person, you know, maybe it would calm or soothe someone to *be* on a mountain in the mist or whatever, but looking at a picture of it? Why? *Why?* Who opens up a book to look at a picture of a beach? People who hate their lives. The anxious and the weak. This isn't art, it's fucking lidocaine.

It's a goddamn book, he muttered, pushing his chair away from the table. You don't like it you can leave it.

Why, so *you* can look at it?

He turned his head away and stood up and reached out his hands for familiar furniture. Immediately I was filled with regret. The comment had come out of my mouth too suddenly, too reflexively. I'm sorry, I said.

No no no no, he murmured, groping toward the kitchen with his mug.

I put the book down on the table and followed him into the kitchen, where he was feeling for the coffeepot on the counter by the stove. Come on, I said, you'll burn yourself.

I got it, he said.

Let me do it, I said, reaching toward him as he reached past me for the coffeepot.

I got it! he snapped—and grabbing for the pot he knocked it from its heating plate. The glass fell to the floor and shattered, spilling coffee and shards all over the tile. Damn it to hell! he shouted.

Don't move! I said. I'll clean it up.

Louise, goddamn it—

I made my way to the cabinet where he kept his rags and cleaning things. Broken glass squeaked on the tile under the pads of my slippers. I came back with a few thick rags and a spray bottle and a paper bag. When I looked up at him again he was standing still amid the mess. Coffee steamed up from the cold floor.

Don't move, I repeated. I crouched down and began to wipe it up, placing broken pieces of the coffeepot in the paper bag. He stayed where he was but against the countertop his hand was trembling.

He said, I want you to be a decent woman, Lu.

Shards of glass clinked against shards of glass in the paper bag.

He said, You don't have to like the book. I just want you to be decent about it.

I paused and stood up, the bag of glass in my hand. Behind the fogged-up perforated plastic his eyes, those shapeless black pools, were vague and restless.

You can't see at all, I said. Can you?

He was stoic, he was distraught. He pressed his lips together.

Oh, Dad.

I put down the bag of broken glass and put my arms around him. He smelled like coffee and salt and sleep. He grasped the back of my shirt with one hand as if he'd forgotten how to hug.

I stepped away. I crouched back down and continued cleaning up. The coffee had cooled on the tile and stained the grout. We both had spatters of it on our pants and slippers. As I cleaned he quietly made his way out of the room, hand-over-hand on the counter. I heard his bedroom door click closed.

I made a list that morning of all the things I'd have to do before I went back to New York. Call the doctor and schedule a follow-up appointment for Toby as soon as possible. Call Martina and see if she could come in every day. Find other help if needed. Call Medicare and the VA and see if either of them would cover in-home care. Pay Martina for her work so far.

I began trying to build out a budget. It made my head spin.

Around noon Toby appeared in the hallway frowning, his face naked without the plastic bug-eyes or the thick glasses I was accustomed to.

Seeing the raw red bruises under his eyes gave me a visceral reaction. I looked away.

Don't know how long you're staying, he said, but we can go to the bookstore tomorrow if you like and you can pick out something else.

No, I said, that's all right. I went back to my arithmetic. Thank you, I said.

He shifted uneasily on his feet. I don't want to let you down, he said.

You've never let me down, I said—and so quickly I'd barely thought the thought before speaking it aloud I added: *Mom* let me down.

Self-consciously I looked up at him to gauge his reaction. He stepped forward, keeping a hand on the faux-wood-paneled wall, which was really just paper glued to pressboard with a wood grain finish.

What made you think of her? he said.

I took off my glasses and pressed my thumb and forefinger against my eyes. I don't know, I said, a little impatiently. I was just going through all that crap in the garage yesterday. I don't know. I just. I don't know anything about her. I don't even know her maiden name.

Okienka, he said.

I put my glasses back on to see him more clearly. Okienka, I repeated.

Holly Okienka, he said. The name in his voice was foreign but he said it with such familiarity I felt a pang of envy.

What is that, Russian?

Czechoslovakian, he said.

She was from Czechoslovakia?

Her parents.

Like Martina, I said.

That's right.

It was just one small piece of information, just one tiny morsel to feed my hungry mind, but it was so odd and unexpected I had to savor it.

Do they know each other? I asked.

No no. No relationship.

I was quiet a moment.

You want to know who she looked like? he said.

Who'd she look like?

Lizabeth Scott.

Who's that?

Oh. Ah. He wiped his mouth with the back of his hand. Lulululu. Are you in for a treat. Do me a favor and go look in the videos. Find one called *Dead Reckoning*.

Practically all his VHS tapes had been reused several times, film after film recorded off the television, the titles crossed out and rewritten on stickers on the sides. If you watched one to its conclusion you'd often see the last few minutes of the one that had been recorded previously, sticking out at the end like a long shirt under a short sweater. I found the one marked *Dead Reckoning* in Toby's back-slant scrawl and turned on the old tube TV and slid it into the tape player while he made his way to his stuffed chair in the corner. There was a glare from the window on the TV screen and it was hard to see but if I lay on my back I could look up into the story from an angle. *Dead Reckoning* turned out to be a B movie from the late forties. Humphrey Bogart plays a WWII veteran paratrooper turned amateur detective, determined to figure out what happened to his war buddy Johnny, who's jumped off a train and quote-unquote *turned up dead*. Lizabeth Scott is Johnny's desperate young widow.

The recording was awful. Every few moments a staticky horizontal would crawl up the screen. Yet the moment I saw her I saw what I hadn't been able to see in the woman at the gas station or the woman in the shearling coat. It was like finding a game piece that had been lost for years under a sofa gathering dust. All the features I hadn't gotten from Toby Rile were there. Thin upper lip, high nose, long philtrum. An almost involuntary expression of defiance. Finding fragments of my own face in someone else's was at once vindicating and unnerving.

In an early scene Lizabeth Scott is in a nightclub and the men are asking her to sing. She's crabby and petulant but she agrees. In a deep, unpolished yawning sort of voice she launches into a cheesy ballad. *Either it's love or it isn't. There's no compromise.* Her dusky tone exaggerates her boy-ish features.

Embarrassed by the schmaltz I glanced over at my dad and saw he had his fist balled up at his mouth, pressed up against his nose.

I spoke loudly to break the spell. This is what she looked like?

He turned away.

It took far too many romances to teach this fool to be wise.

People said she was the poor man's Lauren Bacall, he said when he recovered. I always hated that.

She's no Lauren Bacall, I said.

I hated to see him that way, hated to sit there with him. But what I hated most was how mediocre the film was. The characters were flat and the plot made zero sense. I couldn't keep track of it at all. It was barely a story. In the tense rela-tionship between Lizabeth Scott and Humphrey Bogart there is a misogynist recurring theme about how nice it would be if a man could put a woman in his pocket. As in so many sexist movies she resists the idea at first but at the end when she is dying—I won't apologize for spoiling it, couldn't spoil it if I wanted to, it is already so bad—she embraces it at last. As if to symbolize her soul leaving Earth there is some overwrought footage of a white parachute against a black sky, and at last the whole thing's over.

It was two p.m. Toby was sitting by the window with a forlorn expression on his blind old face. I got up to eject the video and leave the room.

Put on the hockey game, he suggested in a strangled voice.

You can't even see it, I said. I was meaner than I meant to be.

Louise, he said patiently. Put the game on, would you.

I changed the channel.

That afternoon the beach was cold and bright and the waves came fast and high. The ocean was black but for the blinding whitecaps and the sky was a clear mean blue. A gull was pecking in flip-book gestures at the carcass of the horseshoe crab I'd overturned. Didn't gulls ever get cold? Why didn't they fly south like other birds? Up in the dunes a couple of small men drunk as skunks and bundled up in blankets were sharing a case of beer and hurling the empties against the boulder-built jetty. Broken glass flew into the wind. I had to get out of my father's house. I was being poisoned by mediocrity.

|||| |||| |||| ||||

The day after Christmas my energy was renewed. I called Martina and explained the situation and asked her if she could come in seven mornings a week. I could hear children screaming in the background and she asked a little pitifully if she could bring her son with her until school resumed. I said of course. I asked if she could drive Toby to the doctor when necessary. She said she could.

Then I called the doctor and left a message and two phone numbers: my father's and my own. I said it was urgent. I said call back as soon as possible.

I called Medicare and listened to a recorded message about their holiday hours. I called the VA and got the same thing.

I finished my budget and figured that if I worked five days a week at Summerland and three at the 24-Hour Photo, assuming I could substitute at KCA on average three times a month, didn't buy any food, and put off paying Phantom Lawyer Glenn Delaney, I could cover the cost of Toby's surgery via an installment plan. That was the critical expense. I was not under any kind of contract to help pay Glenn Delaney and I could manage without buying food. But I could not neglect the ophthalmologist no matter how much he'd fucked things up, and I could not neglect Martina. Growing up poor hadn't taught me nothing. If you don't pay a person she'll stop showing up. If you don't pay your bills the collections agencies will come after you.

I explained the plan to Toby over dinner, minestrone soup and English muffins. His vague eyes searched vainly for something to land on. No food? he said. You got to eat.

I said, I can take what I need from Summerland.

Mayor of Tofu Town.

Right, I said. The mayor gets discretionary funds.

Take some staples with you when you go, he said. I can get that stuff from the VA. The coffee's pretty good.

The coffee's terrible, I said, but I'll take it. Thanks.

We ate slowly. We didn't know what we'd do when we were done. It was just after five o'clock and already the sky was dark. The soup tasted like its aluminum can and I wondered how long it had been in there. The thought nauseated me. I put my spoon down. There was quiet where the clink of spoon against bowl had been and he noticed.

Not hungry?

I don't know, I said. I wanted him to stop listening, to stop paying attention. I wanted him to take care of himself and leave me the fuck alone.

He continued eating in silence. When the jangle of the phone cut through the quiet I startled.

He tilted his head. She don't usually call during dinnertime.

I picked up the handset from its cradle on the table by the door. Hello?

Lu? Lu, is that you?

Kate!

That laugh! I felt it in my chest and heart. The connection was itchy with static but as her words tumbled from the handset they brought with them all the freedom of my other life. Oh my god, she was saying, I wasn't sure I had the right number! I called someone else twice before getting you, god, they answered in Spanish, it was awful. Your nines look like fours or your fours look like nines, I don't know.

It's so good to hear your voice.

Yours too. I feel like I've been away for ages.

It's another world, isn't it? I said.

Another world for sure. How are you?

I'm—fine.

I glanced at Toby.

How are you? How was Minneapolis?

Oh god, I just got back. Lu, can I tell you? It was a goddamn nightmare. Do you have time to talk?

Sure, of course.

Polly—my brother's wife, you know—

Yes.

I'm just going to say it. I'm going to say it. I can't stand her. I mean I understand why Tom married her. She's pretty, she's accomplished, she's midwestern. She's a Christian! She doesn't *come* from a broken home, she doesn't *do* the whole self-pity thing. She isn't a tragedy, you know? She's every-thing my family has always wanted to pretend they were but could never be. But god, she's irritating. She's like a fucking Girl Scout. She *was* a Girl Scout.

Kate sounded like she hadn't talked to another human being in weeks. Of course she was, I said.

And she hovers over that baby like a *specter,* I swear to god.

Brittany.

God, Baby Brittany. My brother is adorable—it's his first so he's totally over the moon, goo-goo eyes and everything—I've never seen that side of him. That part was nice. But Polly has complete control over the domestic sphere. It's no smok-ing in the house there, everything must be kept pristine and perfect and smelling like a fucking rose garden, so half the time I was freezing my ass off on the fucking patio, which was obviously just a giant snowbank, smoking in my pajamas and an overcoat and snow boots, at ten below zero. I felt like such a fucking addict.

You're not an addict, you're a New Yorker.

She laughed again. I was greedy for that laugh.

Oh my god, Lu, no, I'm sick is what I am. I'm completely sick.

We're all sick. You just have the decency to admit it.

It isn't decency. I have no shame. I mean I have no pride. Is that the same?

I don't know.

I watched Toby feeling around his mostly empty bowl with his spoon. He found a bean and pushed it around the bottom of the bowl, trying to get it into the spoon without success.

If there's one thing this whole nightmare has done for me it's made me utterly shameless. You know except for Christmas dinner I basically wore pajamas the entire time. Meanwhile Polly's playing perfect new mother with her pearls and her lipstick and her fucking perm.

She has a perm now?

I *know*. At some point the tension got so bad I told her she could go to hell. I really did. She was fussing around about the baby, getting the bottle just the right temperature, doing load after load of laundry on high heat to kill germs. She thinks she's killing germs.

Insane.

Meanwhile the baby's crying and Tom's out and my mom's napping so I go over to pick her up and Polly just about bites my head off. *Did you wash your hands? Be sure that you wash your hands!* I just said, Polly, go to hell. She was stunned. She looked like I'd hit her over the head with a hammer.

Kate was talking fast, too fast, as if something terrible might happen if she slowed down. That's funny, I said.

Tom at least had the sense to treat me like a normal person, to give me a little space. He basically ignored me, which is exactly what I wanted. But my mother. Jesus, Lu, my *mother*. Waterworks the whole fucking time. She'd pick up the baby and then she'd look at me, she'd just *look at me* as if she were afraid of what I might do. I'm like, What? What are you waiting for? What are you concerned about here? Do you think I can't handle being in the same room with another person's baby? How crazy do you think I've become? And then her eyes would well up and she'd leave the room. *I'm sorry I'm sorry,* this whole dramatic production just to prove that she's having a hard time, to prove that she's so sensitive and everything.

What a performance.

I smoked four packs of cigarettes. Four packs in three days.

You must feel like shit.

Honestly I'm just so glad to be back in New York I can't feel a thing.

At last Toby gave up, set the spoon down, and felt around for the last of the beans with his fingers. Did he know I was watching him? I shifted the phone to the other ear and turned away toward the window.

How's the Cape? Kate asked. How's your father?

I said, It's okay. He's okay. Not so great actually. Not great.

Bad time? she asked.

Yeah. I heard Toby's chair against the floor as he pushed himself away from the table.

Does he have anyone taking care of him there? Anyone besides you?

Sort of, I said. Glancing over my shoulder I saw he was making his way down the hall. Honestly, I said in a low voice, I'm sick of it.

What? I can't hear you.

I said I'm sick of it, I repeated a decibel more loudly.

What's that? I'm sorry.

I'm sick of it, I said, I'm sick of it!

You're sick of what?

Of being here, I said, lowering my voice again. Of seeing him like this. Of taking care of him.

I'm sorry, Lu, it must be a bad connection or something, I can't hear you at all.

At a normal volume I said: It's all right. We'll catch up when I'm back home.

Home, she repeated, and we let the word linger between us.

Oh my god, she said, I almost forgot the whole reason I called! You had a message. Two messages, actually.

Fumbling, crinkling. My heart jumped. Who?

You'll laugh at this. The first was Chad. He wanted to know where you've been. He said you've missed five shifts?

Summerland! God I meant to call. How did he sound?

How did he sound? Uh, *put out.*

Was he firing me? Do you think I'm fired?

I don't know, you should call him.

He'll live.

Do you want to know what the other one was? The other one is exciting.

Tell me.

Get excited.

I'm excited. Who was it?

Are you ready for this?

I'm fucking ready! Who was it?

Fiona Clay.

I swallowed.

Called long-distance. From Paris.

I gripped the phone cord.

To say.

Jesus, Kate, spit it out!

That someone dropped out of the annual spring group show at Cherrystone Clay and so they have a vacancy and would you like to show *Self-Portrait #400*.

Hello?

Lu?

Lu, are you still there?

I'm here.

You know, Kate said, I've heard the word *speechless* before but until this moment I don't think I've ever actually witnessed speechlessness.

I made a small sound, half laugh.

Do you want her number in Paris? She said to call as soon as you can.

No, that's all right. That's fine. I'll call the gallery. I'll speak to Jessie.

Okay.

Wow.

Yeah.

Kate. Wow.

That's the spirit!

It's happening.

You're goddamn right it's happening!

I can't believe this. This is unbelievable.

You've worked hard for this, Kate said firmly. It's not unbelievable at all.

It's not unbelievable at all, she said. With complete confidence. It was a glimpse, I imagined, into her relationship with Steve. Her comfort in the role of steadfast supporter. I felt a wave of nausea and tasted minestrone in the back of my throat. I swallowed quickly. I said, I gotta go.

Go, she said. Call the gallery.

I gotta go.

Go! I'll talk to you when you're back.

I hung up quickly and ran to the sink and choked up a flood of bile and beans. My head lurched forward, my glasses fell off my face into the basin, and I vomited on them. My throat stung, my eyes watered, my hands trembled. Gripping the edge of the sink I felt Toby's presence in the kitchen doorway.

With a shaking hand I turned the faucet and ran the tap. I'm sorry, I said hoarsely.

I got some Maalox here, he replied.

In the dark kitchen I cleaned the mess off my glasses. I'm sorry, I said again.

I slept fitfully that night and woke convinced it had all been a dream. But when I called Jessie at Cherrystone Clay the next morning she told me it was true. Someone had dropped out of the spring group show—some prize artist who I gathered had been snapped up by another fancier gallery. She said they had been scrambling to fill the spot and Fiona decided *Self-Portrait #400* would be a decent fit. She warned me Fiona wasn't going to take me on officially. But she said if *#400* generated some interest they might reevaluate.

I hung up in a daze and went out into the cold without a coat. The freezing air stung my face. The sun was bright on the dead sandy earth. This was it. There was no turning back. I squinted at the bright white sky until my eyes teared up.

In the afternoon we piled the things Toby wanted me to take—coffee, canned tuna, bars of Ivory soap, a bottle of off-brand Ibuprofen—into the car along with my bag and a few things I asked for: two extra blankets; a ratty wool rug; the green glass pitcher, washed and wrapped in newspaper.

I called Martina twice to make sure she would be there when I left. I didn't want my dad to be afraid, blind, and alone. When she finally showed up it was late in the day and she had her boy with her. He was seven or eight, chunky and sullen. He clung to her leg when he saw me and refused to take off his coat.

Gesturing at my dad I said: He has a doctor's appointment tomorrow. You can bring him to that?

Yes yes, of course, she said. Hello, Toby, she called. Happy Christmas!

He's not deaf, I said.

Merry Christmas, Martina, he replied.

We have little present for you. Danny, can you give Mister Toby his present?

Out of politeness Dad had on his giant black presurgery sunglasses, which hid his wounded eyes. The boy took one look at him and shoved his chubby face into Martina's belly.

Don't be shy, she told him. You remember Mister Toby.

Hello, Danny, my father said, inclining his head in the direction of Martina's voice. Addressing the boy he used a tone I hadn't heard since my own childhood.

I've got to hit the road, I said.

Martina leaned down toward her son and gestured at a paper bag by the door, which she'd set down next to her coat and purse. The boy detached himself from her and shuffled toward the bag. From it he retrieved a prettily wrapped but slightly smushed collection of pastries.

All the way from Czechoslovakia, she told me.

You shouldn't have, I murmured.

I don't want them in the house. Every year my sister sends bushels. Jerking her head toward Toby she added: He loves them.

We both watched as the boy brought my father the package and together they unwrapped the ribbons and pink-and-green cellophane.

She insisted I try one before I left so we each took one, except for the boy, who took two. Mine was sticky and filled with cream, and too sweet to finish. I left most of it on a napkin on the kitchen table and washed my hands while outside the bathroom door my father and Martina made cheerful conversation. *Are you my mother?* I shooed the thought away. Focus, I told myself. Don't think of the past. Think of the future.

They all clustered at the top of the porch steps to see me off. The car took awhile to start in the cold and the three of them watched from above without speaking as I turned the key again and again and the Pontiac shuddered. After a minute I stopped and grabbed my Pentax and leaned out the car window. They were all huddled together above me on the porch, silhouettes against the sky. Martina and Danny looking down at me expressionlessly, Toby facing vaguely the wrong way. I snapped a photo and again tried the car. At last the motor engaged and I pulled out of the driveway into the road between the dunes. In my rearview mirror I could see them bustling back inside.

‖‖‖ ‖‖‖ ‖‖‖ ‖‖‖

The drive was long. By the time I reached New York it was past eleven. I drove slowly over the icy cobblestone streets, the bumps in the unpaved road rattling my teeth, and turned right on River Street. It was immediately clear that something was wrong. Half pulled up onto the curb was a fire engine, its lights rotating silently. In the spinning dark in front of 222 a crowd was gathered. A couple of firemen stood by, passively vigilant. The front door of the building was propped open with a brick.

I pulled up to the curb and got out slowly. Bob Maynard was slumped against the wall near Nancy Meister, whose gray dog stood pressed against her. Uri and Etta Rainer nodded at me solemnly over their kid, who was rubbing her eyes and whining. Erika Kau was speaking urgently with Cora Pickenpew and Kate and Steve.

Steve. So he was back. Okay.

Philip Philips and Tammy Day were underdressed and looked utterly miserable. Everyone's breath steamed in the cold.

What's going on? I said to Philip in a low voice.

Fire inspection, he replied.

In the middle of the night? I said.

He nodded grimly. In the middle of the night.

We can't figure out who called them, Tammy said.

Ten bucks says it was Fat Nancy, said Philip.

But why would she? said Tammy.

Trying to get us evicted, said Philip.

Fat Nancy? I said, glancing at gaunt gray Nancy Meister.

Tammy said, Fat Nancy Sinatra. He means Carmela Mola.

I watched a fireman make a few marks with a pen on a clipboard. Kate caught my eye and waved. I felt a little surge of nausea.

I guess Carmela does look like Nancy Sinatra, I said.

Philip began talking very quickly: I was minding my own damn business—listening to a little music, heating up a little water to wash up—when I hear this fucking banging on the door. I honestly thought I was hearing things. I thought, This can't be happening. But I open the door and there are four massive fucking firemen and they come right in and start snooping around. Checking my sprinklers. Going out the window to check the fire escape. Measuring the distance of my fucking *shelves* from the fucking *ceiling*. Knocking shit over and moving everything around. Getting dirt all over my white rug.

But *why* would Carmela call the FD on us? Tammy said.

Because she can't hand the building over to a buyer while *we're* still in it.

But the building's already sold.

What?

The building's already sold, Tammy repeated. Or it's about to be.

What are you talking about?

This is what happens when you don't come to loft board meetings, Philip. Cora told us two weeks ago. She said they were about to sign. She said we're not going to drop the suit, but that it might be a good idea to start negotiating buyouts.

Philip's eyes flashed. Why hasn't anyone told me this? Did you know this, Lu?

I've been out of town, I said.

All right, folks, said the fireman with the clipboard. I apologize for dragging you outside so late on a cold night. I have here a checklist which will tell you which apartments have been found to violate the fire code. If your apartment is on this list! You have until the first of the year to make the necessary repairs or renovations, or find another place to live.

This is bullshit, Nancy Meister said.

I repeat: If your apartment does appear! On this list! You have until the first of the year to make the necessary repairs or renovations or find another place to live.

Who called you? demanded Erika Kau.

The first of the year is in four days, said Tammy Day.

Bob Maynard said: The landlord is supposed to be responsible for keeping the building up to code. Where's the fucking landlord?

Who called you? Erika Kau repeated.

We received an anonymous call reporting numerous fire code violations and per due diligence we followed up. This isn't personal. Believe me, I don't want to be out here freezing my ass off either.

This cannot be legal. Philip laughed angrily. How could this possibly be legal?

With all respect, sir, the fireman replied, this is not a legal residence.

But we're fighting for it, said Tammy.

Cora said: There is an active lawsuit pending *as we speak.* We've been fighting for years to change the zoning here. For decades! I've lived here since *nineteen seventy-eight.*

Ma'am, the last inspection, let's see, it looks like there has been one other inspection since '78 and that was in 1983. So with all respect you must have been aware that this was a possibility.

We worked with Gary, said Nancy Meister. We made all the upgrades we could.

The fireman flipped through a couple of sheets on his clipboard. According to my records, he said, there were just four inhabited lofts in the building at that time. Since then the number of apartments has almost tripled and the building has not successfully achieved the status of a legal residence.

But that's not our fault, Tammy said. The landlord's been dragging his feet for years.

Whatever the reason, said the fireman, the fire code is the fire code. It looks like some of you folks have been living in unsafe conditions for quite some time. I'm going to put this list up in the hallway where everyone can take a look. If your apartment is on this list!—

Jesus fucking Christ, said Philip.

We followed the fireman back into the dim building, muttering and sullen, and crowded around as he taped it up. He turned and trudged out the front door, removing the brick as he went. The door slammed behind him, blocking the light from the street, and we were left in darkness.

Someone had a flashlight and switched it on. We crowded closer. As we checked the list for our apartment numbers expletives and furious noises mingled with sounds of relief. I didn't know everyone's apartment but it was clear from the sounds in the hallway who would leave and who would stay.

Steve's voice in the darkness: Thank fucking god. Philip and Kate: two gratified sighs. Nancy Meister: No no no no no. I *made* those repairs. I did everything they wanted me to. Tammy Day let out a sharp sigh and ran upstairs. Erika Kau was defiant: Whatever. I'm not fucking leaving. They can't make me leave. Let them try.

Beside me I could feel Etta and Uri Rainer hold a short hushed conference over the head of their sleeping daughter before Etta left and started up the stairs.

Hey, Lu, Uri said.

Hey, Uri.

You safe?

I'm safe, I said a little guiltily. You?

They got us, said Uri.

I'm sorry, I said.

It's all right, said Uri. We've been thinking of moving. It's just too cold in this building for the baby. And she's always touching the walls, putting her hands in her mouth. I worry about the lead paint. I worry about all of it. It's no way to live.

I nodded in the dark. Where will you go?

We'll probably stay with Etta's sister a little while. We'll see where we can go from there. Hey, you got the car key?

Oh yeah, I said, reaching into my pocket.

You still got all your stuff in there, right? It's okay, you can give it to us in the morning.

Okay, I said. Thanks again for lending it to me. It was really a godsend.

Uri shook his head. It's what neighbors are for. Anyway you saved it from being broken into over the holiday.

The crowd thinned and with it went the flashlight. In the dark I could hear Tammy crying by the mailboxes and just make out the dim outlines of Philip and Kate beside her, and Steve a couple of feet away. As I headed toward the door, car key in hand, a long arm reached out to stop me.

Lu, hey—

I stopped walking, swallowed. Hi, Kate.

Hi. Welcome home.

Thanks, I said.

Quite a greeting, huh.

Quite a greeting.

I stood there a moment longer, then opened the front door to the freezing night. A rush of cold wind was sucked into the hall and I stepped out and let the door slam behind me. To unload the car would take several trips up and down three flights of stairs and across the passageway, but I was grateful for the task, grateful for a reason to expend a little physical energy. It was late but the events of the night had left me wide awake. I felt as if a wire of nervous power were coiled inside of me, waiting to spring.

|||| |||| |||| |||| |

I don't know what I expected to happen when I showed up at Summerland a couple of days before New Year's. I mean of course I know. I expected my job. In retrospect I'd like to submit for the record that I have grown at least in this one particular way: it does seem crazy to me now that I thought I could waltz back in after missing five shifts without warning and just pick up where I'd left off. In my defense my behavior came not from privilege but from what turned out to be a fairly accurate assessment of my boss's personality.

Chad Katz spotted me as soon as I walked in from the canned goods, where he was up on a ladder taking inventory. He climbed down hurriedly to meet me, clasping his hands together as if in prayer or plea. Lu, he said, knitting his brows and performing a little bow. Everything all right?

What do you mean? I said.

We haven't seen you for a while.

Oh, I said. Yeah, well. The holiday and everything. Which,

listen, are there any overtime shifts coming up that you need covered? Like maybe New Year's Eve? I could use some extra cash.

Chad sighed deeply. You missed five shifts, Lu. I never heard from you. I assumed you'd quit.

I held out my hands like, *ta-da*! Here I am! I said.

Lu, what we're trying to foster here is a sense of community. Can you tell me what it means to be part of a community?

I waited.

He waited.

What? I said.

It's like this, he said. You are one of seventy-two people, each of whom is carrying a small part of a very large load. Okay? Each of these seventy-two people carries what he or she can. Some carry a little more, some a little less. If one person has to leave for some reason—for *any* reason, really, but let's just say in this case to run off for some *holiday*—that person has a duty to let the other seventy-one people know. Because even though this load is spread across all these bodies, when this person takes off, her load falls on the people around her. And if *everyone* has to run off for some reason—let's say it *is* a holiday, a pretty widespread national holiday, which some ninety percent of these people celebrate, or more—if more than ninety percent of the people in this *community* all ran off at the same time, no warning, suddenly there could be just one guy, just one poor guy, shouldering *seventy-two times* what he had to carry before.

His eyes were wide and his brows were knit and sweat was beading on his nose. All around us the well-hee⌐d residents of the Heights were buying caviar and cheeses for New Year's Eve.

Do you get that? he said.

I waited.

He shook his head, defeated. Fact is, he said, I am short a few bodies on New Year's Day. I was counting on Sam but he just told me he'll be in Long Island. So yeah, if you could come in for opening, and actually if you could stay for closing, that would be great.

Cool. What about the afternoon shift on the thirty-first?

He sighed. It's a short one. We're closing early. But you're welcome to it.

I nodded. Okay, I said. See you. I turned to go.

You're on probation, Lu! he called after me.

I kept walking.

So my primary job was safe. *Self-Portrait #400* was safe. For the time being my loft was safe. And it turned out my secondary job was safe. Apparently no one at the 24-Hour Photo gave a shit if I showed up or not. They'd pay me if I did. They wouldn't take me off the books if I didn't. But other things were beginning to unravel. For example we'd noticed a strange stink in the building, something between rancid oil and smoke.

I returned to 222 River Street one morning in January after a night shift at the 24-Hour Photo and pushed open the front door to be hit in the face with pure stench.

On the stairs I ran into Erika Kau. She was lugging a heavy chair with the broad-shouldered strength of a weight lifter. We wrinkled our faces at each other with a look that meant, *That smell, right?* She set down the chair on the landing.

Seen Bob Maynard lately?

No, I said, surprised. Why?

She shook her head. He owes me eighty bucks. I haven't been able to get ahold of him for days.

He's not home?

If he is, he's pretending he isn't.

Why would he do that? I said.

Who knows. He's a shady motherfucker.

Nice chair, I said. It was sturdy and wooden with vertical slats in the back and four swivel casters, the kind of heavy-duty thing you might find in a library.

She nodded. Surprised Nancy left it behind.

Sure she's not coming back for it?

If she does she won't find it. It'll be at my place. You should go up there and take a look around. She left a bunch of shit. So did Tammy. Uri and Etta didn't leave so much as a scrap. You wouldn't even know they'd been there.

Where *is* Tammy? I asked.

Erika laughed. She rented a studio on Jay Street where apparently a pack of wild dogs is roaming the hallways.

Jesus, I said.

She said it's fucking terrifying. For a while she was borrowing Nancy's dog for protection, although between you and me that animal is about as fierce as a bath mat.

Did they say we could take their things? I asked.

Erika heaved the chair up over her shoulder. Didn't say we couldn't, she replied, and disappeared into the dark.

I changed course and went up to Nancy Meister's place on the fifth floor. I'd been in there only once—on a New Year's Day, in fact, two years before. Every year she'd make hoppin' John and have people over for what she called an open house. I recalled a crowded loft full of conversation, a couple of kids running around. Talking with an anarchist named Simon who wore a safety pin in one ear. The apartment was so warm that I'd left after less than an hour, having perspired through my shirt. Now it was cold and mostly empty but trashed. Going in alone gave me an uncomfortable sensation of trespassing. With mixed feelings I went through each living space. There was a bare bed frame in one corner. Crushed boxes and broken glass scattered all over the floor. A few pots and pans were left out on the counter and a broken picture frame rested against one wall. Several books still lay on the shelves, horizontal: an economics textbook, a book of baseball stats. Howard Zinn, Suzan-Lori Parks, a few poets and playwrights whose names I didn't recognize. Nancy hadn't been gone more than a couple of days. The place still smelled like her dog.

I checked the cabinets in the kitchen and found a tin of sardines, a box of crackers, and some powdered milk. I'd never used powdered milk before, but desperate measures. In the bathroom I found a mostly full bottle of Lubriderm. I stowed my findings in my bag and headed toward the door.

Tammy Day's place was on my side of the building on the second floor. I'd been there a handful of times, mostly with Kate. The fire door to her floor was ajar and the lock on her loft door was broken. She had left behind the heavy curtains she'd nailed up at the windows. In a cabinet with a broken door I found a few old VHS tapes: *Blue Velvet, Stranger Than Paradise,* and one labeled with a sticker that read in Sharpie: *Kids in the Hall.* I didn't have a VHS player, let alone a TV, so I left them. In the bedroom closet still hung a couple of button-down shirts. I was surprised and disgusted to discover a pile of feces in one corner of the closet beside a broken high heel. I turned to go.

I was passing the kitchen when I heard what sounded like laughter. Startled I turned and quickly discovered the source. Slumped against the kitchen cabinets, half reclining on the dirty concrete floor, was a man. One of his hands was resting faceup on his thigh and the other was moving slowly back and forth under the tented crotch of his stained sweatpants. He was staring straight at me, dirty face grinning, with a laugh that was slow, quiet, and mean.

I made an involuntary noise and ran out of the apartment, into the stairwell, and up. I pulled the fourth-floor fire door open more quickly and with more force than I ever had before. When I had made it back into my own apartment I felt dizzy. I locked the door behind me and stood in the entry a minute getting my bearings. When I'd caught my breath I dropped my things and went to the bathroom. I checked behind the door and in the curtainless tub. Went to the kitchen. Stood still, waited, and listened. Went to the living space. Checked under my bed. Soothed myself with the thought that there weren't actually so many places to hide. Went to the studio. My heart fell when I saw the heavy curtain that hung around my makeshift darkroom. Because it was insulated it was relatively warm in there compared to the rest of the loft. It would be a perfect place for a squatter to sleep. I approached it slowly, listening. My whole body was listening. My fingertips, my neck, my knees were listening. I threw open the curtain and immediately saw a sudden movement and smelled a sudden stink—

Rats. I felt the mother brush my shoe as she ran past me. I heard limp squeaking and bent down to see a whole nest of them behind the pipes of the sink. They were babies, each not even the size of my fist, pink with sightless eyes and squirming feet. They were curled together in a pile of rags and torn photo paper and shredded cardboard. The mother was squeaking shrilly, concealed somewhere behind me. I rose up again and left the darkroom to retrieve my Rolleiflex. I came back in and squatted down and focused in on their tiny groping hands and open mouths. The mother was going out of her mind, squeaking wildly as if she were a much larger beast, hunkered down and ready to attack. I took a picture, then got up and left her to her brood.

I stood at the window and looked out at the skyline, its promise of order and civilization. Looking out that particular window, though, was not—could not be—a comfort. The left pane was still covered with plastic and duct tape, a dull reminder. I didn't know what to do. What the fuck was there to do? Call pest control and have the rats all killed? Call the police and have them arrest the masturbating squatter? It was only a matter of time before I could expect another infestation. For that matter, technically I was squatting too. We were all squatting. We were all just an infestation standing in the way of real estate. There was nothing I could do. My home was a nightmare. 222 River Street had become a pestilential haunted madhouse freak show.

I almost jumped out of my skin when this dark line of thought was interrupted by a voice at the door. Lu Rile!

My first impulse was to pretend I wasn't home.

Lu Rile?

I tuned in and heard for the first time that for several minutes now someone had been knocking at the door.

Who is it? I called.

Courier from Cherrystone Clay? Delivery for Lu Rile?

I unlocked the door and opened it to the same skinny kid who'd visited me a month before to take *#400* off my hands. His face was bright and red from the cold, and his nose was scrunched up in disgust. Smells like low tide out here, he said.

Building's falling apart, I said darkly.

He stepped in. Your pad's pretty tight, though.

I just found a nest of rats in my darkroom.

No shit.

Got any advice on what I should do about that?

He sighed and looked up at the ceiling. I don't know, man. I'm a pacifist.

Ideally I'd like all species to live in harmony too, I said. But not when they're making nests and stinking up my darkroom.

Guess you'll have to set them free, he said.

Where, in Cadman Plaza Park?

Wherever, man.

I'm afraid the mother will attack me.

He nodded. That's a possibility.

We stood together a minute.

Last place I lived had rats, he said.

Where was that?

Alphabet City.

What did you do about them?

Nothing, man. Kept my food in garbage bags. Slept with the blanket over my face.

That's disgusting.

It was all right. They're kind of cute.

You want to take mine?

He laughed. You're a funny lady.

This kid was no help. I said: What do you have for me?

Delivery from Fiona Clay, he said, slipping his bag off his shoulder and unzipping it. He produced two thin squares of shirt cardboard neatly taped together. Inside were the slide of *#400* and the test print.

I can't take this stuff, I said.

She said she can't keep it.

I can't keep it either.

He looked around. No space for it?

It's not about space. It's about—

I stopped myself.

It's a religious thing, I said. I mean, not religious but spiritual. It's part of my artistic practice. I'm just going to destroy these things.

He nodded with a look on his face that meant, *And I should care?*

I changed my tone. You know, I said, since the medium was invented, photography has been undervalued, thought of as a second-rate art form. People tend not to understand the technique involved. We can see the artistry in an excellent painting, can see it in the brushstrokes. In a photograph, the artist's touch is more invisible.

Totally, said the courier. His attentiveness encouraged me.

Part of it is also that the nature of the photograph is to exist in multiples. The value of a painting or a sculpture is higher because there is just one painting, one sculpture in the world. Dealers can sell it for all this money because it's one-of-a-kind. Because a photograph can be reproduced again and again its value is inherently lower. I'm trying to work against that. I'm trying to create one-of-a-kind individual prints, which stand alone. It's an artificial way to increase their value, sure, but in and of itself that is a commentary on the inherent artificiality of the art market.

He'd stopped nodding.

It's a conceptual thing, I said.

So why didn't you destroy them before? Why send them back to Fiona in the first place?

I thought for a moment. It's like if I give the gallery a chance to save the slide and they don't, I've implicated them in the process of valuing the work.

But they're already valuing the work, he said.

I thought for a second before replying, Exactly.

Thanks for trying that out on me, man. The best part of my job is getting to talk to artists. I'm an artist too.

What kind of work do you make?

Audio collage, he said.

What's that?

From his front pocket he produced a small handheld voice recorder. The little red light was on. I record conversations, he said.

You were recording this?

I record pretty much every conversation I have. Then I go back and sort of chop them up, throw away the bullshit, keep the good shit, and string them together. It's kind of like a record of my life. Kind of like: my life, redux. It's conceptual art. Like yours.

He pressed stop and rewind and then play and I heard my own voice played back to me: -*dividual prints, which stand alone. It's an artificial way to increase their value, sure, but in and of itself that is a commentary on the inherent artificiality of the art market.*

He pressed stop again and fast-forward.

It was a decent argument. I almost believed it. I might be able to destroy both the slide and the print and stand behind it.

Not bad, I said.

I'll send you a tape, he said, putting the recorder away. I make these mini-cassettes. They're totally vérité, totally unselfconscious and real. People like them. I have seventy-eight subscribers at the moment. It's totally donation based. I'm like an anarchist. In the original sense of the word. I don't believe in charging set prices for shit. One guy pays like a hundred bucks per tape, meanwhile I have friends who get them for ten cents or whatever.

I'll take one, I said.

Cool, man. All right, man. I'll put you on the list. Well, good to see you again, Ms. Rile. I'm sure I'll be seeing you again soon. He stuck out his hand and added: My name's Casper, by the way. Casper Alvarez. In his hand was a handmade business card, just a rectangle of card stock with his name and beeper number printed in Sharpie.

I took the card. It tickled me that an artist only six or seven years younger than I was had schmoozed me so hard. I was impressed by the power of my own bullshit artspeak. Remembering the gallery talk I'd stumbled into years before at Cherrystone Clay, I thought of the disdain I'd had for Steve's performance as a kind of color filter. I was seeing that memory through a filter of another color now: something like camaraderie. Something like respect.

Also, Casper added, Fiona says give her a call. He shifted his weight from foot to foot.

All right, I said, I'm sorry I don't have any cash to tip you right now. I don't have any money at all.

Right on. We all hit hard times. Catch you later.

There was a buoyancy to his step as he turned and walked out the door. I stuck his card to my fridge next to Fiona's with my one magnet: Trudy's Auto Truro.

After Casper left I locked the door and brought the print and slide into the living area, along with a book of matches and a Pyrex baking dish I'd never actually used for baking. In the middle of the concrete floor I struck a match and held it up to the top right corner of the print. It didn't catch at first. The match burned down to my fingertips and I dropped it into the dish. I struck another one and held it up to the bottom right corner of the print. It burned and smoked but immediately went out.

Eventually the flame caught and the emulsion began to dissolve. As the melt crept up into the image the pale suspended nude on the right side of the composition began to ripple and warp. The flames licked her little foot, then ate into her leg, her crotch, her trunk. The fire consumed her. The flame was halfway through the print now, absorbing the paper and transforming it into smoke, singeing its way toward the falling boy.

I could feel him watching me before I looked up. He appeared at first as a shadow on the duct-tape-covered plastic. I dropped the photograph, letting it burn in the dish, and stood and walked to the edge of the window. I could see him through the right-hand pane more clearly than ever before. No longer did he seem as if he could be a mirage-like trick of heat and wind. He was somehow more solid than ever before—as if during the months since he'd died he had been somehow *learning* solidity, *practicing* how to fill in his colors, textures, and dimensions. He was almost opaque. It was almost as if a real flesh-and-blood boy were standing outside my window, standing on nothing, and I was struck by the fact that he was still in his summer clothes out there in the cold, just jeans and a thin unzipped sweatshirt and untied shoelaces. With a horrible exhalation I noticed those shoelaces as if for the first time and realized he must have tripped on them up there on the roof all those months ago. He must have dared himself to walk along the edge of the roof, as a balance beam, and stepped on a shoelace and tripped and fallen. He stood there on nothing and looked at me, and the photograph burned behind me and I worried that he was cold out there—it was winter after all and all he had for warmth was a thin unzipped sweatshirt—and was he shivering? The photograph burned in the Pyrex baking dish and as if in a trance I held out a hand to the window. I had the vague intention of opening it, of letting him in, the vague thought: *He's cold. He just wants to warm up.* I was raising one arm, reaching for the latch, when the fire began to engulf him. I stopped short, transfixed and horrified as the flames licked his legs. He raised his hand toward me. The fire ate away at his feet, rippled his jeans. What was that expression on his flickering face? Was he in pain? I watched as the fire destroyed him. It was hypnotizing. It was unbearable. It reached his sweatshirt and he looked at me with an urgent expression. I'm sorry, I said reflexively—I'm sorry, Max—and I tried to unlatch the window but my hands were shaking and I was not looking at what I was doing, so transfixed was I by him. His face and raised hand were the last to go and as they seemed to melt and disappear I yelled: I'm sorry! I'm sorry!—and the chimerical fire consumed the last of him and the window shook violently in its casing and with a surge of energy he thrust *through* the glass, *through me.*

It was as if I had stuck my finger in a socket or touched a live wire. I felt him pass through me and the force of him knocked me to the ground. I had time only to feel as if in slow motion an undulation of energy as powerful and disorienting as the ocean's undertow after a hurricane. I was knocked over by the force of the wave and sucked below—and then I was out cold.

I woke up I don't know how many minutes later. The first thing I became aware of was an intense pain at the back of my head and, radiating from it, an all-consuming headache. Slowly, half expecting to be surrounded by broken glass, I opened my eyes. Everything was blurry and far too bright. I groped for my glasses, which must have fallen off when I fell. With effort I found them, put them on, and raised my throbbing head, clutching at it as if somehow I could stop the pain. No dice. I felt for blood on my scalp but there was none. Just a nauseatingly painful bruise. I half crawled toward the Pyrex. In it was nothing but illegible scraps and ash. Yet beside it was the intact slide.

Jesus Christ, I said aloud. The sound of my own voice in my head was too loud. I got to my feet and hobbled toward the bathroom, where I swallowed four of Toby's off-brand Ibuprofen one after the next.

||||‌ |||| |||| |||| ||

called the gallery. For the first time, Jessie put me right
through to Fiona.

Lu, she said. So you saw Casper. Great. Listen, I'm going
to need you to get the print framed for the show. Jessie will
give you all the details—the type of wood and dimensions and
everything—and arrange a time for you to pick it up. She'll
give you our framer's information. He's terrific. I know your
schedule is inconsistent so we can work around you. She can
stay late if necessary, et cetera.

I was taken aback. You need *me* to frame it?

Well, yes. We can't exactly pin it to the wall with tacks, can we.

How much do you expect that to cost?

For a piece that size? It would likely come to three hundred, four hundred dollars. Will that be a problem?

Actually. Honestly. I am having a bit of a cash-flow, uh,
situation. My dad . . . and I don't know if you've heard about
what's going on in our building.

No I haven't, she said, and it was clear she didn't care to. Right. Well, generally speaking, just for your own edification, it is customary for artists to cover the cost of framing their own work. There are exceptions of course, but.

I was quiet. I had less than a hundred dollars to my name. I wouldn't get my next check from Summerland until February 1 but that would only be another couple hundred at most. If I could pick up some substitute teaching and pick up a few shifts at the 24-Hour Photo I might be able to make three or four hundred. . . .

Okay! So I'll transfer you back to Jessie then. Hang on—

Fiona—would it jeopardize my piece being in the show if I told you I couldn't afford that?

Well. Not exactly. We can do it, and then we'll just take it out of the final price of the piece if and when it sells. After commission and pricing you'll end up getting less than fifty percent of the final profit. Of course if it doesn't sell you'll still owe us that fee. But! It's a great piece. And we have some very loyal buyers. I can think of two or three buyers actually, just top of mind, who might take a real interest.

You can?

It's a question of pricing, I think. We'll set it low enough so that people feel comfortable taking a chance on an unknown, but high enough that they really feel they're getting something special. And since it's just the one piece, not an edition—

I wanted to talk about that, actually. So you returned the slide and the test print—

Yes, I'm sorry, Lu. We're not able to keep things like slides around here. I wouldn't want them to get lost in the shuffle. You understand.

The thing is though. I was thinking—since it is not an edition it will be more valuable, right?

Well, theoretically. Although really that sort of thing is more of an issue with more, you know, established artists.

I'm going to destroy the slide.

Why would you do such a thing?

To increase the value.

I told her what I'd told Casper Alvarez, more or less. I talked about the artificiality of the art market, the devaluation of photography. She cut me off.

Lu, that's not . . . I would caution against taking that kind of approach.

Can I give it back to you then? Can you make an exception?

I make it a policy not to be responsible for my artists' source materials and other valuable things. Being responsible for the work itself is one thing. But if I start keeping things like slides and test prints, where do I draw the line? Where does the gallery stop and the storage facility start? We're really running out of space around here. It's kind of a dire situation in fact. We have a storage unit uptown that is absolutely packed. Besides which it brings up all kinds of other issues. I don't want an artist knocking on my door in the middle of the night because she's had a fit of inspiration and has to print a series of a hundred *right now*. For example.

Fiona, with respect, I have to get this slide out of my house. I cannot have it around.

Look, why don't we just wait and see how the large print sells, and if it turns out to be a popular piece and the price is right we can talk about a series?

No. I don't think so. I don't think so. No. I think it's just going to have to be this one photograph. I'm going to destroy the slide.

Good grief, Lu, this is all rather dramatic. I don't know if you grasp the magnitude of the opportunity you're facing right now.

I can't burn it. I can't let that happen again. Maybe I'll throw it in the river.

Why! Why?

Because he's haunting me.

What?

He's haunting me, Fiona! Max is haunting me.

Fiona exhaled slowly. There was a long pause. I listened to her breathing. I felt her weighing her options, deciding how to direct the conversation, how to proceed. The bruise in the back of my head throbbed with each beat of my heart. I considered telling her more, telling her how real he was. But I couldn't take that risk.

I'm sorry, she said at last, I hadn't really considered how awful this must be for you. You must feel terribly. Close as you are with Kate and Steve.

I do.

How did they take it when you told them?

Here was a question for which I was unprepared.

You did tell them. Didn't you?

Of course. Kate's my closest friend.

How did she take it?

She. Was shocked. She was emotional. She looked at the image a long time. Eventually though she told me that she understood that the image of the falling boy is a separate and distinct thing from the son she loves and remembers. She told me she appreciated what I was trying to do. She has a great eye, you know. She can see it's a terrific photograph.

And as your closest friend, she wants the best for you, I'd imagine.

My throat closed up. Yes, I managed.

Well. That all sounds positive.

It was.

Good then.

Yes.

All right. Well, Jessie has drawn up your contract. You don't have a fax machine, do you?

No.

Why don't you come in then to look over and sign the paperwork. And when you do come in, feel free to bring the slide. I'll let Jessie know we'll be making an exception for you. And, Lu? I'm sorry I wasn't more sensitive to the nature of this work. Forgive me. You seem like such a tough cookie. It never occurred to me how much this whole nightmare might be plaguing you.

Inside my studio the baby rats squeaked like tiny chew toys. Thank you, I said.

All right, Lu. See you soon. Happy New Year.

I had taken the phone from my ear and was just about to hang up when I heard her voice, small and tinny in the earpiece: Oh, and, Lu?

Yes?

We're changing the title.

What do you mean?

Self-Portrait #400 doesn't do anything for the work. We're changing the title.

I was reluctant, baffled. But *Self-Portrait #400* is what it is, I said stupidly. It's the four hundredth in a series.

If I take you on and there's demand, perhaps we'll alter it again, she said. For the sake of the spring show, it will have a stand-alone name.

A self-portrait a day for four hundred days, though. It was such a long series. Isn't that some kind of accomplishment? Doesn't that say something about my work? About me?

Lu, as far as I'm concerned, those three hundred ninety-nine days were your basic training. The day you took this photograph? That was the big game.

I didn't know what to say.

What are you changing it to? I asked at last.

Self-Portrait with Boy.

I called my dad.

He answered on the fourth ring with a clatter in the background and a shout: Damn it to hell!

Dad, I said.

Ah, hi, I just. Goddamn it!

What happened?

I knocked over the. I don't know. There was a plate or something on the counter and I knocked it.

What do you mean a plate or *something*?

Don't know *what* it was!

Dad.

And now it's. God*damn* it! All over the goddamn floor. I got to call you back, pal.

Dad. Hang on. Calm down. You couldn't see it? You mean you still can't see?

Well, I.

Quiet. Breathing.

Oh, Toby.

They say it takes some time, he said weakly. To recover.

Not this long! Let me call the doctor.

No need.

Let me call the doctor, Dad, and find out what—

No, Lu.

Some kind of *cure*, there's got to be—some kind of *balm*?—an operation—

I'm not going in for another goddamn operation!

If it's about the money I can make it back.

I'm an old man, kiddo. Let it be.

I felt my face crumple. I took off my glasses so as not to get them wet. It's not right, I said. That doctor, Jesus. People sue over this sort of thing.

We're not going to sue.

I listened to the mewling baby rats. I rubbed my eyes.

Hey, he said at last. Why'd you call? His tone was tender.

I wiped my nose, put my glasses back on, and took a breath. How do you get rid of rats?

Rats are so intelligent. When you have an infestation you have to get them used to eating from the traps before you set them, to trick the rats into thinking that they're safe.

I had just one adult rat that I knew of, plus her brood. I

went out and bought a trap and a box of latex gloves like a pre-meditating murderer. I baited the trap that night with peanut butter, but didn't set it. In the morning the peanut butter was gone. I baited it again and left for work. When I came home the bait was gone. I baited it a third time, and set it.

In the middle of the night I woke up to her screaming. The sound she was making was like a tiny child. Her screams awoke her babies and they all started squeaking in response. I stumbled up from bed and found her. Her bald tail and one hind leg were caught and clearly broken. She thrashed her head and front legs, panicking. I watched her, panicking myself. Now what? Toby had not prepared me for this. The trap was supposed to kill her.

I retrieved a bucket from the bathroom, turned it upside down, and put it over her, a junky bell jar. Her weird screams echoed inside the plastic cylinder. Then I put on a pair of latex gloves and pulled open the thick fabric curtain of my darkroom, gagging on the stench in there. On the floor the bald pink babies were crawling blindly toward their mother. I tried the tap of the darkroom sink. The water was on, thank god. I plugged the drain, filled the basin, and picked up one scrambling animal. I dropped it into the water, where it flailed and splashed. I picked up another and dropped it in too. Soon the sink was full of tiny squealing baby rats. My heart pounding, I pushed their heads under the water. One by one I drowned them.

Once, walking by the river on a morning thick with mist, I saw a fleet of pink blots bobbing on the surface of the water. I was not wearing my glasses and at first I thought they were a school of massive sea creatures—who knew what kind—belly-up, all dead. Putting on my glasses I saw that they weren't slick like fish but tufted, cotton-candy fuzzy. Someone upriver had dumped a bunch of fiberglass insulation into the water—quite illegally of course—and it was floating out to the Atlantic. This visual memory is what I hung on to as I fished the small dead blots out of my darkroom sink and dropped them into a garbage bag. I could not let myself believe that they were animals.

At last I returned to the mother rat under the mop bucket. Using a broom as a kind of awkward shovel I tilted the bucket and pushed her into it, trap and all. She clawed wildly at the plastic walls around her. I felt as if she knew what I had done. I'm sorry, I whispered down at her. She was a large and dirty creature, restless nose and whiskers. For one crazy moment I thought: Maybe I could keep her. Maybe I could make this feral animal my own. A desperate pet for a desperate woman.

That would have been insanity, of course. But I also could not drown her among her own dead babies. I set the bucket underneath the tap in the bathtub. The trap would weigh her down, I figured. She would not swim. I turned it on. With the first drop of cold water she flipped out, turning herself over and over, clutching at nothing, squeaking. I hurried out of the room, closing the door on her pathetic noises, which rose in volume and agitation, then ceased.

||||‌ ||||‌ ||||‌ ||||‌ |||

I t is hard to say in retrospect whether or not we knew our
last tenants' meeting was going to be our last. It was certainly a sad affair. It was late in the day in early February.
The clouds were dark, the skyline bright. Kate and Steve and
Erika Kau and I were up in the so-called Penthouse, drinking
Budweisers that Steve had brought. Cora Pickenpew had put
out nothing. It was an emergency meeting. The source of the
stink had been found.

Steve and Erika told us the story with teenaged enthusiasm, cutting each other off to interrupt and take over, to verify
or amplify or interject various details. Apparently earlier that
week they'd made it their mission to suss it out. They explored
the whole building top to bottom and determined it must be
coming from below. As Bob Maynard had a key to the freight
elevator, they'd decided to break into his place.

You could have used *my* key, Cora said, bemused.

Erika glanced at me. Was her expression a little guilty?

Hadn't she said something about Bob owing her money when I'd run into her in the stairwell with Nancy Meister's chair? I wondered whether she'd had an ulterior motive.

Erika lived next door to Bob. They had brought a long ladder out to Erika's fire escape, which was maybe ten, twelve feet from Bob's, and laid it over the tops of both iron railings. They lashed it to the railing on Erika's side with rope. The men in Erika's family were all marines, she added. She could tie an excellent knot.

Cora was listening with bright-eyed anticipation, inter-jecting a campy gasp here and there at the appropriate times. Kate was watching her husband coldly, clutching her beer can with both hands. She looked as if she'd heard this story before. If she'd had anything to say about how Steve had put her in danger of losing both members of her nuclear family the same way, she'd already said it. Now her mouth was pressed tightly closed.

So, they continued, as Erika held the ladder steady from her own fire escape, Steve began to shimmy across the divide, making his way slowly over the three-story gap.

Jesus Christ, Kate exploded, you couldn't have broken his lock or something?

Steve grinned and swigged his beer. It was more fun this way, babe.

Safe on the other side he jimmied open one of Bob's back windows, knocking a collection of empty bottles to the floor in the process. He made his way to the front door and opened it for Erika, and they hunted through Bob's abandoned loft for the key to the freight elevator.

Incidentally, Erika added, Bob left behind some good shit. I got an eight-year-old bottle of Scotch out of this.

Cora laughed. Are you sure he's not coming back?

Where *is* Bob anyway? I said. No one answered. They found the key on a hook by the door—

You could have just used *my* key, Cora repeated.

—and took the freight elevator down from the third-floor storage space. With every floor they descended the stink became stronger. They were definitely on the right track. Rodents scrambled as they opened the gate to the dark basement. They stepped into a lake of inch-high, half-frozen stagnant water and a thick layer of stinking smoke. The odor was so wretched it stung the backs of their throats. In the middle of the space was a gas grill and on the bare ruined grate was what had once been a fish. The animal was rotten now, its bones exposed as its flesh had burned and decayed. Flies teemed in the smoke. Coughing and covering their mouths with their shirts they sloshed through the slush and turned off the gas. They slid the rotting fish into a plastic bag and threw it in the Dumpster outside, then carried up the grill and left it on the curb.

You really shouldn't have left it there, said Cora when Steve and Erika were done. You could get a ticket for dumping. We could all be fined.

Who the fuck cares? said Erika Kau. We got it out of here, didn't we?

The real question, said Steve, is who left it down there? This was an act of aggression, no question. That grill and that fish were down there for days. For a week, even. Whoever planted it *meant* to make a stink. They *meant* to make it even more unbearable for us to live here. They're trying to push us out.

It's got to be the new landlord, said Erika.

Kate said, I completely agree.

Who *is* the new landlord? I asked.

Pinnacle Partners, said Erika—and at the same time Kate said: Wayne Salt.

I raised my eyebrows questioningly.

Steve laughed. Does she live under a rock?

Cora said: Wayne Salt, who founded Pinnacle, is one of the biggest real estate developers in New York right now. Great patron of the arts.

Patron of the arts my ass, said Steve. Wayne Salt negotiated down the price of one of my paintings so far I barely got a dime.

Kate said, Wayne Salt owns this building in TriBeCa where a friend of ours lived since the seventies. Since the neighborhood has been improving lately, he's been raising the rent. When artists can't afford it anymore, they move out and he renovates their lofts. Sometimes to speed up the process, our friend told us, his lackeys pull the same kind of shit over there that they're pulling around here. Locks and windows are mysteriously broken; there's graffiti on the artists' doors. Now that building is chock-full of yuppies paying a thousand dollars a month. Of course, there's never any graffiti on *their* doors. Our friend was priced out of there last year.

She also got a half-a-million-dollar buyout, said Steve. She bought a farmhouse in Rhinebeck. So she's doing just fine.

My point is, said Kate, it's got to be Pinnacle that planted the fish. Who else could it be?

Cora said, My lock was broken last week.

Erika said, Someone broke into my place and destroyed some of my work.

No! I exclaimed.

Yeah, said Erika. This bowl, this enormous bowl. It was like sixty pounds, clay. It had twelve layers of glaze. I worked on that thing for weeks. It could have sold for several thousand. Someone broke in and just smashed it. I'm still finding shards of clay all over the floor.

Erika, said Kate, I'm so sorry.

Erika shook her head heavily. The fucking price we're paying.

Cora said, Maybe we should look into installing an alarm system.

Steve said, To keep out our own landlord? How long would that last?

And how long are we staying? Kate added. Is it worth it to install an alarm system to be safe for a matter of months?

Erika said: I don't know how long *you're* staying but they're not going to drag *me* out of here till I'm dead.

There was a knock on the door and Cora floated away to answer it. Kate leaned in toward the rest of us after Cora was out of earshot and whispered: Did you hear that? *Great patron of the arts?* I'd bet money she's already in negotiations.

And not telling us? said Erika.

I'd bet on it.

Cora reappeared with Philip Philips. He helped himself to a beer and announced: Big news, everyone! Baby got a buyout!

There was murmuring of congratulations all around. Kate clapped. I said: How did you do it? What happened?

I'd had enough, he said. Enough. The stink, the broken locks. It used to be a beautiful place to live. Far away from everyone and everything. A spacious gorgeous getaway. People would come over, they'd say, *I didn't even know this neighborhood existed! Oh my god, the view is amazing!* Now it's hideous. Every day is some new trial. The day we had no more hot water, no more heat, that was bad. The day I found roaches in the kitchen, rats under the bed? That was worse. But *squatters* in the storage space? Strange men shooting up outside my door? The midnight visit from the FD? All of us standing outside shivering, being subjected to these arbitrary laws? No. No! This was our home. I was helping Tammy pack up her things and I had a motherfucking revelation. I realized: I can *leave.* I realized: I can *refuse* to live like this. I can *refuse* to be humiliated in my own home. So I marched right up to Pinnacle Partners' offices in the Heights. This cute little yellow clapboard house. I talked to the boy behind the desk. I said, I demand to speak to Wayne Salt. He said, that's perfectly fine but Wayne's not in today. I said, I know how you people work. I demand a buyout. He said, we can give you two thousand dollars. Cool as can be. Didn't even bat an eyelash. I said, I'm sorry but that will not be enough. For this pain and heartbreak, for this fear and aggravation? No. I said, ten thousand or I'm going to the police. He said, I think you'll find what we're doing here is perfectly legal. I said, the broken locks? The sub-standard living conditions? He looked right at me and said, and I quote: *Sir, I think you'll find what we're doing here is perfectly legal. But as you know, offering buyouts is standard practice. I can give you six thousand.*

Way to go, Philly! said Kate.

My heart was beating so fast, Philip said, I was so nervous! But I have the check right here in my wallet, it's here in my wallet and it's real.

Nice work, said Erika.

You could have gotten more, said Steve.

Don't be rude, said Kate.

I'm just saying, Steve repeated: He could have gotten more.

Kate said: Philip just had the chutzpah to walk in there and demand what he wanted and he comes back feeling like he's really accomplished something and you have to go and tear him down.

Philip said, It's all right, Katie.

How do *you* know he could have gotten more? Erika said to Steve.

Because Maynard got twenty.

Bob Maynard got twenty thousand dollars? I said.

Sure did.

That motherfucker, said Erika.

How do you know? Kate repeated.

He told me.

When? said Kate rather aggressively.

I ran into him at Kiki's.

Bob was at Kiki's? said Kate.

Sure. They're old friends. We chatted, caught up. He said they offered him fifteen initially; he talked them up to twenty.

They *offered* him fifteen? I said.

How did he negotiate? said Philip. What leverage did he have?

He offered to move out quietly and not tell any of us how much he got.

But he told you, said Philip.

Erika added: And you told us.

I don't owe that guy anything, said Steve. I don't owe *them* anything either. Fuck them. And fuck him. This is war. You understand that, right? We are at war. We can't afford to be *nice* here. We can't afford to be *polite.* Steve shot a look at Kate. When there are thousands of dollars on the line we've got to be looking out for us and our own. Knowledge is power. You could have gotten more.

I just wish you'd told me before I went over there, said Philip quietly.

Should have said something before you left, said Steve.

You should have said something as soon as you got back from Kiki's, Kate exclaimed. That was last week!

All right, Cora said, all right. I don't know about all of you but I have somewhere to be tonight and I've got to get dressed.

We filed out of the Penthouse in a collectively sour mood. How much could I get, I wondered? The longer one stayed, theoretically, the bigger the buyout. Erika Kau was playing the long game. Maybe if I played the long game too I could make out with enough to quit working at Summerland and the 24-Hour Photo and take some time to look for a real job, a job I cared about, a job I could be proud of. Enough to pay Toby's ophthalmologist in one swoop. Not that the guy deserved it. Enough to make a down payment on a place of my own, with a darkroom that was actually a room.

I pulled open the fire door to the fourth floor and was met with the stench of excrement. I stopped short in the doorway. I could hear heavy congested breathing. I waited for my eyes to adjust to the dark.

It was not the same man I'd seen in Tammy Day's place a month and a half before. It was another man—larger, with a deep cut over one eye. He was lying down asleep with his back to the wall. A syringe lay beside him.

I almost laughed. Everything had become so insane. Get up! I yelled. Get out of here! This is my house! Get out!

He craned his head over his shoulder and half opened his eyes, squinted in my direction. In a foggy voice he said, It's my house now.

It is not, I said. Get the fuck up and get the fuck out of here or I'll call the cops.

He let out a wheezing laugh. The cops, he repeated.

I will, I'll call the fucking cops, I said. Get out of my house.

Girly, he said, rolling over slowly, propping himself up on one elbow. If this *your* house, why they paying *me* to be here?

What?

He pressed up onto his hands and knees and staggered slowly to his feet. He was at least a foot taller than me. I stood where I was, determined not to be afraid.

If this *your* house, he said again, why they *paying* me to be here?

The smell was overwhelming. He stood there a moment, wavering a bit—and then with a startling bark like the *woof* of a massive dog he lunged at me. Without a thought I turned and raced back upstairs.

I stopped at Steve and Kate's floor and knocked urgently, heart beating hard. A minute later the door opened and there was Steve, a glass of whiskey in his hand.

Can I come in? I said.

He frowned at me.

There's a squatter in my hallway and he just barked at me. He *barked* at me.

Steve stepped back so I could enter. It is truly the end of days, he said.

I'm not saying it's the end of days, I said, I'm just saying I didn't want him to fucking bite me.

Is he human? said Steve.

Far as I can tell, I said.

Sometimes it's difficult.

He took a shit in there.

So you got scared and ran up here to cry to Mama Katie.

Do I look like I'm crying? I said.

Steve took a sip of his drink and smirked.

Is she here? I said.

She's indisposed. He looked away. I heard muffled staggered crying coming from the bedroom. He said, Some people have bigger problems.

I would never dream of comparing her problems or your problems to mine.

His icy expression melted. I'm just giving you shit, Lu. You know that, right? Let me get you a drink. What do you want?

I said, Whatever you're having.

He poured me a whiskey and we went out to the living area, where I'd sat with Kate that first night. Steve put on a record—some band I didn't recognize, droning and atonal and tense—and lit a joint. He offered it to me but I declined. There was something about him that made me feel I should stay on my toes.

I said: He said he was being paid to be here.

Who? said Steve.

The squatter. The barking junkie.

He said he was being paid? Who's paying him?

I didn't have time to fucking interview the guy.

Steve inhaled. The joint crackled. Those motherfuckers, he said. I fucking hate this place. It gives me the creeps. On top of everything—the cold, the vermin, the homeless—it gives me the fucking creeps. He leaned forward and looked me in the eye. It feels haunted. Know what I mean?

Hesitantly, I nodded.

He leaned back again, annoyed. *You* don't know what I mean. How could you know?

I sipped my whiskey. What does it feel like?

Like he's just around the corner. Like no matter where I am in the fucking building he's just around the corner from me. Some nights I have to walk around the loft four, five, six times, sometimes ten or fifteen times, just to put myself at ease. I keep thinking: *The next corner I turn there he'll be.*

Do you ever see him?

He looked at me a long time, taking a slow inhale from the joint. See who? he said at last.

Oh, I said. Who were you talking about?

He exhaled. My son.

Yeah. Okay. Me too.

Do I ever *see* him? The fuck does that mean?

Never mind.

Of course I never see him. He's dead.

Sorry, I said.

Slow inhale. Slow exhale.

Keep thinking I'm going to though. Keep thinking I will. Keep *feeling* him. That's why I have to keep walking around. Around and around just to see. I had this thought: If I installed a bunch of mirrors, if I could just see the whole loft at once, maybe I could stay here. Maybe I could sleep. Know what I mean? A whole bunch of rearview mirrors so I could see every part of the space at once. Then I wouldn't have to keep patrolling the place. I even drew up a floor plan, tried to figure it out, whether with just the right setup I could see the whole loft at once. But it wasn't worth it. It doesn't work. With this layout you just can't. I don't know why Katie stays. I've been trying to get her to leave with me for ages.

Why won't she go? I asked.

Who knows, he said, but his expression darkened. Doesn't want to be alone with me, probably.

I am not a natural conversationalist, but this scenario was particularly taxing. You've been staying with your parents? I asked at last.

I was, he said. I was. But not very long. To be honest I couldn't fucking handle them for more than a couple of months. My parents drive me fucking nuts. No, a few years ago we got this summer place out in Pennsylvania, by a lake. It's not totally insulated but there's a wood-burning stove that heats things up pretty well and the kitchen and bedroom are fine. I'm just holed up there alone right now. Days go by when I don't talk to anyone at all. I mean I talk every day or two to Katie on the phone. I've gotten to know the locals. Couple of guys who go to the bar in town; the guy who sells firewood. But mostly I just draw. I've been drawing a lot lately. My work is totally different these days. I'm just drawing my son. From memory. I'd say it's therapeutic but it isn't. It's the opposite of therapeutic in fact. It's like cutting into a scar over and over every fucking time. Instead of helping me remember him it makes me realize how fast I have forgotten. It's amazing how quickly the brain forgets. Like I was trying to draw his eye, right? And I have in my mind a feeling of that eye. I know what that eye feels like. I remember the gestalt of it, you know? The way it moved and how I used to feel when I looked at it and how the lashes felt up against my cheek—

He stopped. He dropped his head. He stayed very still like that. I was afraid he was going to cry or fall asleep. After what seemed like a long time I leaned forward and opened my mouth to ask him if he was all right but before I could say anything he raised his head and continued where he'd left off.

—but I don't remember how it looks. I can't remember what it looks like. It's the weirdest fucking thing, man. It's so fucking frustrating. I'm *known* for my draftsmanship. I can draw anything from life. But from memory? Forget it.

He took a last drag of the joint and put it out in an ashtray.

It's peaceful though out there. No sirens. No honking horns. No fucking junkies in the hall.

He laughed, then laughed some more, then looked at me and laughed even harder.

Fuck, he said. That's the fucking funniest thing I've ever heard in my life. He took a shit in the hallway. And then he barked at you. He *barked* at you!

I had to smile.

He rose, still laughing, and went into Max's room, where he retrieved a blanket and pillow. The pillow was in a Teenage Mutant Ninja Turtles pillowcase. The blanket was printed with different kinds of vehicles: cars, trucks, trains, and planes.

She'll probably kill me for giving you these, he said. But I don't know what else we've got or where it is.

Thanks, I said.

You can sleep on the couch, he said. We'll kill that junkie in the morning.

I must have looked alarmed.

Kidding, man.

I woke in the early light to a figure standing just feet away from me. I felt for my glasses on the floor beside the couch. It was Kate, her hand over her mouth, her unbrushed hair glowing in the winter sun. I started to get up but she gestured for me to stay put and sat down on the edge of the couch. She put her hand on the blanket and touched each truck and train as the tears spilled over her lower lids and ran down her cheeks and nose. Overwhelmed she lay down beside me and took me in her arms. She was taller than I was and so thin. When she held my head to her neck, held my body to her body, and cried, I submitted to her completely. I let her crush my face, my glasses, my nose. I let her wet me with her tears.

I knew she did not love me, not really. I knew that to her I was just a puzzle piece that had to be forced to fit. And yet as she held me too close, squeezed me hard enough to bruise my ribs, as she cried into my hair, as her tears pooled in my ears I felt: this is what it is like to be loved.

Kate told me so much about Max that morning. And other mornings. And late some nights after a bottle of wine. Sometimes in the afternoon around three or four p.m., when she would have been coming home with him from school, she'd knock on my door and tell me more. She told me he'd been tall for his age, nearly as tall as I was. She told me she was irrationally proud of that because it was something that he'd clearly inherited from her, not Steve. She told me that one summer in Teaneck he'd caught a bunch of fireflies and put them in a jar. But he had neglected to puncture the jar's lid and so the next morning all the fireflies were dead. Grave with regret he buried them one by one in the sand at the edge of the driveway.

She told me he collected rubber balls, that he had nearly a hundred of them and that it was his joy to bring them out into the stairwell and throw them all at once, hard as he could, and watch the chaos. She told me that when he was three years old he'd had a nightmare about something called the Glub Glub Guy and woken up screaming, inconsolable. The Glub Glub Guy haunted his dreams for years after that, she told me. He had another nightmare when he was four, another when he was five. Six was all right but he had two more dreams about the Glub Glub Guy at seven. When she'd asked him to describe the Guy a look of horror had come into his eyes and he'd said: *Fish man with claws and teeth.*

She told me that in first grade he'd had a crush on a girl named Rachelle. They'd run around playing Ghostbusters, zapping ghosts with cardboard poster tubes. But in second grade Rachelle got a little girlier and when he wanted to ghost bust with her she told him he was dumb. He replied that she was fat and bad at running and that made her cry. It was his first and only breakup.

She told me about the time he sprained his wrist flying off the jungle gym in Pierrepont Playground. She told me that although he couldn't concentrate for five minutes in school he could spend hours wandering through the dinosaur skeletons at the Museum of Natural History. She told me that when he was born, for months she'd felt more distant from, not closer to, Steve—until one morning when Max was six months old and she'd walked in on the two of them napping together. She'd fallen in love with Steve all over again that day, more powerfully than before. She told me all of this and more and despite so many opportunities, despite her candor with me, I never told her about the photograph I'd taken. I never told her about the visits I was paid by her dead son.

I have spent these many years trying to explain to myself why not. The gallery show was already in motion. There would be no going back. Kate and Steve would not have been able to prevent Fiona from showing the work, not really. I could have told them, *I have this image. It is going to be shown. I thought you should know.* I could have dealt with the consequences, whatever they were: the shock, disgust, fury, all of it. I was not too weak to face any consequence. I was strong. Bullheaded, even.

Maybe I never told them because I imagined that if they did ask Fiona not to show the work she would have done as they wished, a favor to good friends. Maybe I feared what would happen if word went around that I—*an unknown,* in Fiona's words—had done such a thing to such a cool impressive figure as Steve Schubert. I might have been excluded far longer, perhaps forever, from the world of which I wanted so desperately to be a part.

Yet I must have known that the art world loves a scandal. If they'd told Fiona and she'd agreed to take the piece out of the show, someone else would have taken it, if only for the story. I'm sure of that now.

Maybe I never told them because I was afraid that if I did they would finally begin to see what Steve expected to see around every corner. Maybe I suspected that Max would torture them the way whatever he'd become had tortured me. Maybe I felt that with my silence I could contain him. Maybe I knew that if I told Kate about those visits she would stop at nothing to try to see him herself. Maybe I felt I could protect her.

But as much as I would like to say that that was it, my silence does not feel that noble. It feels cowardly.

More likely I never told them because my guilt and greed ate away my spine. More likely I was afraid that if I told her Max had been visiting me, Kate would resent me.

Most likely I wanted to preserve that feeling of being loved a little longer.

spring

┼┼┼┼ ┼┼┼┼ ┼┼┼┼ ┼┼┼┼ ‖‖‖

I t was just recently, just a year or two ago, that I discovered Pinnacle Partners had renamed my old home. I'd driven down to DUMBO with Franke for a book launch. The independent bookstore where the party was held had new brushed-steel detailing and floor-to-ceiling windows. The coffee table books on sale were displayed as preciously as sculpture. I turned to Franke's friend. I said, I thought the publishing industry was dying? How do they afford this place?

She rolled her eyes. You know Pinnacle Partners?

I said, There's a name I haven't heard in years.

Wayne Salt gave these guys a deal. They pay a fraction of market value; in exchange they make the neighborhood look good to billionaires and multinational corporations. You know the Italian shoestore down the street? For years they got that space essentially rent-free.

The next day while Franke was doing some research at Columbia I wandered New DUMBO alone. It was a beautiful spring day. Coffee shops offered homemade Pop-Tarts and nitro iced coffees. Boutiques sold linen T-shirts and satin trucker hats. There was a doggie day care where trainers would teach your animal sign language and a day care for children where your progeny could learn Mandarin. There was a store that sold records on vinyl and kitschy Japanese toys. The only place I recognized was a Mexican restaurant around the corner from 222 River Street, which had clearly upped its game. Micheladas, palomas, and jalapeño margaritas appeared on the menu. An eager sign on the door read Open Late! Good for them. A sandwich board outside a tapas bar across the street advertised an art exhibition. I went in to take a look at the work. On the walls hung a series of collages: magazine photographs surrounded by wreaths of mixed media, then shellacked. Dolly Parton in a nest of colorful rhinestones. RuPaul embedded in silks and gauze. Richard Nixon in a sunburst of little dildos. Irony and camp can make any dumb idea seem clever.

On Jay Street I found a storefront for a real estate agency and went in. It was seventy degrees outside but they had the air-conditioning on at full blast. On a table near the door were laid out ten or twelve glossy brochures. I picked one up and flipped through the pages of high-res photos, architectural renderings, and ad copy.

A visit to The Boerum is a trip back in time. Take a ten-minute walk to where Whitman penned Leaves of Grass. *Drift down the street to pick up one of the best baguettes in America. With in-unit washer-dryers, solid oak floor-*

ing, and European fixtures and finishes, The Boerum imports the past into the present for that authentic Old New York feel.

Who wrote this shit? Wasn't *authentic feel* a contradiction in terms? I picked up the next one.

Steps away from Brooklyn Bridge Park, in the epicenter of Brooklyn's flourishing arts-and-culture community, 99 Bridge Street is packed with the world-class amenities you require. Caesarstone countertops, preinstalled solar shades, and tons of closet space mean one thing: luxury. 99 Bridge. At the hub of the vibrant world you crave.

What actual New Yorker could take this seriously? The copy was appealing to an audience of tourists and foreign investors. Next:

If you're ready to take living to the next level, Be First! at Triple-Two Tower. Your new place in the luxury DUMBO building will put your friends' apartments to shame. On Triple-Two Tower's stunning roof deck, the only thing between you and the skyline is wind. Be First! to head over, scope it out, and make your move.

I scanned this last brochure to the bottom of the page and found the address. What do you know? It was called Triple-Two for its address: 222 River Street.

I waved at an agent who was sitting at a laptop at a perfectly clean white desk. Hey, I said, I'm ready to take living to the next level.

He laughed and got up. He was Korean, slight of shoulder, wide of smile. Terrific, he said. What kind of budget are you working with?

No budget.

He took in my scuffed boots. Huh, he said. Well, great.

We walked together toward the river and my familiar street. Though private companies had done all they could to transform the neighborhood, the city hadn't gotten around to paving over the potholes and broken cobblestone. If there hadn't been a row of luxury cars parked at the crumbling curb we might have been walking right back into 1992. But as we approached 222 I saw that its brick walls had been cleaned up and painted and a new door had been put in that was level with the sidewalk. A security guard nodded at us from behind a glass desk when we walked in. The real estate agent brought me to the second floor, where carpeted hallways contributed to my sense of disorientation. I could not tell which way we were facing or whose former space we were standing in. All the lofts, which had been a couple thousand square feet each, had been subdivided into studios of a few hundred feet or so.

Note the exposed brick, the agent told me. It's all original.

Uh-huh, I said. I knew it wasn't.

The studios *maximized space* with *lofted beds, concealed storage,* and *foldaway counter space.* It would never occur to the wealthy renters of such a place to wonder why space in a two-hundred-year-old warehouse would have to be *maximized.* To recognize that in fact their management had *minimized* square footage on renovation.

We went up to the roof so I could see the *stunning roof deck*. It was divided into small private areas and a larger communal space. The private areas were accessible by their own doors and set off from one another and from the rest of the roof with incongruous picket fences. Each featured a couple of matching patio chairs and a grill. They were small and antiseptic and strange, like poorly designed stage sets. The public area had a bigger grill, a semicircle of couches upholstered in some waterproof material—hue: inoffensive gray—and a stand-alone fireplace. The fireplace is gas, he told me. It gets nice and warm in the winter.

The edge of the rooftop was lined with a rib-high wall, punctuated by tiki torches. I wandered over and peered out at the view I thought I knew so well. It had changed, as everything had. Gleaming new developments rose up all around us. Where the boxy stalwart Twin Towers had been was now the Freedom Tower, that 1,776-foot-high Fuck You, phallic and shining in the American sun. It had taken a couple of decades, but Wayne Salt's vision had been realized.

I thanked my friendly real estate agent and told him I was looking for something with a more *authentic feel*.

||||| ||||| ||||| ||||| |||||

Somehow despite the pestilence and squatters, despite the fact that most of my neighbors had left or would soon leave, I stayed at 222 River Street months longer.

I was not the last to go. Cora Pickenpew held out for nearly a year and got a hundred thousand dollars in buyout money, or so I heard. Erika Kau was the very last. She hung on through the bitter end. In the great battle of River Street she was the last survivor. A late casualty in the war between art and real estate. The demolition crews came in and still she stayed. They began knocking down the walls around her and still she stayed. I picture her standing her ground as a wrecking ball swings toward her, bringing with it a wad of cash. And Steve—

Well. I won't get ahead of myself.

Spring made it easier to stay. The weather warmed early that year. By March there were buds on the trees and we could go outside in sweaters.

It was on a cool blue day when the trees still looked like

cracks in a windowpane that I took my favorite student, George Washington Morales, to the Cloisters. We went up on a Friday around noon. He said his math class was canceled and I didn't ask questions. After a few attempts at conversation, finding he'd give me nothing more than one-syllable answers, I stopped trying. We rode the train together in silence. George Washington spent the whole ride drawing on his pant leg in ballpoint pen.

Emerging into the light at the end of the hour-long subway ride we could feel the difference. The East River is not actually a river at all but a saltwater tidal strait, all quick dark current glistening under bridges and out to sea. In comparison the Hudson, a true glacial river, is vast and stately, surrounded on both sides by deep cliffs, its blue-green depths penetrated by long slips of sun. We made our way up the hill to Rockefeller's castle and I paid a dollar's donation for each of us. George Washington hunkered down to open his backpack and retrieve a sketchbook and pencil. I hung back, following his lead.

We went into a tall chapel first. It was empty except for a six-foot crucifix. Christ's head hung limp and his arms were thrust open wide. I stood in the doorway and watched as George Washington knelt down to sketch. He was the only person in the room and so small in the giant space, crouching there before the Christ, making his own kind of prayer. I had brought my Rolleiflex, the better to capture the colors and detail of the stained-glass windows. I held it at chest height and looked down into the viewfinder and focused in, adjusting the exposure so that more light could flood in from the peaked windows. It was beautiful.

We walked quietly through rooms full of relics, bones set in gold and ivory, supposed splinters from the cross preserved in vials encrusted with gems. We saw illuminated manuscripts and he stopped more than once to copy a shining letter, coiled with serpents or half concealed by lilies of the valley. We wandered through silent empty colonnades and dead little gardens. At last we found the Unicorn Tapestries, and George Washington Morales sat down on the carpet just to look.

I sat down beside him.

This shit is so *old,* he whispered almost reproachfully.

He needed no instruction in creating a composition. He started with the most complex tapestry, one of the hunting scenes, and made a light grid on the paper, then began to fill in the angles of the spears and unicorn horn just so. I got up and left him to his drawing. He would be a while, I could tell. I left the building to wait for him outside in the chilly sun.

I was wandering the perimeter of the wall when I encountered another woman alone. She was striking, with coarse hair, pale skin, and a large knobby nose. She was standing in the middle of the drive with a perplexed look on her face, staring up into a tree. I followed the direction of her wide light eyes. Above us, caught in the branches of a tree like a manifestation of sunlight itself, was a golden scarf.

She sensed my presence and looked down to see me watching her and laughed, revealing a set of long crooked teeth. I don't know how it happened! she exclaimed. Her voice was deep and she had an accent of some kind, though I couldn't tell from where. I was readjusting it, she said, and—*poof!* Up it went in a gust of wind. So strange!

Very strange, I agreed.

Now I am at a loss, she said. Shall I call the fire department? She laughed again. Scandinavian, I guessed—or German? Austrian? I wasn't much good at accents.

Do you have an umbrella? I asked.

No, she said, the weather is so beautiful today.

What we need is a long stick, I said. I went back to the edge of the drive and hunted for a few minutes among the shrubbery and grasses. She hunted too on the other side.

Will this work, do you think? she called, holding up a branch about four feet long.

I said, Worth a try.

She handed it to me as if it was completely natural to expect me to do it for her, though I was shorter than she was by a couple of inches. After I reached up and waved the branch around a bit, though, it was clear I'd continue to miss the scarf.

Here, she said, and when she took the branch from me I could smell her perfume in the eddying wind. Reaching up she was just able to graze the edge of the scarf. Its fringe hung tantalizingly.

Jump, I suggested.

She looked at me with those eyes and laughed again and her laugh drew back a curtain. I laughed too, suddenly able to see that the whole situation was the silliest thing in the world. I can't believe it, she said—and then, waving the stick above her head, she jumped, catching the scarf on the end of the branch at last.

I yelled an inadvertent cry of victory and she yelled too and we both laughed again, hard, standing there together hundreds of feet above the world. Suddenly self-conscious, I pushed up my glasses and turned to see George Washington Morales in his backpack and baggy scribbled jeans, standing at the bottom of the slope, watching us.

Her scarf got caught, I told him.

He didn't move or speak.

I gave her a little shrug. Well, I said. There you go.

Here we are, she replied, smiling. Those crooked teeth.

Unsure what else to say I turned to go. George Washington and I walked together down the slope. The whole way back to the subway I could feel her standing there behind us, watching us from the middle of the driveway.

My little field trip with George Washington Morales did not go unnoticed. The next time I was at Kings County Academy I was called into Gideon Isaac's office. He was standing with his back to the door when I went in. Do you know, he said—and as usual all I could think of when he spoke was Don Quixote and Rembrandt's (or not-Rembrandt's) *The Man with the Golden Helmet*. Do you know, Ru Lile, what would be the legal provisos were you to take a student under the age of eighteen off school grounds during the school day?

Lu Rile.

He spun around. *Je demande une réponse.*

Excuse me?

Do you know. Did anyone in this madhouse tell you. Anything. About the legal restrictions vis-à-vis removing an underage student from school grounds while he is supposed to be in school?

Ah, no.

Any fool can make a rule, and any fool will mind it. Thoreau. *The golden rule is that there are no golden rules.* George Bernard Shaw. And yet in our little castle on a hill we are beholden to several simple guidelines. We must feed the little demons, of course, and keep them warm in the winter, and provide running water so that they may wash their grubby hands. How do we do these things. How do we do these things, Ru Lile?

I . . . I'm not sure, sir.

Sir! Oh please. Call me Idion Guysaac.

I laughed nervously.

She doesn't know. Of course she doesn't know. How could she know? She is the quintessential starving artist. Look at her homemade haircut. She's never had two pickles to rub together. Isn't into pickles at all by the looks of her. Well, I'll tell you. We do it, my little destitute dyke—we do it, my little cash-strapped strap-on—by charging their parents boatloads of money. Not the parents of American Fabius Morales of course. But the parents of his cohort, certainly.

I was speechless. *Dyke?*

In the future, Petite Naive Ru, you will need a signature, a go-ahead from the Mr. and/or Mrs., if you are to remove a child from our unsavory tower. Is that clear?

I nodded.

That said! And yet! *Corvus oculum corvi non eruit.* We are birds of a feather. Far be it from this old corvid to pull out *your* raven eye. Honor among thieves, am I right?

I'm. I'm not sure, I fumbled.

She plays her cards close to her chest. What I mean is

Unheard-of combinations of circumstances demand unheard-of rules. Brontë—Charlotte, of course, that hussy. While your methods were questionable, the lengths to which you went—for art, for beauty, the quest for knowledge, the pursuit of context, for context is everything, don't you agree?—were admirable. Not since I founded this madhouse in 1969 have I seen such poetry in motion. That isn't true. My teachers are a brilliant, impulsive motley crew. Because they cannot stop for paperwork it kindly stops for them. So?

He was staring at me expectantly, his gray eyes dark. A thread of spittle wavered between his lips.

I'm sorry, I said, I don't follow.

Rubicon Lile! You are about to pass the point of no return! Hercu-Lu! You have slain the Nemean lion! Your first labor is complete! Do you understand? Are you picking up what I'm putting down? She is not a wordsmith, is she? More a smith of the silver salts. Perhaps she requires me to communicate in images. Shall I pantomime it to you, young photographer? Shall we play charades?

I don't think that's necessary—

What I'm saying, my young hero, is that you are one of us now. How would you like to join our faculty full-time, effective immediately?

Oh! You're offering me a job?

Yes, my snail. Yes, my tortoise. Be one of my lost boys. One of my orphans. One of my sprites.

I'd love to, I said.

He stepped back and rubbed his hands together happily. *Felix culpa,* eh?

Sure, I said.

Good. Go forth and prosper! You'll be making just pennies above minimum wage but the intellectual feast you'll gorge on is unmatched anywhere in this fine city. Plus you'll have health insurance! And three glorious months' vacation! *La vita è bella!*

I walked out of that meeting gratified, in glory. It was the second time I'd been rewarded for breaking the rules. I felt invincible. I felt like a predator. A she-wolf among sheep. I marched right down to the 24-Hour Photo and announced to the dwarf with the teardrop tattoo that, effective immediately, I was tendering my resignation. He looked at me as if we'd never met before. I never showed up again.

Quitting Summerland, though, was satisfying as hell. I still remember the grin I wore when I waltzed in. I remember making a beeline for Chad Katz, who was counting persimmons in Produce. I remember the awkwardness with which he took my resignation in stride, the relief in both our eyes, and the pure joy with which I waved good-bye and shouted to no one in particular: So long, suckers! Have a great life! Sam of the leased Jeep called out as I left: Been a pain in the ass working with you! Don't let the door hit you on your way out!

And yet the full-time gig at Kings County Academy did not come guilt-free. A year or so later I ran into Nancy Meister on the street outside the Strand. She was carrying a book on mediation. Her dog was waiting for her, lying on the curb, his leash tied loosely around a No Parking sign.

So you got my friend's job, she said.

I wasn't sure what she meant.

At KCA.

That's right, I said. Your friend. He was in the hospital. How is he now?

She said, He's dead.

I tried my best to make polite concerned conversation. I'm sorry, I said. Did he suffer?

He was sick for about six years. Had nine or ten bad months at the end.

I'm so sorry, Nancy, I repeated. At a loss I added, Thank you again for helping me out when I needed the job. I love it there.

A strange dismayed expression soaked into her face. Lu, I hope you appreciate how much my friend meant to those kids. I hope you appreciate how much you'll mean to them.

It. It means a lot to me that you'd tell me that, I said.

Don't let it go to your head.

What?

She lowered her voice. Lu, I *never* trusted you. I don't believe in letting my personal biases get in the way of my human relationships. We all struggle. We all try to be good people, as well as we can. But I *never* trusted you. The way you swooped in after that child died. The way you ingratiated yourself into Kate's world, Kate's life. You made her care about you.

She leaned closer in and pointed at me. I wouldn't say anything except for the sake of those kids, she went on. I've been teaching in the prison system for twenty-eight years. Take it from me: Any teacher needs clear healthy boundaries—but you? You need them more. Make this your mantra: *It's not about me.* Because it's not, Lu. It's not about you.

I remember her untying her dog and walking away. I remember feeling dizzy and blindsided. I remember riding home on the subway distracted by a wild superstitious feeling. The feeling of being cursed, or of being a curse. The guilt and horror of having benefited yet again from another person's death.

But that was afterward.

####### |||| |||| |||| |||| |||| |

The snow thawed to rain and the days were brighter, the skies brilliantly clear. Birds appeared to usher in the mornings with a cacophony of song, crocuses to sprout bluntly from the black dirt in gated gardens. Tiny bright green leaves budded on the bare-branched oaks and plane trees. The kids at Kings County Academy had a new manic sort of energy, were full of laughter and yelling, could not sit still, would not pay attention, and as the days stretched out into the evening hours time seemed counterintuitively to speed up, rocketing me toward April, and the opening.

In mid-March Fiona called and said they'd printed up announcements. Would I want any? I told her yes and went to the gallery to pick up a box of a hundred. They were large simple postcards with a grayscale image of someone else's work on the front. They read:

GRAVITY
Spring Group Show
2 April–11 June, 1992
Opening: 2 April, 6:30–9 p.m.

On the other sides of the cards was an alphabetical list of the featured artists. The list was surprisingly long, and justified on the left and right margins so that it filled the cards entirely. Most of the names I didn't know, though I did recognize a few. One I knew personally: Steve Schubert, of course.

I wish I could say it excited me to be featured in a group show alongside Steve and other artists I knew by reputation. In fact it unnerved me. I held the announcement and read it over. I felt dizzy and strange. I found my name and read it, then read it again, several more times. It didn't say Louise or Lulu or anything else. It read Lu Rile. It was spelled correctly. There hadn't been any crazy mistake. It hadn't all been some elaborate prank. And yet my heart was racing.

I called my dad. Martina answered. I could hear the voice of little Danny in the background, whining. She handed the phone over to Toby.

Well, well, well. What's the news from Tofu Town? Give me a minute—I got to get my good slacks. Don't want to greet the mayor in dungarees.

Actually I quit that job. I was just hired full-time at the school.

Oh ho, Professor Rile. I like the sound of that.

I'm not a professor.

Miz Rile then.

Mostly they just call me Lu.

Sure, sure. Just Lu. Nice work if you can get it.

Listen, Dad, I have another bit of good news.

Lay it on me. No, Martina, that's all right. Any more coffee and I'll get the jitters.

One of my photographs is going to be in a group show.

A group show.

At a gallery in Manhattan. A gallery with a really good reputation.

Is that so.

Yep.

How'd you pull that off?

It's a long story, I said.

Everything's coming up Lulu.

Ha-ha. Yes. Okay, but the thing is, Dad.

I told him I was worried. That some of the other artists in the show were relatively famous and I was intimidated. That the gallery hadn't formally taken me on and that my picture could really make a stir. I told him it was the best photograph I'd ever taken and I told him what it looked like in as much detail as I could. The vibrancy of the colors, the energy of the movement, the perfection of the composition, the death of Max Schubert-Fine. I told him about my friendship with Kate and about Steve Schubert's reputation, and how I'd gotten involved with the gallery in the first place. I wanted to tell him everything—but I didn't. One thing, maybe the biggest thing, I kept to myself: the fact that Kate didn't know about it.

When I stopped talking he took a deep breath of his own. Well, kiddo, he said. It sounds like a beautiful picture.

I wish you could see it, I said.

He made a vague sound, half regret, half assent.

Dad, I said. I hate to say it but I'm afraid. These people. They're rich. They're educated. They're mean. If this doesn't go well I could be worse off than where I started. It could destroy me.

Let me tell you a story, he said. When I was first dating your mother she brought me to her parents' house for dinner. They weren't well-off, the Okienkas, but they were educated as hell. Back in Czechoslovakia her father was a professor or something, I don't know. The word she used was *intellectuals*. They'd meet in the middle of the night where the government couldn't find them to discuss philosophy and revolution. Their English wasn't great. I guess because of that I'd thought maybe we'd be all right, maybe we'd meet in the middle. But all they wanted to talk about was books. Her father brought out a book of poetry and read from it, and he was so. There were tears in his eyes, real tears. It embarrassed me. I kept quiet the whole meal. I don't know squat about poetry. Poetry? You kidding me? I said I had indigestion. I left early and went home alone.

Holly never said a thing about that, never mentioned it at all. I was grateful to her for that. But she never brought me back there either. Two more years we were together. She never brought me back. I thought I'd disappointed her. Thought she was ashamed of me. Blockhead I am it took me years to figure out she wasn't the one who was ashamed. She could tell I was uncomfortable. She was trying to keep me safe. She thought it's what I wanted, not to be invited. Because I left.

What I'm saying, Lu: If you tell 'em you don't belong, they'll believe you. They won't ask you back.

I wound the curls of the phone cord around and around my index finger, considering his story. Considering this new image of the grandparents I never knew I had. A couple of Czech revolutionaries. Lovers of poetry.

Why have I never met them? I asked at last. Didn't they want to meet me?

He cleared his throat. He was quiet a long time. Didn't know about you, he said.

When I spoke again my voice was almost a whisper.

Why did she leave?

Oh, Lulu, I don't know. We weren't enough for her. What am I saying? That's a terrible thing to say. Truth is *I* wasn't enough for her. I'm not *sophisticated*. I wasn't going to be an *intellectual*. She was young. She was smart. And tough, so tough. She had her own dreams. She had a future. She was going to build something. She was going to do something great. Like you, Lu.

So I sent an announcement to Toby in his house on stilts, though I knew he wouldn't be able to read it. I sent an announcement to Martina, what the hell. I brought a stack of announcements to work with me at KCA and put one in each faculty member's mailbox, even the ones I didn't know. After much deliberation I taped two announcements, one frontways and one the other way around, to the inside of our own busted front door at 222 River Street.

The week before the opening I took the train to Century 21, seven floors of discount clothing downtown near the World Trade Center, to buy a dress for the occasion. I wanted to look good.

I browsed the racks for a long time. Around me women with long acrylic nails clicked through the hangers like pros. The long public changing room turned out to be just a bunch of mirrored doorless stalls. It was crowded with Hasidic mothers snapping at their miserable teenaged daughters, lipsticked older women fumbling with the zippers on skirt suits, thin Chinese twentysomethings wriggling into high-waisted acid-washed jeans. I stripped to my underwear and hung my street clothes from the hook on the wall. In front of my body—bony with unshaven legs—I held up a silver Calvin Klein. It was incongruous, certainly. I almost laughed. I didn't even try it on.

A dark blue, long-sleeved Betsey Johnson dress was all right but had a bunch of lace and nonfunctional buttons going on that put me off. I tried on a skintight dress that clung at the sides and smashed down my tiny tits, creating cleavage where cleavage had always been impossible—but it was embarrassing and I pulled it off without even looking at how it fit all around. I tried a black tank dress that worked great but cost over a hundred dollars and looked exactly like one of the two dresses I already owned.

The last of the bunch was a short silk olive-green number by some Israeli designer I'd never heard of. It was cut like a button-down shirt. I checked myself out in the mirror. Big black glasses and shaggy hair, skinny legs skinny arms skinny neck pretty dress. With its covered buttons down the front, no sleeves, and a collar like a men's dress shirt, it felt both masculine and feminine. I tried it with my boots. I rumpled my hair and took off my glasses and squinted at the blur of me.

Behind me a short big-breasted girl trying on a floral baby doll dress pointed to my mirror. With a Long Island accent she declared: You've got to buy that.

I turned around. Me?

Two stalls down a Hasidic woman and her daughter were having a passionate argument over a Chanel skirt.

Yeah, you, said the girl. Here, try it with my lipstick. She picked up her purse from the floor and rummaged through it. A heavy woman with an orange weave looked on with interest, adjusting her bra and slip.

I never wear lipstick, I said.

She retrieved the tube and held it out. Try it, she commanded.

I took the tube obediently and looked back in the mirror. The lipstick was bright pink and smelled like plastic. I put my glasses on and applied it carefully, then stepped back and looked at myself.

Hovering at my shoulder the girl in the baby doll dress said: See what I mean? She held out her hand and I dropped the tube into her palm.

She's right, said the woman with the orange weave. That's a good look for you.

It had become chaotic in the changing room. A new influx of people was on its way in and the attendants were trying to get us out. The baby doll turned away and was almost trampled in a stampede of septuagenarians whose arms were laden with off-season discount sweaters.

I turned toward the mirror as the crowd swelled behind me. I saw a woman who looked like a woman but I also saw myself. A strange but perhaps attractive person. Green silk and tumbleweed hair. Pink slash of a mouth that expressed both severity and amusement, determination and patience, familiar ugliness and unpracticed beauty. This was me. This was Lu Rile. I hadn't taken a self-portrait in months but now I lifted my Pentax from the hook on the wall where it hung with the rest of my things and focused it properly on the woman in the mirror, on myself. Then I raised it up—the Statue of Liberty raising her torch—and as the bewigged Hasid and her whining teenaged daughter argued behind me, and a changing room attendant shouted to get their attention, and the woman with the weave turned around to check out her rear end in the mirror, I pressed the shutter. This was me. Lu Rile, constant observer. Lu Rile, neither bad nor good. Lu Rile, eye of the storm.

The other thing about that dress was that it was relatively cheap. When I bought it I took that as a sign it was the perfect choice, but when I brought it home and tried it on again a few days before the opening I discovered that in fact it was cheap because it was damaged. A seam in the back was torn just below the zipper.

I tried a safety pin but it crimped and buckled the fabric. I nearly tried duct tape, my old cure-all, but worried it would damage the silk. I tried on my old black dress and found it lackluster. Beyond pulling heavy waxed thread loosely through emulsified paper I did not know how to sew. In the end I brought it upstairs to see if Kate could fix it.

She answered the door in dusty sweats and a ripped T-shirt, her hair pulled back. Lu, hi, she said, but her enthusiasm seemed forced. I asked if it was a bad time.

No no no, she said, come in. I am just in the middle of something. I'm just cleaning.

She was in the middle of cleaning out Max's room, it turned out. It was late afternoon and sunlight was pouring in through the west-facing windows. She had on the classical station WQXR. Strings and brass sang out Beethoven and in her resonant loft the music sounded almost wet. Outside the door to Max's room were two piles of toys, broken and intact; two piles of books, used and lightly used; two piles of laundry.

I can come back, I said. I'll come back.

No, she said, it's all right. This is good actually. It's needed to happen. I had an argument about it with Steve yesterday. I got frustrated with him going in and out of there all the time, treating it like just another room. He told me I was treating it like a shrine. No, not a shrine. What word did he use? Like a reliquary. He said when was I going to start moving on.

I thought of the relics in the Cloisters, splinters of wood in gem-encrusted vials. How people need their relics. That's a little harsh, I said.

I know, she said. I said look at *you*, you know? Are *you* moving on? Drawing his face over and over and over again? But then I thought maybe he's right. We're not going to be here forever. We probably won't be here very much longer at all. I've been putting off cleaning this room for months. If I leave it until the last minute I know it will feel like too much. Meanwhile there are all these perfectly good toys and clothes that aren't doing anyone any good just sitting in there. Maybe it will be a relief to give them to Salvation Army so some other kid can use them.

Her words were optimistic but her tone wasn't convincing. Sure, I said. Yeah.

Anyway, she said, it's something to do. It's keeping me busy. It'll get me out of the house. She nodded at the silk in my arms. What do you have there?

Do you know how to sew?

I know the basics.

I bought this dress for my opening but turns out it's ripped.

A dress! I don't think I've ever seen you in a dress.

I wear dresses sometimes, I said a little defensively.

She took it from me and held it out, inspecting it. Oh, that's easy to fix. Piece of cake.

She sat on the couch to mend my dress and I lay on the carpet in a warm pool of sun, hands behind my head. We didn't say much. We were listening to the music. We were companionable.

When she was done she held it out to me. Put it on, she said.

Now?

Of course now. I have to see how it falls.

I took it into her bathroom and changed and looked at myself in the mirror. *Puny* was the word that came to mind. Though I was no different from the person I'd been in the changing room mirror I suddenly felt supremely self-conscious. What had been simply skinny before now seemed like a cartoonist's caricature: scarecrow arms, lizard neck, stick-figure legs. I came out reluctantly, barefoot on the concrete, hyperaware of every hair on my body. Kate stood and put a hand to her chin, considering me.

Turn around, she said.

Is it too much? I said. It's too much, isn't it. It seemed like a good idea at the time but it was a mistake. I have a different dress I can wear instead.

Turn around, she repeated.

It's black, I said as I turned. It's much simpler. Less fussy.

I was facing away from her when I felt her hands on my back smoothing the silk from the top of the zipper to the bottom at the base of my spine. I exhaled quickly, involuntarily.

Stay there, she said. Let me just—

She grabbed her needle and thread and came back and without asking put one hand up the back of the dress. I could feel her draw the thread through the fabric, feel her thin arm between the fabric of my underwear and the fabric of the dress. The back of her hand on the small of my back. My skin prickled with goosebumps. I realized my mouth was open. I closed it.

All set, she said, standing.

I turned around again to face her.

She laughed at me—neighed, more like. What's the matter? she asked. You look terrified.

I do? I don't know. I guess I'm nervous, I said. About the opening.

Don't be nervous, she said. You've been working toward this for years. It's going to be a great night. And you look pretty.

I knew I didn't. Pretty was not a way I could look. But the word in her voice was a gift. I felt almost dizzy. My heart hurt. You don't have to come, I blurted.

What? she said. Of course I'm coming.

But you don't have to, I said. You really don't.

Lu, she said. It's going to be okay.

It might not, though, I said, it really might not. I felt almost as if I might cry. In fact, I said, don't come—please don't come—I don't want you to come—

Kate stepped toward me and put a hand on my shoulder and looked down at me kindly. Lu, she said. You are freaking out. Stop freaking out.

Okay, but don't feel like you have to come—

I am coming. I will be there. Steve has a piece in the show too, remember?

I exhaled. Right. Right.

Right, she echoed. So I will be there. And you will be there. And Steve will be there. And probably Phil will be there and maybe Tammy and Erika and Cora and Bob and maybe even some other friends. We'll all be there rooting for you. And the dress fits perfectly.

She kissed me on the top of the head as if I were a child. I went to the bathroom to change again and looked at myself in the mirror. Outside the door the music was playing and the sun was shining. Inside my face was flushed and I did look utterly terrified. You are an asshole, I told my reflection, and my reflection mouthed the same four words back at me.

|||| |||| |||| |||| |||| ||

The opening was on a Thursday evening in April so cool and sweet you could have bottled it and made it into perfume. I bought some lipstick of my own for the occasion, a shade of maroon that's pretty awful now but worked then, I think. I wore my heavy boots with the green silk dress. I did not own heels. I told myself the boots were part of my signature look, along with the thick glasses.

I walked in at six thirty exactly and stopped in my tracks. There was so much to look at. Just like the spring show I'd walked into the year before, this show was hung salon-style, white walls crowded with framed work of different sizes, the art like stalled traffic on a many-lane highway that ran from ceiling to floor. It took me five minutes just to locate my own piece. It was on the eastern wall of the gallery, eight or ten inches above eye level, in a simple white frame that effectively covered the small abrasion from the broken glass. It had been hung between a black-and-white photograph of a window and a gouache sketch of a dancer. Below it was a mixed-media assemblage of sticks, twine, and clay. Above it was a blue canvas that had been punctured with violent holes and cleverly extended my violent sky.

It was breathtaking.

I smelled a whiff of amber and pepper and orange blossom.

Left Johnny Depp at home tonight, have you?

I turned to Fiona with what must have been a confused expression.

She laughed. Come on, no one's ever told you you look like Winona Ryder?

The compliment left me speechless.

She went on unperturbed. Arms wide open, taking in her whole little queendom, she said: So! What do you think?

There's so much to look at, I said. It's stunning.

Your photograph looks terrific, she said, it really does. The piece just gets more powerful the more you look at it! It was a bit of a challenge figuring out what to hang it with. I didn't want it to undermine any of the other work, you know? But I think I got it in the end.

She clasped her hands together and I felt as if I could see in her the girl she'd once been. A well-bred perfectionist, she'd never been easily delighted. But when she did feel delight it became a pure, whole-body joy.

Fiona, I said abruptly—

She raised her penciled eyebrows. That little crease appeared between them.

Thank you, I said. Whatever happens, thank you.

How ominous! She laughed. Lu, sincerely: I know I was

reticent at first but the piece speaks for itself. It is very strong. Now it just has to do a little work for *us*! Right?

She gave me a wink and turned to greet another guest.

I said hello to Jessie at the front desk and took a sheet of paper from the stack. It was a map of the work on the walls. Each frame had a little number inside it on the map that corresponded to a list of titles on the other side of the sheet. My number: 36. As other guests came in and the conversation behind me rose in volume, from two or three distinct voices to a complicated din, I walked round and round the gallery space, plastic cup of wine in one hand, list of works in the other. The sheer density of work was breathtaking. The curatorial decisions were oddly superficial. All of the hundred or so pieces had been hung, as far as I could tell, according to visual echoes. I made a game of finding the similarities between each artwork and its neighbors. Steve's piece, a small sketch of a nude that lay diagonally across the paper from the top right corner to the bottom left in that classic Steve Schubert style, tangled multicolored strokes, had been hung between a simple abstract painting that was also divided diagonally and a readymade: a children's bead maze.

I tried to memorize the name of each artist in association with their work. I wanted to be able to have something to say to each of them. I wanted to be able to speak seriously with them, and for them to speak seriously with me. I more or less succeeded. For years afterward when the name of an artist who'd been in that show came up in conversation I could picture not only his particular work but also what hung adjacent to it. But those images have faded somewhat over time. The thing about remembering is that to recall one memory is to suppress its neighbors. In order to remember you must forget.

The thing about remembering is that each time you retrieve an event from the past it alters the memory itself. If to tell a story is to repaint the past, to remember is to crumple; to fold, unfold, refold, and inevitably rip. If to tell a story is to renovate, to remember is to destroy.

Here is what I do not remember when I think of that spring opening at Cherrystone Clay. I do not remember the encounter I bungled miserably by confusing the artist I was speaking to, who was black, with another black artist. I do not think of the humiliated deference with which I would treat that artist for years going forward, despite the fact that she may not even have known what I meant.

Though she probably did. I'm sure she did. Of course she did.

I do not remember the brief conversation I managed to have, despite being starstruck, with Patti Smith. I do not remember the surreal disagreement I got into with an elderly man who told me the current interest in women artists was just a fad.

I remember none of these moments. And in fact, though I associate them with that night, they all may have happened at different openings, at different galleries—in different cities, even.

This is the moment that comes back to me in dreams. That still wakes me in a cold sweat, even now, even as recently as last night:

A crowded room. A complicated din. Plastic cup of wine

in one hand, list of works in the other, I turn from some forget-table conversation to see the glass door open at the front of the room. Kate walks in, luminous in red lipstick, her hair lifting in the wind. Behind her, holding one of her hands loosely, an inch or three shorter than she, is Steve. Paint-stained T-shirt, long hair pulled into a ponytail at the back of his neck. I drop my mostly empty cup and its remnants splash back up, leaving several small dark drops on the green silk of my dress. I look around to see if anyone has noticed. No one has. When I look back Kate has left Steve to chat with someone near the door. She has disappeared into the crowd.

Some time later—I can't tell you how long; in my memory I've been stuck motionless and silent to the same stained spot since I saw her at the door—I locate her again. She's caught up in conversation. She's taller than her interlocutors and has to tilt her head down to hear what they are saying. Feeling me watching her she looks up to catch my eye and smiles a last bril-liant smile before her gaze leaves me, rises past me, to the wall behind me where *Self-Portrait #400* hangs. No—*Self-Portrait with Boy*.

I see her disengage. She moves through the crowd so smoothly, so unhaltingly, she might be on a conveyer belt. She stops at the photograph and fixes herself in front of it. She glances down at the title sheet in her hand, then looks back up. All the noise goes out of my ears. Around us the crowd melts into a vaguely shifting liquid. She turns her back on the photograph and finds me. There's pain in her eyes so pow-erful I feel it shove me backward. Her expression changes. There is betrayal. It changes again. There is fury.

She turns and walks upright and resolute toward the door. I call her name. She pushes past a hundred strangers. People notice. Heads turn. I push past them in her path, following her to the door. Steve notices. She is shoving her way out of the glass door. The crowd of smokers on the sidewalk has spilled over the curb into the street. She is walking so quickly, those long strides, that I have to run to catch up. I am calling her name. I am babbling something about her son. It is all spilling out. Suddenly she halts and spins around. She holds an index finger up to my throat like a weapon.

Don't, she says.

Please, I say, let me explain—

Don't!

I'm sorry I didn't tell you, I tried to tell you, I couldn't bring myself to—

No.

It was such a beautiful picture, you could see that, right? It was beautiful and—

No. No!

And he'd been haunting me, Kate, he was fucking haunting me. It isn't my imagination. It isn't guilt or shame or worry. It was real. He was real. At first I didn't know what he wanted. But then I made the test print and I saw him there and I knew—and there he was—right outside my window, looking in, Jesus Christ—

The fuck are you talking about.

The fury in her eyes.

I know I sound crazy, I know it sounds crazy, but please— the best I can do is this—I think when I took the picture right before he died I captured something essential in him—

No.

—stole something from him and he came back for it, he wanted it back, he couldn't rest—I know it sounds crazy but he's been visiting me, Kate, he's been coming to my window.

The fury spilled over. Tears pooled and overflowed, ran over her lower lashes.

I'm so sorry I didn't tell you. I'm so sorry.

You, she managed.

And I will be ashamed of this until the day I die but I half expected her to say: *You . . . thank you.* Or: *You . . . I understand.* Or even: *You . . . I love you.*

But instead she said, still pointing at my throat: *You.* Are dead to me.

She turned and continued walking up Grand Street. Her hands clenched and unclenched and clenched again at her sides. I watched her walk away and I was empty. I had been emptied of everything and all that remained was shame. Shame had hardened to a shell around my emptiness. Shame was my exterior, shame was my skin, my scales. I turned slowly back toward the smokers, who had all gone quiet watching us. They were staring at me, strangers all. Smoke rose from them in the yellow streetlight. From among them emerged Steve, holding a full cup of red wine. He came right up to me, so close there on the sidewalk that I could smell him. He was breathing heavily. He smelled sour and frightening. I was paralyzed. I thought he was about to pour the contents of his cup all over me. Instead, leaning toward me in a gesture as deliberate and private as a kiss he gathered the phlegm at the back of his throat and spat in my face.

I gasped.

He continued up the street, following his wife.

I removed my glasses. I wiped the spit from them and I wiped my face. My hands were shaking violently. Slowly the crowd of smokers turned back in on itself to discuss what it had seen.

I don't know how long I stood out there alone before Fiona found me. She reached out a hand and clutched my arm and with an oddly motherly gesture fixed my hair. You did warn them, she said.

I swallowed.

You did all you could do.

I nodded mutely.

She gave my arm a sympathetic squeeze. It's a horrible tragedy, she said.

I looked into her perfectly lined eyes.

Now come on back inside, she said. There's someone I'd like for you to meet.

||||| ||||| ||||| ||||| ||||| |||

Probably you already know this. *Self-Portrait with Boy* was a sensation.

Spirit Photograph Draws Admiration
and Ire at Cherrystone Clay
Bob Mather, *The New York Times*
April 3, 1992

A lively and densely hung spring survey gave way to controversy last night when the gathering of work by fresh faces and veterans including Elizabeth Murray and Jeff Koons was overshadowed by an entry from newcomer Lu Rile: her *Self-Portrait with Boy,* a five-foot-square color photograph of the artist, en déshabillé, caught in mid-jump à la Philippe Halsman. But what startled viewers is an apparition of a falling child, perfectly framed in midair outside the window behind the artist's figure.

As in a spirit photograph of the later 1800s, depicting ghosts of loved ones, Rile's image seemed to have caught a glimpse of the other world. One wondered: Does she employ photographic trickery like her 19th-century predecessors? Or—more disturbing—does the image show an actual child falling to his death? Noticeably angry words outside the gallery during the opening were followed the next day by a demand from a lawyer for artist Steve Schubert, also represented in the show, and his wife, Kate Fine, that the photograph be removed. They say it exploits their child, Max Schubert-Fine, who accidentally fell to his death from the roof of their DUMBO loft building—where Rile also maintains a studio—last June. They claim it is a violation of their privacy. Cherrystone Clay Gallery did not immediately respond to a request for comment.

Fiona called and told me I had to print more work immediately. What else do you have? she asked. The buzz is unreal!

I said, I have things. I have stuff, I think. I can get you prints as soon as tomorrow.

I want big ones though. Can you do big ones? People love the size.

Can you give me an advance?

Oh, Lu. Sure. Sure. I can give you *an advance*.

Thank you, Fiona.

You're welcome. Oh—Lu? Listen, if anyone wants you to talk about it you know what to do, right?

What do I do?

No comment.

That's it, no comment?

No comment. No comment. Your new catchphrase is *No comment*. Talk about your approach to the work by all means. Talk about your process. Give them the spiel about the art market that you gave me once. But when it comes to the probing questions, the personal questions, the *questionable* questions, just say *No comment*.

Small articles ran in all the newspapers and art publications. A headline in the *New York Post* read Art World Riled Up—as if we hadn't all seen *that* coming a mile away. I received a hundred phone calls and tried my best to sound sophisticated when they asked about my work. When they asked about Max Schubert-Fine I responded dutifully, No comment. Rereading those interviews today I feel I come off at once arrogant and naive. Like a person in ill-fitting clothes who saunters into a party thinking she looks great.

And suddenly I had friends—or if not friends at least acquaintances who knew me by reputation. Over the next few months my life transformed from haunted solitude to the whirlwind of society. I was put on the guest lists of other galleries and invited to openings all over the city. I was asked to speak on a panel at a radical high school on the ethics of street photography though I knew very little about the subject. I was asked to guest curate a show at SVA though I knew next to nothing about the work of my peers and nothing at all about curating. I was invited to dinners at the homes of people

I barely knew where I made stilted confused conversation and was laughed at as an oddity. *It thinks it's people.*

At a rooftop party I ran into Philip Philips. He had on pale purple lipstick and a mesh tank top. He spied me from across a table of drinks. Lu Rile. Well I'll be.

I said hello. I asked him how he was doing. I asked where he was living.

Oh, he said, I'm crashing with a friend. Seen Katie lately?

We haven't spoken, I said stiffly.

Of course you haven't. Philip laughed. Oh, Lu. Poor Lu. Listen, honey. I respect you and everything? But you're a cunt.

At an opening at the Whitney I ran into Bob Maynard. He was there with a friend, a man with a mustache whose name I don't recall. Bob told me he'd read about *Self-Portrait with Boy* in *Art in America*. The mustache told me I had cojones.

I said, What's cojones?

He laughed and turned to Bob. Who is this kid?

I asked Maynard about his buyout. He told me about his negotiation with Pinnacle Partners but petered off in the middle of the story, distracted by a tall tanned man with a mane of white hair by the drinks table. Speak of the devil, he said.

Devil indeed, the mustache muttered.

Hey! Bob called. Wayne Salt!

The man heard him, gave him a vague nod, and wandered over. His left pant leg was rolled up in a neat cuff to expose a prettily polished wooden leg. With his right arm he leaned on a cane, the staff of which seemed to be made of beveled glass. He held out his left hand to shake Maynard's. I hate events like this, he said. I'm only here to see what I can buy and get the fuck out. His voice had a hard, mean edge. I could easily imagine him in a boardroom, surrounded by other white-haired men, laughing about money.

Bob Maynard held out his hand to shake. Bob Maynard, he said. Remember me? You gave me twenty thousand dollars.

Wayne turned to shake hands with the mustache. Frankly, he said, I give a lot of money to a lot of people.

Two twenty-two River Street.

Ah, DUMBO. Love DUMBO. It's my newest conquest. Mark my words, twenty years from now the whole skyline will be glass and steel.

It became clear no one was about to introduce me. Lu Rile, I said, holding out my hand.

Salt turned to me with an amused expression and shook.

Lu still lives over on River Street, said Maynard.

Hey, another thorn in my side. How much do *you* want? Ten million? Twenty?

Five hundred thousand, I said.

Salt laughed, revealing a row of impeccably straight white teeth. Honestly, he said when he'd recovered, it never ceases to amaze me that people actually live in these shitholes. These buildings weren't made to be lived in. They're literally toxic. I had one woman, mother of two, in a warehouse in Williamsburg. Real pain in my ass to be honest with you. She wanted to sue me because her youngest kid was retarded. I said you think it's my fault the kid's been picking at the paint and sticking his fingers in his mouth? You think it's my problem he's slow? I've been trying to get you to move out for years.

Some people can't afford anything else, I said.

Some people, huh? Let me ask you something. What do *you* do?

I'm a photographer.

She's everyone's favorite new enfant terrible, said the mustache.

Cute, said Salt, sizing me up.

Rather loudly I said: We were just discussing a picture I took at 222 River Street. It's currently up in the group show at Cherrystone Clay.

Love Cherrystone Clay. Chuck Cherrystone's an old friend. Our sons play tennis together.

Then you must know my photograph.

Maynard raised his eyebrows.

Salt looked pointedly at Maynard, then at me. Refresh my memory.

Self-Portrait with Boy.

I don't recall.

Airborne nude on the right, falling boy on the left. Vivid blue sky. It's hanging on the east wall of the gallery.

Oh, right, right. Though I don't recall a boy—

We all went silent.

It was Steve Schubert's kid, Maynard said darkly.

Steve Schubert. Steve Schubert. Why do I know that name?

You bought one of his paintings, I said.

Salt snapped his fingers, brightening again. Right! Interesting piece. Totally overpriced. Ever since The Cherrystone Gallery became Cherrystone Clay they've inflated all their prices. That gal Fiona: She's got an eye, but she overvalues the work. I had to talk her down.

We were interrupted by another white-haired man in a beautiful blue suit. He touched Wayne Salt on the elbow and Salt turned away from us, sucked into another conversation.

Smooth, Maynard said to me. It should have been a compliment, but he said it with contempt.

I looked at him with confusion.

Stay classy, Lu, Maynard said by way of good-bye, and the two of them turned to go.

There were still so many things I didn't understand.

It was a heady time. After an opening at ICP I ended up at a party at the home of a young collector, the heir to a small fortune in weapons manufacturing. He lived in a sprawling loft in the deserted unruly Meatpacking District. His massive windows were left open to the spring chill. Beyond them lay the wide shadowy Hudson. Beyond the Hudson lay New Jersey. There was champagne and cocaine and velvet and silk. I found myself engaged in a fatuous conversation about the Democratic candidates for president. I argued hard for something or other, forgot what I was arguing about, and realized that neither myself nor any of my companions had any actual information. Someone brought up that drawling, swaggering guy from Arkansas. Whoever it was seemed sure this guy could beat Bush.

Beat bush, one of the men said, laughing, and slapped the crotch of a good-looking woman beside him. Beat bush!

I wax, she replied haughtily.

He laughed harder.

I was feeling uncomfortable, wondering as I often did in such situations how I'd ended up there, and what I was doing there, and whether I should go home—*that thing in the corner*—when I caught a glimpse of a sunlight scarf in the crowd.

I left the political conversation without excusing myself and followed the scarf through a crowd of men lighting cigarettes, past a pair of redheads kissing, through a dense and aggressive argument about the nature of consciousness. I lost sight of it near the kitchen, where five or six people were sprawled on the floor eating handfuls of chocolate sheet cake out of a paper box. Did you see a woman in a gold scarf? I asked, and they looked up at me like feral children, mouths smeared with mud. Something glinted in the corner of my eye and I looked away toward the line for the bathroom. A cluster of skinny Cure types who'd been smoking a joint caught sight of the cake and made their way toward the kitchen, revealing behind them the gold scarf. There, third in line, was my old friend from the Cloisters. We locked eyes and smiled and the party fell away like a veil, leaving just the two of us.

You again, she said after a moment.

Lu Rile, I said.

She reached out her hand, palm facing the floor like royalty. Franke Angenent.

I took her hand. It was larger than mine, long fingers, no rings, short nails. Is that . . . I foundered. French?

Dutch, she said.

The line for the bathroom had somehow cleared and made way for her. She shrugged at me and released my hand. Before going in she said: Don't move. I'll be quick.

When she reemerged she seemed to have a plan. Let's take a walk, she said. The cigarette smoke is making me dizzy.

We left without saying good-bye to our host. It didn't matter. We took the freight elevator downstairs, watching door after door rise past the ceiling. At the lobby we hauled open the gate and left the building. We walked together to the west edge of Manhattan by the loading docks and elevated train tracks. Her scarf seemed to glow.

I said, Do you mind if I take a picture of you? Right here under the streetlight?

She laughed a little and shrugged. Do I mind? No I don't mind.

Picture a woman like a column lit from above, standing in a pool of light. Her scarf and dress are wrapped around her long body in dramatic folds. Most of her face is obscured in the shadow cast by her cloud of hair. But you can just make out a smirk on her mouth, the glint of an eye. You can see from the way she stands upright and mocking that she knows what you're up to.

I released the shutter and let the Pentax down from my eye. She said, I know who you are, you know.

Who am I?

She found that funny. I mean I read the newspaper, she said.

We crossed the West Side Highway quickly, dodging traffic. A chain-link fence separated us from the Hudson. We walked slowly a foot apart but I could feel a pull between us, a certain magnetism. To our left the river sparkled darkly under a foggy sky. To the right cars flew past on the Hudson River Parkway, illuminating us in the sweep of their headlights, then leaving us dark again.

You were friends with them, she said. Weren't you?

Yes, I said. With her. Close friends.

And now?

She won't speak to me.

Quite a sacrifice, she said.

A man slept in a pile of blankets next to the fence. We gave him a wide berth.

How do you feel now? she said. With all the hubbub?

I feel, I began—and then stopped. How do I feel? I don't know exactly. I don't regret it. I feel like I had to do it. I feel like it was the only thing I could do. There was really no such thing as a right choice. I made a choice and I followed through on that choice and I mean it did what I wanted it to do. It bought me these fifteen minutes. The fifteen minutes I needed to gain traction, to move forward again. I was stuck for so long.

You are how old? she said.

Twenty-seven, I said.

At twenty-seven, how stuck could you have been?

I said, What else could I have done? I took this photograph and it expressed everything, everything. It was the most beautiful thing I'd ever done. If I had kept it to myself I would never, I could never—

She said, I think I see. You had to do what scared you most. To begin to become yourself.

Yes, I said. I stopped walking and turned to face her. Yes, that's it exactly.

No matter the cost.

Yes, I said.

She looked at me with a strange expression. There was pity in her eyes but affection—amusement, even—in her mouth. After a moment she turned again to continue walking and I continued beside her.

So that's how you felt you ought to proceed. But how about now, after it's all done, after all the press and your lost friend and the—what's the phrase? The tempest in the teapot. How about now?

I said: I feel some pride. I feel like I have finally accomplished something. But now that I've done it it doesn't seem like what I wanted at all. Like all this time I've been hiking up this very steep mountain and I've finally gotten to the top— but now that I'm here I can see that in fact I've been stuck in the foothills. The mountain itself is still up ahead.

The mountain is endless, she said. There is no top. It rises all the way up.

Right, I said. Or maybe it isn't a mountain at all. Like maybe I thought I was hiking but now it turns out I was swimming all along. Or taking a spaceship to Mars.

You've been making a different sort of journey, she suggested.

Yes, I said. And I feel so deflated. I thought I was on this path—and yes I've made progress—but now looking around I can see other ways I might have gotten here, better ways. You don't *hike* to Mars. You don't *swim* up a mountain. I can see other ways now that weren't quite so . . . dangerous. Or quite so . . . sad. I feel . . . I feel really sad. I loved her, you know?

My own words shocked me. I stopped walking and listened to myself. I loved her, I said again. A lump rose in my throat.

She stopped too, and turned toward me. Did she love you?

It was difficult to speak. Somehow I managed: I don't think so.

The passing car headlights threw Franke's handsome face into quick relief. The deep crevices below her cheekbones, large nose, full lips, pale eyes, long lashes, all of her was illuminated at once and then it was gone again, disappeared into darkness. The effect was dizzying. The way she listened to me was dizzying. I closed my eyes. I felt her dry lips on my lips. I raised a panicked hand to her shoulder. I felt her hand on the small of my back. I touched her neck. She tasted like apples and rosemary. I didn't want it to stop.

We dodged the traffic again and she hailed a cab going uptown. When it screeched to the curb she grasped my hand and we fell in together laughing. I had never fallen into a cab with another person laughing. I had never grasped another person's hand that way. We took the cab all the way to the Upper West Side, where she rented a tiny room in a cramped apartment. We rode the elevator up laughing silently as thieves and she slid her key into the lock in a pantomime of caution.

What can I say beyond: It was beautiful? What can I say beyond: Delicious. I could tell you about the rows of books on her shelf, the stacks of books by her bed, how she used stacks of books as stands for more books. I could tell you about the way she laughed and put her hands over her face. I could tell you about the cartoons of sea creatures and plants on her sheets; I could tell you I felt at once completely exposed and completely safe—but I won't. To say so would be to ruin it. And besides, to this story, none of that matters.

But I will tell you this. She was right. I had begun to become myself.

卌 卌 卌 卌 卌 IIII

Franke and I spent a heady glorious couple of weeks together. It was May and the sky itself seemed to have woken up again. Over fourteen days we didn't spend even one twenty-four-hour stretch apart. We took long walks up and down the West Side in the fresh wind and stony sunshine. To Riverside Park, where the tulips had pushed out of the dry earth and bloomed, where she'd read while I wandered, taking pictures, or dozed with my head on her thigh under an elm tree. To Saint John the Divine, where we sat together in the cavernous church and leaned our heads against the back of the pew and marveled at the sound and smell and feel of its space. She was writing her dissertation on pre-Christian Netherlandish folklore—specifically moss maidens, which she said were a little bit ghost, a little bit wood nymph. I asked her, Do you believe in them? Do people believe in them, I mean? and she laughed and said: It's not really like that. Belief or disbelief. That is not really what legends are for.

In the mornings when she'd leave to teach or go to the library, or whatever she had to do to piece together her life of the mind, I'd linger at the cluttered dining table with the professor of Slavic poetry who owned the apartment, reading the paper and talking politics over coffee and toast with black currant jam. He was a kind, crabby man who suffered from bad acid reflux and had no patience for corruption. Reading the paper with him was terrifically entertaining. When I had to go to teach at Kings County Academy or get a new roll of film or—god—change my clothes, she'd squeeze my hand and kiss me on the cheek and say, See you soon, *Egeltje*.

Little hedgehog. Because once over dinner she told me about the fox and the hedgehog and when I'd asked which one I was she'd said, Hedgehog! so quickly and with such conviction that I'd been a little offended. We'd argued about it, playfully enough. I said I could be a fox because as a photographer I had to be open to seeing and understanding a wide variety of things. The decaying carapace of a horseshoe crab had to be as important and meaningful as a boy falling to his death. She said, No no, it is not about what you see; it is about how you see it. And you see everything through the camera. You are a little hedgehog. *Egeltje*. You have just the one point of view, just the one lens.

It was a forty-minute ride on the subway plus a twenty-minute trudge from the Upper West Side to Brooklyn Heights to DUMBO. Sometimes I'd do that trip and its reverse twice in a day. It didn't matter. Where once it would have felt like a waste of time to spend so much of the day underground now it was as if time itself had shifted to accommodate her. My days breathed differently. They were expansive. Because every hour was an hour I could spend with Franke, the hours changed their shapes. They made room for me.

I was taking one of these walks back from the 2/3 train, through the Jehovah's Witness compound under the pounding bridge, late on a brilliant afternoon. I was buoyed by thoughts of Franke. Small memories of our moments together, tentative hopes for our future. I turned right on River Street to find six or seven police cars pulled up around the entrance of 222, their lights swinging silently. My heart dropped. I had the urge to turn away and go back to where I'd come from, to the safety and civility of my newly discovered world uptown. If DUMBO was the Wild West, lawless and plentiful with undeveloped land, the Upper West Side was Vienna.

What neighbors I had left were standing outside with the klatch of cops. The only sound was the murmuring of questions and witness statements. No one seemed to notice me. Erica Kau, in a long smock covered with white handprints, was talking to a policeman, who seemed to be taking down a statement from her. As if in a dream I approached the front door of the building, which was guarded by another cop. He was thick and blond and very young. He blocked my way and asked me what my business was.

I live here? Lu Rile, 4D.

He looked down at a pad of paper in his palm. Four-D, you said?

Four-D.

All right, Miss Rile. Mind if I come along up with you.

It was not a question. He followed me up the deserted stairs, past a dead rat on the second-floor landing, past a pile of blankets and a collection of bottles among the wreckage in the third-floor passage, up to the fourth floor, where my fire door had been left open. The door to my apartment was open too and cordoned off with orange tape. POLICE LINE DO NOT CROSS. Another cop stopped us. This one had a black goatee and thick eyelashes.

She's the resident, said the blond cop.

Name? asked the other.

Lu Rile.

This your apartment?

I think that's been established. Can I come in? What is this?

When's the last time you were here?

A couple of days ago.

A couple meaning how many? Two, three?

Two. A couple means two. What the fuck is going on?

Come in, Miss Rile. The detective would like to speak with you.

I ducked under POLICE LINE DO NOT CROSS and was escorted to my dining table, where the detective had shifted my piles of papers and old mail and photographic prints so she could put her own things down. She turned toward me and I caught a whiff of coconut in her dense curly hair. Miss Rile, she said, reaching out a hand. I'm Detective Lynette Sanchez.

I was increasingly frantic. What is going on here?

She retracted her hand. How close were you with your neighbor upstairs, Katherine Fine? Her voice was thick with some outer borough accent, Queens or Staten Island.

Were? Am. What?

I hate to be the one to inform you of this, but Katherine Fine was found dead on the rooftop below your window early this morning.

What, I said. No.

I'm afraid so.

No you're mistaken, I said. Kate's *son* was found dead on the rooftop downstairs.

Yes, Miss Rile, we're aware—

He fell from the roof and got stuck in an air vent. But that was ages ago. You're like, eleven months late.

Miss Rile—

Would you stop, would everyone stop calling me Miss Rile? I'm not a fucking home ec teacher.

Okay. Louise—

Lu, my name is Lu.

Lu, would you please take a seat?

I will not take a seat. What the fuck happened to Kate?

Detective Lynette Sanchez put a hand on my arm. Her grip was warm and firm. She guided me toward my window, the window that faced the river. The left pane, which had been broken, was still closed and covered in plastic and duct tape. The right pane was open though I never left it open, had not opened it for nearly a year. We stood together in my living room, Lynette Sanchez and me, as cops wandered the space around us and swarmed on the rooftop below.

Can you tell me where you were, the detective said, between midnight and seven a.m. this morning?

The wind was blowing in. There was no boy in the wind. My hair blew in my eyes.

Can you tell me where you were, she said more gently, between midnight and seven a.m. today?

Uptown, I managed. At my. At a. At a friend's place.

Can you tell me how Katherine might have gotten into your apartment?

Kate, I whispered. She goes by Kate.

Can you tell me how Kate might have gotten in?

I don't know, I said. I don't know.

Did you leave your door unlocked maybe, or . . . ?

Oh, I said, realizing. She had my keys.

Why would she have your keys?

To check my messages when I was away.

Away where?

In. With my dad. It was over the holidays.

That's months ago. You never took them back?

No. Why would I. No.

So you were close with Katherine.

With Kate. Yes. For a while. We were close. I mean I felt close to her. There was a fall . . . I mean a falling . . . we haven't—hadn't—talked, not lately.

Lu, I'm sorry, I can tell this is hard for you. But I have to ask these questions. You understand.

Were we close? I think we were.

Did Kate ever come down to your apartment to hang out, let's say, for a drink?

Sure. I mean not really, no. Mostly we went to her place.

Did she ever come down to spend time here when you weren't here? Having your key and all.

I . . . don't know.

To your knowledge did she ever come down here to hang out, have a drink, take a nap, let's say, get away from the husband when you weren't around?

Not to my knowledge. I guess it's possible.

Did anything ever seem different when you got home? Out of place?

I scanned the room, taking in my ratty old butterfly chair, the bookcase made of planks and crates. The line where my latest prints were clipped to dry. The tally marks on the drywall, my running total of self-portraits.

How stupid I'd been.

On the low shelf that ran over the radiators under the window was a wineglass. An inch of wine still in it. Kate.

Below it on the floor were two bedroom slippers, the cheap but pretty embroidered kind you could get in Chinatown for a dollar. Kate.

Miss Rile, said Lynette Sanchez. We'd like to bring you into the station for questioning.

On the floor was a photograph of Max I'd never seen before. It was just a standard four-by-six snapshot taken in some summer place. He was mid-jump, hovering over a trampoline, surrounded by young forest. Mugging for the camera, two thumbs up, hair flying up around him. The photo wasn't in great shape. It had been folded and refolded. A jagged crease ran down its middle. On Max's face there was a smudge of fingerprints. Oh, Kate—

Lu?

Kate, poor Kate. The glass, the slippers, and the photograph. I realized I knew what had happened, knew almost

357

exactly. When I'd told her at the opening that he had been haunting me, that he wanted himself back, I had given her a way out of her grief, shown her a tiny door out of her darkness. So she had let herself into my apartment when I wasn't there. To wait for him. To see what she could see.

Miss Rile.

She might have called me to see whether I would pick up. If I didn't pick up she'd have known she could let herself in. I hadn't been around much lately. She'd have had ample opportunity. She'd have crept down the filthy stairs in her cheap slippers with a glass of wine and sat on the floor in front of the window looking out urgently at the bright lights and polluted sky. Maybe she'd spoken his name.

It wouldn't have worked the first time. Maybe not even the second. How many times had she come back? In the middle of the night, maybe drunk, certainly desperate? Surely it would have taken her several visits to realize she could bring the snapshot as a lure.

Lu?

So she'd returned with this photograph and watched and worried it in her hands. At last he had appeared to her: her nine-year-old boy, fiercely beloved, long dead. Hovering just beyond the window and reaching toward her, reaching toward himself, toward life. And when he'd finally appeared she had run toward the window and opened it deftly, the same way she opened her own window upstairs. How many times had she seen him? I imagine they must have had several rendezvous here, mother and ghost. Meeting after midnight, when Steve was in bed. When the boy reached out to her she'd reached out toward him in kind. Her boy, her apparition. And maybe she'd reached too far. Maybe it was an accident.

But I don't believe it was. I believe he beckoned her out into the wind and she agreed to go with him. I believe over the course of their visits she managed to overcome the part of her that wanted to live. Kate was so full of grief but she lived so well, she was so *good* at living. And yet. Her love for him was greater. So she'd stepped out onto nothing and joined him.

They brought me in for questioning that day and I responded to their strange irrelevant questions as a robot to the Turing test. Emotionlessly I told them about the ghost. I told them about the photograph and the calamitous gallery opening. I told them she wanted nothing more than to have him back, that she might have believed she could meet him. I watched their stone faces flinch ever so slightly at my mention of the supernatural. Now she was gone I had no trouble talking about it frankly. I did not say *I know this seems crazy but.* I did not say *I can't explain it* or *You won't believe me* or *I don't know what I saw.* I didn't sugarcoat the fucking thing. What did I have left to protect? Not Kate.

Finally the interview ended. I signed some paperwork in the dingy station. I walked out of the 84th Precinct into the sunlight on Gold Street and burst into tears.

Back at home again in the fading day I began packing up my things. I left the window open. The cops had all left; there was nothing to hear but the wind and the sirens, the gulls and the boats' low defeated horns. I would leave that place as soon as I could. I made a pile of belongings I would keep: my photographic equipment, which I wrapped carefully in Bubble Wrap and cardboard; my portfolio; a backpack full of clothes; my blanket; my radio; the green glass pitcher that I'd salvaged from Toby's garage. The furniture—my futon, my ratty butterfly chair, the dining table—and the few books I'd saved from graduate school I'd leave behind. If I was going to negotiate a buyout I had to preserve the impression that I still lived there.

I called Franke from my kitchen phone and sat on the floor and told her everything. She asked the Slavic poetry scholar if I could stay with them for a while. He said as long as I didn't drink all his coffee or leave clumps of my hair in the drain.

Then I paged the courier Casper Alvarez. The phone rang less than five minutes later, filling the silent loft with its jangle. I reminded him who I was and he remembered me immediately.

Hey, man, he said warmly. What's up? I owe you an audio collage.

I agreed. I asked him about my photo equipment. You have any friends who could help me transport some things?

Sure, he said, sure. How soon do you need it done? I could get some people together, get your shit out of there as soon as tonight.

I was impressed. Do you know of a storage space?

For a small monthly fee I can store it myself, he said. I guarantee no one will touch it.

I hesitated.

Here's the deal, he said. I need steady income. I live in

this massive place out in Red Hook. It's a former factory and there's lockers downstairs where the workers used to store their shit. I'll rent you as many as you need. You can lock it up yourself and take the keys. No one will touch it.

I can give you ten dollars a month, I said.

Ten dollars! For maximum security with your buddy Casper? What are you storing?

Photo equipment, I said.

Shit, he said. I'd say that's worth fifty dollars at least.

Casper, I'm broke too.

Think of it as an insurance policy.

How about twenty?

Forty.

Twenty-five.

Thirty-five.

Thirty, and that's as high as I'll go.

Thirty, huh? All right, I'll give you a deal 'cause I like you. But you got to promise to talk up my audio collage to Fiona.

Okay, Casper. Sure thing.

We'll be there in a couple hours.

While I waited for Casper and his friends I called Fiona to let her know I'd be staying elsewhere for a while and to give her Franke's number in case she needed to get in touch with me. She had already heard about Kate. I didn't ask her how. She expressed a great deal of sympathy. She seemed a little tipsy.

And from *your* window, my god, she said.

Yeah, I said. I really need to get out of here.

I don't blame you, Lu, I don't blame you. Where will you go?

I'll stay with a friend on the Upper West Side.

That'll be a good change of scenery.

Yes, I said. Hey, Fiona, I said.

Yes, Lu?

I know you must have other artists who've had to negotiate a buyout. Do you have any advice for me?

That's a tough one. Do you know what your neighbors have gotten?

I heard Bob Maynard got twenty thousand.

Then ask for twenty thousand. Say you're not going to budge until you get it. When you aren't home, lock the doors and leave the lights on. Who's your landlord?

Pinnacle Partners.

No kidding! Wayne Salt is a friend of the gallery.

I know.

He's a character.

He sure is.

Mention Cherrystone Clay. Tell him you're one of ours. Chat him up a little. You can do that, can't you, Lu? Remind him of your work. Remind him it was made in that building. He'll get a kick out of that. He's not sentimental but he is superstitious. Ask him about what's branded on his wooden leg. Don't worry, he loves to talk about it.

Casper arrived with two friends who looked just like him. Long hair and flannel, ripped jeans, earrings, tired eyes. They carried my equipment out into the hall and down the stairs and across the third-floor passageway—where the community of squatters had multiplied, was now a kind of cardboard village, littered with the stuff of death and life: bottles, syringes, a hot plate, wrappers for Ho Hos and Sno Balls—and down into the dark street where they'd parked a beat-up van. It had seemed like so much to me, what with the beastly enlarger, the gallon jugs of developer and blix, and so on and so on, but it took them less than fifteen minutes to get it all out. We piled into the cab of the van and they blasted the Melvins and we drove like hell to vacant Red Hook, where feral cats ran through the dim cobbled streets like shadows. Their home was just as Casper had described it, a flaking old warehouse that smelled of spray paint, dust, and weed, with lockers on the ground floor. I had brought a combination lock but one of Casper's friends shook his head and got me a couple of hardier ones, which opened with keys. The locks were brand-new, still in their packaging. These kids were in the business of storage. They had done this before.

When everything was secured I handed them some cash, including a ten-dollar tip for each. They offered to drive me home but it was really only a forty-minute walk and I needed the air. I made my way through the empty streets under the shadow of the BQE, under the Brooklyn Bridge, and through the park by the spice factory. It was a cool damp night and the air smelled of salt and pepper. I felt as if every pore in my skin was open to the chill. In DUMBO instead of continuing up toward River Street I turned toward the river. I got as close as I could to the water and looked up and out, skin prickling. I wanted to feel them. I wanted to feel her. I whispered: *Kate.*

Above me a plane made its automatic way through the sky, taillights blinking.

Kate, I said more loudly.

Nothing.

Max, I tried.

I waited a long time at the river, listening to the sigh of traffic and clatter of trains on the bridge overhead. To the odd cry of a sleepless gull, the periodic groan of a barge. My knees were weak and my glasses were fogged and my face was wet. I kept turning to go, then stopping myself—*not yet*—and turning back toward the water. I waited for them but there was nothing but wind in the low spring wind, nothing but dust in the air.

||||| ||||| ||||| ||||| ||||| |||||

My very last morning in DUMBO I marched over to Pinnacle's offices in Brooklyn Heights determined to get a buyout. The office was on the ground floor of a yellow clapboard house on a stately street named after some fruit or other. Cranberry maybe, or Pineapple, or Orange. A young man in a pink button-down shirt and wire-framed glasses sat at a glass desk in front. He greeted me coldly.

I'm here to see Wayne Salt, I said.

He looked me up and down, taking in my scuffed boots and ripped jeans, my secondhand leather jacket. And what is this regarding?

Two twenty-two River Street, I said. The waterfront property he wants to convert to luxury condos but is unfortunately infested.

Infested? The young man looked a little alarmed. With what?

Tenants. And other animals.

Aha. And you are?

Lu Rile. The photographer. Mr. Salt and I met at the Whitney.

I'm afraid Mr. Salt is pretty busy at the moment but I can tell him—

Just tell him I'm a thorn in his side.

The young man in the pink button-down had me wait in an Eames chair by a white orchid while he disappeared into a back office. When he came back out he seemed to be suppressing laughter. He'll see you, he said.

Wayne Salt's office was in the back room. Two windows behind him looked out onto a shaded garden. The iron bars outside the windows were a tangle of morning glories. He was standing at a massive bean-shaped desk poring over what looked like architectural plans, leaning on his glass cane, his suit jacket thrown carelessly over the back of his chair. His shirtsleeves were rolled up to his elbows and his wild white hair wanted combing.

Let me ask you something, he said without looking up. Would it disgust you to have a bathroom right next to a kitchen? My architects keep giving me these absurd blueprints where the bathroom is right—but *right*—next to the kitchen. I find it revolting. Don't shit where you eat. Right? But apparently I'm fastidious. Apparently not everyone feels this way.

Not getting an answer he looked up. Oh, it's you, he said. The enfant terrible. How can I help you?

I want a buyout, I said.

That's right, he said. Five hundred thousand, if I recall?

Good memory, I said.

Not going to happen, he replied and directed his attention back at his blueprints. Now a bathroom off of a bedroom? That makes sense. You freshen up before sex, you wash up afterward. That's reasonable.

A hundred thousand, I said.

The problem is when you have guests over you don't want them tramping in and out of the bedroom to do their business. The key, really, if you've just got one bathroom, is to put it *beside* the bedroom off the main living space. That's the most discreet option. I'm not an architect, mind you. I'm just a wolf.

He looked up and grinned at me, baring that mouthful of perfect white teeth.

A hundred thousand, I repeated.

Oh, little thorn. This is not how you negotiate. See, you begin by telling me something *I'll* get out of the deal. Make it appealing to me. Offer me something I want.

I'll leave the building.

But I happen to know you're going to leave regardless.

I won't budge unless you pay me.

Really? Is that so? Because I happen to know a beautiful woman recently fell out of your window. And it's none of my business, I know, but it's my personal theory that you and this beautiful woman happened to like each other very much. I'm no more a psychologist than I am an architect but if I were you I'd certainly want to get out of that apartment ASAP.

I swallowed. It doesn't bother me, I said.

Really. Huh. So you didn't recently hire Van Halen to move your things out in the middle of the night?

How did you know that? I said.

Listen, Ms. Rile, he said. Let me tell you who I'm going to buy out of your rats' nest on River Street. A sculptor by the name of Erika Kau. That woman is a rhinoceros. She is not going to move until she damn well wants to. And she's not going to want to without a lot, and I mean a *lot*, of money. We're in a cold war, myself and Erika. Fortunately I happen to *have* a lot of money. Eventually I will throw some of it her way and she will vacate the premises so I can start transforming that rats' nest into actual value. But I'm in no rush. It could be years before she budges. There's plenty to do without antagonizing the ungulate on the third floor. I've got architects to consult with. I've got zoning issues to negotiate. I'm a busy man. You know what makes me the best at what I do, Ms. Rile?

I waited.

He leaned forward and looked at me intensely.

I'm a conquerer. You've got to be a fucking conquerer in this business. I've also got impeccable intuition. You're not really a thorn in my side. You're actually in the process of removing yourself, just as naturally as a splinter dissolves over time, or slides out from the skin of one's palm.

What could I say? He wasn't wrong. I was outraged and silent. But I would not turn to go. I was determined not to leave until I had gotten something in return for the nightmare I'd lived.

At last I said: It's haunted, you know.

He looked up.

The building. It's haunted. A nine-year-old boy comes to look in the window.

What window?

My window. The window from the photograph.

What photograph?

My photograph. You saw it at the spring group show at Cherrystone Clay.

He snapped his fingers. Right! Right. You've been getting some attention for this, haven't you?

I have.

Huh, he said, seemingly to himself. Maybe not such a bad idea.

I waited.

Give me a minute, he said. I want to make a phone call.

He picked up his cordless phone and held it between his shoulder and ear while he flipped through his Rolodex. At last he found the little card he wanted and dialed the number. There was indeed something wolflike about his face, I thought. That long nose. Those wicked teeth.

Hello, he said at last. Chuck! How you doing, buddy. Fine fine. Ha! What's that? Oh yeah, the wife is beside herself. I told her it's nothing. Shit happens all the time. We'll make it back. It's the nature of the beast.

Behind him a tortoiseshell cat slunk between the iron bars of the windows and sniffed at the morning glories.

Listen, Chuck. I'm calling about one of your artists. I'd like to make a purchase. Yeah. No no. No. I'm talking new blood. This young woman. Lu Rile? Interesting print. Funny story. That building? It's one of mine. I know. Pretty interesting coincidence. She's sitting right here—standing actually. Rather awkwardly. Staring at me as I talk to you. She waltzed in about five minutes ago demanding a buyout. Ha-ha. Right. Well, listen. I told her that's not how it works. I'm not going to give her a dime. She's already leaving. But what I will do is I'll do this. I'll buy that photograph off of you.

He raised his eyebrows at me as he arranged the deal, framing, shipment, and all. I sank into a chair. I felt like I'd wandered into some other story. Through the windows I watched the tortoiseshell squat and piss in a flowerpot.

Deal made, he hung up. He cocked his head at me. Satisfied?

What could I say? Was I satisfied? Maybe. I was sure weirded out.

All right then, he said, scram. I have a meeting in fifteen and I need to caffeinate. He pushed a button on his phone and without raising the handset said: Charlie, be a good little fag and get me a coffee.

Slowly I got up.

What's the matter with you? he said to me. Did I not tell you to beat it?

That was my first sale, I managed.

He leaned back approvingly. No kidding. How old are you?

Twenty-seven.

Twenty-seven. You know, I was twenty-seven when I bought my first property.

Wow, I said.

It was a thrill, let me tell you. It was a great fucking feeling. Better than anything. Better than sex. Congratulations, kid.

Thank you, I said. As if in a dream I turned toward the door and reached for the handle. Then I remembered and turned back toward him. Fiona told me to ask you about your leg.

Fiona?

Clay?

His laugh was short and hard. Oh, Fiona! She gets a kick out of me, I can tell. He made his way around the desk and pulled up his pressed pant leg to reveal the finely polished wood cylinder underneath. I stepped closer to see what it said. *Aut Vincere Aut Mori.*

He translated for me: Conquer or Die. When I was a young buck in the air force I had my leg blown off in South Korea. You don't know how an episode like that will change you until it does. I'm not ashamed to say it. I got real low. They transferred me to the First Tactical Wing—which happens to be the oldest major air combat unit in the force, by the way. Over time I got sick of moping around. *Aut Vincere Aut Mori* was that unit's slogan. I had it branded on this fucking peg leg of mine. Since then it's been my shibboleth. My good luck charm. My little bit of sorcery.

Charlie appeared at the door with coffee and Wayne Salt waved me out.

I walked home through the lush tree-lined streets of the Heights, down the hill, and toward the water. When I got back to 222 River Street my answering machine was blinking. There were two messages. The first was from Fiona, happily sharing the news that *Self-Portrait with Boy* had been sold and telling me she needed more work to bring to Artexpo later that month.

The second was from Steve. It was simple and direct. Kate's funeral is this Sunday, he said. Do me a favor and don't show up. I don't want you there. I don't ever want to see your face again.

‖‖ ‖‖ ‖‖ ‖‖ ‖‖ ‖‖ |

So that's the story. What else do you want?

A coda, maybe.

Here you go.

A few years ago I went to an exhibition of Steve's work. He was with a new gallery by then, one of those cool spots that had begun sprouting up in Brooklyn. I went early, just after it opened, thinking it was likely I wouldn't run into him at ten o'clock in the morning. The show was called *Max*.

I was right that he wouldn't be there. The room was empty save for a young man behind a computer at the front desk. I walked the perimeter of the room slowly, stopping for several minutes at each piece. They were all drawings and paintings on paper. Many had been done in simple charcoal but some had been done in tender watercolor, or had wrestled with streaks or splashes of gouache. Most were about eight by twelve. Each was a portrait of the artist's dead boy. Though they were all the same subject they were all quite different.

Here was Max in profile, looking up, white face luminous against a dark background. Here was Max with his eyes closed, half his face in bruise-purple shadow. The title of each was a question: *Are Eyes Skin? Do Fish Think? Why Doesn't the Sun Go Out?* They were the questions of a living boy, a boy who was still learning the world.

In the back corner of the gallery by the door to some private room was the only portrait in the show that was not of Max Schubert-Fine. It was a painting: a woman in a doorway, half turned away. Her profile lit with a fine yellow-white line. Her hair fading into black shadow. It was Kate of course. Our Kate.

So he had painted her after all. Not as the girl who'd challenged him at seventeen but as a woman in her thirties. A thin woman possessed by stillness with circles under her eyes.

I went to the front desk and inquired about pricing. Of course it was wildly out of my budget. I bought it anyway on the condition that we keep the purchase anonymous. The guy didn't seem to care. He wrapped it up for me in acid-free paper and cardboard. I said I'd frame it myself.

I chose a wood frame, light-colored ash. She hangs over the garden sink now in the house that Franke and I bought in Beacon. Beacon because Franke liked the name. She said every time we went back we would feel as if we were being guided home. That sink is where she washes her gardening tools and where I wash my hands after I've been working with chemicals in my garage studio. It is right next to the back door, which leads out to our long green lawn, where our cat, Turtle, stalks finches and field mice, prizes he drops on our quilt in the morning with a vague look of pity. Across from the sink is a window and on its sill we keep a row of other treasures. A jar of shells, my father's glasses. A sketch of a moss maiden. The green glass pitcher I found that year.

I hung her above the garden sink because it is a private place. I can look at her in quiet moments, washing my hands after working or coming in from a walk. I find that when my mind is at its quietest I can remember it all most clearly. That year in DUMBO. The boy at the window. The first woman I ever loved.

Acknowledgments

I have so many people to thank for helping make this novel into a book. To the team at Scribner—Nan Graham, a legend and a dynamo; eagle-eyed Kara Watson; Emily Greenwald; and Rosie Mahorter, thank you for your patience, your enthusiasm, and for believing in this book. Thanks to visionary Jaya Miceli for the most beautiful cover. Thanks to Meredith Kaffel Simonoff, who is surely some kind of sorceress, and to everyone at DeFiore and Company, particularly the lovely Reiko Davis.

For their memories of DUMBO and the New York art world circa 1991 I am indebted to Susan Leopold, Lance Rutledge, and Nancy Princenthal. For answering my questions about photography, cameras, and analog printing, thanks to Pieter M. van Hattem, Mikael Kennedy, and the generous guys at Duggal. Thanks to DW Gibson and Writers Omi at the OMI International Arts Center, where I first began researching the East River and its ghosts. It was at OMI that I wrote what I then thought were a few incongruous pages about a young woman driving up a wet road to visit her father.

Thank you to so many kind friends who read this story in its early drafts and fragments and who gave me love and support during the crazy-making process of completing it, including Kendra Allenby, Jena Barchas-Lichtenstein, Max Bean, Sarah Beller, Evan Bollens-Lund, Maria Bowler, Sarah Bridgins, Emily Cressy, Lawrence Detlor, Molly Gandour, Zack Graham, Brent Katz, Carmelo Larose, Ben Lasman, Mojo Lorwin, Wah Mohn, Julia Phillips, and Rachel L'Abri Tipton.

A deep-hearted thank you to my family. To my generous and thoughtful cousin Jane von Mehren. To my brother Ben, whose frank vigor is an inspiration. To my husband, John, for reading everything I've ever written—often in multiple drafts, multiple times—with intelligence and insight, and for always expecting the best of me. To my mom, for your memories, your eye, and for reading the book all at once, just like I wanted you to. And above all, to my dad, "Bob Mather." Your sneaky contribution enriches the story, but your wise editorial guidance helped transform it.

About the Author

Rachel Lyon attended Princeton and Indiana University, where she was fiction editor of the *Indiana Review*. Her work has appeared in *Joyland*, *The Iowa Review*, *Electric Literature*, and other publications. A cofounder of the reading series Ditmas Lit in her native Brooklyn, Lyon has taught creative writing for the Sackett Street Writers' Workshop, Catapult, Slice Literary, and elsewhere. *Self-Portrait with Boy* is her first novel.

Self-Portrait with Boy

Rachel Lyon

This reading group guide for Self-Portrait with Boy includes discussion questions and ideas for enhancing your book club. The suggested questions are intended to help your reading group find new and interesting angles and topics for your discussion. We hope that these ideas will enrich your conversation and increase your enjoyment of the book.

Topics & Questions
for Discussion

1. In the opening paragraphs of the novel, Lu Rile references an article that describes her as "ruthless." A few pages later, she explains she was "hungry" (page 12). How did you react to Lu's ambition? Did you find your own moral compass shifting over the course of the novel? Discuss the author's decision to begin the novel with Lu looking back on the moment and why Lyon might have picked this structure.

2. The physical format of film is crucial to the plot of *Self-Portrait with Boy*. From the beginning, Lu explains, "If I'd had a digital camera back then . . . I might have just deleted it" (page 18). Waiting for the image, the monetary costs of printing, and how the image reveals itself to Lu

greatly influence her decision. Discuss the impact of the medium in the novel. How might this novel be different if it took place in today's digitized culture?

3. Lu describes first encountering Max's ghost as "more like an afterimage than an image. More like a handprint than a hand . . . simply there, static and lifeless but reaching, all of its curvature quite clear," and recognizes that Max's ghost is reaching toward her (page 105). What, if anything, is suggested by Max's haunting Lu?

4. Lu takes photos of mourners gathered, customers at Summerland, and her father when he is blind and recovering from eye surgery. She is never without her camera. Discuss the ethical implications of photography. How is it different from other artistic mediums, painting for example?

5. One evening as she is having dinner with Kate and Philip, Lu is suddenly overcome with social anxiety: "I began to feel very much as if I did not belong, as if I were worse than a third wheel" (page 172). Discuss these thoughts in the context of Lu's feelings for Kate, the photo of Max, Lu's loneliness, and her need to be behind the camera. What does it mean to play the role of observer over participant?

6. Steve begins working on portraits of Max "obsessively" Kate says, "but the work was so much better than anything she'd ever seen him do before. What made it better

was its utter lack of stylishness, of stylization" (page 173). Discuss the role of grief and expression in art.

7. On page 110 Lu expresses fondness for the community she has found through Kate: "Now because of my friendship with Kate I was no longer the weird little photographer downstairs. I was a part of things." Lu places much importance on her friendship with Kate and her desire to belong. Discuss the coexistence of Lu's love for Kate and Lu's artistic aspirations.

Enhance Your
Book Club

1. If you live in the area, pay a visit to DUMBO and observe how much the neighborhood has changed from the days of the novel.

2. Lu and her father watch *Dead Reckoning*, a Humphrey Bogart movie from the late 1940s, so Lu can get an idea of what her mother looked like. Get together with your group and screen the film.

3. Like Lu, artist Diane Arbus used a Rolleiflex camera—and like Lu she took many, often unsettling, self-portraits. Reread the epigraph that opens *Self-Portrait with Boy* and research Arbus's own self-portraits. Discuss these within the context of the novel.

4. Brueghel's *Landscape with the Fall of Icarus* is mentioned in the novel and shares themes of death and falling; however, the painting's primary focus isn't Icarus but the landscape itself. Look up Brueghel's painting and discuss the connection between it and the book.